A Wasp in the Fig Tree

A Wasp in the Fig Tree

—⫘—

Mary Bryan Stafford

ISBN-10: 1507736606
ISBN-13: 9781507736609

Published High River Ranch Press

Library of Congress Control Number: 2015901532

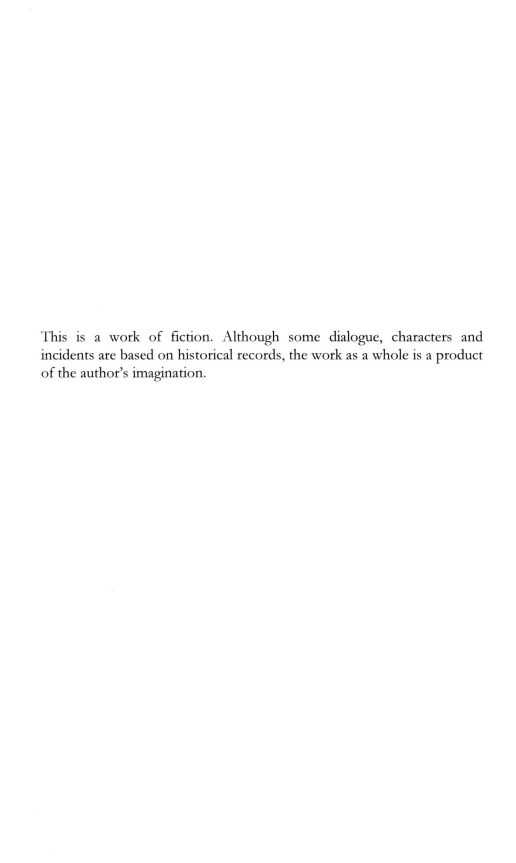

Acknowledgements

To my daughters who listened over and over to different versions of the story.

So many people have helped me along the way. My deepest thanks to my critique group—the Novelcrafters.

Part One

1958

Duval County, Texas

"People live longer down here if they keep their mouths shut."

Anonymous

The Camileño

1958

I was fourteen when I learned to keep a secret.

I should've stayed away from the *Camileño*, but it drew me like the moon draws the tide. *Caballeros* a hundred years past camped at the outpost while they dipped cattle for ticks and castrated bull calves. And even though the ranch hands grinned above our heads, my best friend Burt Charles and I believed their stories about *vaqueros* calling spirits forward to dissolve their fears. Only then would the deserted bunkhouse accept the engraving of their names on its stucco walls.

We rode out with every intention of signing our names on its antiquated stone, but Burt Charles pulled up his horse. "I'm not going any farther, Isabel Martin," he said. "You can make fun of me all you want to. I am not going." He was already turning his horse back to the barn. "Those old stories sound scarier in Spanish," he called over his shoulder, managing to flaunt his fluency in the language while dignifying any qualms he had.

Here in South Texas, he was easily identified as a gringo with his hazel eyes and light skin. And his smile, wide and genuine, robbed you of all misgivings. He tanned golden. Despite the fact that I too was a gringa, I tanned the color of a wet pecan. Seeing my dark hair and eyes, most strangers who came up to the house let loose with a tornado of Spanish. I hated that. As Atlee Parr's niece, I saw myself as different from the local folks—special. I followed Burt Charles back that afternoon, but I had much to prove when I was fourteen. Even as a dark flower of premonition blossomed in my belly, I said, "I'll be going back out there, mister—with or without you." Had I written my name that day, I would not have had to return. And that would have made all the difference.

—⁓⋙⁓—

April Fool's Day, I lay in bed plotting my crime while the light at the edge of the earth began its slow bloom. Riding out alone to the *Camileño* was dicey. If I got caught, Mama would rant about the possibility of my lying unconscious and dying while the horse galloped off to the horizon. From Aunt Hilda, the likelihood of window washing escalated exponentially. But the hardest punishment to take would be the silent spell in which Tío, my uncle Atlee, cleaned his fingernails with the small blade of his knife.

Although he wasn't blood kin, but my uncle by marriage to Aunt Hilda, he treated me more like a daughter than my own father had. Disappointing Tío would hurt more than all the punishments Aunt Hilda and Mama could concoct. But that was *if* I got caught. I considered myself a smooth operator.

The night air sifted through the open windows and seeped deep into the cotton fibers of the sheets. Though ironed and fresh the day before, the fabric lay limp and heavy on my legs. I kicked it aside, slipped into my jeans, and waited for the mourning doves to croon before I tiptoed out into the dawn.

All I could think about was the look on Burt Charles' face when one day he might see in neat block lettering on the *Camileño* wall—"Isabel Martin was here. April 1, 1958."

Holding my breath, I lifted the handle of the heavy door to the patio. No sleepy voice called out, "Isabel?" No grumbling or shifting weight on the beds from other rooms. I eased my way onto the *pasillo* that surrounded the patio of the house and in ten long seconds sprinted to the white walls surrounding the hacienda.

Squinting east, I imagined Marisol and her mother Estela patting down tortillas, scooping scrambled eggs and *chorizo* into them. They wouldn't look toward our hacienda till they pushed open the screen door of their white adobe house. Not till they started out across the sandy distance to our place, tying aprons around their waists, pulling their long black hair into knots at the back of their necks. By then, I'd be past the open space to the barn and saddling my old mare, Canela.

We took the back way, where the road dipped down through creek beds and cooler currents misted. In South Texas, fog collects sound the way water in a cave does. It holds memories of javelinas, their curved tusks carved from their jaws and the flash of white-tailed deer. It hangs like ghosts of *conquistadores* in thickets and drifts like smoke among the trees. This morning the air was still enough to hear the scream of a red-tailed hawk and the rustling of underbrush where an armadillo worked its way back to its hole in the ground.

In the sunlight, shadows knifed long across the road and I caught sight of a jackrabbit. He sat up on the ridge, his over-sized ears so translucently pink against the sunrise that I could have counted my fingers through them.

A perfect morning.

I leaned back and laughed aloud into a pale blue sky.

From the hill, the walls of the *Camileño* appeared opalescent, but as I moved closer, it looked like a giant had spit chewing tobacco down its sides. Screeching and grinding, the windmill drifted in a slow spin that coaxed up precious little water. Only the pond scum retained its green. The hoof-pitted mud gave off a rich and fetid smell.

A prism of light flared from the mesquite. When I shaded my eyes and squinted in that direction, the silver crest insignia of my uncle's Cadillac flashed in the morning sunlight. Another car sat nearby at the old corral, the midnight blue Chrysler Imperial of Tío's brother, George. My uncle stood hunched over the driver's window.

"Shhh…." I shushed Canela as though she were capable of talking. Kicking out of the stirrups, I slid down her side and led her back to a copse of scrub oak where I tied her out of sight. I untied her. I re-tied her. I should be heading back toward the house now, but there was an intensity in the way Tío's arms had flexed against the doorframe of his brother's car. What was Tío talking to George about *now*? Hadn't it all been said and done? George's trial was over but for the sentencing. He had sidestepped a charge of election fraud, but a determined federal jury convicted him of tax evasion for a second time. He was supposed to be standing in front of a federal judge this very minute, taking his punishment like a man, instead of hiding out in the bushes. Never mind I was hiding out in the bushes as well.

I threaded my way through the brush to within ten yards of the car. Still thinking about backtracking to the house before Tío could return, I reconsidered. I chose to do the sensible thing. I hunched over and scurried like a possum into the *Camileño*.

Skidding into the open hull of the ruin, I hugged the wall, and slid down to a squat. I clamped my eyelids shut in relief and waited. They had not seen me. Their voices rose above the drone of the wind. Crawling under the window, I pushed myself up on the other side to get a good view.

George's knuckles wrapped around the top of the steering wheel. The brim of his hat bobbed as he spoke. "They can't do this to me. I'm county judge!" George slapped at the steering wheel with both palms and glared up at my uncle. "But you could—couldn't you, brother?"

Tío stood, his forearms braced against the car's open window. His Stetson hid his face. Shaking his head back and forth, he looked down between his arms.

"At least I took care of Papa's Mexicans, didn't I? While you...you were playin' cowboy!" George mimicked the phrase in falsetto and laughed before falling into a coughing jag.

Tío spoke so softly, I couldn't make out what he was saying.

Amplifying as it ricocheted, George's tirade rebounded off the hot fender. "And I know you gave me a hand every now and then, sure, but to make up for it, I gave you that horse that coulda made you a million."

Tío straightened and walked to the Cadillac and picked up a package bundled in butcher paper from the seat. He glowered at his brother. "You gave me a lot of things, George. Mostly grief as I recall. I hate to see you go to jail. I'd hate to see you die there."

George spit. I couldn't see how close it came to Tío, but I tasted the tang of copper pennies bite deep behind my jaws.

Tío did not flinch. He did not gauge the distance between the spit and his boots. He *did* measure his words. "Take this. It's all I can do for you now." Tío shoved the package toward George. "Use it if you want to. Or take the jail sentence. But I don't want to ever see your face again, George."

"A little farewell present. Well, ain't that mighty kind of you, Atlee. Bon voyage in a bag." He didn't bother to open the wrapper. "Probably a dram of hemlock. Or maybe a pistol. You'd like that wouldn't you? Like to see me disappear off the place forever."

Tío studied the ground before staring back up at his brother. "Your call, of course. Your call. You're an old man. The years they give you in prison will seem a lot longer this time. An eternity. I doubt another Truman will come along to give you a presidential pardon." Tío pounded the roof of the Chrysler with his fist. "Use it or not, George. I don't give a damn."

I rocked back. Never had I seen him hit anything the way he punched his brother's car. And what did he just give George? Would he really give him a gun? *Use it or not, George. I don't give a damn.*

With quiet viciousness George said, "You'd be the one with it all then—you sonofabitch." He was shaking his head back and forth. "And if you think you're gonna take over this county and my judgeship without my support, you're...you're.... You couldn't even... aw.... Get your goddamned hands off my car!"

"You bet, brother. You bet. In fact, I'm washing these hands of you altogether as of this morning." Pinching his cigarette between his fingers, Tío took one last drag, threw it down and ground it into the dirt with the heel of his boot before he stepped away and pushed behind the steering wheel of the Cadillac. He slapped the car into gear and was gone, dust spewing behind him like a fighting cock's tail.

I closed my eyes and slid down the wall.

Against my back, heat filtered through my shirt. Thinking my clothing singed, I shrank away from the wall. Chicken scratch markings scraped the surface. Maybe they *were* confessions of fears scarred into the stone, festering like fossils. And as long as they remained there, they could not cling to the inscriber.

George's Chrysler growled to life. Wheels spun into dirt as George throttled the car in reverse. He braked hard and cut the engine. Then nothing but the hot, still morning and dust roiling up from under the bumper of the Chrysler Imperial.

He had precisely blocked my path to Canela. I scrambled to the farthest corner of the room, hoping for George to leave. But he sat there, his chin sagging on his collarbone.

I waited.

Sweat slid down the small of my back. *Maybe he's sleeping. If he is, I can make a run for it.* I couldn't stand it any longer. Too afraid to stay, too fearful of getting caught, I slunk low, trying to avoid George's rearview mirror. If I could get beyond the row of mesquite, I could slip around the back fender to see if he slept. Then it would be safe for me to get to Canela and make a run for it. I squirmed through the scrub oak and prickly pear, squinting ahead through the bramble, watchful for agave plants waiting to take out my eye. This country could strike any moment, its self-preservation so lethal.

The sun climbed higher. I scuttled to the rear of the Chrysler where I braced myself, hands on my knees and sucked air. When the panting stopped, I leaned out to the edge of the fender. I took a chance and checked the rearview mirror. There he was, motionless. But not asleep. He stared out toward the windmill.

The bawling of an old cow and the repetitive chirp of a cardinal chipped away at the silence. I imagined my mother shaking out my covers and putting out a search party. With my forefinger, I traced the letters spelling Imperial on the raised spare tire compartment and waited.

A snap of the glove compartment and another click. At last he would start the engine. George's eyes shifted to the rear view mirror. He saw me. I knew he did. He would tell I sneaked out. No other choice occurred to me. I must smile, come forward to be polite. Say hello, like I'd been taught. Just say I was out messing around and wondered if this was his car. Just say for him not to feel bad about Tío. Something like "Oh, you know how Tío can be...quiet." Ask if he was gonna come over for breakfast. And if he would, please sir, uh...not mention he'd seen me...that I'd been out looking for...for a surprise for Mama and Aunt Hilda. And did he know about the spirits in the *Camileño*?

In the reflection of his side mirror, George's grey eyes pinned me to the rear fender. My repartee caught in my throat. I was sure what George had to say would change my life, would pockmark it with a truth about my uncle that would finally erase all hopes of Tío's innocence in George's election fraud. But there were no words.

From the rear-view mirror, a glint of steel sparked in the morning light. Just a flicker.

Searing into my face, his eyes left the fevered burn of standing too close to fire. As though he were enlisting me as a co-conspirator, George put the pistol to his head. He pressed his lips together in a straight line, fine as a knife blade, depositing blame at my feet. Never taking his gaze off mine, he pulled the trigger.

A covey of bobwhites burst from the underbrush, but no shudder of wings buffeted the air. A bull opened his mouth in what should have been a leaf trembling bellow. The sound—the only sound—was a cherry bomb exploding. Nothing but the hot white roar of a single shot.

I stood there, wide-eyed, as if viewing myself from somewhere high above the mesquite—a small figure standing behind a dark car with her hands to her ears.

Until the full impact of the scene punched me into motion.

Flailing through the thicket, I pitched over the top of a low branch and fell flat on my back. I screamed once, I think, although I could hardly hear it. It was as though a nest of yellow-jackets invaded my ears. Crab-like, I scrambled backward against a flowering huisache tree. Its orange-colored blossoms drifted down dreamlike and filled the light about me. I swung at them and may have cried out "Stop!" It seemed I did. I flipped and belly-crawled yards before I could still the convulsions in my legs. I flattened my cheek against the sandy earth and became oddly aware of its comfort, a cool hand to mitigate the hot, hot light spearing through the sagebrush. Grit and blood in my mouth, I focused on a dung beetle's single-minded bustling, a small white butterfly's tentative probing of milkweed.

Silence.

Tears muddied my face.

Gripping branches, I pulled to my feet and stumbled back to the car. Maybe it hadn't really happened.

A few steps closer revealed George's slumped form, the thin strands of his grey hair smearing sticky color across the Chrysler's sleek finish. Close enough to make out his liver-spotted hands twisted like dead sparrows. Close enough to recognize the crosshatched handle of a .45 Colt pistol cradled in his lap. Close enough to see brain matter splattered against the early growth of April.

I wheeled around and charged back through the chaparral. A mesquite thorn caught the flesh on my arm. Feeling the pull of it but not the pain, I cocked my elbow across my eyes and parted branches with the other till I found Canela. Breaking loose from her tie, she had trotted several yards away and consoled herself with green grass in a patch of sunlight. She didn't leave me.

I clung to her. Sucking up heaves and tears and swiping my nose across my shredded shirt, I gulped air. It came in fits and swallows. "Okay, okay, we can do this." I flipped the reins back over her neck and dragged myself up. My hands shook, but I clucked her on and we moved into a lope.

The lope accelerated to a gallop, a better rhythm to match my heartbeat. *Don't tell. Don't tell. Don't tell.* The thoughts tattooed themselves in my mind. My head bent so low over Canela's neck that her mane struck me in the face like so many whips. I tried to match her strides, pick up the cadence of a dead run. *Don't tell.* She grunted with each lunge. Her sweat and my own stung my skin. I turned Canela across the pasture for a more direct route. She veered crazily around bunches of yellow flowers and tried to go back to the path. I kicked her then and hung on. Daring a glance over my shoulder, I saw blossoms scattering in our wake—a slow-motion shower of buttercups strewn behind us to make a pretty curtain to hide the horror I'd seen.

Canela skidded to a stop in the corral. Slinging the gate open, I ran her into the barn. I stripped off her bridle in one quick pull, loosened the cinch, but left her dripping with sweat and saddled. Joaquín would take care of her and never say a word to Tío.

I ran the hundred yards to the house until, of all people, Marisol Villanueva sauntered across the distance between our houses. "Ooo, look at you, girl. A horse run away with you *again?*"

I forced myself into a long-strided march.

"They've been looking for you. Better run faster." She stopped and pointed in mock horror. "Oh, look! Even the sheriff came out to find Mr. Parr's niece."

The sheriff's car loomed in the driveway. It couldn't even be nine in the morning. How did he know George was dead?

"Hey! Where *have* you been?" Marisol squinted at me. "You don't look so good."

I felt the intensity of her eyes on my back. She would never follow me—too proud—but her suspicions would slither along to be extracted from her subconscious whenever she needed them.

Skirting around the house to the bedroom wing, I found it quiet. I tore off my shirt and stuffed it under the mattress, ran cool water over my face and arms and covered up the scratches with Aunt Hilda's Erase make-up stick. *Erase it all.* I pushed too hard and the stick crumbled onto the dresser. A long sleeve shirt looked conspicuously hot, but it covered the rivulets of red that lined my arms. Plucking briars and leaves from my hair, I combed the top layer and pulled it back into a ponytail.

As I leaned my forehead on the vanity mirror, a hot print of sweat and breath blurred the image of my clamped lips. I jerked back and scrubbed at the worry line between my eyes. I wondered if the eyes that stared back at me could hide what I had to keep secret. I practiced a new look—blank and innocent.

Maybe I should tell. Maybe it was against the law *not* to. After all, I wasn't supposed to be out there. Crazy thoughts shoved all reason aside. What if Tío *had* helped George with that election last year and George threatened to expose him? And didn't Tío just hand George the weapon that would guarantee his silence? I remembered wishing that George might die before he ever got out of prison. But not like this. Never with my uncle standing in a puddle of guilt.

Dread for my uncle metastasized into selfish fear for myself. What would happen to me if he went to prison? Guilty or not, he'd given me a safe haven when my own father had been incapable. "I will never tell," I said to the mirror. I was no April fool.

Spider veins of blood seeped through the thin cotton of my shirt. I spit on the hem and smudged the stain to pale rust. I thumbed down the door lever and stepped into the veranda and on into the breakfast room.

Mama and Aunt Hilda sat staring at each other over eggs and bacon. My aunt raised both eyebrows at Mama and nodded in my direction.

"Where've you been?" Mama asked without turning around.

I pretended I didn't hear.

Mama turned to stare at me. "Cowboys would say you look rode hard and put up wet."

"Yep." I made the corners of my mouth turn up, but my lower lip hung heavy and trembling. "Warm." I nodded toward the April sunlight. I tried to say that breakfast looked good, but when I mumbled, "Mmm," it burbled on my lips. One-syllable words were all I could force into speech without losing control.

The swinging door to the kitchen scraped open.

"Atlee?" Aunt Hilda's eyes shot up in question.

Tío stepped into the room. He looked over our heads and out the window, his eyes unreadable. He spoke in monotone. "Looks like my brother cut out for the border." Tío put his hands in his pockets and took them out again. "He missed his sentence hearing this morning, but...uh...." Focusing on his empty plate, Tío took his place at the head of the table.

Why was he lying? I poked at the scrambled eggs. Tío's words resounded in my mind: *"Use it or not, George. I don't give a damn."* My fingers trembled like stuttered consonants. I set the fork down and twisted the linen napkin in my lap around and around my forefingers till they stung.

Act normal, I thought. Normal was ravenous, frequently requiring reminders of good manners. I could not eat. Not a bite. But I was so thirsty. "Orange...." I nodded at the juice. Mama placed the pitcher in front of my plate. I unraveled the fabric from my fingers and reached out. Whether it was my numbed fingers or the chill of condensation on the glass, I did not know, but I saw myself lifting the pitcher to pour, and then it was slipping in a slow glide from my hand and crashing onto my plate in a flood of juice and uneaten eggs.

I screamed. "No!" I pushed away from the table and jumped to my feet. I felt the hot flash of tears in my eyes. "Sorry." I grabbed my napkin and tried to sop up the mess. "So so sorry!"

Mama, Aunt Hilda and Tío lunged back from the table, napkins pressed against the rush of orange juice. Mama recovered quickest and rushed around the table to grab my shoulders. "It's all right, honey. It's all right." She pulled me to her and I saw the confusion in her eyes. "I'm sure Aunt Hilda understands. Don't you, sister?"

Already out of her chair, Aunt Hilda hovered near us. "Why sweetheart, how could you imagine this such a crime?" She squeezed my hands.

I looked up at her and broke down again.

"Now, it doesn't matter." Mama gave my shoulders a little shake. "Can you stop crying?"

I smashed the orange-juice soaked napkin to my mouth and bumped my head in a nod.

"Estela!" called Aunt Hilda.

"*Mande?*" Estela appeared from behind the kitchen's swinging door.

"Would you help us out here? It seems we've had a little mishap."

"Oh, of course, Miz Parr." And to me, Estela said, *"No te preocupes, mijita. No importa."* She handed me another napkin and patted my arm.

I tried to bear up as Marisol stepped into the breakfast room with more towels. She sucked air through her teeth. *"Chihuahua."*

I could feel Mama and Aunt Hilda looking at each other over the top of my head. I glanced up in time to see Aunt Hilda mouth the question—*hormones?*

"Oh, and look sweetheart, you have really scraped your knuckles." Mama gripped my fingers till they whitened at the tips. "Oh honey, no wonder you're upset. Your ring...."

My birthstone was gone.

Mama was making excuses for me and I let her. Losing my special black opal would have made me cry under any circumstances, but I couldn't register the significance. I raked my thumb over the gold prongs that splayed like hawk talons.

Tío cleared his throat and scooted back the chair with a screech on the tile. I could not keep my eyes off him. He stood and frowned out at the grounds. Morning light danced across the windowpane and reflected in his fine, clear eyes like sun on shallow creek water. We followed his gaze until a hum in the air became a roar that buffeted the fig trees, the pecan, the orange and tangerine. I slammed my hands against my ears. Helicopters, in search of George Parr, swarmed like angry red wasps over *Rancho de Las Higueras.*

The Funeral

Newspaper reporters poked microphones in our faces and blinded us with camera flashes. I watched my uncle make a furtive swipe at his eyes, but I couldn't read him. "A cup of coffee?" I asked, eager to do something for him. He smiled and pulled my ponytail, but he never answered. He looked over my head and walked away.

George's widow, Eva, draped in black swaths of crepe de chine, buried her face in Tío's shoulder. "Please, you do it, Atlee. You keep him here. My little girl, Georgia, she cannot see this." Eva produced a high keening wail that made me hold my ears and back out of the room.

Mama spoke to me about it later. Funeral decorum. I did not have to sit in the living room reserved for George in his casket. I did not have to stand in line with the family to receive hundreds of mourners who made the sign of the cross and milled past the coffin. But I was not to "exhibit a negative reaction" to people expressing their sorrow. Mama turned to walk away but stopped, her face soft with understanding. She took me by both arms. "I know this is difficult to understand, sweetheart. Just be extra polite for your aunt and uncle. Pretty soon, things will get back to normal."

I made my cheeks push my eyes into tight little crimps to manufacture a smile. *Things will never be normal again.*

For two days, the teak and bronze casket stretched in front of the fireplace like a fine vehicle to heaven or hell. I was pretty sure which. It was never left alone. From where I chose to stand, George's profile surfaced above the white satin like a shark's dorsal fin. Late into the night and early morning, the Tejanos lingered, speaking in subdued voices. "You know? Señor George? He send my boy, my Carlos, to college." The man's speech lilted as if he were asking a question.

Another dark face with pocked skin interrupted. "*Y mi esposa? También, él pagó* the hospital bill when she was too sick. I tell him, what can I do to pay you back? He pat my shoulder and tell me not to worry. *Paisano*, he call me."

The discussions lapsed into Spanish. I listened for Tío's name, but didn't hear it. He sat in one of the folding chairs among the roses and lilies when Mama called me to my room for the night.

I lay staring up at my bedroom ceiling. Was Tío left all alone in the living room with his dead brother? Knowing others had given up the vigil earlier, I decided to look for a window where I could peek in.

It was quiet. An April night full of orange blossom and starlight. Even if George was a crook, it was a shame to be dead on a night like this. Rolling on the balls of my feet, I made no noise on the outside tile. Someone had not completely closed the drapery. Through the gap I saw Tío. He sat alone. The candlelight danced macabre figures on the wall, but barely illuminated George's corpse. Still I wondered how his wound could be so well disguised. From what I remembered, nothing could ever put back the pieces of his skull.

Tío did not look at his brother. He leaned forward, his forearms braced on his thighs. Then suddenly, his head dropped. He cupped his face in his hands, pressing his fingers hard into the flesh around his eyes. His shoulders shook, but no sound escaped the room. My heart broke for him then. So what if it *was* a gun he gave to his brother? Maybe he knew that for George, anything was better than going to jail again. A kindness—like putting down a badly wounded horse. It hadn't sounded like that, of course. It sounded like "Here, take this and go kill yourself."

Tío stayed like that, slumped from the waist. I slunk back to bed, no wiser, feeling no surge of intuition to answer my question. But I loved my tío too much to tell what I'd seen. For all these years he had taken the place of my father. That meant everything to me.

—�⟩—

When I wandered among the visitors the next morning, Tío, stood hands in his pockets, staring out the window again.

Bob and Daisy Taylor, Burt Charles' parents, came. Burt Charles studied me too carefully. I bit my lip and understood that the shake of denial on my face probably resembled a tic. Snatching my gaze away, I fumbled with the prongs of my ring.

The Parr sisters came with their falcon noses and high cheekbones, silver-white hair stretched tight into chignons, their speckled hands heavy with gems. I was sure they could have balanced books on their heads, even when they stretched out their necks to kiss their youngest brother Atlee.

George's widow huddled at the coffin. You could not see her face or hands for the yards of dark fabric. She spoke to no one, but when quiet conversation swelled to gasps, she raised her head.

The new senator, Lyndon Johnson, his Stetson pressed to his heart, strode like John Wayne into the living room. Tío stood to offer his hand. The senator swept him into an embrace, pinning my uncle's arms to his chest for a long moment. He spoke so intimately with Tío that none of us heard, but left my uncle open-mouthed and rubbing his arms. With a grace uncommon to big men, Johnson knelt by Eva. She nodded her head and touched at her eyes with a lace-trimmed handkerchief, but to my relief, uttered no sound.

His mouth sober, Johnson searched the eyes of the mourners. The gasps of surprise hushed. I turned and followed the path of his gaze. It was as though he was a telepathic medium choosing a receiving agent for a message from the dead. As he spoke, his stare reached the Tejanos at the back of the room, and he continued person to person to the gringos standing closest to the coffin. He paused at the sisters, but his eyes flickered away till he came to me. Burt Charles stood behind me and I swivel-headed, hoping Senator Johnson meant him.

But there was no doubt. The senator rested his hand on my shoulder.

Oh god. What does he know? How could he possibly know the secret I shared only with mesquite and huisache? What did he want me to say? That Tío wished it so? Was Johnson psychic? Or was the horror written all over my face, clear as the *Corpus Christi Caller* headlines?

"And this young lady knew George Parr. This girl…."

"Isabel Martin," Aunt Hilda supplied.

"Yes! Isabel. Come here, Isabel." He bestowed a charming smile upon me, took me by the shoulders and turned me around to look at the crowd. He had no idea what I knew, I told myself over and over.

Placing his hand on my head, he spoke in the elevated tone of a Baptist preacher. "George Parr was a fine man. He served his county well and we all mourn his passing." He patted my head enthusiastically enough to make me blink. "Isn't that right, Miss Isabel?" I sought out Burt Charles in the group. His head bobbed like mine till he caught himself and replaced the action with popping all the bones in his neck.

Johnson's words soared, but all I heard was droning, on and on. I forced my mind into a white fugue. He would never, *never* get me to spill my guts. Nobody would.

At last, I was released. I tried for nonchalant, but I stumbled to stand by Burt Charles. He elbowed me, but I grabbed his hand and pinched it between my palms.

The senator posed with a regret so artificially bright that it reflected in the lenses of photojournalists' cameras. I stood gaping at the spectacle till Burt Charles unwrapped my fingers from his hand.

Burt Charles and I headed for the dining table laden with tamales, brisket, cakes, pies, and *pan dulce*, a sweet bread.

Lyndon Johnson mingled.

—⁓—

"Whadda ya think about that? *The* senator!" Tamales muffled Burt Charles' words. "How come he likes *you* so much?"

I shrugged. Stuffing my mouth with *pan dulce*, I gagged when I tried to swallow.

Behind us, a grown-up from town said, "Takes *cojones* for Johnson to show up here."

"Maybe he thinks he'd look guilty if he *didn't* come around," said another. "Beats me. I stay busy trying to keep my own nose clean. You know as well as I do that people live longer down here if they keep their trap shut."

I knew what they meant. *Don't cross George Parr.* My mouth still full, I turned around to survey the faces of the men—not particularly friends of the family. I recognized Mr. Barrera and Mr. Alvarez who merely glanced at me and kept talking with enthusiasm.

"Johnson sure knew what he was doing when he picked George for his dirty work." Mr. Barrera smirked as he lopped a large spoonful of salsa onto his plate.

"You'll have to hand it to the ol' son of a bitch. Parr was a goddamned genius on controlling the votes in Precinct 13."

Barrera snickered. "Damn bad about paying his taxes though."

"Ya gotta wonder what he was thinking. The Feds were all over him."

"Hah! Oh hell, you know he couldn't help himself. Liked to show off too much. Looks like we're at the end of an era."

"Don't bet on it," said Alvarez. "This is mesquite country. You know how hard it is to kill a mesquite tree; you can chop it, you can burn it, but the roots go way down deep and it'll keep coming up again. And there's more than one Parr."

I moved to the other end of the table so I didn't have to hear.

"Would you make up your mind where you're gonna stand?" Burt Charles followed me.

"Shhh. Not so loud. It's those guys." I jerked my chin at the two men. "They're at a funeral for heaven's sake! You're not allowed to talk bad about the dead person, are you?"

"George helped a lotta people out, but he made a good many people mad, too, you know." Burt Charles stripped the cornhusk from a tamale.

"Oh. I know. I *know*! I'm just tired of hearing about it all the time."

The men didn't seem to care who overheard them. "You'd think Johnson wouldn't come struttin' down here, just the same. That's one big ego."

"Let's go. I think I'm gonna throw up." I bumped into Burt Charles' shoulder to get him moving.

But the words that I feared the most came out clearly across the table. It was Barrera again. "Maybe he wants to stay in good with Atlee. Maybe he'll need another election in the bag."

Pan dulce wadded up in my throat. I spit the bread into my hand. Trying to seem very adult—polite, but determined to defend Tío, I said, "My tío would never do that, sir."

I glanced back at Burt Charles for support. Cheeks full of tamales, he blistered red. The men locked eyes and turned their bodies to face me. My last word, "sir," lay suspended in a line over the enchiladas and guacamole. Quiet for a moment, the men snorted and dismissed me like a bothersome horsefly.

Burt Charles touched my shoulder. I wheeled around, doubt spinning with me. "Well, he wouldn't!" Damp bread squished through my fingers.

"Nobody's saying nothin', Izzie. What's the matter with you?" Burt Charles glanced at the men over my shoulder. "And you're gonna get in trouble for talking rude to grown-ups."

"So? You gonna be the one to tell Mama?" I stared straight into Burt Charles' eyes and tore my napkins into tiny pieces. Glancing back at them, I intended to stay on track of their conversation. At least they had moved on to the subject of the drought.

"If we don't get some rain, there ain't gonna *be* enough money to buy off any more Mexicans for a good ol' boy politician." Barrera guffawed, but cut his eyes over at me before he strolled off.

Aunt Hilda, her high heels clicking on the tile, advanced into the dining room with Senator Johnson hot on her trail.

"Hilda, Hilda, honey…." He touched her shoulder and she turned to face him. "I just wanted to tell you how upset I am over this. Your husband is a gentleman and I hope we can continue to count on your family's support, despite this terrible…terrible turn of events."

"I leave the politics to Atlee, Senator." After all these years she still retained that sweet East Texas drawl.

Leaning forward and holding on to the tips of her fingers, he said, "Lyndon, honey. You call me Lyndon." He stared long into her blue eyes. When he noticed Burt Charles and me with our mouths agape, he jerked to senatorial correctness.

Turning his interest on me, he offered his hand. "Now, how *are* you doing, Miss Isabel? I am so sorry for this tragedy, but you must be proud to be a part of this fine family."

Written all over her face were Aunt Hilda's expectations of impeccable manners.

"Yes, sir. Thank you, sir." But as hard as I tried to remember the firm grip I was supposed to deliver, my hand went weasely. I focused on the white rose Senator Johnson wore in his lapel. I could not look into his eyes, so confident of his office, so sure of his charm. I could see how George or even Tío might be moved to do whatever Johnson wanted. So this was the power some men had. It nearly brought me to my knees.

A man in dark sunglasses and a Stetson he had forgotten to remove signaled the senator from the doorway. Johnson twisted his hat in his hands and manufactured an expression of insecurity about what to say. "Looks like I have to go, my dear friends, but I couldn't leave for Washington until I told you the depth of my sympathy and hope for a better day. You let me know if you need anything, you hear? *Anything!*"

Oh, he knew exactly what to say. We all watched from the veranda windows as he marched away, turning to salute at the last minute.

As soon as he left, I scooted into the kitchen and into a chair at the island bar.

"Izzie," Estela said. It always sounded like "Eeesy" when she said my name. She slid a mixing bowl of chocolate chip cookie dough over in front of me. "Make big drops on the sheet." She attempted a smile, but couldn't bear up. For a moment she sobbed into her apron. When she looked up, she said, "You know…el señor George? I know he have many enemies. Somebody else, *they* kill him. He don't kill himself."

Without ever looking up, I slammed a gob of cookie dough onto the baking sheet.

—◊◊—

Stretching its full length along the two miles to the highway, the black snake of one hundred fifty limousines and cars wound down the ranch road, displacing dust and sucking caliche under its belly. Rusted trucks and shiny sedans followed. I could barely see the hats of the men in the front seats or shadows of women's *mantillas* in the back. As the county constable led us onto the main road, cars and pickups pulled over to the side to wait for our motorcade to creep past them. At fifteen miles an hour, the six-mile journey seemed interminable.

Cars and great standing wreaths cluttered Benavides Cemetery. Velvet drapes concealed the dark below the coffin. Rows of folding chairs puckered the green felt carpeting with their legs. Aunt Hilda's high heels sank into the dirt, but she kept her eyes on Tío who guided the widow Eva and her daughter. They sat, shoulders hunched on the front row seats. Aunt Hilda pressed her knees together and leaned toward Tío. Mama held her hand.

I sat next to Mama, my fists wedged in the folds of my skirt that looped between my knees. I stared at my uncle. Behind Tío's sunglasses I imagined tears of relief seeping along the rims of his eyelids. "*Use it or not, George. I don't give a damn.*" Oh, but he did give a damn. I tried to look at things from my uncle's viewpoint. Maybe he gave George this gift as a way out—an escape from the humiliation of prison. George was pretty old and everyone knew this time the judge would not send him to the white-collar, country-club institution. He'd pile George in with rapists and child molesters. Mama nudged me. I riveted my focus straight ahead at the priest.

Throughout the graveside ceremony, I took note that never once did Father Antonio bring up the subject of suicide. Never once did he direct the parishioners to the section in the Bible where suicide condemns one to eternal purgatory. I wondered what kind of deal George had worked out. Wondered if he posthumously held some rank with God. From George's perspective, purgatory probably looked like a mighty lovely place, considering the alternative.

Father Antonio was finishing up. Ashes to ashes. Dust to dust. Six pallbearers stood by, their hands folded respectfully. Two men in white Stetsons joined the lineup. Bolo ties and circled-star badges identified them as Texas Rangers. Their jackets hardly concealed pistols holstered at their hips.

Tío ignored them. He escorted George's widow and daughter to the limousine; Mama and I followed. Through the dark glass, I watched as the men stood on either side of Tío and took his elbow.

And though I never asked the question, Aunt Hilda answered. "He'll be back later tonight. Just business, darling." She pulled down her veil, but not before I caught the rush of tears that filled her eyes.

—〰—

The house, devoid of visitors and help, echoed our footsteps. Mama and Aunt Hilda wandered to their bedrooms without speaking. I followed Mama.

"I've still got to finish that paper on Melville by tomorrow afternoon's class." She exhaled one long sigh. "Guess I'll get to it."

That's when I knew I'd better make my petition quick. Once that door was closed, it became a sanctuary. Do not disturb.

"Mama!" I skidded right behind her before she could shut herself in.

"Izzie, honey." Mama's sighed. "You know I have got to get this paper done. It's been so crazy for the last few days…." She studied my face. "What is it, then? What is so important other than what we've all been through this terrible week?" She paused. "If you don't want to go to school tomorrow…oh all right. You can stay out one more day."

I leaned into her line of vision. She had to listen to me for a change. I couldn't fathom what I might say to her that wouldn't open me up like Pandora's Box.

"Mama?"

"Izzie, what is it?" Mama rolled paper into her typewriter and shuffled through files.

"Mama…."

She turned and glared at me, a wad of notes in her hand. "You better spit it out, girl."

"I want to go home."

Part Two

1951

The Ranch, the First Time

1951

Maybe I shouldn't have said *home*. Seven years back, I couldn't wait to get *away* from home. Before daybreak, I sat on my suitcase where I'd packed jeans and boots and waited for my parents' alarm to go off.

When we made that first long hot drive from Waco down to South Texas, it consumed eight hours in the wide windy backseat of a Ford—eternity in the mind of a six-year-old. I tickled Mama's neck and when she turned around, I produced what I hoped was an excruciating look of emergency. "I gotta go." I cast a quick glance at Daddy.

"Quiet now," she said. I could barely hear her. "Daddy said no." Even then I'd become sensitive to the slight pleading tone in her voice when it came to enforcing his martial law. "Just balance on this little potty." She handed me a Folgers coffee can.

"That's not a—"

"Well, pretend it is!"

I became an expert.

Even with a five a.m. departure, the heat pasted strands of my French braids to my temples. Funneled down the road like the white rabbit in *Alice in Wonderland*, I closed my eyes. I tried to imagine what this ranch would be like. The palette of light and shadow flickering across my eyelids sent images of Roy and Dale. And Aunt Hilda's husband. I had heard my grandmother fussing about the age difference and about their living so far away. I had seen their wedding picture. He wasn't a handsome man; he had smooth white patches on his face and neck. I sat up.

"Tell me what happened to Uncle Atlee again, Mama," I asked.

She sighed with frustration at the number of times a kid can ask the same question. "You remember." She draped her arm over the seat and shifted so she could watch my face.

I did remember. Powered by natural gas piped from the underground source, water jetted into his swimming pool. He stood watching while the pipe gushed. He lit a cigarette. And the whole earth exploded around him. I had not met my new uncle, but I was fairly traumatized. I'd backed into our bathroom heater enough times to know how much a burn hurt. And I had only suffered crisp grate stripes across the back of my legs.

"You can't smell gas, you know, that comes out of the ground," Mama told me.

I knew Tío threw himself down and rolled in the grass to put out the flames. His man Joaquín came running to help him and called the doctor who rushed him in an ambulance all the way to that San Antonio hospital.

I remembered how Mama shuddered when she said that nurses spent hours picking the grass out of his skin before they could bandage him up. Then they had to do the grafts.

"It was awful, but he is all better. Now!" She slapped the seat like a judge gaveling a decision. "Don't let it worry you. He's an awfully nice man."

Stretching out across the back seat, I fell asleep for a good while, until the rubbery smell of coffee pushed me out of a dream. Smoke from Daddy's Lucky Strikes and the odor of over-ripe bananas made me gag. I perched over the front seat to quell the nausea. Mama frowned in concentration as she poured Daddy a cup of coffee from the thermos.

He slurped half of it before he shoved it back at her and said, "Goddamnit, Helen, throw it out! It's lukewarm!" And there it would go from Mama's hand—a dark spray of liquid fanning against the wind. "It's hitting the car." He yelled this time. "Reach farther out!"

Pressing my forehead against the frame of the car window, I took a deep breath and tried to shut out his anger. Mesquite fence posts, each its own unique totem, marched ahead of us down the roadside. I leaned back and let my hand rise and fall against the wind draft, but my eyes studied the horizon.

Up ahead an old truck filled with Tejanos limped along the road. Kids hung from the bed and waved as Daddy honked for them to move over to the shoulder. The father waved too. Daddy blared again and before he swept around the family, he punched his hand into a fist. When the driver spit out what sounded like a Spanish insult, Daddy's face paled to a dumbfounded look I had never seen on his face before. Something about it made me smile.

Forever my signal that we were almost to *Rancho de Las Higueras*, a water tower tottered on spindly legs. In black paint: *Benavides*.

A railroad ran through the town. Two drugstores, two clothing stores lined either side of the tracks. Two movie theaters, one for the gringos, the other for Tejanos. Two grocery stores, Piggly Wiggly if you were Old Party and Hinojosa's if you were New Party. One large bank. The tall tin structure of a cotton mill shimmied in the heat.

Cattle brought most of the gringos to the area. Running cows made them a fair living, but oil gave them a glimpse of wealth and power. In Duval County, most Tejanos voted Old Party, the party of those in power who, despite their light skin, spoke the Spanish language from birth.

The old gringos made their home on the arid land. Like the bougainvillea and the orange tree, they flaunted their charm and made no excuses for the thorns. They surpassed "make-do." Although I did not know it then, the men in my uncle's family were the *patróns* of South Texas, beginning with the senior Parr, whose popularity with the Tejanos put him into the Texas Senate. Along with the benevolence came power. Like the barbed wire that twisted along the mesquite posts, the family held its ground and ruled its domain with a megalomania seldom seen since.

We slowed to a crawl. I suspected my father had no idea where he was going, despite the authority with which he wielded the wrinkled map. Mama sighed with relief when, at last, flinging the map on the seat, Daddy screeched into the only filling station in town.

"Er uh…*hola*," he said to the attendant. "*Dónde está el rancho de Atlee Parr?*" He pronounced the words like gringos who learned the language in college classrooms. When the man stared at him with amused patience, my father deepened his tone. "Can you help me out here or not?"

"*Más allá, a la izquierda.*" The attendant wiped his hands on a red rag and nodded down the road to the south. "*Seis millas.*" He held up six fingers.

Daddy forgot to say *gracias* when he drove away. "Speak English, for God's sake," he said to the windshield. He drummed his fingers on the steering wheel. "Helen. Look up *izquierda*. The book's in the glove compartment."

"I think it means left, Roger."

"Look it up."

She thumbed through the *Traveler's Guide to Spanish*, then held the page out for Daddy to see. I thought I saw a small charge of satisfaction cross her face, but when Daddy cut his eyes over to her, she erased the expression.

Rancho de las Higueras
Ranch of the Fig Trees

From the last hill the white stucco house and walls of the hacienda trembled like a mirage in the Texas sun. It was a pearl in the distance, luminescent with promise.

At last, we left the highway and chugged the two miles of washboard road to the hacienda. In a whorl of dust and squeals of "You're here!" Aunt Hilda let fly with her Cherries-in-the-Snow lipstick smile and swooped us into her arms. She wore her black hair pulled back in a tight, low chignon. She reminded me of Snow White: black hair, blue eyes and fair, fair skin. She wore a quilted circle skirt that she cinched to her twenty-three inch waist.

Uncle Atlee stood back with his hands in his pockets, but humor flickered in his eyes. I stared at his face even though I knew it wasn't the polite thing to do. The white areas didn't move much when he talked and though it had been over a year, I wondered if it still hurt.

Aunt Hilda led me by the hand. "This is your uncle Atlee, Izzie. He is very happy you've come to visit. Isn't that right, Atlee?"

"Sure is." He squatted down to my level. "You can call me Tío. It's Spanish for uncle and you can say it faster than 'Uncle Atlee' if you ever need me in a hurry."

My smile probably had a toe-in-the-dirt shyness to it, but my uncle carried a peace about him that comforted me. "Yes, sir." We were eye to eye. I scanned his face. I wanted to ask if I could touch it, but I knew that would be the wrong thing. I hesitated, and looked in his grey eyes. "Ti...ti...."

"Tío." He offered his hand the skin stretched and pale.

"Tío." I knew to return the gesture, but at the last minute I skimmed my fingers across the scars on the back of his hand.

The twinkle glimmered again. He stood but did not move away and he laid his hand on my shoulder.

"C'mon, Atlee. Show me around this place you've got here." My father slapped his arm around Tío's shoulders. "What's that famous brother of yours up to anyhow?"

Her voice breathy and proud, Aunt Hilda grabbed Mama's hand and pulled her across the portico. "Come see." She reached around my shoulders to usher me to the front of the house.

"We never come in this way. We always go through the kitchen, but I want you to see the place from this entrance just once." A broad stone sidewalk led to the massive walls of the house. Three-inch thick mesquite-wood doors opened onto a cloistered patio. The *pasillo,* an outdoor hallway of tile floors and beamed ceilings, skirted the U-shaped courtyard.

Nodding toward a magnolia, Aunt Hilda said, "I know it was silly, but I missed East Texas so much, I begged Atlee for that tree. He had it shipped from Tyler." She glanced up at the afternoon sky. "I hope it survives down here. Atlee promised the men would keep it watered for me…even with the drought."

Barely above my head, shiny, waxed leaves looked like they might put up a battle. For Aunt Hilda—anything.

"That's the bedroom wing," she said with a sweep of her arm toward the left. Nodding to the right, she said, "Come into the living room."

"Good golly, Mama, lookit!"

Mama pressed her lips together. She had a funny look on her face, but managed to squeak out, "Oh…oh…Hilda. It's…it's beautiful."

Rose-colored Italian tile ran the length of the thirty-foot room. Heavy beams supported the ceiling. Dumbstruck, we followed Aunt Hilda to the billiard room. A squad of cue sticks and ivory balls stood in wrought iron alcoves.

Like a dark Amazonian flower, a chandelier hung over the table in the formal dining room. I counted twenty chairs. Hilda smoothed her hand over the elaborate nymphs carved into the backs. "Atlee had this work done by a man from Mexico. It took him five years."

Mama shook her head, her lips tight. She was still standing there when I yelled from another room.

"Wow! Mama! Look at this!" I stood mouth open, pointing at the painting of a yellow bikini-clad brunette draped across the wall in the bar.

"Is that you, Aunt Hilda?" The dark hair, the blue eyes, the slim form were more than reminiscent of my aunt.

Mama gaped at her younger sister.

"Why, of course not!" Aunt Hilda flushed a deep red. "Don't be silly! Atlee had that painted by a local artist long before he met me." She quickened her step and opened the next door with a grand sweep of skirt.

Mama body-blocked my view of the painting and scooted me along into the veranda. I still managed to twist backwards and peer under her armpit to get one more glimpse. Oh, it was Aunt Hilda, all right.

The veranda, a screened-in porch that stretched across the back of the house, looked out over the grounds shaded by huge pecan trees.

"Tío filled the swimming pool for you, Izzie. Your mama told me you learned to swim last summer."

"Yes, ma'am." I bobbed on my heels. "Yippee!" I slapped my hand over my mouth. The image filled my mind. Water gushing into the swimming pool. Gas jets exploding like geysers. Tío tumbling down its embankments, his skin on fire. Swimming there? I wasn't so sure.

"And Helen, you are going to adore this." Aunt Hilda grabbed Mama's wrists. "Look over there." She swept her arm toward the edge of the grounds. "The fig trees! I know how you love figs! And that's what the ranch is named for. Figs—*las higueras*." She waved her hands. "Oh, I can't say it right. Atlee can. He speaks perfect Spanish."

For the first time, Mama's eyes regained their brightness. "Oh, that is wonderful! You know, I think I'll pick some for breakfast in the morning."

"No, I want to, Mama. Let me pick you some figs." I clapped my hands. "I'll get up early!"

"Oh, honey," Aunt Hilda said, "let Estela or one of the girls do that for you. They'd be happy to."

"Estela? Who's—?"

"Why, the help, Helen."

"Now I just want to make it clear that we can pick our own figs, for goodness sakes." Mama stood straighter.

"You better be careful, honey. Wasps hide in sweet figs and eat out the centers. I bet you didn't know that, Isabel. Just when you think you are going to get a sweet ripe fig, a dang ol' wasp will get you good." Aunt Hilda's speech trailed off as she headed through the breakfast room to the kitchen. She held the swinging door for us.

Drying her hands on a dishtowel, a small woman stood peeking at us from under her eyelashes.

"Helen," said Aunt Hilda, "I want you to meet Estela Villanueva. She and her husband Joaquín live here and help us out. They were actually born here right on the ranch. Isn't that sweet?"

Mama stuck out her hand. "It's a pleasure to meet you, Estela."

Estela looked back and forth between Aunt Hilda and Mama before she offered her fingertips. "*Mucho gusto, señora.*"

Three children stood by the kitchen island to greet us. The girls' black hair fell long and straight down their backs. They wore dresses, not shorts like me, and their thin socks sank into the heels of their scuffed black and white oxfords. They held their hands behind their backs and looked at their feet.

Aunt Hilda rushed on. "Here we have Emilia who is nine and Lupe is, how old, Estela? Almost six?" Aunt Hilda stroked the back of Lupe's head. "And Marisol who is ten. She takes care of baby Ana."

I hung back behind Mama and issued a barely audible, "Hi."

Bolder than the rest, the oldest girl stepped forward. She jostled a small child on her hip like an expert. A band-aid patched her right cheekbone. "You're Isabel." She must have sensed my timidity because at once she gained an attitude of supremacy that she would maintain for years. "I'm Mari. Later, I'll show you the horses."

I gripped Mama's skirt.

"Why, isn't that nice, Izzie? Mama leaned over and peeled my fingers from the fabric. "She'll show you the horses." To Mari, Mama said, "I'm sure she'd love that." And to me, "Won't you, dear?"

I was only six, but I could see the gleam in Marisol's eye.

The Ride

Despite the challenge I read in her eyes on that first meeting, I thought Marisol Villanueva my slave when I was very young. As I grew older, her resentment—honed to a fine blade—aged with me. And so began the series of competitions that kept summer visits to my uncle's ranch in a state of eye-for-an-eye limbo.

By the time I was eight, I understood that twelve-year-old Marisol was not satisfied with her life. She watched my aunt buy me perky little bathing suits with terry cloth jackets to match. She watched my uncle bring me the newest version of Roy Rogers cowboy boots. She was sent to bring toast to Aunt Hilda and me in bed. And all Aunt Hilda had to do was press the intercom button that rang either in the kitchen or at Estela's house a hundred yards away.

Marisol, having an inborn sense of *all things come to those who wait*, hung around till I was ten, and less under the eye of grown-ups, to take full advantage of my ignorance of ranch life. She goaded me into eating *nopales*. She gloated after coaxing me to experiment with a jalapeño. She was full of black lies and skullduggery.

I did my best to align myself with gringos. Burt Charles and his family had begun to come out often, but there were times when I was left without company or supervision. And that was when I risked entertainment at any cost.

When Marisol offered me a ride on an old quarter horse, I gave her a sidelong stare. From the back of that mare, she leaned forward and offered a hand up, *"Sube, gringa."* She ignored my hesitation and cupped her palm to signal me up behind her. When she squinted down, that scar under her right eye feathered out.

"No te preocupas." She smiled. The scar crinkled. "Maybe little ten-year-olds shouldn't ride big horses! Maybe your tío will get you a pony, *bobo*, a cute little pony to walk around in a circle."

"And I am *not* worried! It's just, just...."

"I won't tell if you don't."

"What am I supposed to hold on to anyway?"

"Why, me, of course. You just hold on to me." Mari swiveled in the saddle. "You scared of old Canela, little Lizzie?"

"Not *Lizzie*! It's Izzie."

"Oh, excuse me. You scared of this old mare, *Lizzie*?" Mari snapped her fingers at me and offered an empty stirrup.

When I twisted my mouth to say no, out popped, "I'm coming. I'm coming up. You better hold her."

"Oh, you can trust *me*."

I eyed her carefully, but stuffed my bare toes into the stirrup and reaching for Mari's hand, I swung my leg over.

"See? Isn't this better than walking around in the yard?"

And it was. Warmed by the sun, we suddenly were not so different. The light glinted on our skin in the same bronzed sweat. The breeze splashed our hair about us. We darkened and lightened in and out of shade. Both of us, colors of the earth.

Canela picked up to an easy trot and my heart pumped exhilaration like a drug into my veins—a freedom only felt from the back of a horse, I was sure. This was worth every lie I would have to tell.

But in a slow motion graceful leap, like the *chassé* I'd practiced in dance class, Mari's legs swung out to Canela's flanks. With the audible thump of heels against horseflesh, Canela's haunches sank. My head snapped back with the force of her take-off and I nearly lost my grip on the saddle cantle. I imagined myself turning double flips off that mare's rump as she bolted down the road, dust churning under her hooves. *I could break, I could break....* I put a stranglehold on my horror and concentrated on gluing myself to the horse. The saddle offered no security, so I squeezed my eyes tight and made a lunge for Mari's waist. I clutched at the wispy cotton of her blouse. I tried again, clawing at her midriff. Her black hair, horsetail coarse, slapped my face. I spit it from my mouth. I held my breath, dug my chin into her shoulder, issued a silent prayer and hung on.

The sky lost its blue and white complacency. The shade that had just moments before drafted us into a gentle puzzle fit, now blurred into a stream of confusion. I concentrated on keeping my bottom behind the saddle, but my legs flapped about like a hen floundering from the top of a chicken coop.

Jump! I could jump! But caliche stone was a hard landing. *Hang on, then. Hang on!* I could not speak, but hoped God would hear my thoughts. And I pleaded for him to punish Mari.

Goaded by Mari's heels, Canela stampeded past the Villanueva's house, dodging the goats, kicking out at them if they refused to give way. She charged across the entrance to the carport, shoes slipping on the finer gravel there. Regaining her balance, she swerved around cactus. Their flat paddles extended like small green signs to scream, "Stop!" Mesquite reeled past in a whirling blur of images. As a short cut to the corral, Canela cut through a stand of scrub oak. The branches raked my braids and clawed my back. I imagined the rivulets of blood seeping from my shoulder blades. I felt bruises mushrooming on my thighs. *God, make her stop!*

And then she did—inches from the corral gate. I lurched forward, nearly taking Mari with me and tumbled to a heap at the mare's hooves. Scrambling for the fence, I gasped till I had enough breath to yell up at Mari, who now appeared through kaleidoscoped vision. There were several of her sliding through and past each other.

"Liar!" I yelled at one of the Marisols. "I can't trust you! When Tío gets back, you are gonna get it. And he'll give me my very own horse! A beautiful Arabian stallion!"

With a smile like the Cheshire cat, Mari said, "You are a very funny child—an Arabian stallion, huh?" She slipped off the horse, released the bridle and loosened the cinch. I could still hear her snickering as she opened the gate and slapped Canela's rump.

Grinding the balls of my feet into scorching sand, I pivoted, arms pumping, feet pounding, legs still in straddle position. Burrs embedded themselves between my toes. "Crap!" Hobbling to a halt, I balanced on my right leg while I examined my left foot. The sticker stabbed my thumb. "Crap, crap, crap!" I didn't turn around to see if Mari was looking, but suddenly there she was, offering her arm.

Tears fired hot behind my eyes. "No!" Like propeller blades, my arms gyrated and slapped at her hands. I renewed my indignant exit that abruptly broke down into a peppered hopscotch. With the jerky speed of a Laurel and Hardy movie, I minced my way back to the house.

Their hands over their mouths, Mari's sisters clustered and giggled at their front door. Not oblivious to the comic sketch I provided, I promised Mari with each and every step. "I will...I will...get you for this."

I bypassed the kitchen and skulked around the house to the bedroom side, trying to avoid Estela, but the pad of tennis shoes scuffed after me. "*¿Qué pasó, mijita?*" I ignored her and holed up under the lavender velvet chaise longue in Aunt Hilda's room. Huddled there, I intended to plot my case against Mari. Instead, I sniffled until I heard the click of an opening door. Alligator boots accompanied by a pair of high heels and the more practical wedges of my mother lined up in my view.

Worst of all were the hole-ridden Keds, run down at the heels. Estela. *"No sé, señor.* Izzie, she was running around the house fast. I think maybe she was riding the horse. She had sweaty britches and was crying. I call to her, but she keep on running till she get down under the chair. I just wait till you get back. She's not telling me nothing."

"Isabel, I'll see you in the bathroom." The wedges tapped. "Isabel Martin!"

"It's not my fault!" I blubbered. "Mari tricked me!" I threw a side-glance toward Estela to see if she would try to make Mari appear guiltless, but she looked down at her feet.

The bathroom door closed behind us. It was late afternoon by then, but Mama didn't bother to turn on the light. She flipped down the toilet lid and sat. "Look at me." She snapped my chin between her thumb and forefinger. "Why do you think we make rules like not riding horses when we're not here?"

I shrugged.

"What if you had fallen or been kicked? How long would it have taken to get help?" Her perpetual frown line deepened. "If you want to stay here for the summer, you *will* follow the rules." Mama sounded like a guest whose dog had whizzed on the carpet. "And don't think that you can run wild just because your daddy went back to Waco."

I eyeballed the dripping faucet. If Mari had just left me alone, I reasoned, I wouldn't have had the bejeezus scared out of me and I wouldn't be on trial in the bathroom. "Mari made me ride with her...on the back. She said Canela was old, Mama."

"Let me understand this." Mama developed a leathery tone. "You can't be trusted to follow the rules? You have to be watched by a grown-up so you won't fall prey to every little suggestion anyone makes? Is that right?"

I fidgeted. It wasn't going my way, but I couldn't think of a way to save myself. I opened my mouth, but shut it before I dug myself in deeper.

"Now, march yourself in there and tell Tío and Aunt Hilda that you are sorry. If you ever want to ride horses anywhere on this ranch, you will tell them you know you broke the rules and it will *never* happen again."

"Aw, man!" I could handle my aunt. But Tío? What could I say to a man who had only been kind to me? I skulked out of the bathroom and knelt at Tío's armchair where he sat. "I...I... uh...I guess I broke the rules. I won't do it any more."

My aunt arched her eyebrows and opened her mouth to say something, but Tío spoke first. "That's all right, honey. We know you won't." He laid his hand on my head.

A small hard clot formed in my throat and refused to budge. I dug deep down inside me to find the breath that could stop the sob from welling up. My head resting on his knee, I could only sputter out the words, "I'm s-s-sorry." I wheeled around and tore off for the barn.

I grabbed at the top rail of the corral and swung my legs through the slats. In South Texas, the afternoon shadows drift long off the mesquites. The heat cools down and the Gulf breeze picks up strong. You can hear the doves' call that sounds like water over stones. Pretty soon there'll come the sharp whistle of a bobwhite.

The sun lolled on the distant hill and the swelter of the afternoon funneled to a hot bundle behind my eyes. Somewhere as far off as the Yucatan Peninsula, fields burned. Even though it was a long way away, the smoke swiped across our sunset like a red paintbrush. The evening was pretty, despite my mood. I pressed my forehead against the paint-peeled board and spit at a clod of dirt. Tío had trusted me and I had let him down. He sounded like it wasn't so bad, but I knew adults didn't say everything they thought. And Tío hardly ever said anything at all. I certainly had no idea what he was thinking.

Ol' Canela was happy as hell, a description my aunt was fond of using. I glared at the mare. She just stood there with one leg cocked, her eyes half closed. Her bridle was replaced with a scrappy rope halter. The dirt and salt from her sweat formed the outline of a saddle on her back and sides.

Behind me, footsteps trudged in the sand—Joaquín, coming to feed the horses. He carried his head low, his straw hat pulled down against the evening sun. That hat reminded me of Estela's shoes, forced into some grotesque shape by age and use. Joaquín was Estela's husband and Mari's father, but as far as I was concerned at the time, he was the driver for our six-mile, six-kid trips to the Benavides picture show with me standing in the backseat behind him, staring at the carbuncles on his neck and wondering why he didn't do something about them. With that many kids shoehorned in the old Chevy yelling "*Ándale*, Joaquín!" he was probably in no mood to discuss his skin imperfections.

Joaquín looked as bad as Canela with big dark rings of sweat under his arms and around his sides. He'd probably turn her out to pasture. I thought it would be a while until I'd be riding, even in the yard. As far as my mother was concerned, apologies alone did not mitigate consequence. She always found a way to make a direct connection between crime and punishment. I hiccupped and got mad at Mari all over again.

I didn't think hanging around Joaquín would get me any sympathy even though he squinted up from under the brim of his hat and tried to pass the time of day. "*Hola, señorita. ¿Qué pasa?*" He studied Canela as though he were talking to the mare.

"Nuthin" was the best I could muster. I turned and dragged myself back to the house. In the sunset, the white stucco of the walls and hacienda took on a rosy mother-of-pearl shimmer. Boracho, Joaquín's collie that'd been asleep under the banana plants all day, stood at the cattleguard of the walled entry waiting for me. I clucked and patted the tile of the kitchen porch. With a grunt he plopped down like a bushel bag of oranges and turned his dark eyes to me. I scratched his head. He smelled like a mildewed dishrag, but he was always a good listener.

Mama and Aunt Hilda talked to each other in the kitchen. The smell of frying chicken permeated the summer air. They thought I couldn't hear what they said. But over the spit of the hot lard came, "Would you look at her? Out there talking to that dog."

Then a laugh. "Sometimes I wonder about that child."

Mama was quiet for a while before she said, "I'm sorry she pulled that stunt this afternoon. I thought she could be trusted."

"So did we. Atlee was really disappointed. He hates to worry about her getting hurt. He's got to count on her doing what he tells her. He didn't say much to her, but you know how he is." The frying grease hissed loud and I heard Aunt Hilda cry, "Oh, look out, honey!"

I scooted down close to the collie, draped my arms around his matted coat. I guessed it *was* a sin to defy my uncle's rules. Just the same, I could hardly wait to run my retaliation plan past Burt Charles.

The Debt of Getting Even

"Listen, I've got twelve firecrackers left over from the Fourth of July," I said to Burt Charles. I held up a small paper sack. "At siesta, Mari always stays with her little sister at their house. Man, they sure cater to that kid." Ana was three and puny. "Anyway, you and I can sneak around the back window and lower a tin can full of these firecrackers over the sill. Then we'll strike kitchen matches and drop them one by one till it fires off the whole can." The thought of Mari practically wetting her pants sent me into a flurry of giggles.

"What if we get caught?" Burt Charles' blond eyebrows met in the middle like frayed rope.

"Caught? Who would catch us? Estela and Mama will be a block away over at the main house and Joaquín will be in the field. Besides, we can make it behind their outhouse before Mari can open the curtains. It'll be…. It'll be great! You'll see." I grabbed him by both wrists. "You better not chicken out on me. Swear!"

High noon came—that time of day our mamas kept Burt Charles' little brothers company on the veranda while they rested. The kids sprawled out on the rattan furniture like lion cubs in the shade while the grown-ups talked and drank iced tea. We left word we were going up to the barn to see a new litter of kittens. Nobody asked questions.

In the kitchen, I tugged at Estela's apron to distract her while Burt Charles grabbed a handful of kitchen matches off the stove. "You aren't going to make lamb chops again, are you? Can't we just have fried chicken?" She made about the best fried chicken you ever ate.

"You trying to get me to fry the chicken every night, *mijita*?"

"Well…." I stalled till I got the high sign from Burt Charles, and promptly pasted a smile on my face. "We'll love whatever you make though, Estela."

The last stop was the garbage to look for cans. "Pick a good-sized one," I told Burt Charles.

He pilfered through yuck until he found just the right one. Its top still hung by a sliver of tin.

I pushed a fistful of newspaper at him. "Wrap the lid and twist it off."

Burt Charles had a limit to taking orders and when he turned and stared at me, I saw he had arrived at that point. With a two-penny nail, he pounded a hole through the bottom of the can and ran twine through it. He tied a knot so it wouldn't slip out. I had to admit I was impressed.

The sun glared down on us so hard, I thought it might ignite the firecrackers. Its white reflection on the caliche road made us squint and shield our eyes. Joaquín's goats grouped around the piddly shade of a mesquite and one was halfway up the trunk.

"Good grief, those goats stink." I held my nose.

"You wanna get this done, don't you?" Burt Charles gave me a little shove. I shoved him back.

We eased up to the open window and knelt on a sack of onions stacked on the porch. "Listen. I think I hear Mari," I said.

It was Mari's little sister Ana though. She begged Mari to sing her a song. "*Una canción, Mari, por favor, 'Cielito Lindo.'*"

Not likely, I thought to myself. Mari was more likely to shush her and go back to reading her *Silver Screen* magazine. She loved Dolores del Río, a classy Mexican who made it big in Hollywood. I was surprised when I heard the soft "*Ay, ay, ay, ay...canta y no llores.*" The words came out slower than when the mariachis sang it. Quieter.

Burt Charles lowered the can with firecrackers over the sill. Behind the thin, faded curtains that hung straight down in the stillness of midday, the can rested with only the mildest clink on the concrete floor of the bedroom.

Mari's voice lifted in delicate soprano.

"De la Sierra Morena, cielito lindo, vienen bajando
Un par de ojitos negros, cielito lindo, de contrabando."

Logistics of the project suddenly evaded me. I flapped my hand and mouthed the words with exaggerated enunciation. "Wait! We can't...." Burt Charles' jaw tightened, but the can rose silently back up the wall and over the window edge.

"Are you saying light them up here?" he asked in a hoarse whisper. "What are you? Crazy?" He pantomimed a huge explosion, his palms flashing out.

"Okay, okay!" He was probably right. The can, dangling on its string, wobbled back down the other side of the wall.

"Gimme the matches." I kept my eyes on the shadows behind the curtain. I turned just as Burt Charles struck the match and handed it to me already blazing.

Blinking from sulfur sting, I continued my mission. It occurred to me then and there, that I was likely to set the whole house on fire if I tried to drop the match without moving the curtain. By this time, the flame was firing up toward my fingers. I snatched my hand back from the window and blew. Too late. "Crap!" I winced as the tips of my forefinger and thumb swelled purple. I dropped the match, but enough flame remained to ignite the mesh sack that held the onions.

Wide-eyed with silent desperation, Burt Charles and I spit and slapped at the sack. "Stomp it," he said. A little wisp of smoke sputtered and we smothered it with handfuls of dirt from the yard. No use trying to clean up the mess. No one would likely figure out it was us. With all the dogs and goats around this place, anything could have torn up that onion sack.

"Let's git." He already had one leg off the porch. We sprinted for the outhouse and on to the barn.

I risked tripping over myself and shot a look back at the window. Just snatches of "*Cielito Lindo*" hummed through the hot afternoon. Trapped within the confines of the small whitewashed home, tones of the song wavered, but then Marisol's voice escaped and rose to a high lilting note that trembled on the heat waves to follow us. "*Por qué cantando se alegran, cielito lindo, los corazones.*"

We ran and didn't stop till we got to the third tier of hay bales stacked at the back of the barn. Darker and cooler with only the occasional rustling of unseen mice, it had always offered a dusty haven.

"Didn't go too good, huh?" Burt Charles' face was red with the heat and exertion of a hundred yard dash. Silent and bitter with failure, I made no comment. I just sat there blowing on my thumb.

"Oh, crap!" I whirled to face him.

"What?" Burt Charles spun around, as though he were scanning the barn for some vigilante patrol who could have witnessed the fiasco. "What?"

"The can! You left the can!"

"*I* left the can?"

"You dropped the can through the window. You were in charge of the can!"

He could hardly let that stand as the final say-so. "Well, I guess that makes you in charge of the matches. What have you got to say about that?" He stared at me with conviction.

"Aw, forget it, anyway." I relented. Who knew when I might again need a co-conspirator against Mari? "We'll let her off this time."

At a loss for further accusations, we glumly poked a piece of straw at a mud dauber's nest. A small animal stirred somewhere in the corner. In the distance, snatches of a workman's voice pecked at the silence.

Suddenly, Burt Charles' eyes brightened with direction. "Let's go swim! Want to? It's way past lunch!"

"Yeah, let's go." I stood and picked the hay off my shorts. "I can stay under water longer than you!" I called to him as we trotted on back to the house.

"Not unless you cheat."

—◊—

That night before I could sleep, I lay in the bed with the casement windows thrown wide and listened to the coyotes. I would turn on the air cooler in a little bit, but I had grown to love the *yiiii yiiii*—their excited, almost hysterical call whenever they were close to the kill. It had some mystical quality to it that I didn't understand, but could appreciate all the same.

I lay there, my mind wandering back to the afternoon and our unsuccessful coup d'état on Mari. But I remembered, too, not just the corn tortilla smell that emanated from the kitchen of their little house, but the feel of that *casita*. It had pensiveness to it, even when it was full of all the Villanuevas at suppertime. Worst of all was the sadness in Mari's song that she sang to little Ana. I thought it was supposed to be happy. I'd always heard it played upbeat and lively. I knew enough about the song to understand that the words, "*Canta y no llores*," meant "Sing, don't cry." As I listened, Mari had stopped at odd intervals to catch her breath. It took on a different meaning when she sang it the way she did. Soft like a heartbroken lullaby.

A faint breeze picked up through the pecan trees and on it lay a film of guilt that swelled thicker until it filled my heart. Maybe it was just as well that the firecracker deal didn't work out. I prayed that when Marisol examined the unlit string of firecrackers and can, she would not notice its label. I dearly wished it had been stamped Piggly Wiggly Brand Tomato Sauce.

Instead, it read Del Monte Asparagus—Gourmet Quality.

I was sure of it.

A Man in Black Robes

Being back in Waco in time to start school saved me from Mari's accusatory squints and puckered lips. Aunt Hilda promised to visit us early that fall. When the curved fenders of the Cadillac filled our driveway, I stopped my foot-dragging home from class and skipped the rest of the way.

I burst into the door, red-faced, my braids flapping about my cheeks. "Hey!" The door slammed behind me. They all jumped. "Hi, y'all!" I said.

Tío and Aunt Hilda were at our house all right, but it looked like they were about to go to a funeral. Tío had on a grey double-breasted suit and dressy shoes, black and shiny instead of his alligator boots. He reminded me of the actor who played Al Capone in the movies. I was relieved to see his Stetson on the side table, a good sign that he was still my tío. At least Aunt Hilda wasn't dressed in black, but she looked uncommonly serious. In the quietness of the living room, all I could hear was my panting.

"What?" I asked.

If my aunt was known for anything, it was the intensity of her greetings. "Hi, honey!" she typically called in a treble-pitched yodel that ranged over many syllables and reached two blocks in any direction. That day, it was a soft, "Hello, you sweet thing. You just come on in here and sit down by me." She patted the cushion next to her.

Tío cleared his throat. "Well, anyway, Helen, that's what we've got to do. It starts at eight tomorrow morning, so we've got to get on tonight. Wish we could stay a little longer. Maybe on the way back."

Mama had just gotten home from teaching school. Chalk dust swiped across her navy blue skirt. A mouse-brown strand of hair had gotten loose and fallen out of her bun.

I looked back and forth between them. There was bound to be a clue somewhere, I thought. They locked eyes, but I got no feel for what was going on. I finally had to blurt it out. "What starts tomorrow?" I scooted up to the edge of the couch.

Aunt Hilda glanced at Tío and smoothed her skirt around her.

Tío managed a little cough for a laugh. "Oh, nothing for you to worry about. We're going to…going to…well, we're just supportive of my brother George. He just has a little explaining to do to a judge."

God in heavy black robes burst into my mind. A judge! I looked back and forth between Mama and Aunt Hilda. I caught the lift of the eyebrow and a quick twist of Aunt Hilda's smile.

Mama stood up. "Now I know y'all have got time for just a bite. Let me just—"

"Let's eat out!" Aunt Hilda's voice rose to something of its old volume. "Call your daddy at work, honey bun, and tell him we'll meet him at the Elite Café out there on the highway. It's not too far from his office and then we can just scoot off from there. Our treat."

—⁓⁓—

The Elite Café was my favorite restaurant. The yeast rolls, served before the main course arrived, occupied all my attention and kept me silenced and plastered to my seat. While we waited for Daddy to arrive, I sat wedged between Mama and Aunt Hilda and ate all the rolls. But nobody seemed to notice. At one point, Mama escorted me to the ladies' room. On our way back to the table, I could hear Aunt Hilda. As usual, her words carried across the room.

"I want to help George, but this will take all we have. Land isn't money, after all."

Mama sang out, "Here we come!" I knew she was giving them fair warning that the little pitcher with big ears was on her way.

That night after Tío and Aunt Hilda had left, I scooted out of bed and propped myself up against the door to the kitchen where Mama and Daddy sat talking. Their voices were low, but I could make out what they said for the most part. For once, it revolved around something other than how much the light bill was or why Mama hadn't ironed his pants with the crease centered right. That night, like I knew they would, they talked about the judge.

"It's going to be hard on them financially," Mama said. "George never seems to have money when he needs it. That lawyer they're hiring, Percy Foreman? He is supposed to be the best, but I don't know if it'll do any good. This investigation seems pretty thorough." Silverware clunked against dishware. "I think they are really out to get him this time.

I hope that Atlee isn't implicated in any of this. Being County Commissioner always puts him up for public scrutiny."

"Between the drought and his brother's hand in the federal pie, Atlee is gonna have a hard time." Daddy's words lacked the slurs they had most evenings. "Lotsa money going out. Not too much coming in."

"Think George's guilty? I can't bear to ask Hilda." Mama got quiet a moment. "What if he is?"

"Well, I'd bet my bottom dollar on it. If Truman hadn't pardoned George for his last income tax evasion, George woulda never got back into county politics and sure as hell wouldn't have wormed his way back to being county judge. Kinda ironic that a county judge has to explain things to a federal judge, but George has a way of working things out to suit himself. Just costs his brother a pile of money."

Then someone turned on the water and I couldn't hear what they said next.

George was a judge? How could a judge get in trouble? I had no better idea than I had earlier what kind of mess this was, but I did know it was bad. Maybe Tío was helping George because he loved his brother, I thought. Why it should use up so much money, I didn't know. If George was guilty, I wondered if it was bad for Tío to pay for him? I tiptoed over to the dresser and found a crayon in my Folgers coffee can. Pulling the closet light chain so I could see, I wrote, "immplukate" and "screwtiny" on my Big Chief Tablet. The next day I began my own investigation.

The next day was Wednesday—Library Day—my favorite. The musty smell of old books and how you could see the Heart of Texas Coliseum over the tops of the trees from the library window gave me a peaceful feeling. It was quiet and warm up in the library. More than once, I had to fight to keep my eyes open on those balmy September afternoons. But that day, I had a mission. Just as Miss Young told us to line up at the classroom door, I reached in my desk and dragged out my Big Chief. The library had a dictionary that weighed as much as I did. I figured I would surely find out the meanings of those words on my tablet.

First, just to look casual, I scanned fiction. I snatched up *The Black Stallion Returns*. I was reading the whole series and didn't want anyone else to check it out. Keeping an eye on Miss Young, I glided over to the dictionary. I put my fingers on the first letter of the words and traced down the columns, but the words were nowhere. I broke down and sidled up to the assistant librarian.

"It's a special assignment," I said. "It's okay if I get help looking them up. I just have to have the meaning memorized by Friday." I shot a glance at Miss Young.

The librarian took the tablet out of my hands. She mouthed out the sounds: "Immplukate" and then, "screwtiny." All of a sudden, she covered her lips, but her eyes crinkled.

"Well, now," she said briskly. "I believe if we just adjust the spelling a little you might have better luck. Here, try this." She printed out in large letters, *implicate* and *scrutiny*.

Rubbing my chin, I said "Ah," in my best grown up imitation. "I see what you mean. Thank you, ma'am." I turned with as much dignity as I could muster and strode back to the giant dictionary on the stand.

Scrutiny—a careful continuous watch.

Implicate—to show to have a connection with a crime.

I practiced the words as I copied down the meaning, but when I got to "crime," I froze and looked around me. I ripped the sheet from my Big Chief and wadded it into a tight little ball. I headed for the trash basket, but thought better of it.

"Miss Young, I really need to be excused." I twisted my face and held my knees together.

"All right, but you must hurry right back, Miss Isabel."

"Yes, ma'am. I will."

"You come check in with me the minute you get back, hear?"

"Yes. Yes, ma'am."

Down the stairs I loped, holding on to the rail just in case. All I needed was to plunk down headfirst and have the principal, Mrs. Warfield, find *implicate* and *scrutiny* defined on this crumpled paper in the fist of my lifeless hand. I envisioned her grisly discovery.

"Oh, my word," she would say, her gunmetal grey hair twisted tight into a bun so that the pencil she always stuck there lodged like the sword in the stone.

The halls were so quiet my footsteps echoed *click click click* on the stairway. I swung around the banister into the large restroom of the lowest floor. It was weird being there when no one else was. Creepy. I opened the first door I came to and latched it behind me. I lifted each wrinkle from the ball of paper. There it was: *a continuous watch, a connection with a crime*. I shredded the paper best I could, first long ways and then sideways. I balled it up again, slammed it into the toilet and pushed the handle down. I watched it spin and disappear. The echo of the flush filled the room and then it was silent again. I wished I could do that in my mind. Flush the words away and keep them silent forever.

Christmas

For some, December heralded Christmas. For my father, it meant the oiling of rifle barrels and sighting antlers through the scope of a Winchester .30-.30. We could count on returning from the ranch with a tongue-lolling buck strapped to each of the front fenders and a javelina roped to the trunk, his death grimace frozen on his snout. The soft scraping of cloven hooves would graze the paint of our Ford all the way back to Waco, but getting to go to the ranch was worth every gory detail. Almost.

"No peeking." Aunt Hilda said as she led Mama, Daddy, and me into the darkened space of the veranda. Tío let the dark settle around us. And then, "Okay, Atlee!" Her words rang like silver bells. And he flashed on the lights of the tree.

I gasped. "Ohhhhh." From floor to beams, red, green, and blue lights reflected off the polished tile and shimmered back at us. The whole end of the veranda scintillated in a Christmas glow. A radiant angel bowed her head as it brushed the twelve-foot ceiling.

From the swinging door into the kitchen we heard a scuffing of feet and turned to see Marisol shifting Ana from one hip to the other. Mari blinked once, her eyes full and glassy, and then turned away. I thought it may have been the reflection of the Christmas lights.

"Don't you just love it?" Aunt Hilda asked, as she stood with hands clasped at her chin.

"It's beautiful," I said. "What'd I get for Christmas?"

Aunt Hilda kissed me on the forehead and ushered us on toward the dining room. "You won't find out till Christmas morning, funny one. Not till Christmas morning. Let's go in to dinner now. Estela, everything ready?"

Only three months had passed since September when I'd seen him dressed out of character, but that night Tío looked normal. I sat down at his end of the table where I could keep an eye on him. He had on his usual khaki pants and shirt, so I began to feel a little better. At least he wasn't going to have to talk to a judge. He cut off a corner of his T-bone and clucked to Show Boy, their pet dachshund. That dog was the biggest weenie dog I had ever seen. When he sat up for his steak, his long torso wavered right and left, front and back like a fat cobra hypnotized by a flute. He held that pose till he earned his treat. I thought about the collie Boracho. He was really Joaquín's dog and I bet he never got steak.

George's name never came up and I thought that was a good sign. Hands in my lap, I watched while Tío mashed his ice cream and stirred it around and around to make it extra creamy. Satisfied, he patted it down with the bowl of the spoon. He never bit into it really, but swirled it till it flowed like smooth icing between his lips. He looked up once and smiled at me, offering me a spoonful. I shook my head and blushed at getting caught for staring at him.

"When's Burt Charles coming out?" I asked, interrupting the ongoing chatter.

"Oh, the kids will all be out tomorrow right after Sunday School. Bob plans on going hunting tonight," Tío said.

"And I'm looking forward to it, Atlee!" Daddy lifted his goblet toward Tío. I scanned down the table past the elaborate poinsettia arrangement. Daddy's face had that rosy hue that accompanied a fourth glass of wine.

I sat there as long as I could, before asking to be excused. I didn't last an hour after dinner and fell asleep watching TV. Mama let me lie there on the floor till the National Anthem came on. I sat up, hugging my pillow as the men packed their vest pockets with boxes of ammunition for their deer rifles.

"Should be a good night," Tío said. "Turned out right crisp."

"They'll be runnin' all right." Daddy's voice achieved the required macho timbre. As they slid into their hunting vests and bustled out the door, the cold night air rushed into the room.

"Shut that door, Atlee Parr!" Aunt Hilda tossed one of her Cheetos at him.

Tío laughed as Show Boy gobbled up the orange puffy swirl. The heavy door closed and the dark swallowed up the men's voices as they crossed the patio.

—◊◊◊—

The next morning I scrambled out of bed early and ran into my aunt and uncle's bedroom. Tío always left at the crack of dawn to go into town to

De Leon's Drugstore where he drank his coffee and caught up on local goings-on.

Drinking coffee and eating toast, Aunt Hilda sat propped up in bed by five pillows and thumbed through *Ladies' Home Journal*. "Come on up here, sugar pie. There's plenty of room." She scooped a pillow from behind her and punched it up for me. "What are you going to do today?" She handed me a piece of toast cut in a nice diagonal. "They got a deer last night, you know."

"Wow! Really? I wanna go see." I'd never seen one till it was cleaned and neatly arranged on the car fender.

"Run over to the kitchen. Estela'll fix you something. Pancakes?"

— ᴍ —

Taking over-sized bites of pancakes, I questioned Estela as to the exact whereabouts of the deer.

"Joaquín, he clean the deer down at our house. You got plenty of time. Go slow, *mijita*. You going to choke yourself."

By the time I finished eating, Burt Charles and crew arrived. "They got a deer. Let's go!" I gave him an affectionate shove and headed out the door to the Villanueva's.

From a tree down at their house, the deer spun in a slow spiral, north then south, then east. Eyes still soft, there was no flicker of surprise, no momentary epiphany, no startled whites around the brown deepness that still shone with an iridescent glow. The buck's coat flecked black and grey. His ears still stood alert, tufted in cream down, and if he had never rotated west, I could almost believe him alive. Below the flap of white tail, a gap yawned, displaying the ribs from the inside out. A rope of guts braided around organs clumped in a bucket.

My hands went to my throat, then to my mouth. I willed myself to breathe—"Ah…ah…."

"Good," said Burt Charles, "Joaquín got started on this the minute they got back. He cut the musk gland already."

I squinted at the sunlight through the trees, but my eyes returned to Joaquín's hands streaked red, to the dogs circling the bucket. I squeaked out the question like a mouse in a trap, "The musk gland?" Was that something special to eat? It looked like he had disemboweled every conceivable organ, leaving only muscle and skin. I clamped my lips shut and closed my eyes. *Don't cry. Don't you cry!*

"Oh, you know. When the bucks are in rut, they give off a double-whammy odor that will stink up the whole she-bang if you don't cut it quick."

"In rut?"

Burt Charles' cheeks matched the blood on the ground. "Man! You don't know anything, do you?"

"Well, I...well, you...well, never mind!" Dang, he could get so smarty.

Boracho poked his muzzle into the bucket. Laughing, Joaquín reached down and tossed the dog a handful of intestines. *"¡Ay—los perros!"*

I guess that *was* a big treat for Boracho. To heck with steak, and he didn't even have to sit up for it.

Hands bloodstained, Joaquín picked up a long thin-bladed knife and flicked it back and forth across the whetstone. I'd seen Tío do it all the time before a turkey dinner, but his hands were not covered in blood.

"Joaquín, don't!" I cried out, and then feared I'd be labeled an overprotected and prissy little gringa. I whirled and implored Burt Charles. I put all my feeling into my eyes hoping he would read my desperation—please do something! Anything! But he was hypnotized by the whole process. His eyes slid over mine—numbed to my purpose.

Cutting above the flanks, Joaquín's smile widened in satisfaction *"Esto es lo mejor."*

I turned to Burt Charles for a translation.

"He says it's the best part." Burt Charles had his eyes glued on the innards of the poor animal.

"It's the back strap. Real tender venison." Mari stepped into the group. "Your tío said he let your daddy take the shot. He was just being polite. Headlighting's a quick way to get a buck." With a worldly tone, she continued. "Papa, I want to make the next incisions." Mari spoke with her usual confidence. Joaquín handed over the knife like he thought she could do anything.

"Ewwww." I squirmed and looked away. "I don't know how you can do that! That poor deer!"

"Izzie, chica, you have a lot to learn. For one thing, venison tastes better than wild pig. Your daddy only wants the head." Mari gave the knife a few flicks with the flint. "We'll take the rest and make the best venison steaks and sausage you ever ate. Besides, my biology class has been studying dissection. I can practice on this animal. I intend to make an A." Mari shouldered between Burt Charles and the deer. "Excuse me.

I need to get in closer here." She flicked the blade just under my nose. "Run along, Izzie, if this bothers you."

Know it all. I would have said it aloud if she hadn't had that knife and Joaquín hadn't been standing right there.

"Oh well, guts are guts," said Burt Charles. "Anyway, let's check the points!" He touched each tip of the antlers as he counted.

No match for Mari, I stomped off toward the house and left them with their "One, two...." How could they? How could they? Like metronomes, I felt my braids swing in a furious rhythm behind me.

Before I got to the cattleguard of the house, I could hear the crunch of Burt Charles' boots on the gravel and his panting. "Fourteen! Can you believe it? Fourteen! Wonder if he'll have that mounted."

"Well, I guess that's what he wants the head for!" I let my eyes loll around in their sockets. "Isn't that what Miss Expert said?" Determined to make some sense of my morning, I asked, "What's headlighting, anyway?"

"Oh, that's where the hunters wait till late at night when the deer are running. The stupid ol' buck will stop when that headlight beam hits 'em in the eyes. Just freezes right there. So all they have to do is just point and shoot. Pretty neat, huh?"

"Doesn't sound to me like the deer stands much of a chance."

"Nah, but a buck's a buck. Your dad doesn't get down here very often."

I thought about the story of Bambi. I remembered the fear in that fawn's eyes and how all his mother wanted him to do was run and run if they heard the hunters' gun. I didn't care if it was sentimental. Remembering made me need to take a deep breath, but a catch in my throat issued a froggy sound. I coughed to cover it up. Burt Charles gave me a quick look, but once he was telling a tale, there was no stopping him.

"There's the jeep right there!" He pointed to a small double-decker truck. Welded onto the frame of the jeep, the iron pipes supported a bench seat on the second level. A bar to brace the rifle ran across the pipes. "See? Up there?" Standing with his arms cocked for an imaginary rifle, he said, "They can prop the gun right up on that platform, twist that spotlight down the road and bang! They got a buck!"

I glared at him. "And Tío does that?"

"Mostly when he knows a visitor is just dying to take home a deer. Just like your dad. The constable don't say nothin'."

"The constable? Isn't he like the sheriff or something? Is it...?" I chose my words carefully. "Is headlighting like a crime?"

"I don't know exactly." Burt Charles shrugged. "Come off it, Izzie. I mean, after all, it's his land and his deer."

Oh, it matters. Tío might be implicated in...in a crime. *What if the judge would scrutiny him?*

Keep the Change

During the holidays, Marisol carried little Ana with her everywhere she went. While Estela changed the sheets and scrubbed the bathrooms with her next oldest daughter, Mari toted Ana to whichever side of the house they were working in. Aunt Hilda and the rest of us just traded rooms with Estela till the work was done.

One day while I waited for Burt Charles to arrive, I made an effort to amuse Ana. Puckering up my lips I asked, "And what did oo ask Santy Cwaus for, widdle girl? A dolly?"

Ana just blinked up at me, then looked up at Mari for some kind of instruction.

"*No te importa, mama.*" Mari snuggled her sister up closer.

"Wait! Wait! Wait!" I bobbled my head like a dashboard puppy. "Did you just call her, 'mama'? *Mama*? Good grief, she's your sister, not your mama! That's the funniest thing I ever heard of." I let go with an overdose of laughter like the canned stuff I'd heard on the Red Skelton Show. I pushed for outrageous hilarity.

"No," Mari said. "It is a...what you call...when you love somebody."

"Oh, right."

"You gringos call each other 'baby.' Do you think a husband is his wife's baby?" She bumped Ana to her other hip. "Sometimes you gringos think you know everything!"

I stuttered a comeback. "Well...well, you won't even tell me when I ask!"

"Ask what, Lizzie?"

"Izzie, *not* Lizzie!" She was doing it again. "What Ana wants for Christmas, dummy. A doll or what?"

Spinning on her heels, Mari marched into the kitchen spitting out words like watermelon seeds. "A dolly won't fix what Ana needs. "*Un mejor corazón, eh?*"

"Well, whatever." I gave up. "Shoot! I'll just go outside to wait."

A blue norther had whipped in the night before, leaving a crystalline blue sky. I put on my jacket and waited outside for Burt Charles. An orange orchard flanked the white walls that surrounded the five-acre lawn. Boughs hung heavy with fruit. I yanked an orange off a lower branch and dug into it with my fingernails. A fine mist of juice sprayed out across my cheek. It slid down to my chin before I swiped at it with my sleeve. Sectioning the orange, I let juice dribble over my fingers. I took a bite. Pursing my lips and clenching my jaw to suppress the ache of its tartness, I sprawled out on the grass that was still green before the first frost. I wiped my palms and the back of my hands across the wide blades of St. Augustine grass. Bracing my head in the crook of my arm, I faced the sunshine.

The South Texas sun at midday overpowered the sting of the cold air, but even with no breeze, little chill bumps popped up over my skin. Delicious. With eyes squinted tight against the brightness, I lay there almost asleep. Cold and warm, sweet and tangy, the contradictions melded and lifted me out of thought.

A shadow flitted across the backside of my eyelids, but before I could react, I got "Hey you!" And a poke in the ribs. Burt Charles. I hated to be startled. Boys always thought it was the funniest thing. I bolted to a prizefighter's stance, prepared to wallop him if he got into range again.

"Wanna go see what just arrived?" In singsong voice, Burt Charles said, "You're gonna like it. You better come go with me."

"Gimme a hint."

"Well, it breathes fire, paws the air and can go a quarter mile like greased lightning!" Not waiting for me to catch up, Burt Charles jogged off toward the barn.

"Got a flair for whoppers, don't you?" But I picked up my pace to keep up with him.

"Hey! What does *mejor corazón* mean?"

"Izzie, I've got better things to do besides be your Spanish dictionary. It means heart...heart, heart, heart, for Pete's sake."

I rolled the information around in my head. *Well, that did not make sense. Why in the world would Ana need a heart? She already had a heart. These people are wearing me out.* I dismissed the translation.

We couldn't see past the big trailer parked in front of the corral gate. "Keep the Change" was scrawled across the side in bold letters. A man stood with his back to us, one boot propped on the first rung of the corral fence. Without moving his foot, he twisted around to look at us.

"Who's that?" I asked.

"That's George Parr, your tío's brother."

He did have that hawk nose like all the Parrs and he wore the khaki gabardine uniform of ranchers. "So *that's* what he looks like. What's he doing here?"

"Shhh, he can hear you."

"Well, so? I can ask questions, can't I?" Jeez, I thought. Burt Charles could get so constipated.

My annoyance was short-lived. A powerful *bam* cracked against the door from the inside of the trailer. I whooped and jumped back three feet. Burt Charles squealed.

"You scream like a girl!"

"And what do you scream like, girly?"

"Well, that's because—"

"You kids wanna get yourselves killed?" George was suddenly on us. I couldn't tell whether he yelled at us out of fear or aggravation. He stood between us with a hand on each of our shoulders and marched us off about fifty feet from the trailer. At that close range, I could see his eyes were the same color as Tío's—grey—but they lacked the softness. The image of ice over a dark river came to mind.

Burt Charles and I knew when to keep our mouths shut, but we twisted around with Mr. Parr's hands still on our shoulders to see Joaquín coming around the back of the trailer, a lariat in his hand. George called, "Back him out, Joaquín. I don't have all day."

We stepped back two more feet, but kept our eyes on Joaquín who moved slowly in spite of George's order. He looked off toward the house and looped and relooped the lariat. Seconds later the Cadillac pulled up behind us, and the door slammed.

"Tío!" My optimism swelled. "Can we watch? Oh please. Oh please."

His eyes on his brother, Tío patted the hood of the Cadillac and said, "Up here."

Now we were cookin', I thought as we popped up on the car. I made no eye contact with George, but Burt Charles and I smiled at each other with satisfaction. Another loud crack jolted us out of our cockiness.

"Go on ahead, Joaquín, come in through the side door. You can back him out." Tío was giving the instructions now.

"*Sí, señor. Ya me voy.*"

We lifted our chins and stretched our necks in an effort to get the first look. We could no longer see Joaquín, but the frame of the trailer shuddered with great shuffling and grunting from the animal inside.

"*Cálmate, caballo.*" Be calm, horse. Joaquín spoke softly and low. He repeated his words over and over, even though the horse's fear was almost tangible. Great dark red haunches, burnished in the sunlight backed into view. A hard, sudden scramble of shod hooves delivered onto solid ground the most magnificent animal I had ever seen—Keep the Change.

The horse jerked hard against the lead rope. Backing and backing, his hooves clicked against themselves. He blew great punching gusts, the pink caves of his nostrils flaring.

Joaquín murmured the same words over and over in a kind of mantra against the near hysteria of the animal. "*Cálmate, caballo.*"

"Walk him around here a while and then take him into the corral. He'll settle down here in a minute." Tío circled his hand toward a sandy area.

The horse continued to dance, but finally Joaquín was able to coax him through the gate without getting run over, even though at the last second, the horse put on a burst of speed and Joaquín jumped to the side. His crumpled hat flipped in the dust and tumbled under the hooves.

"Put him on the longe line and send him around. Let's see how he moves," said Tío.

Joaquín snapped a thirty-foot line onto Keep the Change's halter, stretched out his arm to the left and asked the horse to move in a circle around him.

"Well," Tío said to his brother with a nod of approval, "There's nothing the matter with that horse."

"Aw, hell, Atlee. You act like I'm trying to put something over on you." George packed his cigarette down on his fist before lighting it. "That lawyer Foreman was worth every penny you spent. Got me off the hook." His laugh reminded me of gravel being emptied from a bucket. "Better'n having your old brother in the hoosegow again, don'cha think?"

Burt Charles' eyebrows shot up and his mouth dropped.

"What's a hoosegow?" I asked, turning away from George and Tío.

"*Juzgado.* Around here, it means, it means…." He kept his head down, but his eyes peered out from under his cap at George.

"Well, spit it out, Burt Charles!"

"Shhh. They'll hear you."

"Who knows, Atlee, maybe you'll get lucky with this hunk of horseflesh." George roared in laughter and slapped his leg. "And you can keep the change!"

Tío propped his boot up on the fence railing and lifted the brim of his hat just past the permanent sun line on his forehead. He didn't share the amusement with his brother, but nodded toward Joaquín who clucked and sent the horse on.

The animal's eyes rolled wide and he charged a broad circle around Joaquín. Around he flew like some wild thing, his hooves pounding the hard ground. I didn't know how Joaquín could have stopped him if he'd wanted to. Even with the cold front, the sweat glinted off the horse's burnt copper hide in the winter light. The proud heavy neck of the stallion arched against the rope as he flung himself skyward. It was like an appeal to God. I shivered. It wasn't the cool air. It was the power, the…the pure…. I couldn't find the words. "Oh, man alive," I said under my breath.

Burt Charles and I shifted to our knees to get a better look as he circled and circled, the whites of his eyes walled out, his head pulled away from Joaquín. Every now and then, he would suddenly wheel to face Joaquín, refusing to gallop. George sighed and trudged over to his truck. He pulled out a long whip and tossed it at Joaquín's feet. "That'll get the sonofabitch moving right."

Tío contradicted his brother. "Let's start him out easy." Then he called out something in Spanish so Joaquín ignored the whip. Joaquín walked slowly at the horse and lifted his left arm. His head down, Keep the Change stared at Joaquín a second or two then wheeled off clockwise. At last, nostrils wide and contracting hard with each breath, his furious gallop became the one-two beat of a trot in great reaching strides. He began to blink and his ears tuned to Joaquín. Sweat foamed up between his haunches and he bobbed his head like he was asking permission to quit. We all watched in silence. Nothing under the sky but breathing and hooves pounding.

Finally, Tío said. "He's calmin' down. Give him a few more minutes then walk him around, Joaquín. And brush him good." To his brother, he said, "You got to admit, that horse has some stamina."

George said, "Course there's a reason why. He races as a quarter horse, but he's three-fourths thoroughbred. You know he set track records, quarter mile in 21 seconds flat."

"I know, George, I know." Tío looked up at us and winked.

George kept talking. "Had to handicap him so much in California, the trainer got to where he hated to see him run. Still, he could carry the extra weight and win. Maybe you'll have better luck down in Laredo or Ruidoso." He slapped Tío on the back. "Well, if this doesn't cover your expenses, maybe it will in time. On the track or at stud. Best I can do."

"This'll be it, right, George?" Tío's mouth twisted a little. "The last time." It was not a question.

George gave Tío another rap on the back and laughed again. "Forget about it, Atlee. I got everything taken care of. Then he patted my shoulder like he hadn't just yelled at us. "And is this pretty little thing the niece you've been telling me about?"

Weary with the evasion of his comment, Tío sighed. "Yes, it is. This is Isabel Martin, Helen's girl."

"Hello, Mr. Parr. Pleased to meet you."

"Well, you sweetheart you. You call me George." He held out his hand and bowed over it like he was going to kiss it or something. And nodding at Burt Charles, he asked, "How are you, big guy?"

"Fine, sir." Burt Charles glowed with the attention.

"Let's go, kids." Tío opened the car door and looked down the road. He turned to George and repeated, "The last time."

We bounced off the hood and slid across the front seat. George called after us as we pulled off. "You can keep the trailer, Atlee. No good to me now!"

Tío shifted hard into gear, even though we didn't have very far to go to the house.

We pulled into the garage and Tío sat there a minute before turning off the engine. "I don't have to tell you kids to stay away from that stallion. He's not like our geldings around here."

"Oh, can't we watch while Joaquín longes him?" I would never get enough of that polished hide and muscle flexing in the sunlight.

"No."

"Tío!" I didn't mean to whine but the words trailed out that way. "Please…."

"No."

Burt Charles elbowed me out of the car door. "Yessir," he said. And to me, "Let's go count our Christmas presents." Some gifts had magically appeared lately. Maybe even some more with our names on them.

Dinner was cooking as we trotted through the kitchen, but we skidded to a halt in front of the big drawers that held breads and cookies.

Estela chopped onions at the sink. The back of her palm went up to wipe away the tears. We smiled at her temporary blindness. Just as we'd each plucked one cookie apiece out of the bag, Mama edged around the corner and snapped them out of our fingertips.

"We're starving." I pleaded, but before I knew it she sliced an apple and handed each of us a half.

"You'll live. Twenty minutes till supper. Run on."

Dejected, we turned for the veranda. "Sorry, Burt Charles. I can't help it. She's always like that."

We wandered off to the poolroom. Aunt Hilda repeatedly reminded me that I was to refer to the large room between the living room and bar as the billiard room. But I loved the swaggering connotation of "pool room" and frequently suggested that we "rack 'em up and hit a few rounds." I never did get the finer points of the game, but knocking those balls around made me feel like a gangster's pal. Not tall enough to chalk up the cue stick without bracing it at an angle between my knees, I squeaked the blue chalk around and around the tip.

"That's enough, Izzie. Good grief." Burt Charles clearly thought pool was a man's game. I leaned over the felt-topped table and forked my finger over the stick.

"Choke it, choke it," said Burt Charles. "You'll never get a good aim holding it out that far."

I closed one eye and then the other. I came to my conclusion as to the best angle and held my breath.

"Jail."

"What?" The cue skittered along the felt leaving a blue-white trail.

"Jail. You wanted to know what 'hoosegow' meant. It's Tex/Mex for 'jail.'" We stared at each other. No click of cue against ivory echoed through the room. We jumped when we heard Estela call.

"Señora, dinner, it's ready."

And then Mama. "Izzie! Burt Charles! Tell the rest of them to come on."

"Well," he said. "You wanted to know."

—⟶—

The next morning was Christmas. My excitement bubbled over like the foam on root beer. Instructed to play along with the Santa farce for Burt Charles' brothers' benefit, I complained, but secretly I got a good feeling from catering to their sweet delusions.

"Santa Claus is a state of mind, Izzie," Mama said. "Get there." If a state of mind produced new roller skates and the fringed leather jacket I had asked for, I could get there.

I was still rifling through my gifts when Tío and Aunt Hilda called Estela to the veranda while she was working on Christmas dinner. "For you and your family, especially Ana," Aunt Hilda said quietly. Tío handed her an envelope. It had a big bow on it. She wiped her hands on her gravy-stained apron and reached forward.

Big deal, I thought. Is that it? Just a Christmas card? Why especially for Ana? Shoot! She was just a little bitty kid. I could have made a silly face, but Christmas was no time to make a costly mistake.

Estela dipped her head. "Thank you, Señora Parr, Señor Parr." She peeled back the flap almost like she was afraid of what she would find. Lifting out a packet of bills that she didn't count, her eyes filled with tears. She covered her mouth, but managed to speak out in that lift Tejana women give their voices, "*Oh gracias, gracias a ustedes, señores. Gracias a Dios.*" Clutching the envelope and paper to her breast, she backed out of the room, shaking her head. Aunt Hilda reached for Tío's hand. She patted it a couple of times before wiping away a tear of her own.

I just didn't get grown-ups. Frequently, they told us kids to stop crying or they'd give us something to cry about, but then they would bawl over something like a Christmas envelope. Just the same, I got kind of a tight feeling in my chest.

—∧∾—

Christmas dinner was a special time I always looked forward to. We ate in the big dining room at the long ornately carved table. The Taylors were always in attendance—all of them, including the two little brothers. Burt Charles' daddy, Bob, checked wells for Continental Oil. He quoted statistics at length and when he ran out of specific details, referred to the rest as "whatnot."

Daisy was Burt Charles' mama and Aunt Hilda's best friend. For Daisy, all happy occurrences commenced around a little something to eat. She was even known to chew on her top lip, smiling when she did it, so I was never quite sure whether it was out of nerves or hunger. Daisy wore the tiniest slings on her diminutive feet and dangled them off her toes for hours. I sometimes had one eye on the clock and one on Daisy's delicately balanced slippers.

When Estela called that dinner was served, Burt Charles and I raced in and lined up behind the first two seats near Tío's left elbow. While we stood waiting for everyone to come to the table, we absent-mindedly ran our hands over the carvings etched along the edges of the chair backs. We had to wait so long for everyone to mosey in that, for once, I took a good look at the hand-chiseled forms. They were naked! I snapped my head around to check on Burt Charles. Sure enough, his palms caressed the chests of the sirens that formed the sides of the chairs. I jabbed him with my elbow and frowned toward the curves that he followed with his hands. He clucked twice and winked. When Tío walked in the room, Burt Charles' sailor imitation snapped to attention.

Twelve plates stacked up at Tío's place at the head of the table. We knew he'd cut us the drumsticks. He whisked the carving knife against the whetstone with effortless figure-eight flicks of his wrist. I tried not to think about Joaquín and the deer, even though Daddy sat down at the far end with Burt Charles' daddy and talked "through the heart and fourteen points." Fortunately, the aroma that wafted from the turkey distracted me.

With a smile for Burt Charles and me, Tío sliced out the wishbone and set it aside. We were just polishing off the pecan pie when Aunt Hilda dropped the bomb.

Overcome with Christmas spirit, she said, "Estela? You go on home now. We'll clear the table and straighten up the kitchen so you won't have too big a mess in the mornin'."

Mama chimed in, "Yes, we certainly will. Thank you, Estela."

Aunt Hilda reached out, touched Mama's hand, and looked at Daisy. "I just hate to ask y'all to help clear the table. You're our guests, after all. But it just breaks my heart that this may be the last Christmas...." She scooted her chair back and dropped her napkin in her plate.

"Don't talk about it, honey." Daisy tapped at a last morsel of crust with her pinky finger. "It just makes us all sad."

Aunt Hilda said, "Izzie? Burt Charles? Y'all leave the china alone, but you can pick up the silver and carry out the trash."

I opened my mouth in indignation. It was Christmas after all.

Daddy came out of his hunt mode just long enough to notice. "Get up! Get up now!" He stood abruptly grabbing for his chair behind him. He missed and it slammed hard onto the floor. "You get into that kitchen before—"

"Roger...." Mama's face had gone the color of the cranberry sauce.

Burt Charles and I both bolted to our feet, overturning a Waterford goblet in the process. Daisy set her fork down on the table like it was made of crystal. Bob stared at the carcass of the turkey, and Aunt Hilda's mouth formed a little red O. Then silence.

Tío bent forward, placed his palms flat on the table and pushed away. And he stood. Slowly. He draped one arm around me and the other around Burt Charles. Crooking my neck, I tried to read his expression. All I could tell was that he looked at my father straight on for an uncomfortably long time. He spoke very quietly. "I bet these kids could use some help taking out the trash." He gave our shoulders a little shake. "What you all think?" We hugged up against him and went with him into the kitchen.

Later that evening, Burt Charles and I climbed up to the roof. I wore my new jacket against the nip in the air.

"Wishbone?" I offered as I pulled the still stringy "Y" from my pocket. "Make a wish."

Burt Charles grinned and gave a mighty yank.

"Well, good grief!" I stared at my short bone fragment. "What do ya wish for?"

"Oh, I don't know."

"Well, then…. I…would…would you wish for me then?"

"Well, Izzie!"

"You mind a lot?"

"Aw, whadda ya want?"

"You know…."

"No, I don't, Izzie."

"A horse, Burt Charles. You know. A white Arabian stallion."

"Well, good luck on that, girl."

"Just wish it! Okay?"

Burt Charles pinched his eyebrows together and closed his eyes. "All right, all right."

"Did you?"

"Of course, I did. You can't say it out loud for goodness sake!"

I crossed my fingers for good luck. "Thanks," I said. "Thanks." I settled back against the chimney and brought my knees up under my jacket. Quiet for a while, we sat back and looked up at the night sky.

"I'm sorry about Daddy," I said. "He's pretty strict…and nervous sometimes."

"It's okay, Izzie. My dad can be…well…tough, too. You okay?"

"Oh, yeah. I'm kinda used to it."

Then I remembered the "hoosegow" word. "Well, what do you think?"

"About what?"

"The jail, for goodness sake!" I shook my head in wonder at the lack of curiosity in the male species.

"I don't know, Izzie. I really don't. All I know is George's been in a lot of trouble and your tío had to help him out. It was bad timing, what with the drought and all."

"But Tío? Is Tío in trouble, too? He had to go talk to a judge you know."

"Izzie!" He went back to impatience. "Lookit. Nobody tells me anything either. Quit worrying about it."

"And if he's headlighting…the constable might decide that he *does* mind if Tío hunts deer that way and decides to arrest him, after all."

"You worried about the constable? The constable's in your uncle's pocket. Forget about it. You don't know how it works down here. It's different." Burt Charles stuffed his hands deeper into his pockets. "How about you just quit worrying till you're sure you've got something to worry about?"

I hoped my sigh, audible in the still cold air, expressed my frustration. Maybe I was over-reacting. After all, Tío practically saved me from a hard whipping that very night. That gained him huge bonus points in my mind. Surely, he was a good man all the way through.

Our heads resting on our arms, we leaned back side-by-side against the chimney arch and were quiet for a long time. I shivered and looked up at the stars. The stars. It was like a matador swirled his cape full of lights across the sky. "Would you look at that?" I whispered, my breath fogging out in little spurts. Then I couldn't resist. I sounded small against the night, but that didn't stop me.

"The stars at night…."

Burt Charles chimed in "…are big and bright…."

We clapped softly four times but didn't finish the song.

Decision

Two more Christmases and two more summers went by. I was locked into adventures with Burt Charles, and Mari was absorbed with the care of little Ana. Mari and I avoided each other for the most part resulting in only minor skirmishes between us. In our case, absence didn't exactly make the heart grow fonder; it just kept us out of each other's way.

I could not say the same for my parents. Mama and I spent whole summers at the ranch away from Daddy—the preferred arrangement. Although Daddy never missed deer season at Las Higueras, being in his company became precarious. We never quite knew what would set him off. We were circumspect in our speech and actions.

At home in Waco, Daddy and Mama both worked long hours, but by the time I was twelve, Daddy was coming home an hour later than he had before and sometimes he went out again at night. I longed for the weekends when I thought everyone would relax, but one Friday night, Daddy didn't come home till 2:30 a.m. The crunch of tires on the gravel driveway woke me. I thought that he'd had car trouble or was he hurt? I worried about *him*. But I shouldn't have.

Mama was mad. Way madder than I had ever seen her. And crying.

"Where have you been this time, Roger?" She opened the front door and slammed it behind him.

Voices moved to the kitchen. Mama opened the icebox door and then slammed it. I heard the rattle of milk bottles from where I crouched at the door. She raked in a sob.

"Oh, shut up, Helen!" His anger stabbed the garbled words into the space between them.

Something heavy fell against the table and it scooted across the room. Daddy must have shoved her.

"I hate you for this!" She screamed this time.

The shuffle of his boots stumbled across the linoleum. Mama shrieked in pain.

I opened the door. Just a crack. "Mama?"

Mama hunkered down in the corner of the kitchen, her arms extended and fingers flared to ward off another kick.

"Mama?" I could hardly push the word from my throat.

Daddy whirled and squinted his eyes at me like he was trying to bring me into focus. He took three steps toward me and losing his balance stumbled against the table corner. "You," he said. "You get to bed. Now!"

I scrambled to the bathroom and locked the door. "Mama, Mama?"

Despite the silence, fear spilled under doors, splashed from transom windows, hurried along baseboards. At last, Mama spoke between the door and the jamb. "It's all right now, Izzie." She seemed strangely calm.

Slowly, slowly I unlocked the door and opened it to a fine line of vision. He sat slouched on my bed.

Mama limped into the living room and turned on the porch light. A siren fluted through the middle class neighborhood.

"Sergeant Sims and Sergeant Thomas, ma'am." While the policemen talked to Mama in the front room, I inched up to my father. His head fell forward, a wisp of his black hair shielding his eyes, his shame. His arms drooped between his knees. Like a lifeless scarecrow, he hung in space seeming hardly aware of who or what he was. He never looked up. He never moved.

"I hate you too." Then I slugged him with all my strength. He never raised his head. He never responded. It was like I hit a zombie. I did not cry. I hit him again. On the shoulder. On his cheek. On his back. "I hate you, hate you, hate you!"

I stumbled back to the window and wrapped the curtain around my knees when the policemen swaggered into the bedroom and stood wide-legged, staring at Daddy. "Mr. Martin?"

No response.

"What did you say his first name was, ma'am?"

"Roger." Her hand over her mouth, Mama stood backed against the wall.

"Ma'am? You're gonna have to speak up."

"Roger. His name is Roger Martin." Her hand moved from her lips to her throat.

"You gonna be able to settle down now, Roger?" Sims adjusted his gun belt. "Ain't no way to treat your wife, is it now?"

Daddy didn't answer.

With a slow wobble of his head from side to side, Daddy finally responded.

"Well now, that's better." Sims smiled up at Mama. "Let's let it go this time, ma'am. Whatcha think? Looks like he's calmed down and I don't see any signs of assault." He straightened, cleared his throat as though he could clear away the problem like phlegm.

Then Mama, who always closed the door when she changed clothes and who wore her robe tightly belted at breakfast, bared her leg. "You don't call this assault?" The bruise had already begun. A dark blue thickening engulfed her knee to the middle of her thigh.

Sims winced and turned away. "We'll help you get him to his bed." The only effort they made to help Mama was drag Daddy to his bed and apologize their way out of the door.

"You just call us if there's any more trouble." They stood with the front door screen standing open and turned to say, "Maybe he's just had a bad day. He's your husband after all."

I wanted to run after the policemen and shout that Daddy had lots of bad days. But the neighbors whose silhouettes darkened the lights from their living room windows silenced me.

Mama never told anyone that I knew of, but she slept with me that night and all other nights. "It'll be all right," she said. She sobbed anyway after she came to bed, when she thought I slept and wouldn't feel the trembling of the mattress. I felt like the rind left after someone had scooped the red flesh out of a watermelon. Too heavy to blow away, but with all the good parts gone. I punched my pillow hoping Mama would think I was fluffing it into shape, knowing all along the punches were strikes against my father.

The next day on my way to school, my next-door neighbor, Mary Jo, caught up with me. I hoped I would be able to get ahead of her by leaving earlier than usual, but she must have been waiting at her window. As she rushed up breathlessly beside me, it was clear she knew about the police car.

"What happened over at your house, Izzie? Who were the police after? Did you get in trouble?"

"Ask your mama and daddy, Mary Jo. I bet they've got all kinds of fascinating ideas."

Mary Jo and I played together, but it was a friendship born of proximity, not common interests. I couldn't remember how many times people asked us if we were sisters. Granted we both had brown eyes and wore our dark hair in French braids, but I thought myself intense and adventuresome like Tarzan's Jane. A frilly girl, Mary Jo was skinny. And she stayed out of trees for the most part.

Nothing much slowed down Mary Jo's questions. Subtleties washed right over her brain like water over rocks.

"Oh, they thought something bad happened. They heard a ruckus. It woke them up and they even thought about calling the police themselves. Did y'all have a fight or something?" She juggled her books as she sped up to keep pace with me.

"Mary Jo?" I tried to sound firm but even-tempered. "Shut up, please."

"I'm telling!" She swished off, her skirt swaying.

I was pleased to note that her slip was showing.

The Tearing Apart

We all moved about each other like robots: "Yes, no, please, thank you." Mama rushed home from school and prepared Daddy's dinner, but she and I stood at the kitchen counter and ate, our backs turned to the dining room where he sat alone. He stabbed at his salmon croquette and it fell apart like mud pie. He slammed his glass of ice tea down so hard on the table, I would sometimes find an ice cube on the floor. Mama and I just kept on eating. We didn't even look up at each other.

One evening when Mama climbed into bed, she spoke into the darkness. She ran her hands across my back. I rolled over and sat up. The light from the street lamp shone in her eyes. "I'll make it right," she said. "I'll make it right." I had never heard her so resolute. In a way, it scared me.

If Mary Jo gossiped, I never knew for sure. I got a few looks but no overt questions. When I was called to my teacher's desk a week or so after the incident, it was not even clear whether or not it was the result of rumors.

"Come sit with me a minute, Isabel." Mrs. Quarles pulled up student desks for herself and me. We sat with our knees touching. "Are you doing okay, honey?"

"Oh, yes ma'am. I'm doing just fine." I wrapped my fists in my skirt.

"It's just that you haven't been, well, quite so…so…. Well, you know yours was always the first hand up when I asked a question. Lately, you don't seem to care."

"Just tired, I guess, ma'am. I've been doing a lot of…of…bicycle training."

"Bicycle training?"

"Yes, ma'am." My mind lifted off in a pinwheel firework of lies. "The way I see it, bicycling will improve my balance for horseback riding. You see, my aunt and uncle have a ranch in South Texas and lots of horses, and I plan to get real good at riding them. Then I will get a horse all of my own. A white Arabian stallion." Unraveling my hands, I dropped them into my lap as primly as possible and looked up hopefully into Mrs. Quarles' eyes.

"I think I understand," she said. She patted my hands. "You know you can talk to me anytime if you are worried about something, honey. Anything at all."

"Oh, yes, ma'am." *Tell 'em what they wanna hear. Isn't that how it's done?* I leaned forward enough to lift my bottom off the chair. "May I be excused?"

"Of course," she said, but she sounded like she had lost a gamble.

I turned back briefly on my way out the door. Mrs. Quarles still sat in the student chair, her knees to her chin. Her lips wrinkled badly when she pursed them. She shook her head slowly back and forth.

I bolted for home. I ran and ran, only glancing each way when crossing streets, clearing sidewalks in broad leaps till reaching our backyard and the mulberry tree where I hung out most of the time these days. I climbed to where I could see the roof of our screened-in porch. Even with the leaves gone for the winter, I felt protected by the mesh of branches that blocked out the fear that lingered in our house and wafted from the windows.

Moving South

Mama began making long distance calls to a school in South Texas. She'd send me on an errand while she stood at the hall phone, but I hung around at the screen door to listen. She made even longer calls to Aunt Hilda. So in May I wasn't really surprised when Mama said it would be a sad summer, but better in many ways. The fights, the tears weren't the way people were supposed to live. They were supposed to love each other like Tío and Aunt Hilda, and that's where we were going to stay. Just for a while. Mama said she would have a chance to work on her master's degree. With a higher degree she could make more money. She'd been meaning to do that for a long while. "That's why I've made all those long distance calls. I'm aware you've been eavesdropping, you know."

I said, "I hope we get to the ranch before Daddy gets the telephone bill."

Mama sniffed an acknowledgement of my dark humor. "Life will be different," she continued, "but like last year in a lot of ways. The way it was last summer. You had fun. We'll be all right," she said. "The new school will be...all right." Her shoulders shuddered just once. She meant to portray something else. But it was relief I sensed. She was glad to leave. I scooted up against my mama's knee and stroked her arm anyway.

I understood too that the words my mother spoke were no guarantee. In limbo, my world shifted one direction and then another—a heavy liquid, sloshing about me like mercury in a thermometer, too fluid to hold on to, too dense for me to sink.

—◆—

On Memorial Day morning Mama stood at the back door, suitcases and boxes stacked on the porch. Still dark, the glow from the backyard light outlined her form—somehow pathetic despite her proud posture.

Standing behind her, my pillow and blanket clutched in front of my belly, I fought a sudden desire to suck my thumb but instead, I took it into my mouth just the same and bit it hard. *Remember this morning. It will change your life.* I feared it. I welcomed it.

Daddy still had not come out of their bedroom. Was Mama going to have to carry out the luggage herself? I threw my pillow and blanket to the floor and charged back to their bedroom.

"Daddy? Are you in there? Are you going to load the car or not?" I knocked with clipped staccato raps. It hurt my knuckles. When he didn't answer, I turned the doorknob, opened the door and banged again. With my fist this time.

The bathroom light was still on. He stood raking through the hangers in the closet. His arm swept across the bar. Right then left. And back again.

My outrage dissolved when I saw him. He gave me a sidelong stare and then sagged against the closet door.

"I'm sorry," he said. He held out his arms. "I don't want you to leave me. You're all...you're all that's left."

I fell against him.

How could I love him when he had been so cruel to my mother, when he had crushed the fabric of our family? Guilt seeped into my skin. Mama stood on the porch alone while I sobbed in my father's arms. How could I?

I broke away. "We have to go." Turning away, I clutched his hand for one last time.

When I returned, Mama had loaded the suitcases. Daddy silently lifted the heavier boxes and set them in the trunk of the car. My things: the pictures I had drawn, photographs, the letters from Burt Charles, my diary. All packed in a smaller box to be put on the floorboard.

Mama and I were already in the car when we heard Daddy's footsteps on the driveway. He slid into the driver's seat and sat there. Dawn lightened the backyard where I had played for years, the tree I'd climbed, the shuffleboard court where I'd ridden my Mobo tin horse, and the fruit trees Mama had chased me around with a peach switch.

Daddy slammed down the clutch and fired up the car, revving the engine till it ground against itself. The tires spun out on the gravel, spitting pebbles against garage walls. We lurched into the street in a backward arc. Neighbors' lights flashed on at the screech of brakes and rubber. It was only then that he dropped the gearshift into first and drove away, sedate and defeated.

I twisted on my knees in the backseat to look out the back window. I imagined the house would miss us. Miss the sound of laughter. Even the sound of tears. We had become part of the structure of the house, part of the glue that held it together. And we were driving off down Highway 6 toward the south. I spoke the words so that no one would hear me, "Good-bye."

Just pretend it's like every summer, Izzie, I thought. What's the matter with you anyway? You are going to see Burt Charles, ride horses, swim, and have breakfast in bed if you want to. What is the matter with you?

If Daddy could have been good. If he could have just been good.

—⁓⁓—

Aunt Hilda must have stood and waited at the kitchen window till the dust rose and sifted down the road toward the house. She and Tío rushed out to the carport to meet us. Neither spoke to Daddy. Aunt Hilda yanked open the door on Mama's side of the car. Mama sat there a moment with her feet on the pavement before she twisted back to stare at Daddy. From the back seat I tried to read what was in her pale eyes. Loss? Defiance? I didn't have the words for it. A long sigh from a down-turned mouth, a soft moan. Resignation maybe. At last, she lifted herself from the car as though pulled by marionette's twine, strung tight and proud, despite the wobbling legs, despite the empty loose arms.

I had stepped out on Daddy's side. He did glance at me as he backed up. His brown eyes blackened with regret. Or was it a kind of relief that filled his empty gaze? I hoped there was accusation in mine.

Mama did not slump into her sister's arms until Joaquín unloaded the suitcases. Until the tires of Daddy's Ford rumbled over the cattleguard.

"It's gonna be all right, Isabel." Tío took me by the hand and we followed the sidewalk around the house. "I'm going to take good care of you."

"Promise, Tío?" I looked up into his clear grey eyes, so limpid I could see no dark specks of lies. I wanted with all my heart to believe.

He paused for a moment, seeming to take in the child's plea he heard in my voice. Dropping to one knee, he took me by the shoulders. He looked straight into my eyes. "I promise," he said as he gave me a little shake. "You can count on me." For a quick moment, he pulled me to him.

Flinging my arms around him, I hugged him as hard as I could and stifled the *please, please* that wanted to gurgle from my throat.

As quickly as it had come, the moment was gone. But the promise had been made.

As if suddenly embarrassed, Tío stood and abruptly pointed at the oldest pecan tree. "A great-horned owl lives there. See her?"

And there she sat, two feet tall in the crook of the pecan. Her body perfectly still, her head pivoted in seamless mechanical adjustments. Her round yellow eyes scanned our approach. We took one step too many and the owl lifted on perfectly soundless wings out beyond the walls to the mesquite brush.

"She'll be back. Got a nest up there. But she's got to watch out. Hilda's been gunning for that owl ever since she heard her hooting at night. If your aunt was any better shot, that big old bird would be a bag of feathers now and that limb there wouldn't be hanging like a door with one hinge loose."

"How come Aunt Hilda wants to shoot her?" I asked.

"Oh, she says it's gonna attack somebody, but I think it's just because that owl is so big and quiet. Silence scares people sometimes."

Just like Tío. Quiet. It did scare me sometimes, but I sensed his power. And what was he thinking when he had so few words to say?

"That owl's not gonna hurt anybody. Oh, maybe she'll get a rat or a...little squirrel like you!" And he grabbed me and tickled my arms and sides.

After my wild screams and giggles, I asked, "Will she stay till Halloween?"

"Well, now, she just might, if we can hide that twenty-two pistol from your aunt Hilda."

"Y'all still got Keep the Change?" I was dying to get out to the corral to take a look at him. Maybe he had settled down some. Maybe he wasn't charging around so much any more and had gotten to where he liked kids.

"Yes, he's still out there. More trouble than he's worth so far." Tío turned around and we walked back to the house.

"How come? He's awful pretty."

"Well, pretty is as pretty does." Tío shook his head. "We'll be sending him up to Ruidoso soon. See if he can earn his keep by winning a race or two."

"Burt Charles coming out?"

"He'll be out. Why don't you run unpack your swimsuit?"

I ran off toward the bedroom side, stopped short and trotted back. "Can Joaquín saddle up Canela in the afternoons? I'd like to practice every day to get really good." I remembered my lie to my teacher—bicycling to improve horseback riding balance. That was a wild one.

Summer of My Discontent

Those first nights in the summer I thought I'd never get to sleep. Cicadas outpaced Spanish castanets. When they were quieter, they still sounded like the rustling of Scarlet O'Hara's starched petticoats. My heartbeat tended to keep time with the chirring and it was hardly conducive to sleep. Finally I talked myself into believing their noise was my grandmother's rocking chair creaking as she enveloped me in her ample breast. And with the cooling of the night air, the furious chatter slowed and the sound lulled me into oblivion—my nights calmed between the sun-dried, ironed sheets.

I became delirious with plans for living there at Las Higueras. It was my favorite place in the world, for goodness sake. Summer would be like summers before. We would swim in the morning, eat watermelon in the afternoon and swim again. Everything would be perfect. Burt Charles and I would be buddies here at the ranch as well as at school. I would have a horse to learn on while I sweet-talked my tío into getting me an elegant mount that could almost fly. Mama could eat all the figs she wanted, get her master's degree and recline in the velvet chaise longue. I would not awake in the middle of the night to hear sounds that wedged a stake into my heart. Instead, I would listen to the coyotes.

—⁊⁊⁊—

Mama drove forty miles to Kingsville every morning. Evenings, she spent holed up in the blue room. A peaceful place, the blue room. Walls and even the ceiling a soft aqua that made you want to lean back with your arms behind your head and wait for clouds to drift by. Aunt Hilda had moved the lavender chaise longue into that room, and Mama sank back into its cushion to write, her smooth Palmer Method script scrolling across pages and pages of notebook paper. Even with the pressure of studying long hours, Mama laughed more and the lines that had deepened around her mouth seemed softer than before.

I understood Mama being dead set on getting her master's degree. I had my own tactics lined up on how to earn a new horse. Not that I didn't appreciate Tío giving me Canela to ride, and I had developed a fondness for her. I thought if I was masterful enough on the likes of Canela, sitting with grace to her choppy beat, Tío would see I deserved an Arabian stallion. I wasn't sure how much a horse like that might cost, but I bet my Tío could get me one if I just showed him how much I had improved. Maybe it would not even be this year, I daydreamed. Maybe not till next summer. I could save my money, just to show my heart was in the right place. I planned to go up to the corral every evening before supper with a carrot for Canela. The first time she nickered when I shuffled down the sandy path to the barn, I realized I was glad to see her too. I scratched her neck and whispered, "Let's get good together. Just you and me."

At sunset, I walked Canela back to the corral. It surprised me that she didn't take off like a maniac to the barn. I thought about our first encounter outside the yard. Of course, Mari had kicked her into a run. "That was that mean girl's fault, wasn't it, Canela?" I knew Canela was dying to get back so she could eat, but she seemed patient now, willing to amble with her head near my shoulder and willing to wait if I stopped to pull a sticker from my sock. Maybe I loved her more than I realized.

—⚹—

Daisy brought Burt Charles out nearly every day. We sat on the roof at night asking each other questions about the heavens and God. I didn't talk about Daddy much. I didn't know what to say.

I almost didn't see Mari that summer. She stayed at home with little Ana. Sometimes, though, she came over to help her mom with dishes after dinner. She sat little Ana in a kitchen chair and gave her some leftovers to eat.

Just to see what was going on, I'd go into the kitchen on evenings when Burt Charles couldn't come out. Estela's hands plunged into steamy water and a light sweat beaded up on her forehead. A stray hair or two stuck there. The soft clink of dishes had almost a musical sound as Mari dried them and put them in the shelves. "Wanna help?" Mari turned toward me expectantly.

"Nah, I gotta go in a minute." I sat on the barstool and swung my legs back and forth. "What y'all doing over at the *your* house all summer?"

"Just watching after Ana." Mari dried the plates in a fury.

"How come she doesn't come over here anymore like she used to?"

"Supposed to keep her at home." Mari said something to her mother in Spanish. I hated when she did that.

"Who said?"

"Dr. Garza. Okay?"

"*Okay!*" With that, I figured I had worn out my welcome in the kitchen. "Jeez, just askin'."

Before I could grab a lonely half of a deviled egg and beat a fast retreat, Mari threw down the dishtowel and left. She slammed the door behind her.

I raised an eyebrow and looked at Estela. "How come Mari doesn't like me, ya think?" I centered my butt on the barstool and gazed with innocent eyes at Estela. "I mean, you are awful nice to me-——bring me breakfast in bed and all, but Mari acts like I oughta bring *her* breakfast in bed." I tapped a spoon against the tiled island.

Estela untied her apron and then re-tied it. "Mari wants to be better than you and you want to be better than her. You two are not so different as you think you are."

Well, that was just crazy. I tapped out a few more rat-a-tats with the spoon and nodded as though I considered the wisdom of her response. If we were so much alike, why did Mari hate me? Estela probably did know the truth, but she would never say. Maybe she felt the same way as Mari but just covered it up. Estela worked for the Parrs after all. What would she do without her salary and the housing they provided. And the doctor bills? Who would pay the doctor bills? Nah. She wouldn't tell me the real truth.

"Estela?"

"*Mande?*" Estela was taking off her apron after all and getting ready to leave.

"Oh, never mind."

—m—

When Mari wasn't there, Estela still moped around. She didn't make little jokes to me like she had in the past. And she didn't smile when I begged her to make enchiladas. There were no enchiladas like Estela's. I even volunteered to chop the onions since that usually made her cry.

"No, Isabel. Sometimes I just cry. *Me entiendes, mijita?*"

I turned to Aunt Hilda for answers. "How come they carry on so over little Ana?" I asked when we sat down to watch television.

Aunt Hilda studied the ceiling and took up my hand and rubbed it over and over. It irritated me. I figured the back of my hand would be raw by the time she got to what she wanted to say. "Well, darlin', she's just been real sick. The surgeons said she had a bad spot in her heart, well, really, a little hole. They've been trying to fix it."

"Well, why don't they just fix it?"

"I don't know, honey. I just don't know."

The Redheaded Stranger

September came.

"I really think the socialization will be good for her, Helen, and you've got to leave early to get over to your classes in Kingsville." Aunt Hilda was determined to assimilate me into the Tejano culture of South Texas. Never mind, she could barely speak three words in Spanish.

Tío and Aunt Hilda spent the two previous weeks talking Mama into attending Texas A & I College full time. "Just think! You'll walk across the stage with a master's degree in no time." Aunt Hilda took Mama's hands in hers. "You can't say no. I'll be here to keep an eye on Izzie. You know I'd love to do that. You wouldn't have a thing to worry about. Please let me."

As a result of Aunt Hilda's suggestion, I found myself waiting for the school bus with the help. It loomed a yellow shapeless animal out of the haze to snap open its jaws. *"Buenos días!"*

I didn't see why I had to ride the school bus with everybody else. All they did was chatter away in Spanish. I was pretty sure I was the gringo topic of the day. Mari gave me a little pinched smile, popped open her school books the minute those bus doors slammed shut and kept her nose in them till we arrived at school thirty minutes later. No amount of razzing could discourage her. When we picked up Burt Charles, even he spent a good bit of time visiting with the rest of them. I counted telephone poles—three hundred and eighteen between the ranch and Benavides. I lost count on fence posts after one thousand. They came faster than I could think the words.

Even well into October, the schoolroom was a steamy cube packed with hot little bodies. Gnats, always bad in the fall, swarmed and stuck to our heads already tacky with sweat. Teachers, most of them anyway, steered the small rotating fans toward the students, but it was still miserable.

As hard as I tried, I couldn't concentrate very well at school, so I was easily distracted when a girl on the third row stared at me every time she thought I wasn't looking. It became a game. I'd look toward the blackboard, but cut my eyes over to see her zeroing in on me. I'd jerk my head around to catch her in the act and she would glance away. The shy type, I thought. And she practically reeked gringa—red hair that fell to her waist in soft folds, freckled arms. I was the only other gringa girl in the room and that must have been of some interest to her.

I caught up with her when we lined up for lunch. Holding up my lunch box as evidence, I said, "I brought my mine. Wanna sit together?"

An inkling of a smile flitted across her lips. "Are you white?"

That hurt, but I wasn't going to give up. "Well, yes. Do you hear any accent here? Are you?"

Her giggle was like a fairy's bell. Absolutely charming.

We spread out our sandwiches and carrot sticks. We laughed when we realized we had the same lunch, even down to the Oreo Cookies. Maybe she'd like to come to the ranch. I wondered if she could ride a horse. I knew she would become my best girlfriend and that we could really take on Mari.

She opened up by the time we got to the Oreos, telling me her name was Sonia, that her daddy worked for Hiawatha Oil Company and asking me what my daddy did.

My throat locked into a hiccup. "He works for the government—Social Security."

"Down here in Benavides?"

"Well, not exactly."

"So where do you live?" Her shyness was fading like fog on a sunny day.

"Out at Las Higueras."

"Las Higueras? Isn't that the Parr ranch?"

"Sure is." My chest inflated. Everybody knew the Parr's place was fabulous.

Scarlet bloomed at her ears. It flooded her face. It spilled down her neck.

"What?" I wondered if I had embarrassed her with my fine standard of living.

Sonia gathered up the napkin and sack, scrambling them together in a hurried, almost frantic motion. "Nothing. Oh, nothing." Like Cinderella running from the ball as the midnight bell tolled, Sonia fled.

"What? Hey, you can have one of my cookies."

"Oh, I can't stay. I'm sorry. Really I am. Daddy just says the Parrs are...are.... I just can't stay."

I sat there, my mouth a loose flap of skin on my face. I glanced around to see if anyone else had heard. Four kids who sat near us stared for a moment before studying their chocolate ice cream Dixie cups with great interest.

Burt Charles had bolted from his table with the boys and buddied up for a baseball game when the teacher called recess. He didn't even look back or holler out for me to join them. This was not like it was when we were here for summer vacation. At the ranch we had the pool and air-conditioning and Burt Charles spoke English all the time.

I found an empty swing and claimed it. I sat there, kicking at the ground enough to sway back and forth and make me look like I was using the equipment. I wondered how school back home was going. Wondered if my old principal Mrs. Warfield was still cracking the whip. It wasn't really like I was sick to my stomach and I didn't exactly want to cry, but I thought about the musty halls of Provident Heights Elementary, the ocean picture outside the nurse's office and Moses, our janitor. Well, I wouldn't exactly mind seeing them again. I even missed Miss Prissy, Mary Jo.

I thought leaving home was kind of like looking off a cliff. You could see the direction you'd fall, and the net at the bottom being held by your mama and aunt and uncle, but you just didn't know what you might ricochet off of on the way down. One thing I was quite sure of—you probably wouldn't be crawling back up to where you started from. And some of the ricochets would hurt.

A New Saddle, Same Old Horse

Even when my thirteenth birthday came and went, no elegant horse with an arched neck and high prancing step presented itself. I even thought Daddy might make a quick trip down. Maybe to bring me a present or take me to the movies. Or even call. But I remembered it was *long distance*. Not that I really expected either and not that the day wasn't nice, but the night before I felt just a little tremor in my heartbeat that kept saying *maybe, maybe*.

Mama made a white cake with chocolate icing that was my favorite. Mama and Aunt Hilda and Tío chipped in together to get me a nice smaller saddle, one that had stirrups that I could reach. The next Saturday, I was eager to try it out.

"Here, I'll load that in the car for you." Tío slung it onto his hip and we started out for the garage.

Canela stayed in the corral all the time now instead of roaming the pasture with the rest of the herd. It just wore Joaquín out trying to find the horses and coax them up. Canela was old, but she was no old fool. She'd trot off and toss her head when she saw his old Chevy truck chugging across the pasture toward her.

"Hey, girl. Look what we brought you!" I patted the saddle.

She lifted her head when she heard us coming and rolled her eyes toward us, but just stood there.

"Oops, we forgot the carrots, didn't we?" Tío laughed as he pushed the saddle onto a rack. "Whew! Saddles are gettin' heavier every year." It was one of those rare times when I remembered how much older Tío was than Aunt Hilda.

Canela angled herself to face the corner of the corral fence. No carrot, no enthusiasm. She stood by placidly enough, though, as I slipped the halter over her head and led her over to the shed out of the wind.

I brushed for some time with Tío supervising and we laughed as she craned her neck when we brushed her from ear to withers. "She likes it." I smiled up at Tío.

"Yeah, she used to get a lot more brushing. She was quite a mare in her time. He gave a pat on her haunches.

We heard Keep the Change call out from his stall in the far section. Tío flopped the saddle blanket onto Canela and yelled over his shoulder at the stallion. "Yeah, you heard me. *Quite* a mare!" He handed over the saddle to me. "Here, give it a try."

Joaquín had always saddled her up for me and I was anxious to learn to do it myself. I grunted and shifted the saddle to my chest, and with one more hard groan, pushed it across the blanket. "Cinch her up gently when she exhales," said Tío. "After you walk her down to the yard, you'll have to tighten her up again. Let's see if you can do it."

I made a muscle.

Opening the gate, he waited for me to wriggle the bridle into Canela's mouth. "Here, I'll give you a leg up." He stooped and waited for me to step into his cupped hands. Those hands. The skin, scarred and whitened, stretched tight over the bones. His bent head revealed his age once again. I leaned forward and quickly kissed his bald spot. I blushed, I knew I did, but he smiled up at me with such obvious pleasure that I realized again how very dear he was to me.

He boosted me up, gave my leg a pat. "I'll give you and Canela an escort to the yard." He started up the Cadillac and drove slowly alongside of us as Canela and I ambled toward the walls of the house grounds.

"Thank you, Tío," I called. From that moment on, I believed he loved me for sure. My heart ached a little less for the father I had given up. In a stroke of generosity, I rubbed Canela's neck. "I bet he loves you too, old girl."

I scanned the expansive vista of the ranch and wondered when I would graduate to open range riding. Soon, I determined. Soon. And then I would truly be qualified for the horse I dreamed of. I just had to keep believing.

—⅏—

It was almost never too cold to ride, and Burt Charles and I could get going midday without having to wait for the summer's sunset. We began our incessant petitions to ride outside the yard. Thirteen was old enough. Just down the road to the front gate and then down the other fork to the Tanka Tierra. It was only two miles. We had walked there before or ridden our bikes, but it was one heck of a trek and then it was time to turn around and go back as soon as we got there. Horses were the answer.

We begged on a weekly basis. Tío had brought over a couple of dead-head horses from Mexico. Burt Charles picked out the pinto and we named him Jigsaw for the patterns on his hide. Of course, by now, Canela and I were a team. I just decided to stick with what I knew till I could get a good horse.

"If we ride together, how dangerous can it be on these old horses?" Burt Charles and I cornered Mama outside the bedroom wing.

"Worst happen is that one'll fall over dead," Burt Charles added. I nodded approvingly at him. What logic. I was impressed.

Mama laughed. "I'll think about it," she called back over as she closed the door to the blue room.

Finally, at dinner one night, Tío interceded with the feminine guard, over-protective as it was. "Bomb proof," he promised Mama when she gasped at his approval to ride out. "I'll send one of the men out with them."

"I do think it will be all right, Helen. Atlee wouldn't let them go if it weren't." My aunt put her hand on Mama's arm.

"Thank youuuuu, Aunt Hilda!" I squealed.

"Two hours. *Two* hours. That's the limit without checking in!" Mama jammed her index finger on the table. Then she narrowed her eyes. "Burt Charles, does your mama go along with all this?"

"She said whatever Atlee said would be all right." He turned and looked at me. "Really."

And then she faced Tío. "Oh, Atlee, do you really think—"

"Helen, honey. I think it's gonna be fine. Why when I was their age…."

"Oh, I know. But you were born and raised here. I know I just get a little…anxious." Mama stood up abruptly. "Oh, all right. Go on. Get out of here." We were out the kitchen door when we heard her yell, "You be careful. I mean it!"

And so it began. Every Saturday and then nearly every day of Christmas vacation, we trekked about the countryside. Our rides extended weekly. Burt Charles talked about hunting. I talked about Mari. I talked about unloading Canela for a younger version and I talked about Tío and how much he hoped it would rain. Our rides began to take the place of night conversations on the roof. The fact that Burt Charles didn't have much to say didn't bother me. At least he listened. At least he attempted to answer. Somehow it did not matter that he knew no more than I did. He was in this with me.

Our freedom was unprecedented. Just so long as we were back in two hours. Sometimes we had to give the horses their heads and thunder back down the road to the barn to make it home on time. That was where Canela performed. She *loved* to get home as fast as she could. And she could crank up those old bones if the situation moved her.

Mama got to where she relaxed about our meanderings and we rode farther and farther down the road. Memorial Day was just around the corner and we would be free all summer.

On a Clear Day, You Can't See Forever

Time was a slow moving cloud that school year. When classes released for the summer, I looked forward to being on nobody's schedule and easy living, but Aunt Hilda was a fairly unpredictable creature. And the fact that she was "going to keep an eye on me" was a scary prospect. As hard as I tried, I failed to accurately interpret the signs of her shift in mood. One Saturday she'd smile indulgently at my sleeping till ten and calling for toast in bed. The next, she'd insist on an immediate response to an eight a.m. exercise of changing sheets: twin bed fabrics ironed to perfection, lace folded precisely back against the blanket like the white collars of Catholic schoolgirls. I never really did get better at making the bed or predicting her climate. She was as varied and serendipitous as the Texas barometric pressure.

The morning after Memorial Day, she buzzed in at eight and raked the drapes across the wrought iron rods. "I envision a vista," she said with a sweep of her arm, "that is limitless and pristine."

I blinked stupidly as I pressed my back into the headboard and tried to make sense of her words. "Where's Mama?"

"Off to Kingsville hours ago. This new class starts early. All right. Hop up. Get dressed. If you have any intention of swimming today, you'd best get a move on. I'm assigning you a window-washing chore. It's a beautiful day and I intend to see it through spotless veranda windows."

Three windows, recently installed to replace the screened-in veranda, now covered the entire expanse of fifty feet across the back of the room. Two-foot wide arches separated the glass. Unlike the casement windows in the rest of the house, these were fixed in place and spanned almost floor to ceiling.

Her smile ruthless, Aunt Hilda snatched the sheets from under my chin and loomed over me. "Burt Charles will be over here to help you. I just talked to Daisy and she was happy for him to come. She picked up some fruit from a roadside truck and she's bringing it over."

Oh, I saw how it was going to work. Aunt Hilda and Daisy would eat cantaloupe and point out any spots we missed on the windows.

"Any chance I could get a little toast before you put me to work?" I pawed the air like a groveling puppy.

Aunt Hilda regarded me like a suspicious cat. "Fine. Just go get it yourself. Ammonia and plenty of rags await."

When Burt Charles arrived, he glowered at me, but kept silent. The morning warmed into afternoon. A long afternoon. Cicadas tuned up as we set our ladders next to the window. We had buckets and sponges. We had rags. Every now and then we'd hear knuckles rat-a-tat on the glass. We'd heave our chests with great sighs and peer into the window of the veranda for additional instruction. Our view consisted of Aunt Hilda and Daisy's faces outlined in scarves and bobby-pinned curls frowning through the glass, and their fingers pointing to areas that were less than spotless. One long afternoon wasted. I could have told her that cleaning those windows would bring only short-term satisfaction, but I figured the cause would be bugs or the lawn mower throwing off dirt clods. As it happened, it was much worse.

Promise of a Windfall

The big excitement for weeks had been the drilling of a gas well. Exploratory geologists had researched the underground formation on Tío's ranch for over a year. T. R. Ray Company came out to dynamite the well site so a machine called a seismograph could scribble out a map of possible gas or oil-bearing sands beneath the surface. When I asked what exploratory geologists were, Tío said they were diviners of squiggly sonar maps that could predict whether or not oil or gas might lie underground.

"Like people who walk around with that Y-shaped stick looking for well water?" I asked.

Tío laughed. "Yeah. Yeah, as a matter of fact. Just about like water witches, except these guys have more equipment to confuse themselves." Tío pumped his eyebrows like Groucho Marx. "Soothsayers, oooooo. They conjure visions of great wealth!"

"Atlee Parr!" Aunt Hilda paced about us. "I wish you'd take this more seriously. Why…why, Morgan and Smith think it's going to be a wonderful well. A well of mammoth proportion!" She spread her arms wide.

"Uh huh, that's right, honey." Tío stood up and cleared his throat. "Wildcatters like Morgan and Smith are likely to promise us the moon to get to drill. Still, they sure beat the percentage the big companies offer. Kinda like playin' the stock market. Bigger the profit, the bigger the risk." He stood up abruptly. "Gotta go." He gave Aunt Hilda a little peck on the cheek and hitched up his britches. "Be back by supper," he said to the door as he settled his Stetson snug over his brow and stepped out into the hot afternoon.

Tío was a gambler.

Dollar signs did shine from the eyes of my aunt and uncle with the promise of money going into their pockets instead of having to spend every last dime to buy hay bales for the cattle. "Oh, Atlee," Aunt Hilda would sing out, "Just think! You can quit worrying about all those ol' cows. Lord, how you stewed over the right mix."

"Crossbreed." Tío looked at me and winked.

"Crossbreed." She flapped a wrist in the air. "The right Brahma and Hereford combination. You said Brahma meat's too tough and stringy, but the Hereford get...get.... What do they get? Hoof and mouth disease?"

"Pink eye." Tío smiled.

"Pink eye. But you can relax and quit working hard as the Klebergs to develop our own strain of beef. Who cares if there's an ol' drought?" Aunt Hilda threw her arms around his neck. "They're drillin' us a gas well!"

"That's right, baby," Tío used that tone when he was ready to move on to a new topic.

Aunt Hilda hugged me up close around the shoulders and led me off toward the kitchen. "You know what, Izzie, if they get lost, Brahma babies are born knowin' to go right back to where they last saw their mamas." Then she added as a second thought, "We'll have to remember that the next time we're out shopping in Corpus Christi. If you get lost in Lichtenstein's, we'll go back to the place we last saw each other. We don't want to be like those Herefords, do we? Guess the right mix of cow—"

"Crossbreed, Aunt Hilda."

"Crossbreed. Whatever. Guess the right mix would make better beef and easier ranching. When I think of all those cows your tío culled—the ones that have to survive without vaccinations and hay bales. A tough bunch. Poor old cows." Aunt Hilda gave me another squeeze. "But we won't have to worry about that when our well comes in. Will we, sugar pie?"

All I could think about was names for the horse Tío would be able to afford to buy me. I tried them out on Burt Charles: King, like from *King of the Wind* or *Black Beauty*. Then there was Champ, like Gene Autry's horse, or Silver. I didn't think I could wait to see what color he would be. Would Tío just surprise me? Would he take me with him to pick it out? I imagined a pearl white stallion, wildflowers threaded through his mane, his soulful eyes claiming me for his mistress. A protector. A steed that would whisk me away from danger.

—⟋⟍—

The rig came out on huge trucks that rumbled over the road in white clouds of dust. Names like Schlumberger and Halliburton. In the afternoons sometimes, Tío would pack us all in the Cadillac. We'd drive down the few miles to the well site. Fighting for a vantage point, Burt Charles and I hung out the backseat window, arms dangling over the side and our mouths open in awe of the project.

Tío pointed at a structure that lifted three long sections of pipe at once. "That's what they call a jackknife."

"Whoa, look at that!" Burt Charles' astonishment said it all. The derrick lifted into the sky like a great metallic erector set.

Tío suddenly shifted his attention to Morgan and Smith who were arguing with the mud engineer. Morgan's hands opened and closed, his dirty nails cutting into his palm. Sunburnt and wiry, Smith illustrated what I imagined a gas field worker to be—driven. And they were unhappy.

"Wonder what all the ruckus is." Tío watched, but his face gave away nothing. The mud engineer slammed his hat to the ground and stomped off.

As he shuffled past our car, Morgan said too loudly to be talking to himself, "Looks like they'll be finding another man to mind the mud." From under the brim of his hat, he shot a quick look at my uncle.

—⁓—

We begged nearly every day to go to the well. "Just let the men do their work now, Tío said. "Y'all go swim or find poor old Canela." But he'd finally relent. "Oh, go get your mama and Aunt Hilda."

Next time we drove out, the roar of engines made us hold our ears. Even Tío winced at the racket. He angled his chin at us to holler, "Won't be long now before they start drilling."

We sat at attention, our fingers wrapped over the car window rims while the roughnecks added another joint of pipe.

"Those boys have to be real careful up there." Tío squinted to get a better look. He never wore sunglasses and even though his skin was tight and thin from the burns, I could make out lines that pulled the skin around his eyes like stretched chamois cloth.

We watched as one big sun-blistered man wrapped a chain around the pipe. Another gripped huge tongs like a giant would use for barbequing and snapped them into place. Motors strained to pull the cable. Mud sprayed. Diesel engines roared like enraged dragons. I remembered the dragon Grendel from *Beowulf*, a book that Miss Young had once read to our fourth grade class. I had drawn a grand picture of him and colored him green with red fire blazing from his nostrils. I chose my best gold and bronze crayons for Beowulf. Dressed in glitter, he flailed a sword at the monster. Just like the warriors who struggled with a mighty monster, the men labored against a force of nature even more powerful.

Up close, you could hear roughnecks in heavy boots and dirty Levis hollering at each other over the roar of two diesel engines. Sweat darkened the backs of their shirts. Black grease and mud smeared across their sweaty biceps. As the men wrestled with pipes to add another joint or adjust a fitting, veins bulged along their necks and temples until they looked like they would burst.

"Get those damned gloves off," the head honcho bellowed. "Tryin' to lose a goddamned finger, you stupid...?"

Mama gasped, turned and clunked our heads together to cover our ears with her palms. "You kids! Get your heads back in this car this minute. And roll up the windows!"

We fell back against the seat, our eyes exaggerated round and hands crossed over our mouths. Our shoulders shook in giggles. Soon as she was distracted again, we inched the window down half way.

In the daytime, it was dust and yelling and roaring, but if we got a late start and went out after dark, the rig loomed above us like some big aluminum Christmas tree covered in lights. When we got back to the house, after supper Burt Charles and I would look out toward the lighted drilling rig from the rooftop. The flat roof had a high curb and we sat there on starry nights, still feeling the heat from the summer sun baked into the stucco.

"Think the warriors of old could cuss like those roughnecks did?" I wondered if heroes had bad habits.

"Nah! They took a code of honor." Burt Charles arched his brows in superiority.

"That was the knights! I'm not talking about King Arthur! Don't you get anything? I'm talking about warriors. Like Beowulf. Wonder if he swore like those guys."

Clearly deflated, Burt Charles countered. "Who cares? We couldn't understand anything they said anyway! They spoke....They spoke....They probably didn't even speak English!"

"Well, of course, they…." I decided to let it go. It was a lovely starry night and I felt like getting along. When the wind was right, we could hear the heavy clang of pipes and motors churning, but mostly the rig was hushed from that far away. It was quiet that night. Its lights shimmered in the damp night air—a soundless sparkling fairy tale castle. Even with the silence, it promised happily ever after.

Blowout

The last night of June, we didn't go over to the well. We all got carried away watching the only television station with good reception. *Hit Parade* was on and none of us planned to miss it. Burt Charles and I grabbed pillows and a spot on the floor. "Once I had a Secret Love" was next on the agenda. Burt Charles and I smiled at each other. He was only thirteen like me, but for a boy, he was pretty cute.

Just after Giselle McKenzie looked longingly heavenward and crooned "…impatient to be freeeee," thunder rumbled. Not from the clear night sky. It belched from deep in the earth. I covered my ears and pivoted to find an answer in Tío's face. With a sound like the earth cracking open, a huge fissure zigzagged across the expanse of nearly seventeen feet of veranda window.

"Blowout," Tío was on his feet. "I gotta get out there!"

"Let me go with you." Aunt Hilda grasped his arm. "Please, Atlee."

"No, honey, men could be…they could be…hurt…real bad."

"But I want to help."

"No." Tío took her by her shoulders. "Burned bad."

Aunt Hilda's blue eyes dwindled in color, like the sun had suddenly faded them. They searched his own marred skin and she lifted her hand to touch his face. Before any of us could call out, he was gone, letting the wrought iron door clank behind him. "Call the fire department!" he yelled back over his shoulder. We heard the Cadillac's tires squeal on the driveway and rattle hard over the cattleguard.

"Atlee?" My aunt held her fingers to her lips. "Atlee?"

Mama ran to the kitchen for the phone. I could hear her calm and steady giving a quick account to the Volunteer Fire Department of Duval County. We could still hear the rumble, but it wasn't one of the big oil trucks coming down the road too fast. It was gas exploding from underground oando.

"I wanna go! Let's go see!"

"Hush. We don't know…. We don't know what we would find." Aunt Hilda spoke barely above a whisper. Then in a far more audible gasp, "Oh, would y'all look at my window?" The crack scrawled across the middle window and shimmered in the lamplight. For years to come it would give the bougainvillea on the hacienda walls a Picasso-like disparity.

Burt Charles and I took advantage of her concentrating on that window to find a better view of the action. "The roof," he mouthed. We skittered off for the garage where the graduated blocks of the house design allowed us to stair-step to the roof in record time. Burt Charles led the way as we vaulted over the rise to the kitchen and then to the roof.

Breathless, I asked, "See anything?"

"Aw man, I'd say so!" His breath caught. He spoke like he was telling me a secret. "Wow! Look at that!"

I looked at his face, then turned to look in the direction he stared. But in his eyes' reflection I had already seen the bright orange flare of the gas well engulfed in flames. It lit up the sky.

—◊◊—

"I want y'all to just look at that!" Like a hell and brimstone preacher, Aunt Hilda waved her fist at the spew of fire that rose above the ruined gas rig. "And it was named after me, the Hilda Parr. Only thing ever named after me, and it goes up in blue smoke like a mushroom-shaped cloud! That's what the one of the truck drivers said it looked like when it first went up, a mushroom-shaped cloud." Her fingers splayed out in a dramatic rendition of an atomic explosion. "Rosemary García told me that at night you could see the glare from Kingsville."

Three days had gone by and we were on our umpteenth visit to the well site. The same scene was replayed time after time. "You are looking at thousands and thousands of dollars going up in flame. Hundreds of thousands." Aunt Hilda's face bore the streaks of dusty tears.

Despite the repetition, we all stood agog at the image of hundreds of thousands of dollar bills aflame, lifting like ashes in the breeze.

The gas flame burned pure and bright, stirring the air above it into whirls of shimmering molecules that danced in the heat. I thought of the horse Pegasus on the Mobil filling station sign. I imagined his wings afire until he himself would be consumed. Like my horse dreams.

She wasn't exaggerating about the money or the folks being able to see the light from way off. People started showing up, carloads, bumping down the road to get a closer look. They made a picnic of it. In addition to the roughnecks' junk, Dairy Queen cups and Lone Star Beer cans now littered the half-mile radius around the flames.

—ᴠᴠᴠ—

Next trip out to the blowout, Tío slapped the steering wheel. "These cowboys can't drill a well to save themselves. And those geologists? Nuttier than fruitcakes! Only psychologists are crazier. Might as well have psychologists running the show." It wasn't the first time Tío had carried on about psychologists and geologists.

At the site, Tío stood looking over the car roof at the flames. "I can't tolerate damn geologists who don't anticipate gas pockets at these depths. And where in the hell are Morgan and Smith? One panic visit after the thing went off and I haven't seen 'em since." He gave the car door a hard jerk. "Let's go."

Mama and Aunt Hilda looked at each other, but got back in the car without saying a word. Burt Charles and I waited. I scuffed my boot in the dirt. "Wish we could stay longer. That's some fire!" I elbowed Burt Charles for a response.

"You better shut up. He's pretty disgusted already."

"You know, we could walk back. It's not but a couple of miles, maybe not even that—"

"Will you hush? You're going to get us killed! Forget about it." Burt Charles was mostly good for an adventure if it was his idea. I thought about going on my own, but it wouldn't be any fun without him.

"Tell me again exactly what went wrong, Atlee?" From the front windshield Aunt Hilda stared bleakly out at the fiery scene.

"Think she's gonna cry?"

"Shhh, Izzie." Burt Charles frowned.

"What?" I thought a perfectly appropriate question deserved an answer.

Tío grasped the top of the steering wheel and leaned his head on his hands. "Okay. Bottom line. The mud Morgan and Smith used was the glitch. Mud gets pumped down the drill stem by one of those big diesel engines over there." He pointed across the site to a blackened lump of machinery. "It lubricates the rotary drill bit at the bottom and brings up chips of rock that's being drilled through." He paused and slid his hands around the wheel. "You getting all of this, Hilda?"

"Yes, Atlee, I'm getting it, for goodness sake." She sighed and looked at Mama, who remained quiet.

"Anyway, the mud runs top to bottom and back. It coats the hole with a layer of mud and keeps the walls of the hole from falling in. The important thing here is that it's supposed to be thick enough to hold back any gas that may start to bubble up. Here in Duval County, we've got lots of high-pressure gas pockets, so the drillers gotta use the heaviest mud they can. 'Course that costs money. And you know what?" Tío chuckled in a not so funny way. "Here's the punch line." He paused a second and swallowed hard. "These wildcatters operated on a shoestring budget! Just took a chance they wouldn't hit any gas at a shallow depth. Thought they'd save the expensive Baroid mud till they were closer to the mother lode. And according to the inspectors, when that mud started to buck, there was no holding it. That mother lode spit in their faces."

Tío sat up straight, started the Cadillac with a roar and gunned it hard before shifting gears. Aunt Hilda and Mama jumped but remained silent. We rode back to the house in silence.

We pulled into the drive of the house to find wildcatters Morgan and Smith waiting for us. Tío signaled all of us on into the house, but he waited out on the driveway as the men stepped tentatively out of their truck. Burt Charles and I cut around back behind the garage pillars and held our breath so we could hear better.

Both men simultaneously reached for their hats and swept them down by their sides. "Mr. Parr." Morgan leaned forward, wiped his hand on his pants leg before offering it to my uncle. "Don't know how we're gonna make this up to you." He shot Smith a look and squinted over toward the palm trees before he started talking again. "We were countin' on that well coming in to pay for the rest of our lease and the road and equipment costs. But we're gonna see that you get something out of every profit we ever make in the future, sir."

"If we ever get a profit," said Smith as he gazed up at a buzzard circling over. With both hands he twisted his hat brim in tight turns. He attempted a smile, but it was really just an up and down flicker of his lips.

"What he means to say is…." Morgan interrupted as he gave Smith an elbow. "Well, you know, sir, sometimes these things take time. We know we promised unheard of profits. Talked it up big. Hell, we knew it was big." He sputtered a hysterical laugh. "By the time the reports came in of that mud bucking, we already heard the pressure thundering up at us. No time to get the well shut down. No time for nuthin'."

"It was just about the worst sound I ever heard," said Smith. He shook his head back and forth about ten times.

Morgan stepped in front of Smith and hooked his thumbs in his belt loops. "Hell, sir, we had to just make a run for it. That steel drill stem flew outta there like some kinda rocket. The damn thing shot up worse'n Old Faithful. Just shot up and broke off like match sticks." Morgan slapped his palms past each other. "When that driller shouted run, we all high-tailed it outta there. Weren't no way to save it, sir. Nearly got our butts blowed off as it was. It's a wonder nobody died. Lucky them two ol' boys just got burned a little and banged up. Of course, I don't know what sparked it, sir, but it went off like a devil's torch. Jesus God. We was fifty yards out and still running, but it was the godawfulest thing you ever seen, up close as we was." Morgan looked down and shifted the toothpick in his mouth from one side to the other. He squinted up at Tío.

I whispered to Burt Charles, "Here it comes. Tío's gonna tear them up."

Tío took out a Lucky Strike and tapped it on the package. Smith scratched a match frantically on his boot to light it for him. I couldn't see Tío's face, but irony flitted about his words. "Thanks," he said.

And then there was silence.

After an uncomfortable span of minutes, Tío spoke through the exhaled smoke. "I'm a rancher. Not an oil and gas man. But I've got enough sense to know there's always a risk in the drillin' business. You boys had a lot tied up in this yourselves—your investment, your time. Never mind the money you paid for that geologist. You'll learn sometimes you just gotta spend money to make a little more. I asked around about what coulda gone wrong. Inspectors said you should have had top grade mud going down to back up that drilling. This area is well known for having extremely high pressure gas pockets."

They looked like they were going to say something before they thought better of it.

Tío continued. "You knew that. Your cuttin' corners with a cheaper, lighter mud has done this project in. Is that why that first mud engineer walked out on you?"

"Well...." Morgan shifted from one foot to the other. "Yes, sir. But who on God's green earth woulda thought—"

Tío spoke over him. "I'll admit it was surprising to find that gas pocket at 4,000 feet, but you set yourselves up for failure. We all just let our hopes carry us away some. Hard not to...with this drought." Tío took a deep drag off the cigarette, flicked it hard at his feet. He smudged it into the cement driveway with the toe of his boot. "Not much use in me saying more, except that I want Kinley's man, Red Adair, out here. You boys are going to have to foot that bill, but it's time that well's put out. You can settle up with me one day when y'all recover, if you ever do."

"Aw, Mr. Parr, that's mighty.... You're a...a good man." They glanced at one another in disbelief. "You won't be sorry, sir. No sir, you won't be sorry," they said as they both pumped his hand one after the other. Morgan's bottom lip trembled. When he cleared his throat, it sounded like an old car starting up. They tapped their hats back on their heads and hopped in the truck for a fast getaway before Tío could change his mind. Morgan put his truck in gear and headed toward the cattleguard. At the last minute, he turned his head and called out, "We're calling Adair tonight, Mr. Parr! Tonight!" He narrowly missed the gatepost. We heard him yell, "Whoa," then look back and smile broadly at my tío.

Tío turned and shook his head at the sound of a missing muffler as Morgan and Smith's truck revved into gear and barreled down the road. "You kids come on out from behind there." Then a little tiredly, "Run on to supper."

Night after night, the evening sky east of the house glowed with never ending fire. If you didn't think about it too hard, from the distance of the house, you could imagine it a campfire that warmed the night. Just about the time Burt Charles and I would get lulled into trying to appreciate the beauty and power of the force, a gust of gas would rumble to the surface and vomit a red and yellow arc high into the night. "Hard to relax with it, huh?" Burt Charles said. Then he got real quiet. "Wonder if that's what hell looks like."

The Dragon Slayer — Red Adair

The flames burned into late July till Red Adair's red and black trucks rumbled down the road. We weren't allowed to go out to the well site while he was in operation. He'd worked two weeks when we heard the dynamite blast go off.

Right before dinner, Mama, Aunt Hilda and I sat at the table. "Good lord, what's going on out there?" She turned her dinner fork from front to back and back to front while we waited for Tío to come in. "Helen, I'm going to talk to Atlee. I've had enough of this oh-so-deep concern about the wildcatters. What about us for goodness sake? Don't we matter?"

"Of course we do. I've seen the look on his face. He loves you with all his heart. Now don't go jumpin' on him."

We heard the clank of wrought iron door. Tío sighed as he took off his hat and wiped his brow with his forearm. He made an attempt at a brief smile and sat.

Mama reached over to pat Aunt Hilda's hand and shook her head with a subtle *no*.

"Would you like some iced tea? Estela had to leave early but I'll get you some." Aunt Hilda worked a conciliatory smile onto her face.

"Be great. Just great." His face made him a liar.

When Aunt Hilda returned with the tea, I quit holding my breath. But then her hand trembled as she set the glass down. She turned away with tears flooding her eyes.

Uh oh, I thought. Not good.

For a moment it looked like she could recover. She asked without much quiver in her voice how things were going. She stared at her plate and pushed the peas into a pile, and maintained a deadly degree of calm. "What's going on out there?"

"Well, I hope he just shut down the fire." He sawed at his steak. We waited. "Oh, it's a long drawn out affair. But Adair's famous for extinguishing blowouts. Been doing it all his life. Last week, he saturated the well site with water to keep things cool."

"Where in the world did he get water around here?"

"Dug a well out there. Just enough to supply his water jets." Tío scanned the table for second servings. "Of course, that was the easy part. If he put out the fire with that last blast, he's still got to get in there in his asbestos suit, and set up his special equipment with raw gas spewing. Pass me the green beans, please." Tío scooped a helping onto his plate before he continued.

Aunt Hilda plunked the bowl of green beans down. "How can you sit here and tell me all this and shovel more food onto your plate? You act like you don't care that we've lost our chance to survive this drought."

Tío stopped chewing and leveled his eyes at Aunt Hilda and then at Mama. Without responding to her jibe, he continued. "Red said some people called him a daredevil, but they didn't understand. 'A daredevil's reckless and that ain't me,' he told me. Said 'Something like the devil is down in that hole and I've seen what he can do.' Said 'I ain't no daredevil at all. I'm a beware-devil, that's what I am.'"

"Beware devil, my eye. Why can't they just—" Aunt Hilda started in.

Mama lightly touched her arm. "Let him tell us, honey."

Tío gave Mama a grateful smile. "That's why we all need to stay out of his way. All he needs is for that baby to fire up again. He'd for sure lose men. Every tool he uses is made of soft copper to keep from creating another spark. If he's lucky, he can get in there and tighten down the valve, and that'll shut down the flow of gas."

"And what if he can't get it shut down, Atlee? What if he can't?" Aunt Hilda spoke in a pinched whisper. "If he does get it stopped, is there any chance we could drill again? Maybe get whatever's left? Any chance?"

"Maybe. Not right away. But I bet he's got it shut down while we're here eating supper. If he can't, then the well just burns till it finally burns itself out. Months maybe."

"Oh, lord." Wadding her napkin into a tight ball in her fist, Aunt Hilda glared out the window.

Tío finished chewing and swallowed. "That hardly ever happens, honey. He's that good. He usually just shows up and collects a great big check. Morgan and Smith are taking out another loan." He scooted back from the table and wiped his mouth. "Gotta get back out for just a little bit. Might check with Adair. See if he's got that thing capped." He stood and reached for his hat. "I'll wait to have that ice cream till I get back."

"Sue those wildcatters, Atlee!" Aunt Hilda slammed her napkin down and followed him into the veranda.

I'd never seen Aunt Hilda go at Tío like that. Not even close! *Leave him alone!* I waited in the doorway, braced against the frame. Mama didn't make me sit back down.

"They've caused us untold financial loss and never mind the ruts in our roads with their big trucks." Aunt Hilda shoved his shoulder. "And all the gas that was on our land…well, it's just gone up in flames. A huge well. Gone! We were counting on it bringing in more than enough to feed the cattle during this drought or better yet, it would let us forget about the damn cattle altogether."

"Hilda…." Tío stopped and faced her.

"Well, I can't help it. God knows it would have kept our heads above water." She paused and turned back toward Mama. "Hah! Would y'all listen to what I just said?" She laughed, but not a funny ha ha laugh. "As if there was water to keep our heads above."

"Hilda…." Tío tried to pull her into his arms.

"Atlee, if you sued, at least we'd have something to fall back on. Some money to pay for hay. Maybe irrigate from what's pitiful left underground. And money to—to just get by." Her last words were too high pitched to sound rational.

"Those boys don't have any money to sue them for. Blame me. I should have taken Humble's offer. They—"

"I don't care if—"

"Now let me finish here, honey. They might not have made the mistakes these ol' boys did. 'Course they wouldn't have offered us the percentage of royalties that Morgan and Smith did either. Guess we all got carried away with the promise of all that profit."

"You're just gonna let them walk away from this, aren't you?" She held her arms rigid at her sides, her hands in fists.

"No. Now they'll repair the ruts in the roads and repay the lease when they can. They had all their money on the line with this, with no extra backing."

I stared at the linen drapes. The scenes were watercolor scenes of rolling hills—a kind and giving countryside. A parody of the drought we faced. I started to shake a little bit. Maybe I could just drift into the scene in the drapery—a camouflage of soft greens and creams.

"Just flyin' by the seat of their pants, these guys. It would have been some gas well if we could have held it." Tío reached for her and pulled her close to him. He stroked her hair. "Naw, it won't do to sue these folks. Blame me for going out on a limb, if you want to. We can't get back what we never really had. What we really lost was just the potential."

Aunt Hilda pulled away and looked him straight in the face. "The potential was everything."

"I know, honey. I know." Tío's words fell into her hair. He sounded calm like he really didn't mind much, but he shut his eyes and pinched his eyebrows together when he thought Aunt Hilda couldn't see him. She banged her head softly against his shoulder. I felt funny watching. It made a knot stick in my throat.

Tío laid his hand on my head as he went out the door. And then very gently, he said, "Don't eat all the vanilla now, Izzie." He tried for a smile, but it appeared more of a rip across his mouth.

I followed him out to the carport. He seemed to be listening for the roar of the blowout. Quiet, except for the grumbling red truck of Adair's that pulled through the gates.

Tío stuffed his hands in his pockets and frowned against the sunlight at the dragon slayer. "Well?"

"Well, what'd ya think?" Adair smiled as he peeled out of the truck cab and strode forward to shake Tío's hand. "I got her down." He looked like a triumphant gladiator who'd been down with the devil, like he'd said in his own words. And I believed him. Grease and sweat and mud smeared his red jumpsuit, his face, his helmet.

Tío's face opened up and his hand went forward. "Red...." He shook his head. "Red, I don't know how to thank you."

"I suppose your boys will be cutting me a nice check, but the look on your face now that I'm finished and packing? It's the best thanks in the world. Nobody's hurt and the well's under control."

Shaking his hand again, Tío said, "I know those wildcatters got a loan to take care of you. And I know it was a whole lot of money for them to go begging at the bank for."

"Well, you can tell them if they think it's expensive to hire a professional to do the job, wait until they hire an amateur."

Tío flinched at that. He kept his smile pasted on his lips, but he flinched.

They talked for a while longer. I had questions, but Tío looked like he had all he could take for a while.

I skulked around to the bedroom side. *Was Tío to blame? Did he care more about those wildcatters than he did about us? They were skimping on mud, for goodness sake! With a name like wildcatters, what did he expect? He could sue them like Aunt Hilda said, but he wouldn't.*

I looked at my scuffed boots. *Guess I'll start school with these crappy shoes. Maybe Mari will give me her hand-me-downs. And I bet she'll be pretty smug about my not getting a horse.* I was wallowing and I knew it. But what if Tío and Aunt Hilda couldn't afford for us to stay here any longer? I wanted to run somewhere to get away from my feelings that whispered—*that'll teach you to dream, Isabel Martin.*

When it was way past sundown, I made my way to the roof. I didn't scramble up fast like I usually did. I sat up in the spot where I had watched the well even though I knew it wouldn't be the same. I still wasn't quite prepared. The flames were out, after all, and the night silent except for a few little squawks of the last cicadas. I couldn't tell if it was the gas well explosion or the drought, but the flat lap of earth out to the east looked as though an old, sad dragon had heaved his last breath across the land. The mesquite was singed and the cactus shriveled. My castle had gone poof, as though the fairy godmother had a change of heart and waved her wand in a fit of pique.

The Campaign

As though the gas well remained afire, the summer heat never faltered. The town of Benavides blazed with excitement—an upcoming election. Flyers and posters lined the announcement bulletin board in the Piggly Wiggly and the post office.

Free Bar B Q!
Free Beer!
Meet Representative Lyndon B. Johnson,
Our next senator from the State of Texas!
Saturday, August 15th
2-4pm
High School Football Field

I gave up on my radio music. Voices pitched thirty decibels higher than tolerable ranted about the sins of the other party. The fifties had been a national disaster in drought; only the Democrats could save us. Or was it the Republicans? Not that anyone should have worried; no one could remember when Texas didn't send a Democrat senator to Washington. And Lyndon Johnson was coming to town.

All of us looked forward to a change in summer venue. Burt Charles and I sat eating watermelon in the shade of the old mesquite that protected the kitchen side of the house. When we heard George's car roar into the driveway, we stopped slurping the melon and tuned in.

"I want you and Hilda to be there, Atlee. Hell, even bring Helen and her kid. Helen can't vote, but wait." George whipped out a little notepad and scribbled something. "We'll make this her permanent residence. I'll take care of that. I already talked to Joaquín and Estela. They'll be there. I'm sending a truck for them. We want this to look good!" George's words pierced the air like rocks from a slingshot.

"I'll admit I've had enough of Stevenson," said Tío, "but he's a tough old bird. How's Johnson going to beat that kind of backing and experience?"

"Well, I'm gonna *give* him backing and experience. Who knows what this ol' boy Johnson can do to help us get through this drought."

George's eyes almost emitted flames. "Got him scheduled in Jim Wells County next month. I'm gonna help him out down here, and anyway, last time I asked Stevenson for one appointment, the sonofabitch—"

"Watch your mouth, George. The kids."

Burt Charles and I acted like we hadn't heard.

"Aw, quit worrying about the kids and think about what's at stake here. I like this man Johnson. He's got *cojones*. I heard he was so sick last month, they tried to stop his campaigning long enough for him to recover. Wouldn't have it. No siree. Lost 30 pounds, but I'm tellin' ya— *cojones*."

Tío threw a cautionary look our way. "I'm willing to listen, George. I always am. You know that. It's probably one of my best faults."

Both men laughed. George slapped his brother on the back.

"What do you want from this guy, anyway? If Stevenson didn't help you out that much, why would a new guy?"

"I can get Johnson elected and he knows it." George patted his back pocket where he kept his wallet. "My favors to these people don't go unrewarded. If an ol' boy's wife needs a hospital bill paid, if his kid wants to give college a try, he knows who to come to. And he'll know who to vote for come election time. It pays to have an understanding with these people. I think I can count on you to help me with that."

Tío shot a glance at us, but then relaxed when he saw our faces, which we had swabbed with ignorance.

—⁓—

The day of the barbeque broke out in the splendid heat we all expected, and Burt Charles and I planned to stake out a shady spot under the bleachers. No food was being served yet, but we could get a cool Dr Pepper out of the ice buckets.

"Good grief, I never knew this many people lived in Benavides. I bet there're over a thousand people here."

"And more will be coming. When George Parr orders up a group, they show." Burt Charles raked the cold bottle across the back of his neck.

"You sure it's not just the free barbeque and beer?" I asked.

"Well, Izzie, if George wants people to come, beer or no beer, they'll get here. Come on and get in the shade."

We threw down our towels and sat down cross-legged under the slatted seats of the football stadium. We looked up. Above us hundreds of shoes and bottoms offered us a place out of the sun.

"You suppose these bleachers can hold all that many?" I had a mental vision of the boards sinking, and then splintering while a wall of rumps descended upon us. "We could be squashed like bugs."

"These bleachers can hold up, I'm telling ya." Burt Charles squinted up at the slats. "Ever seen a football game here?"

"Yeah, but I was always sittin' up there." I tilted my head above us. Suddenly a racket made us cover our ears. "Jeez, run!" I screamed, fully believing the bleachers were collapsing.

"Would you relax?" But Burt Charles scurried out from under the planks right behind me. "Lookathat!"

A helicopter roared from the sky. Dust and paper swirled in dirt devils and cries of "*Dios mío*" emanated from the crowd. As the machine circled above us, a loudspeaker boomed: "I'm Lyndon Johnson and when we get down there, I want to meet every single one of you! And… and…." He paused. Then with a bellow, "I want to shake your hand!"

The bleachers vibrated like a riled-up rattlesnake.

As the machine rocked and settled down to the ground, we all stood with our mouths open. With the blades still whirring above it, the mechanical animal birthed Lyndon Johnson from its innards and he spun his hat out over the crowd. The bleachers above us rocked with people coming to their feet. Their noise swelled in adoration. I imagined that was how the bullfights sounded. "¡*Toro, hombre*!" Burt Charles and I followed the arc of Johnson's hat. It sailed, spinning into our segment of bleachers. We scrambled for it.

"Whoa, look at this!" Burt Charles turned the brim, his fingers holding it in delicate respect. "You know how much one of these Stetsons costs?"

"Nope, but Tío's got one."

"Well, yeah, all the big ranchers around here have one, but they don't go throwin' it out of a helicopter. This thing's a Beaver 6X. It comes in a suitcase when you buy it."

"He's probably gonna want it back, huh?" I searched the crowd for Johnson.

"Wonder if he'd let us ride in the whirlybird if we brought it back to him."

"Burt Charles?"

"What?"

"Sometimes you come up with the best ideas!"

The loudspeaker squawked and Johnson's speech rose over the noise. "My friends! *Mis amigos!* You make me proud to be here." He saluted the visitors. "And I'm gonna make you proud!" Johnson became like the first Spaniard ever to set foot on American soil...a god.

And the crowd exploded into applause. "*¡Qué magnifico! ¡Qué hombre!*"

"But first of all." Johnson paused for effect. "Let's eat!"

Trampling down the steps of the bleachers, the crowd cheered again and headed for the barbeque area.

Burt Charles said, "Let's go shake his hand. He's talkin' to kids, too. We'll give him his hat." He set the Stetson on his head. It wobbled around some, but looked like it would stay on. "C'mon, will ya? You're stragglin'."

I picked up my pace to catch up with Burt Charles. We slowed as we approached Johnson. Grinding out his words, he lectured two of the men. We waited till he was finished. When a man nudged him and nodded our way, Johnson's face rearranged itself—from *I'm gonna kill somebody* to *Well, how are ya?*

We gave each other a quick look, but stuck out our hands anyway and offered our prize. "Howdy, sir, here's your hat. We belong to Atlee Parr."

A huge sigh of relief washed through Johnson's demeanor. "Bates! Hanley! You can stop looking. At least a kid could find it!" He sounded angry, but when he turned back to us, he was jovial. He shook our hands with both of his. "Parr, you say? Why, you kids come here." He nodded toward a chubby redheaded guy with a camera. "Parr's kids! Get this shot!" Johnson hugged us into him and bent forward toward the camera with an I-love-kids look on his face.

Johnson looked like he was going somewhere. I could feel it. He was big and tall. He dreamed and dared and dragged you along with him.

"Mr. Johnson?"

"What is it, little buddy?"

"We thought maybe you'd give us a ride in your helicopter."

Johnson ruffled our hair. "I bet one of these days you'll have your own Stetson!" And with that, he released us into the masses. "Y'all better head up there for barbeque," he called after us. And as a second thought, "Thanks for the hat!"

"Wow, how 'bout that guy?" Burt Charles' eyes, wide and dilated, sparkled with amazement. "I still wish we coulda gone up for just a little bit. Do you think he heard us?"

"I dunno. It was kinda like meeting a movie star, wasn't it? He walks like John Wayne, you know, like this." I swaggered side to side and rolled my shoulders.

"Well, not exactly." But Burt Charles laughed. "He said to eat, so let's do it!"

We lined up behind about fifteen hundred people while Johnson worked the crowd. He had a huge presence. Vital. Dynamic. He was the image of a man who would get things done for the poor people. George pumped his hand, introducing him to gringos and Tejanos alike, his hand on Johnson's back, his other extended in the *embrazo* for amigos.

Mama and Aunt Hilda helped serve. Aunt Hilda wore swoop-tipped sunglasses and her signature red lipstick. Mama squinted, concentrating on filling the plates. Tío stood farther back in line.

Tío spoke with the people in his quiet way. He turned to folks, smiling and shaking hands. "Juan, how's that new job working out at the bank?" His manner was kind with true concern when he asked, "Manuel, you able to keep some crops this summer?"

George, rowdier, pumped hands, but still appeared sincere. The people smiled even bigger and pumped his hand right back, genuinely pleased he had come to talk to them.

Watching while Johnson maneuvered through the Tejanos, we stood speechless. He stopped to visit each one, like that one poor man was the most important person in the world. His magnetism locked in on you, made you special, made you trust and made you believe. Johnson filled himself up with the people's need and turned it into possibilities. That power must have made him feel like he was headed for the White House.

We got to the front of the line. "What kinda meat is this, anyway?" Barbeque sauce disguised its origin. Mama opened her mouth to tell me, but Aunt Hilda touched her hand and while still looking down at the beans she was serving, made a barely perceptible shake of her head. Mama laughed and answered, "It's *cabrito*, honey. You'll like it."

I generally tended to ask more questions about disguised food, but the kid behind me nudged me on with "*Ándale.*"

So we got our barbeque plates and settled back down under the bleachers. Scanning the sea of color above us, I did a double take. "Hey, isn't that Mari up there?" I recognized one of Aunt Hilda's old skirts. "Here, chuck this rock. I bet she'll never know who did it!"

Burt Charles let fly but the stone bounced off the bleachers with a loud crack. Mari pulled her skirt tight against her knees and bent over to look below her. I had to admit she was flexible.

"Oh, hello there, children," she called down. "Izzie, how do you like the goat meat you're eating? I hear it was a very young *cabra*. It's good, no?" She strung out the "o" in "no" and then laughed for an extended time.

"Ewww," I said and I coughed up what I could and wiped my tongue with a paper napkin.

"Oh, you liked it before you knew what it was. Get over it. I'll eat the rest of it if you don't want it." Burt Charles mopped up the last of the barbeque sauce with his bread.

"Fine, but I'm not watching."

Still spitting into my napkin, I cast one last upward glance at Mari. She was busy, talking Spanish baby talk to her little sister.

All of a sudden, the mariachi trumpet blared like the fanfare to a bullfight. The guitars followed with *Jalisco* and somebody yelled, "*Oi, oi, oi.*" The music swelled over the crowd's cheers and elevated a poor Tejano town barbeque to a fiesta of epic proportions. Lyndon Baines Johnson stepped to the podium and after making a weak effort to settle the crowd, he made a quick speech, tipped his hat and slumped into a humble bow.

—◊◊—

On the way home, I asked Tío if he liked Mr. Johnson. "He sure was neat, wasn't he? I mean, woo, he came in like a paratrooper. He was awful nice."

"Except he wouldn't let us ride in his helicopter," said Burt Charles.

Mama whirled around from the front seat. "Y'all asked for a ride in that...that war machine?"

"Well—"

"Well, my foot! I'd a grabbed you by the shirttail, both of you." She looked straight at Burt Charles. "And pulled you off. Don't you ever think about getting on one of those things again!"

Tío looked out the side window to hide his smile. I saw him in the rear view mirror.

I tried to distract Mama by getting Tío's opinion again. "So he's a cool guy, huh, Tío?"

"My measure of a man depends on his honesty, his word. More often than not, you can't tell when you first meet a man."

I scooted up from the seat to just behind Tío's ear. "The other day it sounded like you'd vote for Johnson no matter what."

"We'll see, we'll see. Politicians tend to get what they want, one way or another. Some are real good at it." Tío lit a cigarette and inhaled. "Nope, can't tell by looking."

"But Tío, isn't George a politician?"

Meeting the Carpenter

Entertainment came in the form of Dennis Wiley, retired cowboy. That's how he introduced himself anyway when Burt Charles and I accosted him down at the corral. He'd been over at the house the week before, talking to Tío about repairing the barn. We watched him spit tobacco and stack boards for 30 minutes before we approached. He didn't look up at first, but when he did, he sent an arc of tobacco juice sailing at a horny toad.

Burt Charles did a double take. "Oh, wow, sir!"

Mr. Wiley set down the two-by-four. He leaned over toward his thermos, took a big swig, and wiped his sleeve across his puckered lips. We stood quietly watching.

"Pretty damned hot, ain't it." It wasn't a question. Rubbing his hands across the seat of his pants, the carpenter grinned. "Dennis Wiley, ex-cowboy, at your service." He stuck out a large callused palm. "Whatchoo young'uns up to?" he asked.

Burt Charles stepped forward with equal bravado and met the handshake with what I was sure was the hardest grip he could manage. "Burt Charles Taylor, sir."

"Pleased to meet you, son. Who's your girlfriend here?"

Burt Charles looked confused and then his face fever-flushed. "Izzie? She's not my girlfriend!"

The indignation offended me. "H…heck, no, sir." I stepped forward but I couldn't think of a comeback except, "I'm older than he is anyway." I hesitated. "And my name is Izzie. Isabel Martin."

"You're not that much older. Two months is all." Burt Charles said as he body-blocked the possible handshake I thought I had coming.

Mr. Wiley spit at the ground again. "Heh, heh, now y'all just quit a-worrying about it. You got to learn to take a joke, boy."

Limping over to a bale of hay, Mr. Wiley grunted as he sat. "What's y'all's claim to fame associating with this here Atlee Parr? I know he ain't your pa."

I jumped in quick. "Atlee Parr is my uncle! He's married to my mama's sister." I smiled proudly. Burt Charles is just my friend."

Mr. Wiley glanced over at Burt Charles and his bleary eyes softened around the edges. "Why, I bet he's a mighty important friend."

I looked back at Burt Charles who studied the ground. "Oh well, sure he is," I said.

Mr. Wiley sprawled across the hay and dragged up a wrinkled paper bag. "Y'all mind if I go ahead and eat my lunch here? Breakfast wasn't much and it was early."

"Oh, no sir." Burt Charles jumped in. "You just go right ahead. We don't mind a bit."

Shuffling open a noisy wax-paper wrapper, Mr. Wiley bit into the shriveled sandwich.

I was stunned. "Sir? Don't you have any teeth? I mean, who ever heard of a cowboy with no teeth?" I slapped my hand over my own mouth, fully aware of the etiquette faux pas I had just committed. "Well, uh, I mean, I just barely noticed and my grandmother doesn't have any either and it's okay. And Gabby Hayes is my favorite—"

"She means she's real embarrassed that she didn't have any better sense than to make a rude remark about your teeth, sir. Or no teeth," said Burt Charles as he turned and glared at me with big open eyes.

"Oh, I got teeth, but they're somewheres back in a jar. Damn things drive me crazy." He gummed his sandwich in happy disregard of my comments. "In a minute here, I got to get on back to work, but y'all can hang around some if you're willing to help."

Burt Charles, intuitive enough to see an ally, volunteered on the spot. "Sure, Mr. Wiley, what you want me to do? I can hammer and saw. Just about anything you want me to." He stepped up to a ladder that leaned on the barn wall and narrowed his eyes at me.

I refused to take second seat. "Well, I can hammer, too. Probably even a little better. Burt Charles here, he sometimes hits the nail so crooked, he has to take it out and start over."

Before Burt Charles could challenge that statement, Mr. Wiley laughed out loud. "Hah! 'Bout ten years ago, I saw a movie that coulda featured you kids. Yep, Annie Oakley and her boyfriend sang this song." Mr. Wiley commenced in a rattley baritone: "I can do anything better'n you." He took a last gnaw at his sandwich.

I opened my mouth to ask what he meant about "boyfriend," when he asked Burt Charles to hold a plank for him while he sawed.

"And you, Miss Isabel...." Mr. Wiley handed over some nails. "See if you can't hold these number threes in your right hand and the number sevens in your left and hold 'em out to me when I call for 'em."

I snorted but when Mr. Wiley looked up, I pretended a cough. I had started to ask if he really thought I could manage the chore, but thought better of it. When in doubt, it was best to be polite to a cowboy.

—⟡—

Novelty never failed to intrigue us. We were willing to keep Mr. Wiley company every chance we got. Mama and Aunt Hilda laughed about how enthralled we were by the old codger.

"Wiley's never going to finish that barn if you kids don't let him alone," Mama said.

"We're helping him, Mama,"

She laughed. "Oh, I go out to check on y'all sometimes and half the time, he's sitting down, telling you a story."

"But see, we make up the time by being his assistants."

Pursing her lips and nodding, Mama said, "Oh, I *do* see."

—⟡—

By ten in the morning every Saturday, we set out for the barn. Mr. Wiley could tell some good stories. He'd get to talking about his cowboy days and an hour would go by before we knew it. Our favorite one included a few bad words we knew we weren't supposed to hear, but Mr. Wiley just used them to spice the story up.

"Tell us the one about your friend who drank too much." We sat down to listen, our arms dangling between our knees. Mr. Wiley opened a can and stuffed a wad of tobacco into his cheek. At first, I blinked and wrinkled my nose but after a while I got used to it. Just part of his storytelling.

Mr. Wiley settled in for the story, but admonished, "Now this here is like a parable. There's a lesson in it. That's why I don't mind tellin' it over."

"Yes, sir. We understand."

"One evenin' after me and Roy put in about fifteen hours, we got to thinkin' that a little alkyhol would ease the soreness outta our backs." Mr. Wiley frowned. "Not that I'm a recommendin' this, you understand."

"Oh no, sir." We shook our heads enthusiastically.

Settling back against a tractor tire, the carpenter continued. "That ol' boy never shoulda drank. And that night, of course, Roy, he jest got ornery and got to huggin' on some ol' girlfriend of the local farm boys."

Burt Charles and I grinned at each other.

"Them farm boys said, 'Well, just come on outside 'cause we're gonna settle 'is.'"

Burt Charles held up his hand, like we were in school. "You forgot the part about where y'all were."

"Oh, y'all know where we wuz. Down at the Silver Nite."

We grinned again. We knew where the Silver Nite was. It was a ramshackle bar on the edge of town and sometimes when we came back late from the picture show, we'd see one old skinny guy weaving straight down the middle of the highway. Joaquín would honk loud and long till the man stumbled over to the gravel side and sat down hard, looking surprised as anybody.

"Now, where was I?" asked Mr. Wiley as he spit a stream of brown liquid toward the gate. "Oh, yeah. Well, I seen they'd beat the living hell outta him, so I stepped up to be the peace maker." Mr. Wiley straightened his collar. "Aw, them boys come out the door and you could tell they were stout, good-sized, corn-fed boys, so I got to explainin' real nice that Roy didn't mean no harm, he jest couldn't hold his liquor and if they didn't mind, we'd jest ease on outta the place and we wuz sorry for any upset that we'd a caused."

"Then what happened?" we asked, our eyes wide.

"That boy just bumped his chest at me and allowed as to how he would see my sorry ass wrapped up in a blue bow first."

I gasped the first time he told the story, but by the third telling, I mouthed the words along with Mr. Wiley.

"I seen it was comin'. There was gonna be a fight. Ol' Roy inched on back to where he could lean on the truck. Of course, I'd hoped we'd be breezin' back down the road in that truck instead a nose to nose with this ol' boy. I figgered if I was gonna come out alive, I'd better get in the first swing." Mr. Wiley leaned back and put up his fists. "I mashed that ol' boy's nose against his right ear, but I pretty much saw stars after that."

Validating his story, he pointed to an inch long scar along his left eye. Like always, I leaned in and looked.

"Next morning, I says to ol' Roy…." Mr. Wiley cleared his throat for this part. "Well, Roy, how come you didn't back me up? You's the one they really wanted to whup." He shook his head. "Roy always could think up a good one."

"'Well, now, Denny,' Roy said, 'Look at it this way. I knew you'd be beat to a bloody pulp. And you'd need somebody to drive you home.'"

"Oh yeah, well? Next time I'll just beat you to a bloody pulp and then drive *you* home."

We giggled and snorted even though we knew what was coming next. That was the hilarious part right before it turned sad.

"But now y'all know. There's a lesson in this."

"Yes, sir. We know." We shuffled our feet in the sand.

"Ol' Roy did get his butt beat bad enough to kill him one day. I stood around when they buried him."

"If you were his friend, couldn't you make him do right?" It seemed to me that Mr. Wiley should have stepped in and saved his friend from his bad behavior.

"Well, I wisht I could. I tried even. But when it comes right down to it, a person does right because he wants it for himself, not anybody else. That ol' coot shoulda never drank. Don't y'all do it neither."

"Oh, no sir." We protested the mere possibility, although there had been times when if a glass was left with a tablespoon of wine in it after dinner, we'd swig down the last drop.

On the way back from the barn I asked Burt Charles, "Do you really think a person does right just for himself? I mean, wouldn't a person do something for somebody else?"

"Beats me. You'd think they would, but Mr. Wiley knows a lot about folks. It's complicated, I think—asking why a person does or doesn't do. There's gotta be somethin' in it for themselves."

And back in my mind, although I would never tell it, I wondered if Daddy was getting beat up in bars. Or if I was the only one who had ever punched him.

Run-off Election

After Johnson's big shebang, nobody said much about the results till a run-off election landed on the calendar. Newspaper's featured bold headlines—"Stevenson Answers the Call." And the air hummed with the blades of the "flying windmill" as Johnson pirouetted like a frantic dragonfly through skies above small Texas towns.

George sponsored another barbeque over at his place. Johnson couldn't have stayed more than thirty minutes. Reportedly thinner, with dark circles under his eyes, he still stirred the crowds. A couple of New Party men carried around posters, but surprisingly, no fistfights broke out.

In August, the Taylors spent their usual Sundays with us. After the Gulf breeze kicked up, all the adults sat out under the pecan trees watching us swim. Burt Charles and I dived for marbles, raced the crawl and backstroke until I wore him out long enough to win a round. The little kids bobbed around in their horse-faced rubber tubes and squealed at each other. They were not allowed past the rope that separated the shallow from the deep end. Every once in a while, a hard-backed, shiny black water bug the size of a large roach torpedoed through the water to pinch the delicate skin of our thighs. If one headed our way, we screamed and scrambled for the edge till we scooped it up with the pool net and hit it with a brick.

The grown-ups essentially ignored us. They talked. Except Mama. Sitting with one leg bent under her, Mama chewed on the earpiece of her glasses and stared off into the oblivion that she frequently visited. I wondered if she was thinking about Daddy. And if she ever had second thoughts.

Aunt Hilda, her cigarette poised between her fingers, leaned back, exposing her long white neck as she pursed her lips and blew a delicate stream of smoke up through the low leaves.

Tío tilted his chair, the front legs lifting off the grass. In puzzle-shapes, the pecan leaves' shadows eclipsed the pale patches of his skin. I never knew if he felt self-conscious about the scars. He had managed to marry a young beautiful woman. I thought about the yellow-bikinied brunette across the wall of the bar. He and Aunt Hilda didn't seem to fit if you just looked at them, but they did. Power and beauty. It went together somehow.

Daisy's shoe dangled and Bob quoted statistics on the rate of oil production versus price. Marisol must have made half a dozen trips to the poolside to bring iced tea. The grown-ups drank glass after glass and smiled with absent-minded indulgence at our demands: "Watch this," we'd yell as we competed for the best jackknife dive.

Shaky with exertion, Burt Charles and I sprawled out in the sun. Mari brought out one more round of tea. Burt Charles picked up my glass and took a long slug. When his head tilted back, I watched the muscles in his throat contract while he downed my drink. I let my gaze drift to his chest that was beginning to take on the sculpture of male youth. His swim trunks clung to the shape of him. His skin emitted a golden-brown sheen, despite his blondness. I could not help but examine him, but relied on the anonymity of my sunglasses. He was some new creature evolving before my eyes.

Flopping down on my stomach, I rested my head on my arms, and drifted into a hazy torpor. Not really sleeping. Just daydreaming. I watched the adults for a long while. There they were. The people most important in my life. Except for my father. The divorce was final. Smudged from my life like a chalk mark smeared across a blackboard, he no longer seemed very real to me. I tried not to care, but I couldn't help wondering what he was doing. I doubt he would try to call. He used to get purple in the face at the mention of a long-distance call unless it was an emergency. Even then, he limited the conversation to less than ninety seconds. Clearly, I was no emergency. Maybe I was just someone he wanted to forget.

That day, the topics covered the upcoming calf sale, the price of hay if you could get it and the fiery run-off for the Senate primary. "You have to give it to that Johnson boy. He wants it bad to spend all that money and whatnot to go up against Stevenson. Think he stands a chance?" Bob chewed on the ice from his tea.

Tío drew on his cigarette and turned it to stare at the red tip. "He made a big hit here didn't he?" Tío coughed. "The man's got a powerful personality."

"Hey, rumor's going 'round that Johnson's been dropping by George's office over at the courthouse. George and his bunch are out to help Johnson make it. What do you think about that?"

"That right?" Tío didn't sound surprised.

"Well, I guess all of Duval will be out to vote come Saturday," said Bob.

The Gulf breeze swept away the words and lulled me to sleep. As it turned out, Bob was right. Duval County folk would be out to vote—dead or alive.

———

The next day, the heat at noonday stifled any living thing. Undaunted, Burt Charles and I grabbed two umbrellas and shuffled out to the barn.

Mr. Wiley smiled despite the row of nails in his mouth. "Well, well, well. Who y'all gonna vote for?"

"We can't vote, sir, but we just turned thirteen."

"Aw, I thought y'all wuz nearly twenty-two."

"Nuh uh, sir!" Burt Charles swelled up ever so slightly.

I knew Mr. Wiley teased us, but I still felt pleased. It reminded me of when Mama's smile turned suddenly coquettish when she had to show her driver's license to cash a check and the bank teller would say, "Oh, Mrs. Martin, you *couldn't* have been born in 1914."

I elbowed Burt Charles. "He's kiddin', you fool."

"Uh uh, let's not have any of that 'fool' talk. Seems like I remember something from the Bible about that—'but whosoever shall say, Thou fool, shall be in danger of hell fire.'"

Who would have figured Mr. Wiley for quoting the Bible? It was my turn to feel heat flash to my ears. I was close enough to hell fires as it was. "Really," I said, "I didn't mean—"

"Yeah, you did." Burt Charles bunched his eyebrows and glowered at the dirt.

Unwilling to dwell on a bad moment, Mr. Wiley continued. "Know who I'm gonna mark on my ballot?" Mr. Wiley asked between long slurps of water. "I'm gonna vote for Coke Stevenson-—that West Texas boy who used to be governor. I may be the only cowboy in Duval County to vote for Coke, what with George Parr lined up on Johnson's side.

"His first name is Coke?" said Burt Charles. "You kidding us, Mr. Wiley?"

"Nuh uh," I added. "Nobody's got Coke for a first name!"

Burt Charles and I broke into the commercial song, "All I want is a Coke!"

"Coca-Cola." Burt Charles said, "Hah! *Cola* means tail in Spanish. I guess that means Mr. Coke is a …hahahaha…well, you know…." He gave me a shove and grinned before pulling his hat down over his face.

I covered my mouth, giggling into my hand.

Mr. Wiley smiled a gummy smile. "Well, I imagine that's just about what George woulda called Stevenson. Coca-Cola. A horse's…uh… patootie." And he laughed out loud.

"Oh, we'd vote for Mr. Johnson. Didn't you see him come flyin' in on that helicopter? We caught his hat for him." Burt Charles' eyes glowed with the memory. "Boy! Ya shoulda seen it!"

"Mighty gung-ho fella. Mighty gung-ho. How's your uncle like him?"

"Hard to tell." I jumped into the conversation. "Last time I asked him all he said was politicians usually got what they wanted."

"Well and why not?" Burt Charles intervened. "They want to get elected so they can help run our government."

Mr. Wiley grunted and smiled. "Some do, I guess. I've been waitin' to meet *that* man."

"Well, I bet that Mr. Johnson would. He's like John Wayne," I said. "Anyway, George likes him. He told Estela to vote for him. He's George's friend."

Mr. Wiley guffawed then. "Now if y'all ask me, George Parr's friends *earn* their keep. George was real tight with Coke Stevenson till he appointed someone else's man as District Attorney down there in Laredo. Don't think George ever got over that."

"Did it hurt his feelings?" Maybe George was a more sensitive man than I realized.

"I'll say."

On our way back to the house, we tilted our umbrellas against the sun. "Think it really upset George pretty bad? I mean bad enough that George would get all his friends to vote against his used-to-be buddy?"

"Well, Izzie, you haven't been here long enough to know how George works. If he gets aggravated, he gets even. It's not just his friends he talks to around here. It's every Mexican in two counties. He's got what you call…influence. Anyway, Daddy was laughing the other day, talking about sometime back when the Klebergs supported George's daddy's opponent for Texas Senate. Daddy said George never got over that either." Burt Charles squinted up at the sky. "Man, I can't take this heat. Let's go swimmin'."

—⚏—

That night Tío and Aunt Hilda watched *Gunsmoke*. Mama studied. I studied too—on the matter of George getting his way. I imagined Tío would want to get even with Coke Stevenson and Kleberg, too. He would want to do what his brother wanted.

What You Learn at the Picture Show

To get away from the newscasters' speculation on George and Johnson, we drove to the picture show in Alice, 25 miles away. Forecasters predicted showers but no one believed it. Still, that evening it began to drizzle.

"Guys and Dolls" was showing at the Rialto Theatre. As we turned the corner away from the car, a man stepped out of the shadow of the Rexall Drug Store.

"Señor Parr?"

Aunt Hilda squealed like she always did when surprised, but the man appeared polite and plaintive. Tío spoke briefly to him in Spanish and the man clasped his hat to his chest skulked back into the shelter of the building's overhang.

What did he want? I wondered. I wasn't afraid really. It was just the idea of someone waiting in the dark to step out and stop us.

I pushed it out of my mind. The movie offered something for everyone—gangster appeal for Tío and song and dance for the rest of us. The Rialto was an old theater even then, a remnant of the days when baroque designs embellished movie theatres with velvet drapes, crystal chandeliers that illuminated murals, and carpets of maroon and green irises.

"Can we sit in the balcony?" I begged. "I love the balcony." I glanced up at the sea of brown faces above us.

"Nope, we don't sit up there. You know that. We sit in the main auditorium." Aunt Hilda grabbed me by the hand and struck out down the sloping aisle behind Mama and Tío. "Keep up, now."

We arrived late during the gambling scene. Juggling our popcorn in the crooks of our arms and gripping our drinks, we excused-me past the ten people who had gotten the best seats earlier.

"Shhh…. Down in front."

Mama and Aunt Hilda changed positions twice. "Let me sit next to your tío, honey." Aunt Hilda's stage whisper turned heads for three rows in both directions.

"Izzie," Mama said, "Switch with me. I know you can't see over that man." The man with a bushy head turned to the side to hear more, but someone intervened for him.

A male voice boomed from behind us. "Oh, for crying out loud!" He unnerved me enough to squeeze my popcorn sack and lose nearly half.

I loved musicals and I loved Sinatra. Even though I caught myself nodding every once in a while, I was not about to doze off. The picture show ended. The *Movietone News* came on and "The Three Stooges," and then the movie started all over again. Before I knew it the gambling scene had come full circle. "Isn't this where we came in?" Mama leaned over me to Aunt Hilda.

Aunt Hilda asked Tío, "Atlee, isn't this where we came in?"

"Guess so."

"Yes, let's go," passed back down the line.

"Oh, let's stay through till the end."

Back up the line.

"What for? We know what's going to happen."

Back down the line.

"Oh, please, let's stay."

Back up the line.

"Oh, all right."

The impatient man who sat behind us must have decided not to stay past the scene. He stood up abruptly and cleared his throat like the lion on Metro-Goldwyn-Mayer. We all jumped, but looked straight ahead. As the belligerent stranger sidestepped toward the aisle, Mama yelped and grabbed the back of her head.

Before we could figure out what the problem was, the heads of the theater population swiveled at a high-pitched scream from the aisle. The projector whirred to a stop. The lights came up and the theatre usher scurried to the scene of hysteria.

Flicking furiously at his vest front, a man with a profile reminiscent of Alfred Hitchcock's squealed again. With nostrils flared, uttering piggy-like sounds, the man dislodged a furry mass from a button on his vest.

"Oh my God, Hilda! My bun!" Mama gripped the back of her head with both hands and looked back and forth between Aunt Hilda and Tío. "Atlee? He's got my bun!"

Tío stared at the man still holding the hairpiece between his thumb and forefinger, his pinky extended. Tío looked back at Mama, whose elbows angled at forty-five degrees while she fumbled at hairpins. He put both hands on the arms of the theatre seat and slowly pushed himself to standing. It was hard to read his expression, but his mouth had that twitch to it. He scooted back down the row to the aisle. "'Scuse me, 'scuse me." Tío was not tall and his head just reached the stranger's nose, but he rested his hand on the man's shoulder. He reached out with his palm open. "Be glad to take that off your hands, sir. I believe that belongs to my sister-in-law."

With a flip of his wrist, the man leaned back and tossed the offending piece into Tío's outstretched fingers, then pivoted on the spot, his fists balled up and arms stiff at his side. He stomped up the incline to the lobby in short jerky steps. Their eyes riveted to his retreat, moviegoers' heads bobbed erratically with no attempt to stifle their laugher.

Just as the projector clattered up again and the lights faded, Tío eased back down the row to us and to Mama, handed off her hair bun. "For you, Helen." The twitchy smile returned to his lips.

By this time, Mama and Aunt Hilda started to giggle. Uh oh, I thought. Once they started, at least one of them would have to run for the restroom. People from rows ahead of us turned and stared. *Oh jeez. Y'all get a grip.* I shrugged and jerked my head at my mother and aunt—like I couldn't help it that these two women were nuts.

From the corner of my eye, I saw Mama cover her mouth to stifle laughter. But the harder she tried, the more she giggled. Aunt Hilda gripped the back of the seat in front of her and leaned forward, her head between her arms. They'd get quiet for a minute or two. The minute Aunt Hilda sat up, she'd look at Mama and a hoot would bubble from Mama's throat. Off they'd go again, shoulders shaking. Tío shifted uncomfortably in his seat, but he was chuckling off and on himself.

Even after the gambling scene got going good again, you could hear a snicker or two break out from somewhere in the dark. That set Mama and Aunt Hilda off. Mama flapped her hands and Aunt Hilda held her breath so long that when it did come out, she snorted. Tío sat, glued to the screen, but sometimes I could see him out of the corner of my eye. Just a slow shake of his head.

I slid down in my seat, so I remained just out of sight of the swivel-necks. Even though I was grateful for the dark where my hot face could not be seen, the laughter filled a vacant spot in my heart. A swelling kind of feeling I couldn't describe. I had almost forgotten how Mama could laugh. With the separation from Daddy and the challenge of graduate school, she seemed calmer, but I had not heard her laugh like that in ages. It was a musical run—like a canary escaping its cage. For one moment there in the theatre, I felt like a pea in a pod made up of my mother, my aunt and my uncle.

Only for just a moment did I let the man who waited outside the theater evade my little haven. What could he want from my tío? And why did he shrink back to the shadows so quietly?

I drifted into a dream-like state myself until the music swelled in final crescendo and the lights snapped on. Mama nudged me and we filed patiently with the others shuffling up the aisle.

We stepped out into the warm night. To our surprise, the rain maintained its erratic fall, and the tires of the passing cars hissed on the asphalt street. I leaned back and let the drops fall on my tongue till Mama elbowed me. I wanted to hold out my arms and spin in the mist. We had parked a little way from the marquee. Again, as we turned toward the car, the man blocked us momentarily before stepping away. And again, his hat twisting in his hands, he said, "Señor Parr?"

This time Tío stopped. He handed Aunt Hilda the keys. "Y'all go on and wait for me in the car."

Aunt Hilda opened her mouth to object, but Mama slid her arm around her sister's waist and whispered, "Now, let's just go on now, honey."

I hung back with Tío, but he patted my shoulder. "You too, sweetheart. I won't be but a minute."

Crawling into the backseat, I shifted my view around my aunt and mother. The neon of the marquee shimmered in the mist, and harlequin shadows in red and green flickered across Tío's face. The man had put his hat back on. The deeply blocked creases funneled the rain onto his nose. He pinched and tilted the crown occasionally to drain the water from the brim. He spoke with open palms, his lips moving rapidly.

For a moment, Tío stood, weight on one hip with his fingers in his front pockets. Then he leaned forward, reached into his back pocket for his wallet and pulled out some bills. He folded them into the man's hand. The stranger's head bobbed up and down as he drifted back into the night.

"And what was that all about?" Aunt Hilda asked when Tío slid back into the front seat. "Did you just give him money?"

I was not used to her business-like tone.

"Oh, a little bit," he said. "His wife's real sick after that last baby and he couldn't afford the prescription." Tío started up the engine.

"You're still livin' like we did before the drought," said Aunt Hilda. "Next thing you know, George'll be coming around with his hand out again and you'll be down at the bank writing out another check to that Percy Foreman lawyer."

"It's my business, Hilda. Let's not hear another word about it." Tío's mouth set into a hard line and he dropped the Cadillac into drive and the tires spun on the rain-slick street.

Aunt Hilda glared at Tío while she said to Mama, "Helen, change places with me. I keep hittin' my knee on the gearshift."

"Here, put your legs here." Mama patted the seat as she scooted over. "We better not switch going down the highway." Aunt Hilda slid over rather violently and adjusted her skirt. I noticed she hadn't complained about the gearshift on the ride *to* Alice. Mama put her arm around the back of the car seat and flapped her fingers at me to sit back and quit breathing down their necks.

My good mood from the theatre evaporated in the back of the Cadillac. The three of them sat up front not speaking. Aunt Hilda sat as far over on Mama's side as she could get. Mama, uncomfortable I could tell, was staring out the window into the night. I watched the rain make fine streams across the car window. Now see, I thought to myself. Now see! That's not right. George had to be positive that Tío would help him buy votes for the next election. Why else would Tío give money to some man he doesn't even know?

Helping George always came with a dollar sign.

By the time we got home, the rain had stopped. Tío checked the rain gauge on the carport post. Only a tenth of an inch there at the ranch. Just enough to settle the dust for the night.

Just a tease.

Election Day

Hot. We knew it would be. The highway heat coalesced on the blacktop like an oasis in the Sahara. We rolled the windows all the way down and dangled our heads out like hound dogs, closing our eyes to the flat heat of wind draft. Burt Charles and I had finagled a ride to the snow cone or *raspa* stand that stood by the school where polling booths were set up. Aunt Hilda and Mama intended to vote in the run-off election that would decide the Democrat nominee for U.S. Senator. We all knew how they were going to mark their ballots. Instructions had come down.

Skidding into the gravel parking area, Aunt Hilda remarked, "You kids hurry up now. It's hot and we have no desire to stand out here sweatin' in this sun. While you're at it...." She dug through her purse for change. "Get me a cherry one. You want a snow cone, Helen?"

Mama shook her head and waved us on.

A long line looped around the back of the school building where voters stood sharing umbrellas and wiping the backs of their necks with limp handkerchiefs. They fanned their faces in a dismal attempt to cool off. Before we could get back, the *raspa* flavoring dripped like a faucet. We sucked at the bottom of our paper cones and handed one over to Aunt Hilda.

"Oh, good lord. Helen, help!"

Mama grabbed the cone and squeezed the tip. "You better hurry. I don't know how long I can keep my finger in the dike."

Burt Charles stared at me.

"She means like the little Dutch boy," I said.

"Maybe. But most people don't talk like that," he said while he tried to keep the red sugar drip off his shirt.

"Well, of course not. These women...." I circled my finger at my temple.

The day steamed hotter. Two or three ladies in line came close to fainting and weaved off to the benches set out to the side. Burt Charles and I headed over to a lone mesquite tree and slurped our *raspas* at frantic speed before our shirts were completely tie-dyed with colored drool.

"Can't believe people want to vote so bad in this heat. I mean who cares, really, who wins this election? Never mind what George says." I sucked the sweet iciness of the *raspa*.

"Oh, they care. If George thinks it's a good idea, it works out for them in the long run. I just hope your mama and Hilda can get it done quick. Think I'll just dive in the pool with all my clothes on when we get back to the ranch. For once, Mom might think it was a good idea." He slapped at the stain soaking into the cotton of his white t-shirt.

I pressed my palms together. They stuck like magnets. I elbowed Burt Charles to show him the variety of items from the ground that would stick to my hands: the empty *raspa* paper cone, a cigarette butt and a baseball card that he stripped from my fingers.

"That's a Jackie Robinson! Good grief, give me that!"

"Just looks like a colored man to me."

"Oh....Oh, he's only the best! Number 42 for the Dodgers. He can do it all."

"Whatever you say." I wiped my hands on my shorts. "Let's go before you have a cow."

"I can't believe you found this." All the way back to the car, he kept saying, "Can't believe it!"

"Ah hah! Look at that!" I pointed at my aunt who sidled up to one of the first in the voting line. She smiled prettily at an older man and he shuffled aside with a wave of his hand, inviting the two gringa ladies to step in front of him.

"Oh, she's smooth, isn't she?"

I nodded. I had to admit, she had a knack for getting her way.

We waited in the shade until Mama and my aunt opened the car door to let the heat escape some before starting the engine and heading down the road.

We passed the Villanuevas on the way back. They were taking all their voter-aged relatives to the polls. In the closest thing to a Benavides rush hour, streams of dilapidated cars and trucks, their brake lights flashing, turned into the voting area.

"Boy, everybody and his dog are out today." I pivoted on my knees to look out the back window. I glanced down at Burt Charles who was still fingering the baseball card. "Hope my giving you that card works out better for you than that wishbone trade did for me." I remembered the night when I had begged Burt Charles to make a wish for me instead of for himself.

"You can say we're even. You got the wish and I got the card." With a gentleness I hadn't seen before, he placed the card in his shirt pocket and patted it against his heart. If it hadn't been for the well blowout, maybe my wish would've come true. Maybe I just dreamed for too much. All it took for Burt Charles to be happy was a Jackie Robinson baseball card.

Mama and Aunt Hilda were silent. Unusually so. Then Mama asked, "I'm surprised this many are turning out. How in the world did they get the dollar seventy-five to pay their poll tax?"

Lifting her hair off her neck, Aunt Hilda resettled her sunglasses on her face. "I think George tells them not to worry about it. He'll take care of it." Her eyes cut over briefly to Mama.

Mama was quiet for a long time before she ventured to ask more. "You mean George paid for all these people's poll tax? That's thousands of dollars! A dollar and seventy-five cents times the population of Duval County?"

"Sometimes it's several counties. He wants them to be able to vote even if they can't afford the tax. What's the matter with that?"

Mama snapped her head around to look out at the brown, withered fields. "Well, nothing of course. Just where…where would he get that kind of money?"

"Oh, I don't know. What do I know? Maybe he just excuses it, you know? Maybe he just waives the requirement. It's in his power as county judge, I think."

"Well, what about those other 'several counties?'"

Aunt Hilda whipped across the cattleguard at the first gate. "Oh, what do I know, Helen? What do I know?"

"I'm sorry, Hilda. I didn't mean to be so nosy." Mama patted her shoulder. "I guess I'm just trying to understand things. That's all. Forget I said anything."

In the rear view mirror, I saw Aunt Hilda's eyebrows frizzle together.

She took a deep breath and tweaked out a plastic smile. "I think there's some watermelon left in the ice box, y'all," she said. "Let's cut us a big piece each when we get home. Whatcha say?"

I was disappointed that Tío was not there to cut it for us. I loved watching him flick open his pocketknife, stab the melon and drag the blade in a crisp clean motion through the green hide. So simple— opening the heart of a watermelon.

Dead Men Can Vote — Twice

That night, Aunt Hilda, Mama and I sat watching *Coke Time* with Eddie Fisher. "You don't think this'll jinx the election, do you? Aunt Hilda crossed her fingers and hooted a laugh.

"Coke Time is anytime anywhere. It's always time for ice-cold Coca-Cola." I sang along with the commercial. The cameras zeroed in on a black and white shot of an ice-filled chest of bottled Cokes.

Mama sat up. "Hmmm…that does look good. Izzie, why don't you run over to the kitchen and bring us a coke?" Of course, we knew she meant Dr Pepper. "Coke" was Texas generic for any soft drink. I begged off till Eddie finished his fifteen-minute repertoire of songs.

Aunt Hilda checked her watch on a regular basis. About every thirty minutes, she would find a reason to adjust the outside antenna. Just to make the process valid, she'd yell in the window to see if the reception improved, but I suspected she really wandered out to see if she could hear a car coming down the road.

We sat through *The Phil Silvers Show* and laughed at Sergeant Bilko's shenanigans, but *Gunsmoke* wasn't the same without Tío. The news came on and announced that Coke Stevenson had probably taken the democratic nomination, but not all the votes were counted. By the time *The Tonight Show* aired, we sat and stared alternately at the clock and the television set.

Tío still wasn't back.

Aunt Hilda picked up the phone with the best nonchalant air she could produce and dialed Daisy. "Sorry to bother you, honey, but have you heard from Bob?" Her manufactured smile quivered. "Oh, good. Nope. Everything's fine. Well, of course, I'm sure. George's wife just gave me a call. And you know George and Atlee. They're probably all down waiting to hear election results."

Aunt Hilda got up, dragging the phone cord behind her like a microphone wire. She changed TV channels. "Just wondered if you'd heard anything. Oh, no no. Don't wake him." Aunt Hilda twisted the television dials, oblivious that Mama and I stared at her in disbelief that she had run through the three channels we had. Many times.

Hanging up, Aunt Hilda continued to rotate the channels for a few moments.

"Hilda.....Hilda." Mama spoke to her sister like a psychiatrist to a demented patient. "Let's stick with *The Tonight Show*. Shall we?"

"Oh! Oh, of course." Aunt Hilda turned back to her chair and sat. But she had left the channel on a movie made in the forties.

"Something rotten in Denmark?" asked Mama. She was trying to be clever again.

"Not in Denmark." Aunt Hilda picked up the nail file and sawed away till she winced at the quick of each finger.

I got the high sign from Mama to change the channel back to our show. We all sat there in silence till the National Anthem came on.

"Y'all go on to bed. You don't have to wait up with me. Think I'll just get my pajamas on and read for a while." Aunt Hilda leafed through a mystery novel she had started.

When I woke later, I pulled back my curtain. The light from her room still burned a bright path across the patio. Aunt Hilda still waited.

George Comes to Dinner

The *Corpus Christi Caller* announced that Lyndon B. Johnson would be the Democratic nominee for the U.S. Senate seat, courtesy of Box 13 in Jim Wells County—courtesy of George Parr, the *patrón* who finagled the 87-vote margin tipping the balance for Johnson. Some votes bore the names of deceased citizens. Rumors buzzed in gossip hives and newspaper headlines that George had bought votes for the Johnson campaign. And when they needed more, he bought more.

The following Friday, Burt Charles rode the bus home with me. We wanted time to ride before his parents came for dinner. Just as we ambled back from the corral, George Parr's new Chrysler pulled through the carport gates. As we tiptoed over the cattleguard, George and Tío stood together talking. George cracked two pecans together and picked at the dry kernels. They crumbled in his hands and he slung them out into the grass.

Tío frowned at the ground and shook his head. "We'll talk about it some more, George, but I just don't know."

"You bet, Atlee!" George laid his hand on Tío's shoulder and gave it a jostle. "You bet! We've got time to sit down and figure this thing out. I'm not about to let them get the best of us." He looked up and acknowledged Burt Charles and me with a tip of his hat.

Burt Charles nudged me. "We better walk on up. You know how they are about manners." Before I could detour to the kitchen, he body-blocked my departure. "Go on. Say hello."

"Well, look who's here!" George swept off his hat in the gallant gesture of the three musketeers. "Y'all musta got a head taller since I saw you last." I flinched when he hugged me. With Burt Charles on one side and me on the other, he strolled with us in tow toward the house. Even with our shoulders still scrunched up around our ears, Burt Charles and I managed to make eye contact. Burt Charles basked in the attention. He looked at me and then smiled back up at George. Charmed. To me, George's hug felt more like a half nelson.

"I hear tonight we're havin' some of that creamed corn your aunt makes up special. Mmm. My favorite!" And he gave us both another squeeze. I had to admit his grey eyes were warm now, and he genuinely looked interested in us. "Is Keep the Change still down in that corral? Maybe that uncle of yours will get Joaquín to tame that horse down so you could ride him, Izzie." I tried to swivel around to watch Tío's reaction to that absolutely outstanding idea, but George snuggled me up closer and walked up the steps to the kitchen.

"Hilda," he shouted, finally releasing us. "Hey, you pretty thing! I heard you cooked up some of your famous cream corn for me. Girl, you know how to make a man happy." And he kissed her quickly at her temple.

"Oh, you scoundrel." I noted Aunt Hilda's smile regardless of the complaints she frequently registered against him. "Come on in this house." She leaned against the wrought iron door and held it open with her body as Tío followed his brother into the kitchen. "Dinner's almost ready."

George rubbed his hands together. "Somethin' smells good. *¿Qué pasó Estela?*

"*Hola, señor George.*" Estela tucked her chin and smiled timidly as he gave her a brief hug.

He gently turned Estela to face him. "How is baby Ana doing? *¿Mejor?*"

"No mucho." Estela dropped her dishcloth, and George bent quickly to pick it up for her.

George lifted Estela's chin so that their eyes met. 'We'll help," he said and turned toward Tío. "Atlee! Didn't we call in some favors to get Doc Davidson's boy outta trouble over that..." George glanced over at Aunt Hilda. "...incident? Bet he'd be happy to make some calls on Estela's behalf here."

"Wasn't Dr. Davidson's son charged in that terrible hunting accident?" asked Aunt Hilda. "How did you...?"

"Yes, he was, Hilda." George intervened before Tío could answer. "That was all just a big mistake, just a little misunderstanding. I thought the boy's attorney presented a reasonable defense and I gave the kid probation. But now, quit worrying. You let us ol' boys take care of things." Once again, George turned and with a warm smile and a flurry of Spanish, spoke to Estela. Tears flashed into Estela's eyes as she gazed up at George's face and twisted the dishcloth around her hands.

In the veranda, George greeted Burt Charles' daddy, who leaned on the fireplace mantle. "Well, Bob Taylor!" George stretched out his hand and leaned forward, at the same time grasping Mr. Taylor's upper arm in a brotherly *embrazo*. Burt Charles' daddy was slim and towered over George, but George carried off the encounter with an air of *never-confuse-size-with-power*. "And Daisy, good to see you, honey." George continued his conquests with one of his brief one-armed hugs. Daisy blushed.

George bent to Burt Charles and put his hand on his shoulder. "You have a lovely mama, son. You be good to her, hear?" George's eyes took on a confiding gaze that invited equality between man and boy. By the simple gesture of a hand on his shoulder, George had laid claim to Burt Charles' admiration.

Burt Charles stood taller. "Yes, sir! You can count on that."

Oh, brother, I thought. I'd seen Burt Charles act smart to his mama on plenty of occasions, but I had to admit, George was impressive. Still, it irritated me in a way I couldn't explain. Maybe I was jealous.

"I bet we've got time for a round of pool." George slapped Tío on the back and with the sheer power of his will, shepherded them all to the billiard room, as though this were his house and not his brother's.

"Boy, rack 'em up for us and stand back to watch an ivory disappearing act!" He nodded toward Burt Charles who swaggered around like he had a cigar between his lips and a cue stick between his fingers.

George insisted Tío go first. He stood patiently with both hands wrapped around the cue stick waiting his turn. His grey eyes darted from ball to ball and angle to angle till he finally spread his fingers wide on the felt and began his shot. His hands were small, almost delicate. I watched him sink the last ivory ball into the pocket. It was all in the spin and slant.

—∿∿—

The talk at dinner centered on the drought and a new oil refinery they hoped would be moving to the Benavides area—no politics, just "pass the gravy." Tío didn't talk much, but George held forth with charismatic charm. His jokes sent Mama, Aunt Hilda and Daisy into titters of laughter and made their eyes sparkle. Burt Charles kept his eyes glued to George and chewed with his mouth open. I elbowed him. "Close your mouth."

"What?" He had no idea what I was talking about. I did an imitation of his previous behavior. He frowned but zipped his lips.

I glanced over at Tío at the head of the table. His eyes down, he cut his steak more slowly than usual and slipped little pieces to Show Boy. At last, Aunt Hilda rang the silver bell. Estela appeared at the door.

"You may clear the table now, Estela." Aunt Hilda touched the napkin to her lips and asked if anyone would like apple pie or just ice cream.

Estela moved around the table like she had so many times before, but her hands shook and she kept glancing up at Tío. I guess he finally noticed because he excused himself and followed her into the kitchen.

When he returned we all looked up expectantly. "Looks like you have a little entourage following you, George. The press got wind you were over here and is waiting outside the kitchen door hoping for a few words with you when you walk out."

George tucked his napkin under his chin and scooted closer to the table. "Well, then I guess I better keep my strength up for a long conversation. I'll have that pie and two scoops of ice cream, Hilda, if you don't mind, honey."

We all settled back down to our desserts, but there was restlessness among the adults even a kid could pick up on.

"That reminds me," George continued, "...about the ol' boy who...."

He went on with the joke and everyone smiled, but now we looked at our ice cream instead of his cool grey eyes.

The grown-ups stalled after dinner with coffee, but we kids were excused. Burt Charles and I headed out the door and up to the roof where we could get a look at the reporters.

"What do you think they're gonna ask him?" Burt Charles asked.

"I don't know but, man, that's a lot of reporters."

They had parked their cars mostly outside the carport, but there was a Chevy Bel Air blocking George's Chrysler. They weren't going till they were satisfied.

I was beginning to get a chill when George finally stepped out the kitchen door and the clamor began.

"Mister Parr! What's your response to charges of election fraud?" called a reporter with his hat cocked like Dick Tracy.

"I hear a whole graveyard voted," called another.

"Who was in this with you?" a third shouted. "Your brother?"

George stood on the tile steps and settled his hat on his head. "Now you boys just take it easy. I don't control the votes or dig 'em up. I just pick the man and the people here vote for him. They trust me." He started down the first step but was blocked by a reporter from the *Kingsville Gazette*.

"Just why would the Mexicans trust you so much, Mr. Parr? You've been to the pokey once and indicted again on federal tax evasion. If it hadn't been for Harry Truman's pardon, you woulda never got back into politics." The man waved his pen in the air. "Think the White House will pardon election fraud?"

George moved right along as if the question hadn't been asked. "These people vote with me because I've been their friend all my life. My father was their friend. I spoke Spanish before I could speak English. I sit in their homes and talk with the old ones. My wife is Mexican."

I looked at Burt Charles. "She is?"

"Oh yeah…Eva. I guess she is. She hardly ever comes out here. Shhh."

The reporters milled about like hyenas waiting for the lions to finish. And George continued even more confidently. "I live with these people, work with them, play with them. I go to chicken fights and bullfights with them. I bet on quarter horse races with them. When they need a friend they come to me. I help them get born and help them get buried. I am not like my churchified Baptist enemies. They're too good to go to a Latin-American home. Well, I'm not too good." He stepped down the last step and glared at the group. "Y'all quit worrying about stuff you don't understand."

"What about your brother, Parr? We all know how this *patrón* system works around here. He has deep pockets when it comes to these Mexicans too, doesn't he? I hear he's been picking up some big hospital tabs for some of these people. And they probably vote just like he wants 'em to. *Don't* they? The old Parr technique…a little favor here, a little favor there. Lots of favors owed." The reporter, pen poised above paper, prepared to write down any comments George made. A chuckle circulated among the men.

I gasped at Burt Charles. "Tío *did!*" I said. "He did give that man money!"

Burt Charles shushed me.

"Those votes came from my people, and from what I understand, the electors are going to accept the vote as it stands." George hitched his pants higher.

"But what about Atlee?" The reporter smirked. "Surely, he would wanna help a brother out. And information I have here says he's done it before. Didn't he buy off that judge for you up in Dallas a few years back?"

I remembered Tío and Aunt Hilda's trip to Dallas. *To see a judge. Scrutiny and implicate* on my Big Chief tablet. My heart double-flipped. But George was a judge, too.

"Did your brother help you pick up a few cadavers from their grave, let them make their mark and send 'em back to their grave?" Grinning, the reporter scanned the crowd for appreciation, but most of the other reporters shifted on their feet and gave each other cautious glances. "The Parrs have pull around here. Some say they can even pull votes right outta the county cemetery. Pretty embarrassing behavior for a county judge, I'd say."

"Son?"

"Yessir?" The words came out in a sneer.

"What's your name?"

The reporter's eyes widened and he coughed.

"Spit it out, boy. What's your name?"

"Edwards." He looked at the ground as if he were addressing the grass.

"Edwards?"

The crowd hushed.

"You keep outta my business. I'll take care of this county without your opinion. If I were you, I really wouldn't let the sunrise reflect off your rosy red ass." George punctuated the time with sharp raps to his Rolex. "Never can tell." George exuded a saccharine falseness. "Someone might mistake it for a bull's-eye."

It was hard to read his expression from our vantage point, but Edwards riveted to attention. George lifted his palms shoulder high. "Ya never know. Sometimes these people are hard to handle after a few shots of tequila. Just lose control. And you, being a gringo, might run into some trouble. Know what I mean?"

Edwards looked like he might be ready to leave at that moment.

"The rest of you people, don't fill your heads with these silly rumors. It's just politics as usual. Stevenson's likely to say anything to get the results reversed. He wants this Senate seat real bad and is kicking up a storm, but you can bet your bottom dollar, he can't afford too much scrutiny himself."

There was that word again. *Scrutiny.*

George jingled the car keys in his pocket. "If Stevenson gets his demands through the courts, he can expect a little tit for tat. There won't be any changin' of the guard. You boys just relax." George nodded out at the carport. "That Chevy needs to move. My wife's waiting for me."

With his small but squared shoulders and the click of his boot heels on the tile, George parted the men as though he were slicing cake. He opened his car door, shifted to one hip and leveled his eyes at the Chevy behind him. One of the reporters broke from the crowd, leaped into the car and made two sputtering attempts to start the engine before it caught. He screeched backwards just as George's back bumper brushed the Chevy. The others stood silently for a moment as they watched, then disbanded, mumbling and shaking their heads.

Still crouched on the roof, Burt Charles and I leaned there, shoulder to shoulder, and waited till the reporters backed up their cars and puttered down the road to the highway. In the cool air, Burt Charles felt warm. I wanted to scoot closer, but thought I'd probably scare him to death.

"So George's married to a Mexican?" I asked. This was a first in my experience.

"Yeah." Burt Charles studied his fingernails. "Daddy said there was a shotgun involved. George never brings her over. I've only seen her once in town. She's all right. She's way younger than George though."

"Like Aunt Hilda's age?" I had worked the math and figured Tío had to be twenty years older than my aunt.

Burt Charles snorted. "Nope, not even close. I heard Mama say that Eva tried to look a lot older by wearing her hair in a tight bun and long straight dresses. But she's barely twenty."

"And George is even older than Tío!" I rolled my eyes. "Man!" Still, twenty seemed a fine age to be married, I guessed, even if your husband was old enough to be your granddad.

Burt Charles continued with his cache of information. "And…." He paused for effect. "George and the new wife have a little girl, Georgia, after George. Just like his first daughter."

"You are kidding! He has two daughters named Georgia?" This was another first in my experience.

"Yep, the first Georgia and her mother live on the coast. She and George divorced a good while back."

"Ohhh...." I thought about how I would feel if my daddy got married again and named his other daughter Isabel. When we scooted down the stucco ledges that led to the yard, the idea was so unnerving that I miscalculated my jump from the wall and turned my ankle.

Burt Charles came back to check on me. "Izzie, you have got to watch what you're doing."

I sat on the ground rubbing my ankle. I wanted to cry.

"Oh, here," he said. "Grab hold."

He reached around me and heaved me up. "Put your arm around my shoulder, for cryin' out loud. I can't haul you in without a little help."

The Three Roses pomade Burt Charles used to groom his flat top drowned out the other night smells and the peach-fuzz on his cheek tickled my face. I held on tight and tried to bounce along in rhythm to his step. It was an odd dance. Our first.

The moment he swung the door open to the veranda, he let me go and I hobbled on in without him. He wouldn't make eye contact with me the rest of the night. Oh, he talked, but never once looked me straight in the eye.

The grown-ups sat, talking quietly and then hushed when Burt Charles and I came through. "What happened to you, Izzie? And where have y'all been?"

"I practically broke my ankle, is all."

"Let's take a look," said Mama. "Mmmm. It is swelling some. Put some ice on it, honey. Burt Charles will give you a hand, won't you?"

He shrugged and let me hop to the kitchen on my own.

Not that I minded. The thought of Burt Charles icing down my ankle held an attraction I couldn't quite explain.

Easing into a chair, I propped my foot on a stool. I looked out from under my lashes and asked. "I hope you don't mind."

"Whatever." He busied himself wrapping ice cubes in a towel.

"I've heard that a bag of frozen peas works pretty good."

"Whatever."

I thought I better push him to a more comfortable topic than my rapidly swelling Achilles tendon. "So what do you think? I mean, really think? Those reporters seemed to think even Tío was in on Box 13."

"They didn't call him out, though. That was a good sign."

"Ask your daddy what he thinks."

"You ask your mama," Burt Charles said. "While you're at it, ask how you can get dead people to vote."

—⟋⟍—

I considered Burt Charles' suggestion about asking Mama. I had always talked to my mama, but now it seemed that she burrowed herself in a hole, all in the pretense of getting more education. After her master's degree, she would probably try for a doctorate at the rate she was going. I missed our night whispers and the fragrance of her Wind Song perfume. Even when she wore it too strong.

A few nights later, I waited till the light died under her door—until she had probably faded into some dreamland that I wouldn't be banished from. Holding my breath, I pulled the heavy door open just enough for me to slide through and tiptoed to her bed. Silently I slid between the sheets. They were cool until I eased closer to my mother. I leaned against her shoulder and moved as close as possible without disturbing her. I would stay till the small gasps that came before each breath I took, calmed. It made no difference now. What answers could she give me, really? I just wanted to feel part of her again and not a page she had studied and moved on. I remained longer than I had promised myself. The answers didn't matter really. What mattered was that we stuck together. Even if it was when she slept.

Have You Seen the Newspaper Yet?

For a Sunday morning, the phone rang early. Leaning across her pillows, my aunt picked up the receiver with a singsong "Hell-l-o-o." She listened for a minute before covering the mouthpiece. "Helen, Daisy wants to know if we've seen the front page of the newspaper"

The paper lay untouched on the television console. Mama put down her magazine and walked over to the TV. "What? I don't see...oh." She paused and clutched the page to her breast before spreading out the pages on the bed. "Oh, Hilda."

"What?" I asked. It was like I wasn't in the room. I looked from one to the other.

Aunt Hilda scanned the headlines. "Call you back, Daisy." She dropped the receiver in its cradle, but left her hand on the phone.

"Oh, honey. I'm sorry." Mama laid her hand on Aunt Hilda's knee.

"It's never gonna end, is it?" She leaned against my mother's shoulder just a second, then she snapped up the phone again and buzzed the kitchen. "Estela? Atlee back from town yet?" She waited. "Figures." She sat up straighter, flipped her legs over the side of the bed and jammed her feet into her slippers. "Maybe a bath, a hot bath." And she disappeared into the dressing room.

I stood up and walked over to the crumpled section of the *Corpus Christi Caller*. Under an unflattering photo of George Parr was the caption: "Duke of Duval Faces Possible Indictment on Election Fraud."

That was just the beginning. At least twice a week, reporters drove out to the ranch to cluster for hours in the carport, waiting for Tío to come in from the field.

A Nordic type with his tie loose on his neck waved his microphone. "To what extent were you aware of your brother's involvement with that ballot box business? Two hundred votes! That's a lot of ghosts to dig out of the cemetery."

Tío held up both hands to block the surge of questions and flattened his palms against the microphones they thrust at his face.

"Wouldn't you say that was a lot of ghosts, Mr. Parr? Names in alphabetical order, all in blue ink?"

I stood at the entrance to the kitchen and watched Tío as he shouldered through the group, his lips drawn in a tight line. Holding the kitchen door open for him, I hoped he could escape the microphones and accusations. But one last question stopped Tío.

"Mr. Parr! Mr. Parr! Are you aware Edwards from the *Kingsville Gazette* is missing? Has been since the night he interviewed your brother. Are you aware of that, sir?"

The tile scraped as my uncle halted abruptly. He turned to face the reporter. His grey eyes, not colorless but ashen, shot a guarded stare at the reporter. A long stare. Tío turned back to walk through the door. He did not look at me, but strode straight through to the dining room. He measured his pace as though he faced a firing squad and had refused the blindfold.

Estela's Point of View

Estela wiped her hands on her apron and closed and locked the door behind Tío. Shaking her head, she returned to scooping out avocados, her elbows jerking at her sides.

"Estela? What—"

"Isabel, you want to make the biscuits with me? I show you how."

I couldn't ignore her. Besides, making biscuits was my specialty, even if Estela thought I never set a helpful hand to work in the kitchen. I used to make biscuits all the time. Mama taught me. Those biscuits came out of the oven just as we all used to sit down to dinner in Waco. At exactly 5:20 in the afternoon when Daddy walked through the door. Exactly.

I listened to Estela's instructions even when she got to the part about adding a teaspoon of sugar. *Sugar*? Mama never put sugar in the biscuit dough. Oh well, this was Estela's show. It wasn't any crazier than ghosts coming out of the cemetery and signing their names.

"Is Tío in bad trouble like George?" It seemed like he was…like he knew things he wasn't supposed to know.

"No, *mijita*. Your tío, he is a good man. Señor George is a good man, too. He is different from your tío. He likes the politics. I don't know what this *ruído* is all about. I just know that if anybody need help? These two? They help you." Estela handed me the biscuit cutter. "Their daddy was a good man, too. You know, when he was young, he rode the Chisholm Trail. He built this ranch with his own hands and the help of my grandfather's hands. They work hard for all they got. Work hard and now with the drought and all this *politicos*, it's sad to see. They help when my papa was very sick from the heart and Ana too. They try to help with good doctors. It was just something the doctors could not fix."

"But all this ghost stuff? What do those guys mean?" I sculpted the dough into a big mound and floured it down.

"You know? I don't know nothing. I just think we help out your tío and George. They been good to us. We don't forget."

I kneaded the dough, letting it squash between my fingers till Estela reached over and patted the backs of my hands. "Time to roll it. Your biscuits gonna be tough if you mix the dough too long."

"What was Tío's daddy like?" Hard to imagine a man as old as Tío had once been a little boy.

The swinging door to the dining room swished. I jumped, but it was only Mari who marched into the room carrying a heavy silver tray and coffee service. She banged it down on the kitchen island, then turned to rifle through the pantry shelves. She stood with her back to us, but I knew she was listening to everything her mama said. The silver polish sat right in front of her, and she just stood there staring at it and holding the cabinet doors wide open. Taking in every word.

Estela glanced up but continued. "Well, my papa said Archer Parr, he work very hard. When he was young, they were young together and my papa work right along side of him. They had to ride the fences to check for breaks and find all the new *becerros* to brand. They work all day long, up early and to bed late. But pretty soon, the señor Parr, he have some good years and make some good money to buy more land, and when they beg him to run for state office, he like the idea. He help more people that way. I remember him like I remember my own papa. He make sure we have food and little house. Papa used to say, 'Anything Senator Parr want, you be sure to help him.'" Estela nodded her head. "And I do the same for your tío. He do it for us."

"But George? What about George? He's always going to trial." I thought about how upset Aunt Hilda had been. If they were so good, how come Aunt Hilda cried and asked so many questions?

"George? He take care of us, too. He wants the right man to win the politics. That way he know everything's okay. All I know is sometimes, he come through the kitchen, give me a hug, hand me a card and a little money to help out and say, 'Here, honey. Here's our man. You go give him your vote.'"

"What about Tío?"

"Oh sure, we know who he likes to win the vote. That's who we like, too." Estela rolled out my dough more evenly onto the counter. "Now, you cut out some biscuits for us. Pretty good, Isabel. Sometimes you surprise me."

Sometimes I surprised myself. But it wasn't about the biscuits. Why exactly were all the reporters yelling questions at my uncle? I twisted the biscuit cutter hard with each turn, wadded up the leftover dough and rolled it out again. George Parr was obviously in big trouble and from where I stood it looked like my Tío was right behind him.

"Isabel, you roll it too flat! You gonna have little hard biscuits."

Mari finally picked up the polish and a rag and really went to town on the tray. She didn't look up for the longest time. I cut my eyes over toward her. Without stopping her furious rubbing, she glanced up and held my gaze for an unnaturally long time. She blew an errant strand of hair from her forehead and then at last dropped her eyes and leaned back as if to study the patina of old silver.

I looked down and sure enough, the dough looked as flat as tortillas. I started over again, trying to think about what I was doing and not about the trouble my uncle and his brother were in.

Aunt Hilda quit driving into Kingsville to shop. She sent Joaquín to the Benavides country store to pick up the order she called in. "Put it on my bill, please. No, no newspaper, thank you."

She played bridge with Mrs. Brooks, Mrs. Oliveira and Daisy over and over. No one else. She told Daisy that if the conversation drifted toward politics, Daisy was to bid a grand slam or drop her cards, exposing her hand. "Anything to distract them. They'll get suspicious if I do it. Oh, Daisy, what are we going to do?"

As usual, Tío left before I even got up for school. I didn't know if he came in for lunch like always, but he never came home for dinner before dark, even after the spring days got longer and longer.

The newspaper was conspicuously absent. I followed Mama into her room where she holed up to write critical analysis after critical analysis. It was like she was held captive by her thesis. "Ishmael," she muttered and tapped on the notebook paper to indicate her kidnapper.

I missed my funny pages and asked Mama why we didn't have it anymore on Sundays. "Oh, I think Atlee gets all the news he needs at the drugstore."

"You know, I'm getting pretty old—nearly fourteen, as a matter of fact—in case you haven't noticed!" I spoke with my best adult indignation. "You don't have to treat me like I'm a baby. Tío's in trouble, isn't he?"

"Now you're just going to have to trust your tío." Mama stared at me, then looked back down at Melville's *Moby Dick* and snapped her eyes back up at me. "I do know George has asked for his help again. I don't understand it all myself. This political scenario is way out of my league. Haven't lived down here before. Don't know their way of doing things. Don't want to know. I just want to try to help Hilda feel better and keep my nose out of the rest of it. Let's just do that. Shall we?"

Rumors at the Raspa Stand

Poised at keyholes, Burt Charles and I set about investigating these matters of family intrigue, interrogating anyone willing to reveal a tidbit of information. We struggled with the lack of clarity the grown-ups provided. They were a funny bunch. They espoused the see-no-evil philosophy common to the whole generation. If questions roused a blush, it was flat-out denied. No, Uncle John was not a drunk. No, Mary was not adopted. And there is no way possible for your great-grandfather to have been Jewish. Although we made a game of it, I never admitted to myself that the answer I searched for might leave me fatherless again. If Tío was involved with George.... If Tío....

As closed-mouthed as everyone was at home, seventh graders were like baby birds in the nest. Mouths open—squawk, squawk, squawk. During recess I hung out at the *raspa* stand. Sweet iciness rolled down the back of my throat as I gazed at the sky and tuned in to conversations that might include the name Parr.

Burt Charles pulled me aside to advise me. "Listen, just play like you don't hear those guys, especially the Cadena twins."

"Well, it's pretty hard to just listen to horses' patooties shoot their mouths off about Tío and George." My eyes smarted with humiliation. "Did you hear what they said? Did you?" Dislodging my sleeve from Burt Charles' fingers, I twisted and checked over his shoulder to glare at Jose and Beto Cadena.

"What do you expect? Their family is New Party and all they know is what they hear their dad say. And he's been against the Parrs and the Old Party for years. Ever since he came back from the war, my daddy says."

I didn't care whether or not they were just parroting their parents. "I expect them to think before they shoot their mouths off. That's what I think!"

Burt Charles stepped in to block my view again. "I'm tellin' you. Pay them no mind." He grabbed my elbow and ushered me back to the building.

I shrugged off his hand. I remembered Sonia's cold shoulder in grade school. "They said the Parrs are crooks, Burt Charles."

The Piggly Wiggly and *Time*

By spring, Aunt Hilda quit playing bridge. Mama looked frazzled, but I couldn't tell if that was her thesis paper or the political ping-pong.

I decided that I'd ask to ride with Joaquín to pick up the groceries on Saturday. While he stood at the counter to check out and load up, I scanned the newspaper stand and the magazines as I rotated the comic book carousel. Nothing jumped out at me at first, but finally as I flipped through the magazines, *Time's* cover said it all.

"Parr Delivers in Texas"

I fingered its pages and then glanced at the storeowner who was totaling our bill. It always took her forever. She wrote down the items by hand and then attached the receipt. She looked up quickly at me and smiled. I grinned back. The comic rack blocked the magazines enough so I could lift a comic book with one hand and reach behind me with the other for *Time*. I sucked in a deep breath, slid it under the back my shirt so it lodged at the waistband of my jeans. I grabbed the first *Archie* comic book I came to and strolled up to the counter.

The big fans of the grocery store spun around and around, pushing warm air from one spot to another. The perspiration from my forehead pooled and slid between my eyes. With a quick brush of my forearm, I swiped away the evidence of guilt. It did feel awfully hot. The drops plopped on the hardwood floor and beaded up on paste-waxed planks. I smudged them with my tennis shoe. "Ma'am, do you think it would be all right if we added this to our bill? I...I don't think Aunt Hilda would mind. I could always pay her back." I lifted the comic book up to her with both hands. "I just forgot to bring any money with me. Is that okay with you, ma'am?" I smiled without showing my teeth. I hoped this suggested innocence.

"Well, I'm sure that will be fine, honey. That's a ten-cent one, isn't it?"

I glanced down. "No ma'am, it's fifteen cents. I believe this is a special edition. I love Archie," I said, "but Jughead is my favorite." I took sudden pride in accurately reporting the price of the comic. Maybe I wasn't all that bad, I thought. Maybe I could return the *Time* to the stand after I'd read it. Then it wouldn't really be stealing.

All the way home in the backseat of the car, the slick cover of the magazine stuck to my backside, my sweat acting like glue. It felt like an 8" by 14" stamp somebody had slobbered on and slapped on me for a joke. I squirmed as I planned a safe hideaway where I could read the article. The barn. Relieved and now confident of some success, I leaned over the front seat and asked, "Hey, Joaquín? *Qué pasó?*"

Joaquín smiled at me in the rear view mirror. "*No mucho, no mucho.*"

I figured I was home free.

As Joaquín pulled into the carport, I bolted out of the car door for the barn but slowed to a walk. For all I knew, Mari blood-hounded my tracks. Flexing my shoulder blades, I tried to lift the sticky magazine cover from my back, but it lay there like papier-mâché.

Relief washed over me in the cooler darkness of the barn. Peeled away from my skin, the cover was smeared and wilted, but the inside was intact. No time to read it before lunch. I flattened the magazine back out and waved it in the air a couple of times before sliding it under the second bale on the third level. "Second bale…third level." As I slid down the stacks of hay, I memorized the location and repeated: "Second bale, third level." Then flapping my shirt out behind me to cool my skin, I sauntered back to the house. Burt Charles needed to see this with me. Maybe his mama could bring him out.

I had just enough time before lunch to change my shirt. As I peered over my shoulder to examine my back in the mirror, Mama stepped through the bathroom door.

"Oh, hi," she said, "I didn't know you were here." Then she did a double-take. "What in the world is that all over your back?" She wheeled me around and held me by both shoulders. "emiT?"

"Oh, that!" Just…just…tattoos, I was practicing how to make tattoos." Pleased with my own impromptu response, I relaxed too soon.

"On your own back? How in the world could you reach your own back?"

From force of habit, the words "Mari did it" sprang from my lips. "You know how she is, always experimenting with something." I grabbed a towel by each end, flipped it over my head and furiously scrubbed my back. "She tried to transfer a magazine cover to my back to evaluate the color chemistry. Something like that." I kept scrubbing.

"Actually, that doesn't sound a bit like Marisol." Mama shrugged. I could tell she wasn't going to spend too much time on this. "I imagine you'll have to soak it off in the bathtub tonight." And then you could tell her mind wandered back to *Moby Dick*.

"Probably." I hollered back over my shoulder as I stuffed my head into another T-shirt. "The bathroom's all yours!" I sprinted back across the patio to the kitchen to call Burt Charles.

—⟋⟍⟍⟍⟋—

At the table, I stacked the rice and swirled the refried beans, but as nervous as I was, I still managed to eat most of my enchilada. Some foods just overrode nerves. Burt Charles would be out shortly after lunch. I pasted a pleasant smile on my face and listened to the drone of the adult conversation. Tío mentioned he was sending Joaquín out to burn more thorns off the prickly pear for the cattle. The talk dwindled after that. We all sat staring at our plates.

I asked to be excused and walked to the veranda to plop down on the couch till Burt Charles got there. I picked up a *Modern Screen* and leafed through the pages. Marilyn Monroe posed over a street vent with her skirt circling her thighs. Man, I thought, movie stars got away with a lot of risqué behavior. George was in the category of celebrity if they wrote about him in *Time*. And he was trying to get away with bad behavior himself; only his was not risqué. It was just plain risky.

Daisy's laughter announced their arrival. With the force of an invasion, the two younger brothers barged in the door and Daisy followed. I rushed to head them off. Daisy opened her mouth to ask what we were up to, but I popped up and suggested that if she hurried, she could get in on the ice cream. "They're just finishing up in there. Go on in. I'm sure Estela'll bring you some."

Daisy's lips shrunk to a nice little O and smiling, she swept on through the swinging door to the dining room.

"Let's go." I grabbed Burt Charles by the elbow and headed out the door.

"Well, Izzie, my mama's not the only one who woulda liked a little ice cream." Burt Charles looked hurt.

"Later. You can wait till later." The door slammed behind us. "C'mon. I've found some evidence." I picked up my pace and urged Burt Charles to keep up. "A double dip on a cone, I promise…when we get back."

Burt Charles took a deep breath, but complied.

The barn at midday was still my dim hazy sanctuary, a safe place where secrets lived.

Shards of sunlight wedged through the roof and suspended dust motes. Despite the comforting atmosphere, my heart pounded. "Second bale...third level." I vaulted over the stacks, pushed the bale over with both hands and slid the wrinkled magazine from under the hay. My hands shook. I shoved the magazine at Burt Charles. Maybe I really didn't want to know about my uncle and his brother. What would I do? Tell Mama? Would we have to move away? The enchilada roiled in my stomach. "You read it."

Burt Charles stared at me a minute, then shrugged. He opened the magazine and ran his finger down the featured items. "Parr delivers...Parr delivers...page 23." He pinched the pages apart and finally found the article. Clearing his throat and folding back half the pages, Burt Charles began to read aloud.

Archer Parr and his son George, the first and second Duke of
Duval, were overblown...cari car...ic—

I grabbed for the magazine, but Burt Charles swung it out of my reach.

...caricatures of the South Texas patrón. If Hollywood made
the Parrs' story into a movie, the critics would say they were
unbelievably violent and corrupt.

"Hey, wow...a movie? Who do you think would play us?" Burt Charles' focus had a tendency to unravel. "I hope we get to pick. Maybe—"

"Oh, right, Burt Charles, they'd really want us in the movie. Keep reading." I did run over a few first or second choices: Natalie Wood. She wasn't too much older than me. Or Annette Funicello. She was just my age. We looked a little bit alike.

"Well, every once in a while, you gotta look on the bright side of things, Izzie! Think about the movies. All the outlaws bite the dust after they try to rob the bank." He grabbed his chest and with an "arghhhh" fell back against the hay.

I reached for the magazine but he snapped it out of my hand. "I'm readin' here."

Last week many Democrats from north and west Texas who
never considered the dapper 'Duke of Duval' anything more

than a local political princeling found he had become a powerful kingmaker.

"Kingmaker? We don't have any kings in this country!" I didn't get it. "I know this is supposed to sound bad for George, but it's not making a lot of sense. Keep reading. Maybe something will fall into place."

Burt Charles searched for where he left off and started again.

Despite his financial losses of the past and bankruptcy, Parr has begun to recover from the foreclosure of his half million dollar, 61,000-acre ranch where he often entertained his political associates in baronial splendor. The sale of his 25 blooded quarter horses procured some financial relief. One of the finest however is rumored to be kept in reserve by George's younger brother, Atlee.

I couldn't breathe right. Crushed, dry hay filtered into my throat. I tried to cough, but it came out more like a gag. "Oh God, Keep the Change."

Burt Charles set the magazine down and took a deep breath. "Well, now wait. Sometimes these articles don't get all the facts." He sounded fairly grown-up and convincing, but he had started to chew on his fingernails. "You remember Atlee and George talking, and it sounded like George gave Keep the Change to him for helping him out."

"What? Take your finger out of your mouth!" I slapped at his hand. I had to slap at something.

Burt Charles flicked his fingers at me and frowned. "I *said*, it sounds okay to me if George owed Atlee money and he was just paying him back with the horse. What's illegal about that?"

"Well, maybe he just wanted to hide Keep the Change from the bankruptcy people."

"George said he was giving him to Atlee!"

I snorted. "George said. George said! Oh, that makes me feel better."

Burt Charles took a deep breath and pinched his eyes shut in what I supposed was a desperate attempt at patience.

I gave up. "Okay. Okay. Go on." I guessed that this was not the best time to harass my only compadre.

With another big sigh, Burt Charles plodded on.

Though it may never be proved, the election theft for Johnson has been called the high-water mark of George Parr's reign— the ultimate, arrogant display of his power. Perhaps it will also mark the beginning of the end of his iron-fisted clutch on the politics of South Texas.

"The beginning of the end? That sounds like they hope it is."

"Sounds like they hate George." Burt Charles picked up where he left off.

Despite his forced cutbacks, Parr still maintains his homestead, a luxurious mansion with its walled, lush tropical landscaped grounds with swimming pool, multiple garages filled with 150 trophy animal heads and generous servants' quarters. Against the palatial living all this represents, the way of life of the mass of Latin Americans in the Land of Parr—from whose political control Parr has, to such a considerable extent, made his enormous fortune—is drab indeed.

"Do they mean George or Tío when they just say Parr?" My hands burned. I rubbed them on my hip pockets to dry the sweat.

"Your tío doesn't have all those elk and buffalo heads in the garage! Good grief!"

"Oh." I sighed in relief. "Okay. I guess you're right. Is that all it says?"

Burt Charles waggled his finger down the page. "It goes on about 'Latin shantytowns of Benavides.' It says Benavides is a 'cluster of treeless, grassless....'" Burt Charles sputtered out, "'di...dilap... dilapidated one and two room shacks crowded together, frequently without plumbing or electricity.'"

"Well, Mari's house is like that. They still use an outhouse," I said.

"They got electricity, though."

"Yeah, but they only have two rooms, a kitchen and bedroom." I thought of the little bedroom where Mari sang to Ana. How many people could sleep in that one room? I started to count the members of the Villanueva family.

"But they've got three little houses to spread out in."

"Well, it works out to three people for each bedroom. I guess that's not so bad, if you don't count the two uncles. They probably take up one whole bedroom to themselves." I imagined being crammed into those small bedrooms with two beds and four people. Every night I slept in the luxury of ironed sheets and softly drawn drapes. I slept alone. I wondered if the warmth of family, two or three sisters to a bed, made up for the lack of even a modest standard of living. A family together in one room. A little wave of envy swept through me.

"Whaddya think?" Burt Charles asked. "I don't think it sounds too bad for Atlee. I mean, really I don't."

"What?" I had forgot for a moment what we were talking about.

"I *said*, I don't think it sounds too bad for Atlee."

"Oh, oh that! I guess not. But George's got his tail in a crack." I'd heard my mama use that term when she pointed out the trouble I was in. *You've got your tail in a crack now, Isabel.*

"Yeah, it sounds pretty bad for George. I'm not sure what election theft means, but the magazine makes him sound pre-tt-yyy bad."

"I just hope taking care of Keep the Change is not something illegal. I mean, what if it's not okay? What will happen to Tío?" I hesitated. I didn't know if I should mention I'd seen Tío give that man money. But maybe Burt Charles could explain it. This was different country down here. "Maybe...." I took a deep breath. "Burt Charles? Once Tío gave money to a Mexican outside the Rialto in Alice. And I know he gives Mari's family extra money besides just what they make. That's what those reporters said George did to get people to vote his way."

"He's just trying to be good to people, Izzie. Why do you always try to make something out of nuthin'?" Burt Charles patted my back. "Jeez, I see the Parrs do that all the time. I never did think anything of it. People just knew the Parrs would give them a hand if they got in a bind. You know, I always thought it was a good thing...helping these people. If Atlee and George didn't, then who would? Not many people around here have the money to do that kind of thing." He looked self-conscious and sat on his hands. "You know what I mean?"

"Well, that's just it, Burt Charles. What with the drought and blowout, Tío just has a whole lot of land and cattle he can't feed." I whispered like I was spreading a rumor. "I mean Aunt Hilda got real mad at Tío for giving that guy money in Alice." I realized that no one would be lurking in the barn listening to me. I spoke up, "Oh, she got over it, but she's hardly ever mad at him." I remembered crouching in the back seat. *Don't fight. Don't fight.* Reminded of the blows my father had dealt my mother, I winced.

"Whoa, really? I've never seen them mad...ever." Burt Charles' eyes widened as he took it all in.

"And I never told you this before, but you know that Edwards reporter who kept hassling George? And remember George said he'd better be careful because if he didn't leave town, he might 'accidentally' get shot? Remember? Well, he disappeared. Just disappeared!"

"That doesn't mean anything, Izzie. He probably got out of town like George said to do."

"You didn't see Tío's face, Burt Charles. You did not see his face."

Despite his attempts at logic, I could see Burt Charles was shocked. I put my fears out on the table and his one look validated every one of them. The whole catastrophe fell in on me. A kind of desperate fear rose in my throat and bubbled out into a sob. I hated to cry. Hated it. It made me feel weak, a girly girl. Especially in front of Burt Charles. I sucked it up quick as I could, but it was too late.

Burt Charles reached around my shoulder. "Aw, Izzie, it's gonna be all right. Don't...."

I jumped to my feet and rubbed my nose on the sleeve of my shirt. "Don't forget your ice cream. You just had to have your double dip, remember." I grabbed the magazine and stuffed it under the hay and took giant steps down the stairway of bales.

In Marisol's Opinion

Finally, I had to suck it up and kowtow to my rival. Marisol was bound to have strong opinions about the politics around here. She had strong opinions about everything else. While maintaining my own dignity was high on my list, I also knew I had to make her think she had really won a round. I intended to look composed and unintimidated. As a result of my experience, I had come to the conclusion that sometimes people let their guard down when they're at some mindless task. Grandmother let plenty of family skeletons out of the closet while shelling peas on those long afternoons on her porch.

After careful consideration, I decided to approach Mari while she was helping her mother clean. I wouldn't even offer to help, but just fall in with the action. I did reserve the right to choose the activity. I had no intention of cleaning toilets. Dusting might be just the thing though. It would take a while and conversation would be easy. I wouldn't want her out of breath.

As it was, the opportunity came when Mari was stuck with polishing silver again. My enthusiasm lagged at the sight of all that tarnished silver, but at least it was a sit-down activity. Estela worked in the bedroom wing on the other side of the patio. That was good. I remembered the look on Mari's face that time when I was making biscuits and her mama and she heard us talking about the Parrs. I didn't doubt Mari's opinion would take a different slant.

I sidled up with an old, soft rag in hand and picked up a Francis 1st sterling fork. Mari smirked, set down the serving spoon she was polishing and stared directly at me, her eyebrows noticeably arched. I puckered a smile, slid into the chair next to her and dipped the cloth in the Hagerty's Silver Polish. Mama had told me that silence was sometimes the balm of conflict. I hoped she knew what she was talking about. That *balm* and *silence* and *conflict* all came together in the same sentence was not reassuring. It was a new technique for me.

Mari stared a moment longer at me and then picked up another spoon. I saturated a cloth and rubbed with vigor, occasionally holding the fork out at arm's length and squinting to check the success of my efforts. Every so often I'd catch Mari in the corner of my eye. I wished she would say something. At least twice I caught her opening her mouth as if to speak, but she resisted.

Finally, I guess, she couldn't take it any more. "The tines, Lizzie." she said. "You've got to get between the tines."

I managed to ignore the Lizzie word. I would not be sidetracked in pursuit of my goal. And it was then that I learned the value of incompetence. Some people just couldn't stand to watch it and sooner or later, they would have to speak up.

"The what?"

"The points of the fork," Marisol said with a sigh. "You've got to get between them. Tarnish builds up there the worst because they're hard to reach." She took my fork and demonstrated the technique.

"I got it," I said. "I think I can do it." I held my hand out for the fork and delivered what I hoped was a smile full of warm appreciation. "You know lots of things, Mari." For the next few minutes I polished feverishly between the tines, ignoring Mari's covert glances.

"What causes silver to turn black anyway?" A good question. I mentally patted myself on the back. Not that I cared, but it gave Mari another opportunity to appear knowledgeable about household activities. If I could just get her going, she might not resist the questions I really wanted answered.

Mari leaned back, tilted her head and gazed into the patina of the serving spoon's bowl. With all my might, I resisted rolling my eyes. At last, she snapped up the bait. "Tarnish," she said, "is very much like rust, a chemical reaction with the environment." She took a breath, but before I could say "Oh" and move on to my real goals, she continued briskly. "Actually the term is derived from the Latin word for "gnawing." The same etymology as "rodent." Interesting, isn't it?"

Whatever *etymology* was.

"Tarnish is produced when silver reacts with sulfur in the air, like the smell when you boil eggs."

I wrinkled my nose, but Mari just kept rolling. "Tarnish doesn't really ruin the silver. It just makes it look black. And of course, it just takes another chemical process to undo the change. You can rub all day with Hagerty's or you can take advantage of a little chemical expertise."

"Why are you using polish then if this chemistry stuff is so great?"

"Your aunt Hilda wants it done with Hagerty's. She said she didn't have time for me to show her the other process, so we do it the hard way. We use up a lot of rags with this and it's messy, but whatever Mrs. Parr wants." Mari lit up again. "It's fascinating really. By wrapping a fork in aluminum and putting it in a pot of water and baking soda, you've got a reaction that separates the tarnish from the silver. Amazing, isn't it?" Mari's eyes sparked with enthusiasm.

I shrugged.

Without waiting for encouragement from me, she swept a spot clear of utensils on the table, grabbed a pencil and an old envelope and wrote: $3Ag_2S+2Al->6\ Ag + 2Al_2 + 3S$.

"The reason that this process works so well is that it acts electrochemically." She looked into my eyes for a sign a life. "Get it?"

Suddenly aware that my mouth was sagging open, I shut it. I sat still for a minute staring at the letters and numbers scrawled across the paper. Realizing I needed to respond, I said, "That's nice, Mari." Hoping she had gotten whatever it was out of her system, I forged ahead. "Whew! You see all those reporters here a few months ago?" I tried to remain light and conversational.

She shook her head, her mouth twisting in defeat.

"What?" I asked.

Mari's expression had gone from fired up to flat. "Saw the cars."

"Lots of 'em, huh?" I frowned at the fork and kept rubbing.

Mari picked out another piece of silver and examined the darkened edges. She did not offer a follow-up comment. Maybe she just disliked me. I summoned the effort to try again. Maybe directness was the key. Straightforward. No more monkeying around.

"I wish you would tell me something." I tried to suppress the pleading tone, but suspected it seeped through. Mari put down the spoon and turned directly to me, but I could not force my eyes to meet hers. I polished around and around, slower and slower. "What's all this talk about election theft?" My hand shook, so I polished harder. "You know, what George is in trouble for?"

"Ask your uncle if you want to know so bad."

I twisted the rag and black oozed between my fingers. "I don't think they want me to know anything, but I'm old enough. I'm older than you were when we first started coming out to the ranch." I hoped to build on what seemed like our long history. I could show her that I could forgive and forget. Set an example. Build a new foundation for…well, maybe not friendship. I plunged ahead. "Remember when we first came?"

Mari snickered.

"What? What's so funny?"

"Oh, of course, I remember." She cleared her throat. "You were little, about six, right? All spic and span with your hair done up in French braids, prim white socks, and little ruffled top and matching shorts. Never seen a Mexican before."

I was startled by her last comment. I had been fooled into enjoying her preceding description. I thought I sounded fine till the change in her tone jarred me.

"I…I…. Well, where I grew up, we never…. You've never liked me at all, have you, Marisol?" I slammed down my cleaning rag. My whole scheme to glean tidbits of inside information had flubbed. I was the one lured into her target range. I *did* remember that day.

The three Villanueva daughters had stood behind tentative smiles. Their hair hung long and black and straight. Their dresses faded and mended. Their socks sucked down into the back of their oxfords with the caked-on polish. And it was true. I *had* never seen a Mexican up close. Only gringos went to my school. It was Mari who spoke out boldly with an offer to show me the horses—Mari who thought in terms of long-range plans. I saw that then. From the moment she first met me, she envisioned the offer of a horseback ride, as well as the look on my face afterwards. I was up against a master.

"Oh, you're all right." A twitch of regret flickered across Mari's eyes. "You missed a spot there on the bottom of your fork. You've got a ways to go."

I had no idea what she meant. "How far do you think I have to go?"

"Farther than you can imagine."

"And just how far do *you* have to go, Marisol?"

Mari stood up and gathered the silver onto the towel and deposited them in the sink. They settled into the water with a soft heavy clink.

Without turning around, she finally answered. "Farther than you can imagine."

She walked out of the kitchen, through the *pasillo* and the carport, across the cattleguard and past the walls of the hacienda. I pictured her striding with sullen determinism down the road that led to their little houses.

For days, I mulled over my failed venture. Why did she always have to make it so hard? She could never take anything I said at face value. She always thought I had a scheme in the back of my mind. It occurred to me that perhaps I did. Well, for sure I did, but it didn't have anything to do with her being Mexican. She managed to turn the simple question of election theft around and scramble it up with her heritage.

I couldn't help being born gringa any more than she could help being born Mexican. Luck of the draw. I wished she'd get over it.

Off the Hook

Suddenly the cloud lifted. At dinner two nights later, Tío told his favorite story about the good ol' boys who bought their first motor boat. "Tomato-red Chris-Craft! Pin-stripes! Low in the water and revvin' up. True story, true story!" His chuckle began before he could get the next sentence out. "So this good ol' boy who's driving the boat, revs it up another go-round and yells back at the knees and head bobbin' in the water. 'Ready, Fred?' and Fred, sprawls back on the skis yells, 'Gun 'er, Claude!' And…and…" At this point Tío doubled over and could barely finish. "Claude guns 'er all right, and ol' Fred…hahahaha…. Fred hits the water face first and noses a rooster tail all the way to the Nueces River Bridge." Tío's shoulders shook and he tossed a pinch of chicken at Show Boy who sat up as tall as a dachshund could without falling over. "It was the funniest damn thing I ever saw. 'Gun 'er, Claude!'"

We'd all heard the story about fifteen times, but Tío's jovial mood struck Aunt Hilda, Mama and me with such relief that instead of our usual dutiful smiles, we all laughed. Maybe a little too loud.

The reason for this change in mood became obvious when I was excused from the table to go ride Canela. The *Corpus Christi Caller* lay boldly on the kitchen counter. I hadn't seen a paper in months and there one was. On the front page:

> *State convention declares Johnson wins senate seat*
> *by less than eighty-seven votes.*

And there flashed a four-by-six photograph of Senator Johnson and Governor Shivers, flanking George Parr, their arms around him. The caption read, "The hero of the Democratic Party—the man of the hour—George Parr!"

I folded the newspaper on the bottom shelf of the telephone stand. A ride on Canela would give me time to think.

Each rock I kicked on the way to the corral was a question to be answered. How George could get from villain to hero in a few weeks time befuddled me. Somebody was happy about the election results at least. Reporters were yelling accusations at him one minute and the next,

George shows up on the front page of the same paper, smellin' like a rose. I shook my head and flapped my arms down at my sides. A bobwhite's hard whistle pierced the monotony of the Gulf wind. The stiff breeze was annoying, but it lifted the straggling strands of hair off my neck and made the ninety-degree heat bearable. Maybe George did good for some and not for others. Maybe he *was* a hero.

I clucked to Canela and offered her a handful of sweet feed. Her muzzle was soft and tickled my palm as she rooted for the last bit of grain. There was good and bad in everything, not just people. Take Canela. She ran off with me once, but Mari was in charge. I was nervous for a long time after that, but now when it was just Canela and me, we did quite nicely.

Our ride would be a short one. I wanted to get back to that newspaper. Setting my hand on her head to remind her to drop it for the bridle, I stared off at the rise to the east. The warm humid air made the hills and mesquite vague and soft in the light of sundown. I took a deep breath. Life was good after all. Tío was happy again. Absentmindedly, I pressed Canela's head again. From where we stood, I could see a long ways off in all directions. Safe. I felt safe. I glanced back at Canela. Her poor head was practically hanging to her knees. I got the giggles and then hoped she didn't think I was making fun of her. She was trying so hard to be a good girl.

If I rode alone, the rules directed me to amble in a designated perimeter around the house and walls. A nice enough ride, but I had to stay in clear sight. It still gave me solitude to think and bounce ideas off Canela. I hefted myself into the saddle with a grunt. We didn't even feel like trotting. We just walked and she listened.

"I guess if Tío's telling jokes, things must be looking up. And from the headlines, George's got some big names backing him up." I reached down and scratched Canela's neck. "Don'cha think?"

Her ears twitched front and back.

"Me, too." I hooked my knee over the saddle horn and let Canela circle back around to the corral. We swayed side to side in slow four-four time. I quit thinking and took in the world around me. Sliding quickly now, the sun melted over the horizon. I sang Canela's going home song. "Give me land, lots of land, under starry skies above…don't fence me in." She picked up her walk to a livelier beat to keep time.

It didn't seem all that late to me, but I knew if Mama looked out the window from her lighted room, it would appear dark. I jogged most of the way back to the house after whipping the saddle off Canela and throwing her some hay.

Mama sat with Tío and Aunt Hilda in their bedroom watching *Gunsmoke*. It must have been a bonus night for Tío. The law wouldn't get George, and Matt Dillon would gun down a bad guy. One of those little ironies I noticed was that not all bad guys got gunned down. The really good thing was that if George was in the clear, Tío would be okay.

Mama shot me a warning look when I slid in the door. "See the clock?"

"Oh? Oh, yes, ma'am. Sorry. I stopped off in the kitchen a few minutes." It was more like twenty seconds.

Pulling her glasses down over her nose, Mama leveled her eyes at me.

"Chester staying out of trouble?" I nodded toward the TV as I flopped down on the floor on my stomach. I crossed my ankles and leaned my chin on my hands. Staring pointedly at the television, I commented, "Chester's always running up against something." I didn't turn to look for an answer and was relieved to hear nothing but Chester's scratchy explanation of finding a Miss Sarah under a blanket in the shed.

"Is she dead?" Aunt Hilda winced.

"Looks like," said Mama.

"Well, that awful man!"

Tío made no comment. He focused completely on the black and white screen.

At nine-thirty, I didn't need to be told twice it was time to go to bed. I staggered to my feet as though sleep was already overtaking me.

"Going to bed?" Mama looked a little surprised, but they all lifted their faces for a goodnight kiss on the cheek.

"Sleep tight," Tío murmured.

I shuffled back to my bedroom. It would be a while before Mama came to bed and I'd best go for the newspaper before she did. I put on my shorty pajamas just in case and slipped barefoot out the door and across the patio to the other side. I elected to walk around the veranda instead of going through it. Iron doors clanked and the interior doors screeched on the tile.

The walkway began at the patio outside the bedrooms and circled the veranda to end at the kitchen. My feet collected little sandpaper-like pebbles from the sidewalk, and I curled my toes against the possibility of stepping on a June bug. Even tarantulas were known to tiptoe around out there. A flashlight might have been a good idea if I hadn't thought it would give me away. I followed the curving walk. In the moonlight, the pecan trees fanned their dark embroidery over my path. A mockingbird sang a desperation chorus. Tío said they sometimes sang all night if they hadn't found a mate yet. I felt akin to the mockingbird. I knew how he felt.

Easing up the steps to the kitchen, I turned the knob and slipped inside. I snapped on the small entry light and snatched the paper from where it still lay on the phone stand. Rolling the paper and stuffing it into the bottoms of my pajamas, I shuffled back down the walk. I would have to remember to check my backside for newsprint. Rubbing the bottoms of my feet on my legs to clear the grit, I stepped back into my bedroom entry from the patio.

Cross-legged, with the bed sheet draped over a lampshade, I folded back the front page to re-read the caption under the photograph. George sure looked happy. Everyone in the picture looked happy. *Wow...hero, man of the hour.*

I flipped through to the editorials. An article titled "Parr's Democracy" sounded reassuring. Most of it was confusing, but this editorialist believed with all his heart and soul that Parr's fraud handed Lyndon Johnson the vote to win.

> *With a miraculous 87 votes, George Parr's delivery of Box 13 has ensconced Johnson in the U.S. Senate. Will Johnson be launched into greatness or will the power of George Parr's graveyard constituency stain what should have been an honorable record?*

It went on to say that party heads were "on vacation" and judges and clerks were "visiting relatives" or "suffering the flu." One custodian sadly confessed he had inadvertently tossed copies of the ballots in the trash and another had lost the container. In rapid succession, George vacillated between criminal and hero all in one issue of the *Corpus Christi Caller.*

Tío was obviously relieved that it had all worked out the way it did or was he just glad he wasn't going to have to answer any charges himself? George had gotten what he wanted and didn't seem one bit worried about how he got it.

Back on the front page, George's smile was broad and confident. He must have thought he deserved the pat on the back from the senator and the governor. They owed him. I could read it in his eyes. I hated to believe the worst of George because if it were true, it would tarnish my uncle's reputation as well. I doubted even Mari could come up with a chemical reaction capable of polishing up George Parr. I wanted Tío to be happy. My life depended on his being home day after day. After reading the newspaper, my optimism was still a little shaky. Too easily come by. The whole situation seemed like quicksand. Smooth and seamless looking, inviting an easy way across a troubling course. But something told me—don't believe everything you read.

I twisted the paper into a roll, slipped it down my pajama bloomers and eased back out into the night. The moon slanted off to the west. I squinted into the night and shuffled along the walk.

I replaced the paper and turned to go back to my room. The mockingbird was silent. The cicadas had hushed. The breeze was up again and masked the brush of my bare feet on the walk. I decided to just take the situation at face value. I crept back into my bed. If Tío was happy, I would be happy. Quicksand or no quicksand.

Hurricane Adele

Rain had been a prayer topic for as long as I could remember, but summer sultriness flickered in waves off the caliche and the wind blew hot through the brittle trees.

Crackling like hard cellophane crushed in a fist, the leaves of the fig trees skittered along the patio. Even the pecan trees looked tense, that kind of taut strain that shows life is just hanging on. For over two years, no rain had fallen except for brief showers that barely settled the dust.

I thought about how the drought had affected everything and everyone and how in the late afternoons, cows bawled for more hay. Hay prices were sky-high. Plenty of cactus remained, but burning the thorns off them to feed the herd was backbreaking. I'd as soon be shot as do that. Joaquín left early in the morning before the sun went white-hot and went out again after six in the evening when he could tolerate the heat.

I was glad not to have to ask Joaquín to saddle Canela anymore. Proud I could do it myself. I couldn't bear to see him do one more thing after the cactus. I remembered the carbuncles on his neck, the dirt ground into his skin. The family had outhouses, but where they took baths was a mystery to me. I had seen a metal tub on their porch and they may have bathed in that, but it also doubled as container for onions or jalapeño peppers.

We got to where we just lay around on weekend afternoons. The air conditioners hummed like soft-snoring old men and lulled us into a kind of torpor.

Hot as unmitigated hell, as my uncle would say, the record heat brewed up storms in the Caribbean, but none of that rain roiled our way. Until finally on the second day of September, the weatherman pointed to Mexico—a pinprick of hope. Tropical storm Adele stewed off the Yucatan Peninsula.

"If it comes in through Brownsville, we should pick up at least a few inches of rain." Tío jumped to his feet and paced about the room, rubbing his hands together. "God, we need it! If we could just get a couple of inches...." Like he might jinx the storm if he wished for more, he added, "Don't y'all hold your breaths. It might take it three days to get here if it gets here at all. It's just now crossing the Yucatan." He sat back down with a plop, but his face reminded me of a child on his birthday.

Tropical Storm Adele gained hurricane status. Lacking a crow's nest, Burt Charles and I relied upon our lookout on top of the guesthouse. Avoiding the pools of tar that coalesced on the seams of roof patches, we climbed to the flat roof. We scanned the southwest horizon. Seeing nothing but blue, we scooted down without further comment. I glanced over my shoulder. Tacky with tar, our feet left sooty smudges on the tops of the whitewashed walls. It seemed some portent that I couldn't quite interpret. For an instant I wondered if I would come back years later and find them still there—children's dark barefoot prints on a crumbling wall.

—⟋⟍⟍—

Waiting for the weather report, Mama, Aunt Hilda, Tío and I clustered around the Magnavox. Sure enough, Hurricane Adele approached from northern Mexico, just below Padre Island. Damage to the Yucatan had been considerable. The weatherman expected landfall in Texas sometime early tomorrow morning.

"You never know with these things," Tío said. "Sometimes it's not much to get excited about, but I guess it's our only chance for a while."

As it was, Adele suffered no worries of a jinx. She rolled like a downhill boulder. Next morning, when I crossed the patio, the sky had turned the color of ashes. Estela had the kitchen radio on a Spanish-speaking station, but it was not her usual polka music. In Spanish, the newsman delivered at spectacular speed and pitch. I raised my eyebrows for permission and changed it over to an English version. The radio announced that Adele had moved inland from the Gulf just south of Matamoros early on the morning of the fifth. She struck Brownsville with winds estimated at 130 miles an hour and traveled up the Río Grande before turning sharply east when the barometric pressure dropped in Corpus Christi. We sat directly in Adele's path.

"Woo hoo! We are gonna get us a hurricane." I picked up the phone to call Burt Charles.

Just as I dialed, Aunt Hilda made an unprecedented early arrival to the kitchen. "Is that Burt Charles?" She nodded at the phone. "Tell them to come on over. We'll sit this one out together. It'll be fun."

Her hands moving restlessly about her apron, Estela glanced up at Aunt Hilda. "Señora, can I go home for just a little...to check some things?"

"Why, uh certainly, Estela...." Aunt Hilda paused as her eyes swept over the white tiled kitchen counters. "Oh, sure, you go on. I see the coffee's made."

Without untying her apron, Estela made for the door. She didn't even look back to scan the room as she usually did when she left the kitchen.

The clock read nine-fifteen.

Burt Charles finally answered the phone. "We'll be over just as soon as we finish boarding up these last two windows." He was more breathy than usual, rushed.

The door to the kitchen swung open across the tile. It had made a crescent track that even the floor buffer could not erase. Mama shuffled in, uncharacteristically ruffled from sleeping later than six a.m.

"Hast thou risen from Morpheus' arms?" Aunt Hilda asked.

Mama smiled. "I have indeed, sweet sibling."

"You guys slay me."

Mama ignored me. "It was so nice and dark, I thought I hadn't slept late at all. What a surprise when I looked at the clock. Is it really a quarter after nine?"

"Sure enough, honey." Aunt Hilda stood at the window. "Let's make us some toast. I let Estela run home a minute. Coffee?"

They stood at the window then, looking out into the slate grey morning. Both had that vacuous stare that said morning stupor.

"Where's Tío?" I asked.

"Hmmmm?" Aunt Hilda said, but she didn't look away from the window.

"Tío! Where'd he go?"

"Oh! Atlee? He drove into town to De Leon's Drug as usual, for coffee and politics. Said he'd get back soon on account of the weather. But I guess I better have Joaquín go ahead and put up some plywood between the glass and wrought iron on my big windows. Miss Adele might be tempted to finish up the crack that the blowout started."

She put her coffee on the windowsill, lifted the receiver and buzzed down to the Villanuevas. The phone didn't go through a phone company connection, but when Aunt Hilda rang the buzzer, it sounded at their house and they could talk.

Mama's cup rested on her lower lip till the steam fogged up her bifocals. Frowning and shifting her glasses to her head, she said, "What Mother Nature starts, Mother Nature likes to finish."

To the phone, Aunt Hilda said, "Honey, tell your daddy to come *aquí*."

It never failed to send me into stitches when Aunt Hilda attempted Spanish. Since she'd moved to South Texas to marry Tío years before, she managed to remember but nevertheless bungle about seven words. "Joaquín, *limpia los* floors." She'd wave her hands at the tile. "Estela! *Limpia los* sheets" She'd flick her fingers at the four-poster. Nearly all sentences she started began with "*limpia los*" and then she'd flutter her wrist in the direction of the direction of what she wanted cleaned up. Finishing this conversation with "*Grassus*, honey," she hung up the phone, a satisfied smile on her face. I tried to catch Mama's eye for a shared joke, but she had turned and busied herself with the toaster.

"Good, there's Atlee. He's headed around to the bedrooms. I bet he thinks we're all still in bed." Aunt Hilda banged on the window to get his attention. "We're in here!" She yelled as though he could hear her.

"I'll go." I headed out the door. Just as I rounded the walk, Tío's hat went tumbling off in the wind. "I'll get it." I sprinted after it. I almost had it once till it flitted off just as I grabbed for it. Stumbling over my feet, I reached way out again, but it scudded along another yard before it flipped end over end. Like a butterfly in a breeze, it sailed and paused and sailed and paused. I finally succeeded when it lodged in the fork of the magnolia tree. Breathless, I returned it to Tío, my eyes tearing up with the sting of the wind. He stood patiently, his face relaxed into gentleness.

"You're a good girl, Izzie. You know how I feel about my Stetson." He hugged me up beside him and we trudged back against the wind. When the limb of a pecan tree cracked and split and collapsed against the side of the house, I yelped and grabbed the lapels of Tío's jacket.

Tío covered my head with his arms. "Whoa, that was a big one! Lot to pay for a little rain, isn't it?" He must have seen that the crash really unnerved me. "You know you're going to be all right, don't you?" He jostled me gently as if to warm me up. "You're going to be just fine. I'll take care of my girl."

And for that one moment, I believed every word he said.

A bluster shoved us into the kitchen. "Picking up a little out there." Tío's smile swept across his face. "Did you say Bob and Daisy were on their way?" Without waiting for an answer, he continued. "They better get a move on. According to the weather report, Adele should reach Corpus by four this afternoon. That'd put her over us in less than three hours." Tío dropped his hat on the table and pulled out a chair. "If we're to believe the weathermen."

"Here comes Joaquín now with the boards for the window," said Aunt Hilda. "He must have read my mind. Don't you think?" She cut her eyes down at Tío, but her lips puckered in a teasing smile. "See, Atlee? Not everybody around here has to be perfectly bilingual."

"Hope that sheet of plywood doesn't act like a sail and carry him off down the road." Tío blocked the crown of his hat back into shape but left it on the table. "Reckon I better go give him a hand."

As Tío went out one way, Burt Charles burst in the other.

"I thought I was about to have to send after you all," Tío called back, his hand holding the door open just a second longer.

His face glowing with wind and excitement, Burt Charles gasped, "The rest are still getting out of the car. Daddy had to come hold Mama's door open for her. Wind kept blowin' it shut."

I squinted out the window. The palms that lined the northeast side of the grounds yielded to the wind driving up from the southwest. They looked as if their backs might break with the unnatural bend of an opposing wind.

The moment the kitchen door opened, the wind altered its tone. Instead of the whisper, it dropped into a moan. Daisy and Bob came rushing in. "Wheeee!" Daisy's squeal cut off the conversation. "That wind's a doozy!" She blew the strands of hair out of her eyes and stood like she'd been glued to the floor for a moment, her arms outspread as though she still needed them for balance. The wind had pasted her skirt above her knees, exposing hurriedly tied knots that held up her stockings. Her signature neck scarf looped like a runaway cat's tail by her ear. The little brothers tore around the kitchen, screaming and tackling each other. Bob clutched his hat to his chest and smiled broadly at his wife's discombobulation.

We heard the veranda door slam hard and then Tío, his face flushed around the burn scars, bustled back through the swinging door. Grey strands crisscrossed his almost bald head and peaked around his ears. He chuckled. "What do you think the winds are up to now, Bob? Maybe forty-five or fifty? And I'm not sure, but I think I felt a drop of rain."

Burt Charles nudged my elbow. "He sure wants it to come a gully washer."

"You noticed that, too, huh?" My heart ached for my tío.

Too Much Pizzazz

The smattering of rain made no real promises, but the wind stripped more immature pecans off the trees and rattled the magnolia leaves like tambourines. Our whole world became a fabulous Mexican fandango.

Sent in search of a Coleman lantern, Burt Charles and I hunkered over and scurried to the garage. It took both of us to slam the storeroom door behind us and we stood in inky blackness, thick with the smell of oil rags and mildewed leather. The flash of the 150-watt bulb revealed the red Coleman on the first shelf. Next to it, the fuel can.

"Well, that was quick. Now we've got time to welcome a hurricane." I said. "You know, announce Adele's arrival with a little—" I bared my teeth in a grin "—pizzazz."

"Don't you think that hurricane is speaking pretty well for herself?"

"Oh, come on, Burt Charles. The encyclopedia said that hurricane flags have been raised on the flagpole since...since...a long time. It's the least we can do to announce Adele's coming."

"Well, let me think. Oh, wait a minute. We don't have a flagpole."

"See what I mean? No pizzazz." Ideas spun through my mind. "How 'bout a pool cue stick with a white t-shirt tied on it stuck down a drain hole on the roof? Hmmm?" I tilted my head and stretched my eyebrows to my hairline.

"How we gonna sneak up to the roof, Einstein?"

"Tell 'em we're going to play some pool. We'll be back before they notice." I recognized the look that crept over Burt Charles' face. "Every time I come up with an idea, you look like that—like it's an electric chair offense." Latching my arm around his elbow, I marched us through the kitchen. Out of earshot, I stopped. "Are you with me or not? This is gonna be cool, Burt Charles. They'll think it's neat when they see it."

He jerked his arm out of mine, stepped back and reached around me for the door handle. "I'm gonna do this with you, Izzie, and not because they'll think it's cute. They'll probably kill us for it." He pushed down the door lever. "Because—it's got pizzazz!"

He shouldered past me through the door. Hesitating as the wind buffeted him, he trudged on. I made a fast shuffle across the patio where Burt Charles waited on me. He stood there grinning that lopsided smile.

We cut our flag out of one of Tío's t-shirts and chose Aunt Hilda's lipstick, *Fire and Ice*, to color in the red square. With a plain black marker we inked in the center square. "From a distance, it'll look all right," I said.

"Yeah, guess so. Let's get the cue stick before they start to notice we're gone."

The wind pasted our jeans to our legs and flapped our shirts even in the protection of the courtyard. We skirted around to the billiard room. I held open the door and Burt Charles darted in and out to hand me a pool stick. Even with the door opened for just seconds, blistered little pecan nuggets and leaves skidded across the tile. Stuffing the flag down to the bottom of my back pocket, I lowered my head into the wind with the stick grasped firmly in my fist.

"Hey, Brunhilda," Burt Charles shouted from behind me, "You may want a little help with that."

I turned to hear what he said and the pool stick twirled like a baton, almost beheading Burt Charles, had he not been agile as a colt.

"Gimme that before you kill me!" He grabbed one end of the stick and we marched one behind the other, the pool stick between us, a small battering ram against the wind.

The guesthouse roof seemed the most appropriate location since it could be seen from far down the road. Occasional raindrops hissed on the wall and made it slick. Our Keds slipped, but I got a boost from Burt Charles' knee, and then he vaulted to the roof from the hacienda wall. We broke out in nervous laughter. I had to scream into the wind once to break the cycle.

"Okay, okay." Burt Charles snorted. "Let's do it." His elbows ground into the tarpaper as he belly-crawled across the roof.

Determined to be one of the guys, I scooted behind him to one of the drain holes. Silently we sprawled face to face, the cue stick between us. I tugged our t-shirt flag from my pocket and stuffed it onto the cue stick. Burt Charles held while I directed the base down into the drain.

"I hope it holds!" he shouted.

"What?" I hollered back.

"Hope the flag holds!"

I nodded enthusiastically.

Burt Charles scrambled back down off the roof and waited to help me. I waved him off, but he just stood there.

"Move!" I could get down by myself. I went for a tough face, but he did give my heart a little twitch—him with his upturned face shiny with rain. His lips parted. His arms outstretched. The drizzle coalesced into fat, hard raindrops that sent a chill down my shoulder blades. "Get outta my way!"

Negotiating the first landing made me cocky. And I was laughing, looking down at Burt Charles to celebrate our adventure. It could have been overconfidence or maybe I had just never scooted around on the wet whitewashed surfaces of the wall before, but the stair-step design of the wall took on a different proportion—a slide awash in rain, a slippery creek bed. A foot shot forward, heel first, and I was down against the stucco steps. I reached out for balance—for something. I grasped behind me, but there was nothing but raindrops, and below me on the ground, Burt Charles calling, "Look out!"

Later he told me my head bounced like a mis-hit baseball. Leave it to him to use a sports analogy. All I remembered was stinging rain against my face and Burt Charles shaking me by the shoulder, his eyes brilliant with fear.

I lay there. I would always take a little joy in reminiscing the panic in his face. It was a sweet kind of panic. I probably lay there a little longer than necessary.

"Can you get up? Will you finally let me help you? Here." He reached under my back and pulled me to his shoulder.

I could play it like the damsel in distress or I could set forth with more bravado and fake a profound recovery. The damsel was not in me. Later I regretted that, but at the time I thought I had to keep a stiff upper lip. "I'm fine." I stretched out my hand for a lift to my feet, but that was all I would concede. "Just fine." I brushed away whitewash on my shoulders and marched off to the house.

"Jeez. You sure, Izzie? I mean, you took a wallop." Burt Charles jogged beside me "You don't always have to be so tough. What are you afraid of, anyway?"

That was a good question. If I couldn't trust Burt Charles, who could I trust? The male species was on my shaky list. It was a chancy leap to pin all my faith on one member of that gender. Sympathy never did me any good when I was trying not to cry. I was grateful to the rain's disguise. The wind shoved us back into the patio and we turned to survey the result of our expedition. Standing out nicely from the makeshift pole, the storm warning flag snapped stiff.

Despite the knot I felt swelling on the back of my head, I took pride in our hurricane flag. There it was—square in a square, black on red. Just before we stepped inside the door, I made one small concession. Burt Charles reached up to smooth my damp, mussed hair. And I let him.

Best Laid Plans

Our faces ruddy with the thrill of conspiracy, we strolled back into the kitchen, but no one seemed the least suspicious. Disappointing. A raised eyebrow in our direction would have added spice to our adventure. As a challenge, I let slip with, "Bet y'all never thought to post a hurricane warning." Not even Mama responded.

Estela still hadn't come back and the adults sat hunched over a full course breakfast. The women laughed and poured coffee. Standing shoulder to shoulder, they chopped tomatoes, jalapeños and onions for *pico de gallo*. The men sawed away at their ham and eggs. Smoke from greasy skillets and Lucky Strikes wafted toward the yellowed ceiling.

I glanced at the clock. Ten-fifteen. Estela had been gone an hour.

The clouds were sodden layers in the sky and rain peppered down, but still no downpour everyone hoped for. Still the wind did pick up.

Tío uttered under his breath, like a prayer, "Just about four inches. If we could just get four inches, we'd get through to November, December without feedin' for a change." Tío's face shone a dim reflection in the window glass, his eyes full of expectation.

Where *was* Estela? Ten-thirty now.

Aunt Hilda punched the red button to ring the Villanuevas. "No answer." She hit the button several more times in succession.

"That line from here to there probably went out an hour ago. Not likely they'd want to run over here in this wind," said Daisy. "I wouldn't either."

Leaves fell in flurries. Pecans that had stubbornly stuck to the branches now pummeled the sidewalk around the house. Like green pendulums, the immature oranges convulsed in the wind.

"Sure glad we're here at this house." Daisy said, staring at the ruckus outside. "Oh lord, look at that poor ol' dog!" Daisy pointed out the kitchen window. "Good heavens."

The collie Boracho headed for the house from the carport. His tail whipping under him, he almost floated along. Making it only as far as the air conditioning enclosure under the kitchen window, he stumbled over his own feet and whisked past the small entry. Turning to backtrack, he faced the wind; his lips slicked back, exposing his teeth. He slunk along as he clawed his way into the alcove until we could no longer see him.

"He'll be safe there," Aunt Hilda said under her breath as she turned away to check the clock. With a sigh, she reached for the phone again and pushed the button. "Just static." Still gripping the phone, she drummed her fingers on the receiver. "Do you think they're all right?"

Leaning across her shoulder, Tío took the phone from her hands and set it back into its cradle. He reached for his hat, but put it down. "No use in wearing that." He opened the door and leaned into the wind. We watched from the window as he backed the Cadillac out of the garage. I looked at the clock. Ten forty-five.

Fifteen minutes later, napkins flew and glasses toppled over when the door reopened and Tío carried little Ana and led the Villanuevas through the kitchen. Clothing made transparent by the rain, arms clutched about their hunched forms, they studied the floor as they hustled past us. Everyone but Mari. She stopped for just a moment, stood to her full height and looked me straight in the eye. Suddenly, it was I who examined the floor.

Tío led them on to the old living room that over the years, we had begun to use as a kind of dormitory for overflow guests. Aunt Hilda bustled in ahead, stuffing blankets and towels into their arms and cooing to the kids.

"I tried to come back, señora, but the wind was stinging my eyes, and I couldn't see where I was going. And Joaquín, he said no."

"Oh, Estela, honey, don't you think another thing about it. I'm just glad Atlee thought to go bring y'all over in the car. Why y'all might've been blown clear down to the corral."

"Canela!" I stared wide-eyed at Burt Charles. "She's just standing around out there in the corral!"

"And Keep the Change! Aren't you worried about him, too? He's worth a fortune!" Burt Charles shook his head at my sentimentality over an old mare.

"He has a special stall. You know that."

"Well, that stall isn't much stronger than the corral posts."

"If Atlee was worried, don't you think he woulda done something? That stallion is worth a pile of money. A pile! Don't be a cry baby."

I gave Burt Charles a shove. "You know that shed's tin roof is barely hanging on. What if it blows off? What if it hits one of the horses? After all, it's not your horse out there."

"Did Atlee ever actually give Canela to you?"

"Well—"

"Well, nuthin'. You can't exactly say she's *your* horse! And anyway, maybe Atlee didn't have time to trailer the horses to another barn. Maybe he decided it would be better to pick up the Villanuevas instead."

The logic really annoyed me. Burt Charles annoyed me. This whole situation was starting to blow away my enthusiasm for a hurricane party.

"Come on." Burt Charles tugged at my sleeve. "Let's go play canasta. Want to?"

I shrugged and shuffled off behind him to the veranda. Nothing we could do about the horses now. It wouldn't do any good to go to pieces. Still I couldn't dismiss the thought of Canela with her back to the wind, her tail blowing hard up under her belly. We collapsed on the couch and I picked up the decks of cards.

"She's old," I said.

"Deal," said Burt Charles.

After three hands of Burt Charles skunking me, I threw my cards down and sat back with my arms crossed. "I am through. That's it!"

"Whaaat? Don't be a sore loser," he said, his eyes alight with victory.

"I've got a headache. Go get Mari if you want to play that bad."

Burt Charles marched off to the living room.

I stomped over to the bookshelf and ran my finger across the line of Texas history books. Taking one down, I slouched in the club chair in the corner and hitched one leg under me. I let my eyes close for just a minute and rubbed the knot on the back of my head against the chair's cushion to see how much it hurt. It hurt a lot, and I wondered if I should have asked Burt Charles to check my pupil size.

Ahead of Burt Charles, Mari strolled into the room. Without stopping, she pulled her black hair behind her head and twisted it into a bun. "Oh, hello, *Lizzie*."

Twirling one of my braids up between my nose and lip for a mustache, I glared at her. I examined the ends of my braids and considered letting my hair grow to my butt, too. I crossed my eyes at Burt Charles as he grandiosely offered Madame Mari a few magazines to sit on so she wouldn't worry about getting the couch a little damp.

Outside the rain fell at a forty-five degree angle from the south. The windows seemed to swell ever so slightly with each gust of wind.

I wondered how our hurricane warning flag fared. The only way I could check on it was from the room where the Villanuevas camped. It wouldn't hurt to see what they were up to anyway. Standing up suddenly enough to make Mari call a misdeal, I strode out of the room. Footsteps padded behind me. Aha! Burt Charles couldn't resist after all. I cast a smug glance over my shoulder. But it was Mari. Oh, but then, of course, she couldn't stay away from Ana for more than five minutes. Burt Charles remained on the couch, practicing a fancy shuffle of the cards. His lack of curiosity never failed to amaze me. Well, he would have to ask *me* if he wanted to find out if the flag still flew.

I knocked on the door to the living room and walked in. Not spread out at all like I thought they would be, the family huddled at one end of the room. I felt as though I had invaded their little group. They knelt on the Italian tile and fingered rosary beads.

Mari rushed to Ana, touched her face, her shoulders.

"Would you relax? You can see she's just fine." I said. A fortress of limestone, steel and stucco, this house was not going anywhere. "Just looks like we're finally getting a little rain." Working up a confident swagger, I strolled across the room to the windows to get a peek at the flag. No one gave me any eye contact, and they scooted sideways on their knees to let me pass. Their wet dresses stuck to their thighs and towels covered their heads like the mantillas they wore for mass. I stood to the left of the curtain, lifted the edge of it and frowned out toward the bruised sky. "Yep, it's coming down all right." Rain spattered the window. Wind stripped bark off the pecan trees and flicked it into the bougainvillea like Estela peeled avocados and flipped the skins into the trash. Our cue stick listed severely starboard. I had hoped to see the flag stuck out smartly to the north, but instead, it flapped from the makeshift pole by one corner.

I was turning to the Villanuevas to salute and say, "Well, *hasta luego*, y'all," when a burst of wind and shattered glass sucked away my snappy farewell. Lights flickered and snuffed out. Drapes whipped like sails unfurling. Our screams sailed above the low roar that sent lamps smashing against the tile and books scattering. The smaller children tunneled under beds and the older ones bent down close to them trying to cover their heads with the bedspreads.

I dived across the floor toward Mari. Linked together, we braced against the wind.

She covered my head with her hand. "We'll be all right," she said. "We'll be all right."

I clung to her, trying to absorb her faith, her bravery. We piled together like puppies blindly searching for their mother.

All but Joaquín.

From his duck and cover position, he struggled to one knee. Grunting, he pushed himself to a stand. Black hair slicked to his scalp, Joaquín leaned into the gale. He never took his eyes off the tunnel of wind barreling through the broken window. Lifting a knife from his pants pocket, he snapped the blade open. He raised his hand and sliced down and then across, making the sign of the cross into the wind as though it were a devil force. Joaquín chanted a litany like a priest blessing the wine.

> *Jesus Christo, aplaca con tu ira, tu justicia,*
> *tu rigor y con gran poder compasivo, Señor.*

And the wind calmed.

I sat up. Joaquín had just saved us. And had I really hung on to Marisol to protect me?

I let my eyes wander around the room. The drapes hung heavy and motionless. Lamps lay in pieces, their necks cockeyed. And slung sideways against the far wall, the cue stick, its six-point blue luster inlays chipped but still intact. The warning flag was gone.

My pizzazz could have cost a life.

Clutching the bed covers to my chin, I turned toward Joaquín. In my mind, Joaquín was a common laborer, the father of too many children in too small a space. I thought he did for our family because he had to. He had nowhere else to go. But in that one moment, Joaquín transformed— he became a hero.

The hush, broken only by little Ana's whimper, was relieved when my family charged into the room. Mama clasped me to her, then jerked me back and ran her fingers over my face. "Are you all right? No cuts?"

"Fine. Fine. I'm fine." I cleared my throat, staring at Burt Charles who stood speechless at the door.

Tío shoulder-hugged Joaquín and wrapped Estela in his other arm. He gave a few brief orders and in moments, the men nailed bed slats in a tic-tac-toe fashion to cover the jagged window. Aunt Hilda, Daisy, and Estela and her girls swept up glass and mopped up puddles of water.

Marisol, Burt Charles and I gathered up the little ones and took them to the adjacent billiard room where they rolled the pool balls back and forth across the table. With great care, I lodged the cue stick back into its slot in the cabinet. I never met Burt Charles' eyes. Didn't he recognize our improvised flagpole? I hoped he didn't. The blame was mine. All mine. Me and my stupid ideas.

Burt Charles stared at me across the pool table. "You okay?"

I nodded, still without looking at him.

"Really?"

"Really! I said I was fine, didn't I?"

Mari grabbed one of the towels and frantically dabbed at Ana's dress that draped like sagging skin across her thin frame. Ana shivered. Her teeth chattered. Pressing her face into Mari's side and clinging to her, Ana never cried but moaned a little between hiccoughs. Mari bowed over her sister's form, and furiously wrapped another towel around the child's head. I was struck by how small and frail Ana was for eight years old. She'd always been a skinny kid. I guessed it wouldn't hurt to throw some dry clothes on her.

With the wind still quiet, I trotted across the patio to my room. Branches lay broken and stripped leafless; patio jars too heavy to bring in had splintered into bright colored shards across even the most protected areas. Nothing would breach the three-inch thick wood doors, but the gale had embedded leaves into the screens of the iron doors. It would take weeks to remove them.

Rifling through the bottom drawer of a chest, I pulled out last winter's purple sweater, some striped pajama bottoms and wool socks embroidered with Rudolph the Red-Nosed Reindeer. I grabbed Aunt Hilda's new hairdryer and wrapped the clothes in one of our best fluffy towels and hurried back to the billiard room.

Mari eyed me warily when I offered the items, but accepted at last "for Ana." Lifting her sister who still trembled with cold, Mari disappeared into the billiard room's bathroom. I guessed it was the least I could do. Everybody else sure fell all over themselves to take care of the kid.

When the eye of Hurricane Adele clouded up, the wind nearly bent the palm trees double again. The term "eye of a storm" had little meaning for me, but it drew great commentary from the adults. I knew they were ignorant of the real reason—Joaquín's stand against Hurricane Adele.

And it rained.

With feigned innocence, Burt Charles and I strolled back into the kitchen and hoped guilt did not color our faces. Yellowed light from the outside sky reflected on Tío's face as he gazed out the window at the rising water. Pinching the bridge of his nose, he closed his eyes. He pressed his forehead against the rain-splattered windowpane and rocked against the glass. His eyes held no expression as he watched the pool overflow and the patio flood. The troughs for disinfecting the cattle would be deep enough now to drown a bull. Canela would be standing hock deep in the rain and mud, her ears hanging low on her head and her tail dripping.

Burt Charles and I stood on either side of Tío and glanced at each other when a lipsticked and markered t-shirt slapped up against a tree trunk. I had no words to console my tío. How could I have thought this storm was a game?

Aunt Hilda came up behind my uncle and slipped her arms around him. "It's too much, isn't it? Too much."

Joaquín and his family knocked on the kitchen door and asked permission to come through. They needed to go home to see what damage they had.

"Y'all can't make it across that road now." Aunt Hilda wrapped her arm around Estela's shoulder. "Let's just wait till that water goes down some. Stay here tonight and we'll have ourselves a feast! Come help me and we'll make dinner before it gets too much darker. Who knows how long the power will be out?"

Over the gas stove, Aunt Hilda must have fried half of the meat from the freezer and boiled frozen ears of corn. She made us all drink milk before it spoiled. Mama dug out candles and lit them on the tables. In the candlelight, shadows flickered across the faces of those about me. I glanced at Tío when I thought he wouldn't notice. He cut pieces of steak and tossed chunks to Show Boy, but when it came to picking up his fork to eat, he just shuffled the potatoes to center and squashed the peas to green goo.

Aunt Hilda studied Tío. Mama kept an eye on Aunt Hilda. Burt Charles examined the gold florentine pattern on his already empty plate. Still wearing my Rudolph Christmas socks and purple sweater, Ana sat on Mari's lap while Mari offered her small mounds of Butter Brickle ice cream in a silver demitasse spoon. I just shook my head.

Pushing away from the table, Joaquín excused his way back to the living room. I reached out to touch his back as he went by. I hoped he would never tell exactly what took out the window, but it was more than that.

"*Mande?*" he said. His face filled with question for a chore he must have thought I wanted him to do.

I managed to speak before the catch in my throat halted the words. "You did real good."

Aftermath

The pastures lay glassy with water. The stench of dead cows spiraled into a hot, windless September. No one could drive out to survey the damage so we stood on the roof of the house to view the scene. The goats survived for the most part, but even several of those hardy characters lay swollen on the roads. Trees had felled cattle where they gathered for protection. Buzzards, circling on the thermals, dipped with slow grace to the bounty. Hay bales strewn into bushes would ferment to stinking wads. Splintered in all directions, the corral boards scattered like pick-up sticks. Mother Nature's child's play. All the repairs that Mr. Wiley had made to the barn lay jumbled.

The stallion and mare were gone.

I imagined Canela, too old to fight for herself, struggling in a pool of swampy water. Maybe Keep the Change would try to push her, nudging and nudging till he too gave up and knelt down beside her.

We begged, but Mama wouldn't let Burt Charles and me go looking for the horses. We turned our appeal to Tío, but he agreed with her. "If Keep the Change is out there with her, there'll be trouble. He regards her as his by now. Stallions tend to be jealous creatures."

"And if they need our help, Tío? What if they lie down too long?"

"We'll have to wait and see. Just wait and see." Tío touched my shoulder.

I shook his hand off. I had had it with these people. Just wait and see? Why did they think saying nothing was better than telling the truth?

"Y'all just won't tell me anything, will you? But even I know a horse can crush its organs with its own weight if it can't stand up. I read that, you know!" I choked on the words and neglected to say that I wished I'd never known it.

"Isabel, honey." Tío dropped to one knee beside me. "I don't know what to tell you, that's all. I can't always predict what's going to happen. I just figure there's no use worrying you if I'm not sure."

"That's the problem! Nobody's ever sure about anything! Not a damn thing!"

"Isabel Martin!" Mama's hand shot to her mouth.

"Well, they're not!" I turned and bolted from the room. Where to go this time? No corral to run to, no horse to ride off on. I headed for the roof.

Water still stood in puddles on the flat, tarred top of the house. I sat down on the ledge and jammed the heels of my hands into my eyes. In just a moment, a shuffle of Burt Charles' boots scuffed up to where I waited. I hoped he would come and then I hoped he wouldn't. But there he was. Kneeling beside me, he patted my shoulder, then reached an arm around me, then let me go suddenly and held my wrist till I let him pull my hand away from my face. So timid his actions, so tentative that I was touched and amused all at the same time. Just the same, I let him hold one hand while I disguised my confusion with the other.

—\\\—

Burt Charles and I climbed to the roof of the guesthouse every afternoon after school to scan the fields, but it was not until the very last of September that the two horses appeared on a distant hill. We ran calling for Joaquín. Yelling and pointing, we dragged him by the sleeve to the truck. "*Caballos!* Keep the Change and Canela. C'mon Joaquín, let's go!"

And Joaquín, like the *vaquero* he was, called out, "*Vámonos, amigos!*" We piled into the truck while Joaquín grabbed a bucket of sweet feed. Burt Charles and I both hung out the window, pointing the way.

Canela's head snapped up at the sound of the truck and she began walking toward us with tired resignation. The stallion called to her, but she moseyed on toward us.

Banging the feed bucket on the side of the truck, Joaquín enticed her. Canela picked up to a trot and whinnied. I couldn't stand it any more and called out to her, "Girl, c'mon old girl." My voice broke, making "girl" two syllables. Burt Charles turned and looked at me, so close I could almost feel those blond eyelashes. I hoped he would think the wind had caused my eyes to water.

"I'm glad to see her too, you know." And then he looked quickly away.

Joaquín handed us the pail of grain and jerked his thumb to the back of the truck. "For the *caballos.*"

We tumbled out of the cab and scrambled into the truck bed. Joaquín found a wide enough spot to turn around and started back toward the house at five miles an hour. Canela came in to take bites from my hand, but the stallion was having none of that. He followed at a greater distance, picking up the pieces Canela dropped along the way.

Tío would be real proud of us, I thought. This was important. Keep the Change was alive and after he was fed right and brushed up, Tío could sell him for good money. That would make all the difference. I was so imbued with optimism that I reached over and gave Burt Charles a big kiss on the cheek. We were a team. He was a stunned part of the team, but he didn't wipe it off. He just yelled louder at the horses to come along.

—⁓⁓—

Almost a month after the storm, a hundred cows struggled to the caliche-based road. Tío and Joaquín rode behind the bawling lot on mud-splattered ponies. Leaping in the air, I ran out to meet the scraggly bunch.

"Where'd you find 'em?" I yelled up at them as I jogged beside the horses whose heads drooped to the ground.

"Out past the *Camileño*, over on the south side." Tío smiled for the first time in a week. "They're my experimental group. Didn't burn cactus for 'em or even vaccinate. And they are the ones that made it!" I heard the pride in his voice.

Joaquín let go with a gush of Spanish. Wincing, he swung his leg over the saddle. Tío groaned as he dismounted. Their shirtsleeves were splashed filthy and deep rings of sweat stained their sides. They laughed and shook hands, and then embraced each other.

The flurry of Spanish between them left me out of the goings-on, but I understood happiness and trust between the two men. So much the same. So different. Tío's scars were white against the sun-blistered skin on his nose and forehead, while Joaquín was the color of mesquite bark. I studied them both while they moved the cattle to a makeshift holding pen. Not much talk, more like mental telepathy. They had just dug hope out of the stinking mud.

Hard to understand—this attachment to the land. It would be so much easier to live in the city, put on a nice shirt every morning and come home by five o'clock each day. Have the weekends to go out to dinner, take in a movie.

My uncle and Joaquín were like barbed wire, cactus, the mesquite, and they survived in this South Texas. Maybe if Tío had to break the law a little when he helped his brother too much, it was just his way of getting by. Maybe that's what it took to survive in this godforsaken country—thorns.

George Never Gives Up

Some weeks went by with five or six phone calls a day from George. I thought maybe he was worried about us.

"For you, Atlee," Aunt Hilda would say with a questioning lift of her shoulders.

"Talk to him later." Tío slapped on his hat and headed out the door.

"He can't get to the phone right now, George, but I'll give him the message."

Her eyes wide, Aunt Hilda held the phone away from her ear and stared into the mouthpiece. She called after Tío. "He's says he's tired of your blankety-blank hidin' from him and he's coming out today." To me, she said, "You know, George didn't used to be so...so...emphatic."

Sure enough, as Burt Charles and I sat in the kitchen stacking cheese and crackers, George's Chrysler pulled into the carport. He seemed to be in a better mood and set about sweet-talking Estela.

"Where's that ol' brother of mine, Estela?" He patted her shoulder and pinched off a bit of ham. "Whup, never mind. I believe I see him comin' around the house." And to us. "Why, how y'all doin'? Uh...Burt Charles and uh...uh...."

"Isabel, sir." I said, but he was gone without waiting for a response. We didn't miss a beat getting out the door behind him.

"¡Chicos!" Estela called. But stuffing cheese crackers into our pockets, we ignored her and skidded behind the old mesquite.

George called out to his brother before he even got within conversation distance. "Now I'm hopin' you're over whatever got your drawers in a wad, but I been trying to talk to you for a week!" He stood with his hands on his hips and scanned the grounds—the broken trees, the glass blown out of the garage windows. "Whew! You got quite a little mess out here. Aw well, you'll have it cleaned up in no time." George clapped Tío's back. "I mean, hell...you're not short on water." George snorted. "Like they say, sometimes you gotta be careful what ya wish for."

Tío looked at George with no expression on his face.

"Well, I know you're busy out here, but let's get on over to the corral and take a look at that stallion. Heard you finally rounded him up."

I opened my mouth to take the credit, but Burt Charles grabbed my arm and stared me into silence.

Without waiting for a response, George strolled over to the truck. "Oh…been meaning to tell you. I got an ol' boy coming out with his mare. A thoroughbred. He's done me a few favors, and I said you wouldn't mind letting that stallion cover her. Said he'd give you a call this week. Let you know when he'd be bringing her out." George opened the truck door. "Hop in."

Tío took off his hat and raked the back of his wrist across his brow. Weight on one leg, he ran his fingertips around the brim of his Stetson. "Don't guess he's gonna drop a dollar on this?"

"Why, hell no! It's the damn governor for Chrissakes. He's backed me up on a few deals. I owe the man."

"George, you know as well as I do how much time and expense it is to keep somebody's mare up for a week. Besides the extra feed, there's liability. Breeding can create some downright dangerous scenarios. You never taught that stallion any breedin' manners. There's such a thing, you know."

"Might know. Don't care."

"You know what?" Tío slammed his hat back on. "You just go on ahead and take a look at Keep the Change by yourself. It doesn't feel much like he's my horse anyway, the way you're loaning him out at my expense."

George started the truck and gunned the engine. "Well now, I got a few little debts to pay and that stallion can do it for me. Just get over it, little brother." George waved without looking back as he pulled out of the carport.

"Man," I said.

"Shhh," said Burt Charles.

Tío looked furious when he strode over to his car and climbed in. He shut the door with a hard click and drove off in the direction of town.

"Why doesn't he just tell George to take a hike?" I hated to see my tío beat down like that.

"Aw, it's hard to tell, Izzie. Maybe George helped out Atlee before. Maybe it's just because George is his older brother." Burt Charles pulled me toward the swimming pool. "My little brothers better be respectful of me or...pow!" He slammed his fist into his palm. Somehow Burt Charles' last comment was the most telling.

—⁓⁓—

Sure enough, it wasn't a day or two till out she came, a tail-twitching thoroughbred brood mare, her head so high she could lift me off the ground if I held the rope. Tío took one look at her and muttered under his breath. I tagged along beside him asking rapid-fire questions that he ignored.

"Well," he said, "let's get her settled." Turning to Joaquín, "Come on back out in about an hour and we can see if we can get this thing done."

"I can help, Tío. It's time I learned about the horse business. Next week is my fourteenth birthday, you know."

He stopped, his hands on his hips, and smiled, first up into the afternoon sky and then at me. "Honey, this is, uh, this is uh...well, men handle this part of the horse business. But I appreciate it all the same." He put his arm around me and pulled me to his shoulder for a moment.

I looked up at him, his eyes now focused on the mare that danced right and left of her lead, as if sand blistered her hooves.

"Well, I know you don't really want to do this, and I could help a little," I said.

"Now Izzie, why would I be doing something I don't want to do?"

"You know."

That was the second time I ever saw my uncle flinch.

"Tell you what, you can help us get this feisty thing settled. After dinner, you can put some hay in her run...from over the fence." He turned back toward the house. "Let's go eat."

A six-year-old could do that, I thought, but I knew there was no use arguing.

Although Tío made it clear I was not to participate in the breeding session, I figured what information I could gather might some day speed me toward being the horsewoman I aspired to become. As soon as Tío got up from the dinner table, I ran to the corral, slid through the panels and shoved bales around me to make a fort. Twigs of hay poked my neck and my arms itched, but I was determined to see this "man's job." I left just enough space for a porthole view.

Despite the fact that the mare was a shiny chestnut that could toss her mane like Rita Hayworth, Keep the Change was not totally smitten.

The introduction began innocuously enough. Joaquín and his son held the mare and Tío led the stallion into the paddock.

Tío's reason for my non-participation became astoundingly clear. I had never ever in my life seen a stallion preparing to mate. Keep flared his nostrils, peeling back his top lip like a caricature of a grinning clown. The size of his reproductive organ was stunning.

"Watch animals, if you really want to know what nature is all about," my mother once said instead of answering my questions about where babies came from. But this scene forced air into my lungs and never let it exhale. If this was what it was all about, I was heading for the hills.

I had heard the term "hussy" from my mother and this mare gave new meaning to the word. Postures posed. Necks bowed. Fluids flowed.

Tío was leading Keep into the mare's run when the stallion pivoted on his front feet and drove his back hooves hard into her rump. The men dropped the halters and bolted for the fence. The mare squealed like one of the hogs out back of the Villanuevas and dived at the stallion's neck with teeth bared. Keep spun and kicked out again. Joaquín yelled but the brawl was on. Tío shook his head as he walked over to where I hid. I shrank back into the hay and held my breath. He bent down so close that I thought he would notice the bales were lined up like cockeyed Lincoln Logs. He picked up a bullwhip and moved in toward the love-affair-gone-bad. Tío popped off a warning round and then laced Keep the Change. The stallion backed off for a moment, but the whites of his eyes glared in the dusk. His ears flattened hard against his head. His nostrils blown wide, he reared and advanced on his haunches, his forelegs striking the air. Twelve hundred pounds of horseflesh intended to pound my uncle into the dirt.

Bolting from my hideaway, I screamed, "Run!" Tío's head snapped around. Distracted, he tumbled backwards. Keep the Change was almost on us when Tío regained his balance and faced the stallion. I grabbed Tío's belt loops and closed my eyes, but Tío had no intention of taking my advice. He escalated a battle I thought he could never win. He shoved me behind him and moved toward the stallion, calling for Joaquín to send the mare into an open stall. The air reverberated with the slap of the whip as Tío laid it to the sides of Keep's shoulders and backed him down. Keep the Change wheeled around and charged into his stall, foam and sweat flying from him like the day I first saw him. I stood in the shadows of the hay bales, covering my mouth so Tío would not hear my sobs.

"Damn stallions," was the only thing I heard him say, before he turned to me. "Isabel Martin!"

I plunged into my uncle's chest. "I'm so sorry, I'm so sorry." I bawled as much out of guilt as relief. "It's my fault, isn't it? I wasn't supposed to be here."

I felt the bump of a suppressed laugh as Tío guided me to the house. He called back to tell Joaquín to load that mare up first thing tomorrow morning. "I'll call Governor Shivers and offer to pay any vet bills," he said to himself, but it pleased me to think he was speaking to me like I was a grown-up. And then to the powers that be, he said, "That is it!"

—⚏—

I phoned Burt Charles later that evening. Sometimes he sat in the hall closet at his house as we talked. His mama didn't know he was on the phone so late unless she traced the long black cord.

I was not about to mention the mating fiasco. I wasn't sure just why. It had been worthy of comment—just something I couldn't say to Burt Charles. Too embarrassing. I wondered how experienced he was in such matters. I limited my comments to the danger Tío had been in.

"Good grief, Izzie!" Burt Charles said, "Atlee coulda met his maker! He's getting too old to battle down a stallion like Keep the Change."

Suddenly, it did occur to me that Tío looked older these days. His hair was grayer, thinner.

"And you are not going to believe this, Izzie." Burt Charles' conspiratorial tone made my heart skip a beat. "Atlee is gonna have more bad news than Keep the Change. The Feds indicted George again. I heard Daddy say tonight that he guessed there was more than one way to skin a cat when it came to George. The IRS was tops in the cat-skinning department, he said. Maybe Daddy didn't think I'd catch on to what he meant, but I know what the IRS is and I know they've jailed George before."

"I wish they would get him and leave my uncle alone. They won't get Tío too, will they?"

"Not unless he ain't been paying up. They're a tough bunch to fool, Daddy says."

"But Tío doesn't have any money. All he has is lots of flooded land and a bunch of dead cows."

"The IRS don't care. They can make you sell the land to pay your taxes. And anyway, Keep the Change brought in a good bit over the last few months over at George's track. There was some side bettin'. Even Daddy got in on that."

"Is that legal?"

"Aw, Izzie!"

—⁓—

Tío never did tell Mama and Aunt Hilda that I'd disobeyed him. And I never did tell them that the stallion could have killed my uncle on that late afternoon. But somehow the day marked a change in the man. His eyes took on a hard look. He wore his Stetson all the time. But when he pulled it off at dinner and sat down with a sigh, he'd rake his hand through his hair, even if there wasn't much left to slick back.

Tired. He just seemed tired.

Treks to San Antonio

When no one brought the newspaper home, I figured George must have made headlines again. Once Joaquín did bring in the paper when he delivered the groceries, but it disappeared until Aunt Hilda called for him to burn it.

"Joaquín, take this out to the trash and…." She mimed a match strike and hissed her version of the Spanish word for fire. "Foo egg o."

"Ah sí, señora, *fuego*," His face contorted to keep from laughing.

"Please do take care of it right away." She smiled prettily and straightened as she handed the wadded pages over to Joaquín.

I followed, of course. Vexed by my trailing him, Joaquín crushed the newspaper to his belly. I kept in step, almost tripping him. At the burn barrel, I volunteered to do the work. He probably already knew I was up to no good. "*No, Izzie. Yo.*" He struck the match against the rusty sides of the barrel and let it fall. When he shuffled away and didn't look back, I grabbed a stick to rifle through the pages. Just before the flames caught the headlines, I read "Duke of Duval Indicted on Five Counts of Tax Evasion."

Then came the weeks of Tío in a grey double-breasted suit and Aunt Hilda in her pencil skirts and fur-trimmed jackets. Each morning I watched dust billow up behind the Cadillac as they left for San Antonio where the judge had ordered a change of venue from the too-forgiving jury pool in Duval County.

"Business, darlin'," was all I ever got out of Aunt Hilda, when she kissed me on the head as I sat at the breakfast table. "Estela, take care of our girl. Make sure she does her homework." I rolled my eyes, but Aunt Hilda clucked me on the chin and smiled big. "We'll be late, but your mama'll be home by five."

Tío held the door and sighed. "Hilda, let's go, honey. Long drive." I got a perfunctory smile that had no particular focus. When I heard the motor fading, I scooted over to the window and watched the car speed down the road.

"Well, now what, Estela?" I asked too loudly.

"*¿Pos, quién sabe, Izzie? Los políticos.*" Estela dried her hands with her apron, then bustled me on. "*Ándale, chica.*"

I got the "politics part" and "the who knows" part. I collected my books and headed to the cattleguard where the bus waited. *Well, somebody knows something.*

At least on Saturdays, Mr. Wiley kept us entertained as he restarted work at the barn. And we began to understand that he knew pretty much what all was going on in the county. He liked to present local goings-on in a historical light.

"Them New Party boys have sure got themselves riled up. Kinda reminds me of the Ku Klux Klan. You know the Klan didn't start out to be a bunch of pansies hidin' under their wives' old sheets. They used to be the only law in these parts. They'd take an ol' boy that'd been running around on his wife, drinkin' and carryin' on, leavin' his children without food and decent clothes. They'd run him out of the house at night and rope him to a stout tree. Whup him till he allowed as how he'd better settle on down and do right. 'Course, it ain't the same world now. I believe them ol' boys just lost track of what was right. Nowadays, it's mighty hard to tell the good guys from the bad guys." He shook his head slowly. "Didn't used to be so hard."

That last story got me to thinking what Mr. Wiley might know about the trial even if it was in San Antonio, but when I brought it up to Burt Charles later, he said, "Izzie, I swear. You think some old cowboy is going to know about a trial over a hundred miles away from here? I mean, he's nice and all but for goodness sakes, he doesn't have teeth and he spits." Burt Charles shook his head in exasperation. "Go ahead and ask him if you want to, but don't be surprised if you just embarrass the old guy."

I spent the next week planning how to approach Mr. Wiley without making him feel inadequate and without revealing my own insecurities. As one friend to another we would enjoy discussing the right and wrong of local politics, the good guys and the bad guys and who was who. And why my uncle had to attend these trials. Was it to support a man who deserved a prison term? Was it to protect his own involvement? Probably not income tax evasion, but maybe he didn't want his name to come up in association with his brother's election fraud.

Just when I had my interrogation planned, Burt Charles' mom called to say he was running a fever and she'd better keep him home. Well, I thought, there goes my interview. Mama said she didn't want me to go down to the barn to visit Mr. Wiley unless Burt Charles was with me. I scoffed at her over-protection. But she said she frankly didn't care what I thought.

I sulked some, but Burt Charles was probably right. Mr. Wiley couldn't know much. He was a nice man, but I couldn't see him being too serious about anything. Like he said himself, just a cowboy. As it turned out, Mr. Wiley was gone that week, too. It had been chilly, but I thought he would like cold weather. I wondered if he had a fever as well and if he had gotten it from Burt Charles.

On the bus ride home from school, I sat gripping the bar on the seat in front of me and stared out the window. Dark and grey, the day made me feel just as dreary. Maybe I was coming down with the bug Burt Charles had or maybe I was a little homesick.

The trees here didn't turn pretty colors in the fall. Leaves drifted to the ground when the new ones forced them off. Except for the orange trees, the vegetation turned brittle and colorless. The bus kids blabbered non-stop, and I still couldn't understand half of what they said. I missed Burt Charles. I hoped he'd get well soon. It wasn't like him to be puny for a whole week.

As the bus slowed I looked out the rear window. Tío's white Cadillac was coming up on us fast. I traded seats with a kid at the back and waved and waved. Aunt Hilda finally noticed me, but Tío never responded till Aunt Hilda nudged his shoulder. Glancing up, he raised his hand from the steering wheel. The palm salute, the casual but courteous acknowledgement between drivers on the roads of South Texas, was not the heart-warming howdy wave I expected from my tío.

They drove behind us for a while till we topped the last hill and they could see to pass. Tío floored the Cadillac and they roared around us.

A fine drizzle fell as I stepped off the bus. Mari walked all the way to her house with her head in a book. I stood between our two homes, the hacienda and the squat quarters of her house. No one else was out. Even the cows had gone off leaving nothing but cow patties and hoof prints. Sadness settled over me. The faint rumble of thunder crescendoed across the landscape, and fat raindrops plopped into the dirt knocking up puffs of dust. A cloud that touched the earth moved my way across the fields. Mist collected on my eyelashes as I squinted out toward the barn. Mr. Wiley was loading up some tools and sliding into his Ford truck. I didn't wave. Draping my jacket over my head, I dragged to the house.

"Your tío and Aunt Hilda, they are here," Estela said. "I think they are tired from their trip."

I avoided their room by going through the far part of the patio. I told myself that it was too windy to walk across the open terrace between the two wings of the house, but it was more than that. Something was wrong. Really wrong. They would never hole themselves up in their bedroom. We seldom needed to knock because the doors were rarely closed. We watched TV in there and ate Cheetos. It was our family room. But across the patio, there it was, a sight I never expected to see—curtains drawn tight and their door shut against me.

Mama's Apology

The next day was Saturday and it stayed cool and damp. Mama sat in the kitchen drinking coffee.

"How's Tío?" I asked. "Is he sick or something?" He had not gotten up early as usual to go into town, although Aunt Hilda followed her normal routine of coffee and magazines in bed.

"Hmm?" Mama's breath steamed across her coffee cup.

"Tío! How's Tío? Does he feel bad?" I couldn't really tell if Mama was evading my questions or just preoccupied with her own world of academia. I opened a cabinet door pretending to look interested in the rows of spices.

"Oh. Don't know, honey. Probably tired from all that driving back and forth to San Antonio. Don't you think?"

"How would I know? Nobody tells me anything anyway." I slammed the cabinet door. Mama jumped and coffee sloshed between her fingers and onto the table.

"Well, for goodness sake, Izzie. What in the world is the matter with you?"

"You're gone all the time! Burt Charles is sick! Even old Mr. Wiley disappeared! Aunt Hilda and Tío have been going to San Antonio for weeks!" I opened and slammed another cabinet door. "What did they have to go for?"

"Court business! You know that!" Mama sopped up the spilled coffee with hard little stabs. "And you know what else, missy?"

"What?" I sprayed the words in defiance.

"That's their private affair." Mama pushed away from the table and with deadly accuracy chunked the ball of napkin into the wastebasket. "And any more of that tone with me and you will spend the rest of the day in your room."

I stalked through the swinging kitchen door to bump squarely into Marisol. How long she had been standing at the doorway was predictable—long enough. I shrugged, hoping for her understanding of dealing with difficult mothers, but there was no commiseration in Mari's eyes. She stood her ground, waiting patiently for me to go around her.

"Well, crap," I muttered as I dodged sideways to get past her.

Mama caught me before I got to the outside door. "Izzie, come sit with me a minute. Please." She grabbed my shoulders and hugged me to her.

Suddenly, I wanted to punish her, too. I stood limp in her embrace. Her hands slid down to mine and she backed up, pulling me to the couch. Refusing to look in her eyes, I concentrated on the square designs on the tile. I pressed my lips together and locked my eyes on the coffee table. I found it aggravating that Mama continued as though I were cooperating.

"I'm sorry, Izzie. Truly I am. You do deserve to know what's going on. I want to apologize. I've been so wrapped up in writing my thesis that I know I've not been a good mother to you." Tears bubbled in her eyes.

"Well, you *have* left a lot up to Aunt Hilda."

"I know. I know. I shouldn't have. Partly because engrossing myself in my studies helped me not think so much about...about your father. It hurts."

This time, I took her hands. "I'm sorry, Mama. I...I...."

"And partly because Hilda wants so badly to take care of you. She's always wanted a child of her own and they've tried hard but...she hasn't been able to.... Well, she just hasn't."

Mama didn't have to tell me everything. I stood, reached for a book and leafed through it. "Oh? Oh, well! I mean...."

"No. It's my job to take care of you and I've been all wound up in myself."

"I get that, I really do. But it's all this mess about George. Tío and Aunt Hilda go to San Antonio all the time and don't say a word."

"They're worried about George."

"Well, I know that! Did you ever think George *deserves* to get in trouble? He's done plenty of bad things!" I wheeled to face Mama. "Tío and Aunt Hilda have just knocked themselves out getting him outta trouble since I can remember."

"I know. You're right." Mama slid one leg under her and held on to her ankle—a posture she assumed when defensive.

"I just wanna know one thing."

Mama looked hopeful for the first time in our conversation. "Just one?"

"Just how do you know a bad person when you see him? George can sure be nice when he wants to be. And Tío is always nice, but he gives out money to people—to voters."

"Now you don't know who he gives money to."

"He gives it out though—like bribes! Don't you remember the man outside the movie theater? Who knows how many people Tío dishes out money to? And that's what George got in so much trouble for. Paying people to vote his way and when that wasn't enough, he dug up names from the graveyards. Maybe Tío helped him do that too."

Mama lost her expression of relief. She was in the thick of it now and you could tell she'd rather be drifting on the sea with Ahab. "Well, Isabel, that was never proved."

"*Never proved* doesn't mean anything. It just says you can't tell the good guys from the bad guys."

"I know." She shifted to sit on the other leg. "I thought your daddy was the perfect man for me. I never saw the drinking side of him till after we were married. I wonder sometimes if it was my fault. That's a saying, you know. 'She drove him to drink.'" Mama tried to make it a joke, but she stumbled over the last words. "There were things between your daddy and me."

"What things?"

"Things." She shifted over to her other foot and pinched her ankle in her fingers. "Private things." Mama stood abruptly and started for the door. "And sometimes you *can't* tell the good people from the bad."

I wanted to say, "I rest my case" like Perry Mason on television.

Mama turned back and paced the room. "And you know what else? Sometimes people do bad things for good reasons." Her words sped like her fingers on the typewriter. So fast I could hardly keep track. "Like if you had to steal bread to feed your family or you had to lie to protect someone you knew was innocent." As she walked the floor, she looked at the ceiling as if conjuring more examples. "Sometimes the worst ones are the ones that look so holier-than-thou. A preacher who—"

Well, this was way more than I wanted to get into. She just scared the crap out of me, but she was finally opening up—actually talking to me without her finger holding her place in some book. "I think I understand, Mama. It's okay about you studying so much. You'll get your master's degree soon and then we can talk some more." But I was suddenly in no hurry.

What Mr. Wiley Knows

The feeling didn't last. It was time to explore every possible avenue, even if it meant embarrassing Mr. Wiley. Even if it meant humiliating myself. Even if it meant very bad news about Tío.

I reached for the phone. "You well yet?" I tried without success to hide my impatience. And I hated to give Burt Charles the idea that I really missed his being around. "If you came out, we could probably go talk to Mr. Wiley. I bet he'd let you do some hammering." No immediate response came from the other end of the line. I thought I heard a third party pick up and listen. I tapped my nails on the receiver.

"What are you doing?"

"Gettin' rid of nosy listeners. Would you just go ask your mama?"

"Y'all got any ice cream out there? My throat's still a little scratchy."

"Oh good grief, Burt Charles. Yes! Go ask!"

Having Burt Charles to wait on hand and foot for a week no doubt prompted Daisy to drop him off as quickly as possible. I sat out under the mesquite to wait and in less than thirty minutes, I heard their car coming down the road. He did look a little peaked. Thinner. I told him the cool wet air would probably be beneficial—like the humidifier Mama used when I had a bad cough.

"You'd tell me anything to get me to do what you want."

"Let's go down to the barn."

"See what I mean?" But he smiled at his own accuracy and said, "Sure, why not."

By the time we finally got going to see Mr. Wiley, an early cold front blasted in. Like my uncle said, Texas weather was a paradox. Estela sent some coffee for Mr. Wiley, just in case he hadn't brought something hot to drink. We wrapped up in our wool jackets and ski caps under our cowboy hats and headed to the barn.

"Ol' Mr. Wiley's been gone, too. Saw his truck there yesterday though." I headed toward the sound of hammering.

"That's what you said."

"You've got a lot of homework to make up."

"So?" Burt Charles shuddered. "Dang, it's cold. My lips can't move right." His teeth chattered and he blubbered his last few words.

"Just thought I'd let you know." I tried to keep the conversation light, but all the while, my heart vibrated in my ears.

"Howdy, howdy," Mr. Wiley called. He looked relieved to have us as a diversion. "Woo, that wind is a booger. You kids better get in behind this wall or you're gonna freeze your little butts off."

That sent us snickering. "Butts." Adults chastised us if we ever forgot and said the word aloud. Still snorting a little, I handed him the thermos.

"Estela thought you might like this."

"Why now, lookyhere. Ain't that nice." Mr. Wiley opened the thermos and inhaled so deeply that his chest bumped way out in front of him. "Hmmm mmm. Can't beat that!" The chicory aroma lifted in the air leaving me to wonder why coffee smelled so much better than it tasted.

"Where you kids been?"

"Where *you* been, sir?"

"Oh, down the road, down the road."

"Burt Charles here had the flu. Thought maybe you got it."

"Nah! Too mean to get sick."

"Oh, you're not mean, sir." I thought I might as well wield my charm as soon as possible.

"Why don't you sit down and rest a minute, Mr. Wiley? You must be pooped out."

Burt Charles regarded me suspiciously.

"What?" I asked. "The man's worked hard."

"You got that right, little lady. Y'all sit down, too. It'll feel warmer." We sat down cross-legged and covered our knees with our jackets.

"I bet you know practically everything that goes on around here. Right, Mr. Wiley?" I asked.

"Been around these parts for a long time. Can't say as I know everything. Lotsa folks don't much care for you studyin' their problems. Glass houses, if you get my drift."

"Take my uncle, for example."

"Your uncle's all right. Ain't been an easy time what with the drought—never mind the hurricane tearin' up things."

"Mr. Wiley!"

He looked up, surprised.

"That's not the part I'm talking about!" I couldn't help it. I whined.

"Now, little girl—"

"Don't call me a little girl, sir. Please!"

"Beggin' your pardon, ma'am. I stand corrected. Anyway, your uncle is just plain whupped over this trial business, if that's what you mean, but he's gonna be all right. I know the man." Mr. Wiley craned his neck over his shoulder toward the house like someone might be coming.

"Well, I know him too," I said, "but I don't know what he does."

Mr. Wiley ignored my implication and continued. "Oh, he knows his brother's going to jail. That there appeal they've got goin' won't do no good and he knows that. Won't be much longer…maybe mid-spring till George gets the final verdict."

"What will they do to him, Mr. Wiley? Will they hang him?" I asked.

Mr. Wiley grunted to disguise the laugh. "Now I doubt that. This ain't a hangin' case. Just some jail time. Nuthin' new to George."

"Mid-spring? That means in April?"

"Yes, ma'am."

"April Fools?"

Mr. Wiley looked up at me and then quickly looked away. "Could be. Could be."

La Llorona

Halloween. Trick or treat in town was out of the question, Mama said. We were too old. We could have a little party at the house for Burt Charles and his brothers, the Villanuevas and me.

With a sack of red glitter and a pair of Aunt Hilda's old high heels, I sidled up to her with the sweetest smile I could manufacture. She never said a word, but disappeared to return with the Elmer's Glue-All. Mama braided my hair and I smeared on *Fire and Ice*, the brilliant lipstick of our hurricane warning flag. Squeezing into a pinafore of my childhood, I grunted as I leaned and folded down white anklets. Late that afternoon, I strutted around in full regalia singing, "Over the Rainbow," till Mama and Aunt Hilda said they wished I could make the money Judy Garland had.

Burt Charles decided to be "The Creature from the Black Lagoon." Somehow he came up with green clothes and shredded paper napkins sprayed green to paste all over his body and face: scales and gills. He later confessed he got into his father's John Deere paint.

Marisol tried to rise above the excitement, but Aunt Hilda recruited her to be the Halloween gypsy. Once she got started, Mari exposed a flair for the melodramatic. She wrapped a red scarf across the side of her head, blocking out the vision in one eye. Bangle hoops dangled from her ears and black kohl eyeliner swept from tear duct to eyebrow. She must have used the same pencil to black out one of her front teeth.

I mumbled, "Good grief," but was secretly impressed with the transformation.

What she couldn't achieve with disguise, she finished off with ambience. At the base of the big pecan tree, Mari set up her gypsy tent by tying a blanket's four corners to chair backs. The owl we had watched all summer waited silently for Halloween night. She was just a slope-shouldered shape in the crook of that tree, but we knew she scanned us with great yellow eyes.

"Think they're in cahoots?" Burt Charles cackled. "Get it?"

"I got it," I said. "You go first." I had no reason to trust Mari at this stage of the game. I doubted she'd ever told me the complete truth about anything. She never went to a whole lot of trouble on my account unless she was focused on her own amusement. But despite years of distrust, I lined up with the rest of the kids to hear our fortunes in front of the makeshift tent.

Burt Charles was happily obliged to go ahead. I listened but heard only what appeared to be light conversation.

He stepped out of the gypsy tent and double-dog dared me to stoop into the darkness. "Your turn!"

Marisol beckoned me with a red plastic fingernail.

"What'd she do?" I asked, but he started with the *puck puck* chicken routine so I gave him a shoulder and dived in.

A flashlight propped snug under her chin, she smiled her black tooth grin and motioned for me to sit. Raising her fingers to a point on her chin, she began.

"Beware." Mari growled. "This is not a story to entertain you. This is a story to *warn* you. Warn you of *la llorona,* the woman who weeps late into the night. She walks and weeps."

"Hey! I thought you were going to tell our fortunes!"

"You never know when my story's fortune may become your own." Marisol hissed as she continued. "She walks and weeps."

"You said that already." I was determined to keep it light.

"She was foolish once, this girl María. She fell in love with a beautiful man."

"A beautiful man?" I guffawed.

Marisol subdued my response with her long painted nail held to pursed lips. "Their children were as beautiful as the handsome husband. But one day he left María for another even more lovely than she. He rode about the countryside in his fine carriage with his new wife at his side. He stopped when he came upon his family of old, but he completely disregarded poor María. He refused to even look at her. Now he spoke only to his children because he loved to look only into the eyes that were as beautiful as his own." Marisol paused to issue a raspy whisper. "María seethed in fury."

"She what?"

"She *seethed!*"

I shrugged. I could tell she was trying to scare me. "Yeah, yeah, go on." I shifted to sit on my hands.

"How could María punish him? Her jealousy became so strong, she raged about the countryside, wringing her hands. Night after night, she plotted revenge. At last, in her crazed misery she came upon the perfect scheme. The children! She would take the children away from him forever."

"I *said*, aren't you supposed to tell our—"

"No man would throw her away like trash!"

There was no stopping Mari. I clutched my elbows, then twisted my ring around and around on my finger. She ducked her head to force me to look into her eyes.

"And on a night of the full moon in a fit of uncontrollable fury, María dragged her children to the river and pushed them under the murky stream." Reaching for my hands, Mari kept going. "Just as she left the river bank, she realized with horror what she had done. She turned and *threw* herself into the dark waters, searching and calling her children's names. Too late!" Mari lifted her chin and howled like a coyote. *"Lloroooona!"*

I scrambled to free myself, but she clawed at my wrists. Mari shifted to her knees and gripped both my hands. Her breath blew from her lips like the north wind, *"Lloroooona!* Her children—dead, drowned in the black, swirling waters of the river. And to thisss day, you hear her late at night, *weeping, calling* for her children. A woman in white, like the day she herself was buried, crying into the night. And when you do hear her...*run*, run and hide! She will take you for her own. Down, down into the river's grave while she cries, *'ayi...la llor...ohh...na.'*

I bolted, knocking over two chairs and collapsing the tent over Mari's head. My legs pumping under me, my braids whipping my face, I ran, my breath ragged in the cold wind. In one jump, I cleared the patio ledge into the light. I whirled to look back. Mari stood, the white blanket blowing against her, its cloth clinging to her form. In the shadows of the pecan, she swayed and moaned.

My red glittered shoe lay sparkling in the grass.

The Truth about Ana

Mesquites finally lost their leaves, and citrus trees in the yard drooped heavy with fruit. Estela always made us a jelled salad: grapefruit and pecans and cream. But not this winter. She was never around. And neither was Mari.

"Where are they, anyway?" I prodded Mama since I hated to ask Aunt Hilda. She'd probably just think I didn't like to make my bed or dry dishes. Which was true, but not the only reason.

"Isabel," Mama said in her sit-down-explanation tone, like she did when she explained our move away from Daddy. "It's little Ana, honey. She's just sick as she can be." Mama patted the chair cushion. "Come here a minute." She took a deep breath before continuing. "Ana never has been a busy little girl, has she? Estela always had her here at the house when she was working or Marisol was watching her. Ana couldn't run much or play because she was born with a defective heart. Remember? One of the valves doesn't pump blood the way it should." Mama covered my hands with hers. "And remember that Christmas envelope that Aunt Hilda and Uncle Atlee gave Estela?"

I nodded yes, even though it had been over four years ago.

"Well, that money was for a very important operation. Everyone thought it might help. But now we know it's not going to. Estela and her family sit with Ana day and night. It's just a matter of time, really. Just a sad, sad time."

I looked out at the orange trees. That did explain a lot. I knew Mari coddled Ana because her heart was a little weak. But this did sound bad.

Remembering back when Burt Charles and I attempted our firecracker revenge, I had no intention of asking another question, not one, but Mama went on. "Don't bother Estela with questions. It's hard for her."

I squirmed. I remembered Ana's high, thin little voice asking for a lullaby. *"Cielito Linda,"* the song Mari sang to Ana, trilled through my mind. *"Canta y no llores"*—sing, don't cry. It had bothered me then how sadly she sang that song and it bothered me now. Flashes of my old tricks scalded my face. Guilt washed through me.

"Do you understand, Izzie?"

I looked at my hands cupped in Mama's and bobbed my head up and down.

"We never talked about little Ana with you kids. I guess we hoped she'd get better and it would never come to this." Mama stopped talking for a minute, took a deep breath.

"Can I call Burt Charles to come out?" I popped up and headed toward the phone.

Mama frowned at me. "You do understand, Isabel?"

But I was dialing and pretended I didn't hear her. I didn't have to hear her. Not if I really didn't want to.

—⋙—

It would be afternoon before Burt Charles got there. I waited out on the whitewashed walls of the grounds till his mama's car dredged up dust on the road.

"Javelinas have been coming in the yard at night to eat the pecans. Let's get 'em picked up before they get any more!" I headed out. Burt Charles whipped his hat off his head, and we ran around picking up the few pecans left from the hurricane.

Less than twenty minutes later, we sat, heads together on the patio steps, hammering pecans and stuffing the meat into our mouths. I let things get quiet for a while before I asked, "You hear about Ana?"

"Yeah. Mama just told me."

"Mine, too. What'd they do? Decide it was time to let the cat outta the bag?"

"Izzie!" Burt Charles had a genuine look of horror on his face.

"What? It's not like she's gonna die or anything!" I slammed the hammer down hard on the pecan, splintering it in all directions.

"Oh, Izzie." Burt Charles said. "She is. She is gonna die." His eyes darkened. "Haven't you seen all those cars over there? It's their whole family from Realitos to Laredo."

Shells scattered around us in brittle remnants and I methodically pounded a pecan into paste. The flavor I loved so much suddenly tasted like bitter pulp.

—⋙—

Ana died.

Aunt Hilda and I were sitting together in her bedroom when Tío came in to tell us. I stiffened at the news. "But that can't be, Tío! She was just a little girl."

So I was guilty of the same ostrich's-head-in-the-sand evasion as my family. The signs were all there and I chose not to reckon with them. Little girls didn't really die. They did, of course. I'd been told she would. Why had I refused to believe it? How could my mind just let a curtain fall around the truth so I wouldn't have to see?

Aunt Hilda called me over. "Sit by me, darlin'." She caressed my head and began to brush my hair in long soft strokes. As if she read my mind, she said, "Sometimes when we don't want to see the truth, when it's just too much, our eyes and hearts become blind to it. It's not just you. People do it all the time. I could hardly believe it myself."

I bent forward, feeling the pull of the brush, the nearness of my aunt and uncle and realized that Ana would never feel such things again. Mari would never again hold her little sister in her arms. Estela would never kiss her baby goodnight again. And oh, how I wished I had been kinder. Even if I hadn't *done* anything hateful to Ana, I had *thought* she was just a rotten, spoiled child. Jealous. That's what I had been—jealous of a child who was going to die. And Mari knew it.

"Now I want you to listen to me," said Aunt Hilda. "All the grown-ups need to go down to Joaquín and Estela's to visit for a while. You and Burt Charles might want to stay here. I don't think...." She caught her breath in a choke before she went on. "I just don't....oh, you don't want to see that, honey. Y'all stay here. We'll be back in a little while."

She brushed the same spot over and over. Then stopping abruptly, she put her hands over my ears and kissed the top of my head. I nodded but I knew I had to go.

It was dark before we saw Tío, Mama and Aunt Hilda return. They huddled together, so they looked like one rounded shadow coming back across the road to the house. They settled on the veranda. I heard Mama's and Aunt Hilda's whispered voices and the catches of sadness in them.

Burt Charles and I played canasta in the kitchen. For a long while, it was quiet except for his shuffling the decks.

I waited till I heard their conversation begin again. "I'm going over to the Villanueva's." I grabbed Burt Charles by the sleeve. "You have to go with me."

"Izzie...I don't want.... I don't think we.... Well, I'm staying here."
He made a stab at sounding firm. "You didn't ask permission or
anything." Jerking his arm away from my grip, he flipped out the cards
for solitaire.

"Well, what if I can't remember the right words in Spanish?"

"You know, they have been known to speak English, Izzie."

"With or without you, I'm going." I waited just a minute, facing the
door. "I'm going," I repeated in a little singsong threat.

"Jack of hearts on a black queen."

"Fine. Be that way." I pulled down hard on the door handle. "Fine."

The moonlight ricocheted off the hard, white caliche road down to
the group of small, flat-roofed houses a hundred yards off. I walked
halfway before stopping to look up at the sky. The full moon was so
bright it faded out the stars. I couldn't even find the Big Dipper. Resolve
dwindling and fighting off thoughts of *la llorona*, I thought about tearing
back over the short span. Terror would fill me up if I let go of my self-
control enough to run. "Daddy—" I don't know why I called out like
that, but I still did it when I was afraid. I glanced desperately back over
my shoulder at the ranch house. Burt Charles stood at the cattleguard,
hands in his pockets.

With exaggerated resignation, Burt Charles trudged forward. But he
came. It dawned on me that he was the only friend I had in the world. I
smiled my best smile and reached for his hand. He wouldn't let me hold
it, but handed me my jacket instead. Silent except for his warning tone,
Burt Charles paced beside me. "Isabel...." He dragged out the last
syllable.

A dark huddle of smoke and talk, the men stood outside in the yard,
their voices low, swallowed up by the dark. Boots shuffled in the sand.
Shoulders hunched and collars turned up against the cold. Tequila passed
from one fist to the other. Throwing back their heads, the men made
quick, hard pulls at the bottle. They glanced up at us, nodded in
acknowledgement.

Light from a hundred candles and litany of a thousand prayers spilled
from the casita into the night. Burt Charles and I stepped onto the porch.
"What are they saying?" I asked.

"The Holy Rosary. Hail Marys." His voice was so serious I hardly
recognized it. "This is as far as I'm going."

"You scared?"

"Heck, no. It's just that...well, all the men are standing out here."

"You're scared."

"I came with you, didn't I? I'll just wait here…with the men."

I gave up. I opened the screen door. Someone had made *pan de polvo*, a Christmas cookie of small dough rings formed on the pinkie finger. A licorice trace of anise seed permeated the palpable, thick warmth of wax burning. Against the stucco wall in the kitchen sat a small coffin. As though hypnotized, black eyes in swollen faces fixed desperate gazes on the crucifix above it.

"Dios te salve, María llena eres de gracia." Estela's solitary voice isolated her from the shawled shapes of women. I studied her face, drawn and aged in despair. But it was her hands that mesmerized me. Estela's knotty fingers massaged the rosary pearl. Her thumb and forefinger fumbled down the thin chain of separation and began kneading with dishwater-wrinkled hands the next large round bead.

Then in unison, Marisol and her sisters joined Estela's chant, their voices a bare hum against their mother's lead. *"Santa María, Madre de Dios, ruega por nosotros, pecadores, ahora y en la hora de nuestra muerte. Amén."*

Changing my focus to the play of shadows against the open hearth, I held my breath against the thick sweet smells and tried to count the candles. When the room began a slow spin, I gasped for air. Mari's eyes flashed up at mine. She stood and slipped past the others to stand in front of me. Pulling me over to the coffin, she dug her fingers into my arm. I tried to step away but she stood so close she blocked me. "Now you see, gringa? Now you see?" Borders of the room muted. Candles lost their definition. Shadows enclosed all but the two of us. I pinched my lips together and to keep from looking at Ana, stared at the small scar above Marisol's cheek. She held me tight against her shoulder and then pivoted me to face the casket.

Ana's head rested on a shiny taffeta pillow. She did look like she was sleeping, but her cheeks were too pink, her lips too red, her skin too pale. *"Dios te salve, María llena eres de gracia."* Along Ana's thin shoulders lay her long dark braids that her mama had threaded with blue ribbon, *"El Señor es contigo."* She wore what I thought to be one of her sisters' First Communion dresses, the white ruffles tucked behind to take up the slack, the collar gaping at her throat. *"Bendita tú eres entre todas las mujeres y bendito es el fruto de tú vientre, Jesús."* Past the hem of the too long skirt, I studied her lace-trimmed socks and patent leather shoes. Not one scuff. *"Santa María, Madre de Dios, ruega por nosotros, pecadores."* And delicately among her small, thin fingers, a rosary of wooden beads entwined. *"Ahora y en la hora de nuestra muerte. Amén."*

The crucifix above Ana, the shadows that writhed against heavy plaster walls, all those candles. I searched frantically. Where was Burt Charles?

"Burt Charles?"

Marisol gripped my arm. I couldn't face her. What was she trying to prove?

But finally, there was no option. I couldn't cause a fight either. I had to look at her. There in her eyes, it was. A deep suffering I could only begin to understand. Set grim and tight, her mouth gave away nothing. Her eyes, though, her eyes. I looked Marisol straight on and clutched her other arm. I remembered Halloween night, how I was locked in her grip, but this time I held onto her as well. For the first time, I could see that she would have to fight battles I would not. The prickly pears, the runaway horse, the *llorona* story, all her silly pranks on me seemed unimportant.

"I didn't know how sick Ana really was. I guess I didn't want to know."

Mari's lips pressed together in an almost smile, but she choked as she gave me a hug. "You better run back home, *gringita*. Your family, they'll be looking for you."

I ran, stumbling through the door. Where was he? Where *was* he? There—standing with one boot against the wall. I pushed through the men who stepped aside in surprise. I stopped just before reaching Burt Charles and wheeled around, my back to him.

"Well?" he asked. He touched my shoulder.

"Well, what?"

"Well, was it terrible?"

I finally answered. "We'll talk later maybe." For the first time that I could remember, I was too full of images to talk.

—⚬⚬⚬—

Estela came back to work two days after the funeral. Scrubbing with a vengeance, she took on the copper-bottomed pans. She snapped sheets off the line and onto the beds as if hoisting the mainsails of a clipper ship. But sometimes, when she was cleaning bathrooms and thought she was alone, she gave in to the pain. Her sobs seeped under the door and diffused the air with heartache. I shoved my fist to my mouth to keep from crying with her.

And Mari. She no longer studied all the way on the school bus. She sat at the back like she always did, but she did not pore over her notes. She sat with her elbow propped on the window edge and stared. Even when the glass fogged up.

What could I say to her that could possibly make her feel better? She'd spent all the years I'd known her taking care of her baby sister. And now little Ana was gone. Perhaps I didn't have to say anything. Perhaps I could just sit there. I twisted in my seat. *Just go.* I stood, and bracing myself on the back of the bus seats, I weaved unsteady steps to the back. What if she slapped her books in the seat next to her so I couldn't sit down? What if she got up and moved to another seat? *Take your chances, Izzie. It won't kill you.* I sat. I didn't dare touch her. We rode without speaking. And for once, we really didn't need to. Folding my hands on my book satchel, I gazed out the same window.

—✦—

Joaquín spent hours grooming and training Keep the Change for the race track. He even worked on Canela, trimming her hooves and exercising her. Now that some grass had grown and he didn't have to burn cactus for the cattle, he elevated the care of the horses to a compulsive level. I came out to watch him, and brush Canela myself. He stroked her sides and said, *"Está bonita ella."*

She did look better than even before the hurricane. Maybe a while in the pasture with a stallion did her some good. Made her feel young again or something. Anyway, taking care of the horses seemed to grant Joaquín some peace.

After all that time of being annoyed with little Ana around the house, I missed her. Her absence crafted an even stranger gap between Mari and me. I wanted to be kinder. I wanted to reach out and show I wasn't the spoiled rich kid I'm sure she thought I was, but those years of contest had become habit. Still guilt was a great motivator. Maybe guilt would make me a better person.

Part Three

1958

April 1958

The night after George's funeral when I had begged to go home, Mama kissed me. Said that when she completed her master's degree, we could find a home to ourselves if we wanted. Said she knew how hearing of a suicide must be upsetting to a young girl, well, anyone really. Just give her time to get her thesis done, she said. Take another day off school, go for a ride on Canela; maybe Daisy would let Burt Charles stay home and go with me. "Hush, darlin', run to bed. Tío will be back soon. Everything will look better in the morning. Goodnight now. Let Mama get this paper done."

I was fourteen and I did not need to take her advice. I walked out into that spring night—the air close with faded orange blossom. I grabbed a towel off the line and folded it beneath me under the fig tree, its leaves still delicate and small—not the hand-sized spans they would become.

After I got still, the owl called out—a powerful *whoo*.

"You watch it all, don't you?" I scanned the branches. "What do you know that I don't know?"

Who-who—whoo-whoo

"I know exactly what you mean."

From behind the air conditioning unit crept Boracho. "Whew!" I shooed him off, but he belly-crawled back.

"Okay…c'mon." He moved closer and lay his old head on my knee. "That owl won't hurt you. It's just keepin' tabs."

The fog moved in and obscured the stars. It settled on the grass and collected on the flat surfaces of the fig leaves. Hiking my legs to my chest, I pulled my John Deere cap down to block the moisture that streamed together on the fig leaves and fell in slow flat plops. Boracho stuck his nose in the space between my knee and stomach. Reaching around him I snuggled him up.

Headlights swung in an arc before a sedan pulled into the carport. Boracho pricked his ears and whined. I caught him by the collar and shushed him. Tío stepped from the back seat and spoke to the Rangers before walking to the kitchen door. I watched as he sat at the kitchen island. He didn't eat. He didn't drink. He just sat there. It seemed a long while till he struggled to his feet and crossed through the veranda and out the door to the bedroom wing.

The collie started to shiver. I wrapped part of the towel around him. Old Boracho was managing to get by without falling all to pieces. I guessed I could suck it up, too.

So this is the way it was going to be, I decided. We would all just put one foot in front of the other till maybe the rest of the world would forget about George and Box 13. And whose brother he was. I didn't have to be all that happy. Just go to school tomorrow, tolerate condolences or ridicule, whichever. Smile at my uncle and accept what he told me as the truth. I didn't have to pick apart every event looking for misfit puzzle pieces. Just shut up and make nice. Kiss Tío and Aunt Hilda goodnight and smile at Marisol. What was it to me if the adults around me had their own separate lives? It appeared that I was going to have one myself. Maybe that was growing up—keeping secrets.

"I bet you can keep a secret, Bo." I gave him a good scratch before standing to shake out the towel. I pinned it back on the clothesline, filling in the gap like I would the blank spaces in my life.

Just a little pretending. I could do that. And I wasn't sorry George was dead. If Tío did give him a gun to make a quick exit instead of prison—fine with me. I could keep my mouth shut forever. George didn't even have the decency to wait till I was gone to pull that trigger. Didn't care that I would witness something nobody should ever see. "I hope he went to hell."

Boracho sat thumping his tail like I had come up with the right answer. "You." I snagged the towel back off the line. "C'mon." I coaxed him into the air conditioning alcove and covered him.

Heavy with dew and resolve, I turned to face the house. Mama's light was still on when I tiptoed in, but Tío and Aunt Hilda's room was dark. No glimmer from under the door, no murmur of the late news. They hid in the darkness.

The Trouble with Opals

"What's with you, anyhow?" Burt Charles drilled his finger into my ribs. "Izzie, you are slippin'." He'd come home from school with me every day since the funeral.

"Nah, just trying to keep up with my studies." I frowned and scribbled on a piece of notebook paper.

"Oh, excuse me! Trying to keep up with ol' Mari's A honor roll? I mean, don't let me distract you. You are going to need *hours* of work." He backed off, bowing and scraping.

"Shut up, please," I said, my tone equally obsequious.

"Nah, really, Izzie. You can't kid a kidder. You're making me nervous. Let's get a plan with…with pizzazz!"

I must have flashed my eyes over to Burt Charles just long enough for him to pick up on a brief spark.

"Ah hah! I thought so," he said. "I've been thinkin'."

"Omigod! Not really!"

"Izzie, do you know how much patience it takes to put up with you? Do you think you could just listen for once?"

"Just once? Oh wow, if it's just *once*, I might could."

Burt Charles put two fingers to my lips. "Shhh. I've got something important to say."

Before I planned my retort, I heeded the little frown burrowed between his brows. He meant it. An emotion I had never seen before flickered about his mouth and eyes. His fingers still pressed against my lips.

He talked fast. "I'll go to the *Camileño* with you. I'll sign the wall with you. And we could investigate…you know…the scene."

I shuddered. "Oh…." I strung out the word with a long sigh. "Not this weekend. I've still got that report on Brazil to do. You know, population, agriculture, exports. All that stuff."

"Good grief, girl, we can get that done in an hour. Your tío has umpteen *National Geographic*s we can cut up and glue onto poster board. We'll make you look like a genius."

"What's with *you* anyway?" I asked. "Since when could you be lured out to the *Camileño?* Last time I tried to get you to go, you had a list of excuses."

Burt Charles' face melted just a little before he recovered. "You ain't been yourself, Izzie. I mean, for a while there you were all paranoid. No, that's not the word. You were pickin' to pieces everything that your tío did. And now, it's like you're...you're like.... What's that operation they give you when you go cuckoo? Lobotomy? Like that! It's like you've had a lobotomy. I mean compared to how you used to be."

"You're the one that's nuts," I said.

"Well, that's more fun than a lobotomy. C'mon, let's go. Appreciate my sacrifice here. I'm willing to scare myself to death to get you back to where you are fun to be with." Burt Charles laughed, but he looked down before he said, "I've been missin' you. Maybe that's *my* fear."

I could barely keep from crying. I did not want to lose Burt Charles. He might very well decide someone else was more fun. They probably would be.

"We could look for clues, you know? The Rangers might not have found everything. What if somebody made George's death *look* like a suicide?" Burt Charles cut his eyes over to check my reaction. "There's a rumor in town, you know."

I worked my face into deadpan, but through my head ran—*Confess your fear to the spirits. Who knows? It just might work.* I would try harder this time. Just maybe I could find some clue that would make things clearer in my mind, which would confirm or deny Tío's degree of involvement.

I glanced at my hand where my opal ring had been four weeks ago and was now gone. My tan already covered the pale evidence of ever having worn it. Rubbing the vacant space with my thumb, I wondered once again if I had lost the stone that morning I was out at the *Camileño.* "Saturday morning." I said, making it clear I was doing him a big favor.

"We'll finish your project! I'll bring—"

"Saturday morning we ride." I sounded like a Forties cowboy movie.

"But I thought you had to finish the project, Izzie. You said—"

"Losing your nerve?"

Burt Charles stiffened. "Hell no." But his smile hinted of triumph. "She's back."

One thing I knew: it *was* a suicide. I was probably the only one in Duval County who was absolutely sure. I knew Estela and the girls insisted that someone else was involved. George's wife Eva cried to the newspapers that it was murder. And if you hand a gun to a man going to prison, does that count as murder? Even if you weren't the one who pulled the trigger? Or if George was contemplating suicide, how much sting would a brother's unforgiving comment have? Plenty, I thought.

The Texas Rangers revealed no evidence, but from what I understood, they didn't much care how George died. No longer a source of irritation, he could, like the tombstones said: R.I.P.

Burt Charles frequently identified me as "transparent," but he was the only one who had really noticed. Only the wall had to know my fears and then I could sign my name. Burt Charles wouldn't actually have to *listen* to me, but it would help if he waited for me *outside* the *Camileño*. Close by. I would whisper.

—⟋⟍⟍⟋—

That Saturday, no one really asked us exactly where we were going. I saddled Canela—barely getting the cinch around her belly. I had both horses ready to go before Burt Charles got to the corral. He brought donuts and a thermos of milk with a little coffee in it.

The sun warmed the air by eight a.m. and I was glad I'd worn my cap to keep the heat off my face. The morning was nothing like April Fool's Day when I'd last been to the *Camileño*. No gentleness to the atmosphere. Hard and bright. I guessed the truth would be like that—hard and bright.

Nurturing my bravado, I pretended to razz Burt Charles. "You sure you can make it? There might be ghosts out there after all. Wooooo…." The only ghost I ever expected to see was George Parr's. Canela craned her neck at my legs in curiosity at their trembling.

"Take the back way," I called. We both knew why. Even if by now the adults were less worried about the distance we traveled, we knew there would be plenty of objections to our meddling around the *Camileño*.

A small band of javelinas shuffled across the path in front of us. Repugnant, coarse-haired critters, their piggy snouts grunted a warning. Their equally ugly offspring scooted along among them.

"Hey, you smell that?" I yelled at Burt Charles.

"Oh, man, yeah. Whoof!"

Neither horse shied at the feral scent. Oh, they looked, but just kept moving at a steady walk. The horses either had nerves of steel or were just too old to give a hoot. "Good girl." I patted Canela.

We trotted up to the worn, chalky *Camileño*. The windmill still turned while cows mucked about in the sludge and manure. Out of hunger or some bovine curiosity, they wandered up to us as we approached. They milled about, murmuring in their restless moan. How peaceful it looked.

Rope marking the area trailed off as though dragged by some bull, and sagged down through the mesquite forming an asymmetrical frame around the suicide.

"Whoa! Crime scene!" Burt Charles flung himself off his horse and followed the rope line.

I don't know how I expected him to react. He was just a boy, after all, and Texas Ranger activity excited his every nerve ending.

I hung back, remembering the animosity between Tío and George. I sat in the saddle, watching Burt Charles scurry about the place. He lifted the rope. He scuffed the ground with his boot.

"Not much here to look at." He sounded like Jack Webb on *Dragnet*. "Those Rangers don't miss anything." He knelt down on one knee. "Musta been where the Chrysler sat. You can still see the smudge of a tire. And hey! Lookyhere! Another car was here!" He pointed to an imprint below the broken mesquite. "Man, do ya think—?"

"Oh, crazy, you don't know who all's been out here since then. Probably the Rangers' cars."

"Well, you can sure take the fun outta a mystery."

"Just don't get carried away." Swinging myself off Canela, I inspected the ground about me with great seriousness. Nothing. There was nothing I could comment on. "I'm checking out the house," I called. It wasn't five seconds till Burt Charles was breathing down my neck.

"Would you back off?"

"Jeez, Izzie, this is supposed to be an adventure. Remember?"

"Okay, okay. I'm sorry. I've…I've…I've got a stomach ache."

"Oh." Having become informed in health class of the reproduction cycle of the human female, Burt Charles was probably not taking any chances at further discussion. He made a quick return to inspect the outside evidence. I sensed my advantage in the years to come.

I pressed my shoulder to the doorframe and gazed into the shadows of the *Camileño*. Quiet. Not like the time before when angry voices punctuated the air outside. Stepping inside, I sat back against the wall. The brightness of the day gave a photograph's negative effect to the interior of the crumbling building. The peeling walls, the ragged screens of the windows closeted me in some past world of the *vaquero*. Mud daubers' clumps and swallows' nests caked the windowsills. Cow dung littered the concrete floor. I imagined grimy hombres sitting around the fire, drinking tequila and telling bawdy stories, laughing from their throats in that guttural way Mexican men did, recounting macho tales of how they conquered a wild mustang or wrestled a longhorn to the ground. They must have missed those rowdy days and nights of *machismo* and still liked lurking around as ghosts.

Warm and still, the room emitted a melancholy I'd seldom known. I took a deep breath, sighed and sat.

"Aw, Izzie...." Burt Charles stuck his head through the doorway. He hesitated, but came in and dropped to the floor across from me. He swirled the palm of his hand flat against the concrete, picking up gravel and tossing it at the fireplace. "Sometimes I don't know who you are anymore."

Before I could lift my head and make another excuse for my behavior, he shouted. "Isabel Martin! You are in luck today!" He plucked what looked like a dirty watermelon seed from his palm and turned it over again in the light from the window. "Your opal! It's the opal that goes in your ring! Look!"

"Oh!" I sat up straight and rolled to my knees. "I can't believe...I mean, you found.... That's wonderful! That's great. Thank you so much, Burt Charles." I smiled with feigned innocence, hoping he would not connect the dots like we used to in our coloring books. "You sure do have a good eye." I reached out to accept the gemstone. "Mama will be real surprised."

Full of good will, he leaned forward to present the stone to me. His face suddenly contorted from triumph to suspicion. "Wait a minute now. You lost this around the first of April." He closed his hand around the stone, holding it in a fist. "How? How did it get here? Have you been out here by yourself?"

Reading the accusation in his eyes, I sat very still and settled my hands back down into my lap. I examined my fingernails, then folded my hands like a pious school girl. I couldn't think. What to say? Burt Charles sat very still himself and waited for an answer. Ticking off the seconds, time passed like ice melting. A cow lowed outside by the water tank. Some insect rustled old leaves as it milled about the hearth.

"Oh, after the investigation, I thought I'd take a little look around." I smiled at what I hoped Burt Charles would interpret as fearless detective work.

"By yourself." His hazel eyes leveled on me in that purely honest way he had.

"Well, yeah. Whadda ya think?" I jerked my chin at his skepticism.

"You better come clean with me, Izzie. I am not buying this for one minute." He unclenched his fist and studied the opal. "No way would you have come out here after that suicide and not brag about it. I know you."

I was past lying, but if I spoke the words—if Burt Charles put all the pieces together, he would see it like I did—an indictment of a man he respected and loved. "Burt Charles?" I couldn't say another word.

"C'mon, Izzie." He reached out, unfolded my hands and let the opal drop into my palm. Taking my fingers one by one, he wrapped them around the gem. "C'mon."

I looked into those eyes, the greens and browns, limpid in their innocence. My friend. My only friend in this hard, burnt country. I clutched the opal in my palm and pressed my fist to my eyes to stop the tears, but they sputtered between my fingers.

"I saw it. I saw it all. They fought, Burt Charles. George and Tío. George yelled awful things at Tío and spit at him. He spit! Can you believe that?"

Burt Charles could only shake his head. "Man, Izzie. Then what—"

I kept going. There was no way to stop me now. The truth poured out of me the way it wanted to all along. "Tío handed George a package and he said...he said, 'Use it or not, George. I don't give a damn.' It was a gun, Burt Charles. I just know it was a gun so that George could kill himself instead of going to jail. George even said he thought that's what it was."

Burt Charles was holding my arms now, trying to keep me together. I sobbed.

I stopped and looked into Burt Charles' eyes. "He stared at me."

"Who? Who stared at you?"

"George, Burt Charles. George!" What I had seen came out in hiccups. "And he was just...I was just trying to get home before...before Mama found out and he just *sat* there." I pointed to the spot where the Chrysler was parked a few weeks ago. "He knew I saw him." I stared down at my birthstone. "I didn't know I'd lost my opal till later. Thank you for finding it, Burt Charles." I felt oddly deranged and produced a smile that no doubt confirmed it.

He shook me gently, but I continued in a voice no longer mine. "George stared right at me and...he pulled the trigger."

"Oh, Izzie." Burt Charles pulled me into his arms.

"You can't tell, you know. Promise."

Burt Charles held my face with both hands and pushed aside the strands of hair that stuck to my cheeks. "I promise." He kissed me. "I promise. Don't cry. Don't—." He kissed me again. His lips quivered against my own trembling mouth.

As though someone had said "Shhh," his words dropped to whispers. "Forgive your tío, Izzie. Everything will be all right. It will be all right." He pulled me to my feet and pressed his forehead against mine. "Even if you don't understand what you saw, you can just trust your uncle. He's a smart man…a good man."

"Forgiveness is overrated. I think I read that somewhere."

"It's supposed to make you feel better."

"Well, I'm just going to chalk it up as growing up." I pinched my mouth into a smirk. "Don't have to forgive anything. I'll just get over it. I can sign the damn wall now, can't I? Give me your knife." Backing Burt Charles into a corner of the *Camileño*, I reached into the front pocket of his Levi's and closed my fingers around the Swiss Army knife.

"Just forgive him, Izzie."

I dug my thumbnail into the groove of the large blade and peeled it open. *No matter what he's done, keep my tío safe.* What I said aloud was, "What about *your* fear, Burt Charles?" Without waiting for his answer, I carved *Isabel Martin 4/30/58.*

Mr. Wiley's Surprise

A little fissure opened in my I-don't-care stance and hope for my uncle's innocence weaseled in. Despite doubts of gaining reliable information, I would talk to Mr. Wiley just one more time.

The carpenter looked up when he heard us coming and gave us a straight-arm salute before he started back to unload some planks. "Hope you kids plan on makin' yourselves handy. I'm fixin' to nail these sheets of tin down on the barn here and I'm gonna need a ladder climber and a nail expert so's I don't hafta wear myself out runnin' up and down this here thang." Mr. Wiley slammed the ladder into the dirt against the outside wall. Burt Charles acted like he was trying to hold it for him, but I knew he would pursue the ladder-runner position. In fact, he had already snaked his hand over a rung. I sighed and accepted my role as the "nail expert."

Mr. Wiley lurched up the wooden rungs. At the top, he went into a coughing fit. The ladder shuddered. Burt Charles and I put all our weight against it to steady it. Mr. Wiley wrenched his left hand behind him and wiggled his fingers. "Three roofers!" I whipped out the nails and Burt Charles relayed them to Mr. Wiley's outstretched hand.

"Hand me them cigarettes, boy. Down in the tool kit. Should be lying right on top."

Burt Charles scurried up the ladder as Mr. Wiley reached down. I could see that getting started with my questions was going to be difficult. I lined up ten roofing nails, so I didn't have to think about anything else while I asked. I took a deep breath and spouted out what I needed to know. "Hey, uh, Mr. Wiley, sir, I just wondered if Tío had…well, you know, any trouble with the law?" It all came out too loud and I tried to steady my voice. "After all, he was George Parr's brother."

Mr. Wiley, the nails pressed in his lips, stopped and looked straight down at me. I stacked the nails in tic-tac-toe fashion and waited.

"George Parr's brother? That don't tell me nothing." Mr. Wiley spoke over his shoulder. "Don't you be pickin' on your uncle."

"You have to say that! He's paying you to build this barn!"

Mr. Wiley sighed like a Hereford bull and backed heavily down the steps.

"Now, lookyhere, missy." He took me by the shoulders and directed me toward a sawhorse. Burt Charles straddled alongside me.

Pulling up a bucket and flipping it over backwards, Mr. Wiley groaned as he sat. He leaned forward, both forearms on his knees, a cigarette dangling between his fingers. "How come you think you got an uncle that'll break the law?"

"He does in all kinds of little ways, but mainly he gives out money, Mr. Wiley! I've seen him. Money to people who are gonna vote!" I wished my last words hadn't squeaked out like a parakeet. "Like George did. And Tío was gone election night, you know—the one with all the graveyard ghouls who voted for Johnson." I grabbed a twist of rope and began to shred its frayed end. "And next thing you know, the Feds will get Tío on tax evasion and send him to prison like George." I stopped myself before I cried, "And then where will I be?"

"Where'd you put them cigarettes, boy?" Mr. Wiley patted his shirt pockets. "Oh, here...I got 'em." Mr. Wiley fumbled for his Lucky Strike pack but finding it empty, crumpled the cellophane. "I guess I ain't been real open with you kids."

The words hung in the air.

Burt Charles and I angled glances at each other.

"Atlee Parr and I go way back. Oh, my family came from a different background all right. We wuz s'poor you coulda chunked a cat through the wall, but we had nice enough clothes, ate pretty good. Every one of us kids worked from four-thirty in the morning to school time and till after dark when we got home. Atlee and I got to be buddies in the classroom. Just a minute here now." With a pincer grip, Mr. Wiley pulled a flimsy cotton bag of Bull Durham out of his shirt pocket. Holding the paper between his second and third fingers, he shook the tobacco into place and tapped it down. He lifted up the longwise end and ran his tongue along the edge, but sat there without lighting the cigarette before he continued.

"A few years after your uncle went off to college, I got myself into the army. I was young and didn't know no better, but then I didn't have much of a choice, you know. I weren't no rancher so I was up for grabs anyway when we finally got into the war." Gripping the kitchen match in his fist, Mr. Wiley flicked the head with his thumbnail. It fired up. He took a hard draw on the cigarette and smiled through the smoke. "Maybe

I liked the uniform. So soon as I got out of the military, I signed on as deputy sheriff. I hafta admit the Parrs put in a good word for me. Did my time just waiting till I could up and join the Texas Rangers." Wiley leaned forward and reached into his back pocket. "They let you keep it even if you're retired." He cupped the badge of the Texas Rangers in his palm. "Captain Dennis Wiley, retired, at y'all's service."

I slapped my hand over my mouth. "You're a spy!" I tried to get up but slipped, my legs churning under me to regain my balance. "Oh no, oh no." I turned to grab Burt Charles' shoulder.

"No man in the wrong can stand up against a fellow that's in the right and keeps on a-comin'." He polished the insignia on his pants' leg. "Spent thirty-some-odd years wearin' that badge with a star. I kinda miss it and then sometimes I don't. Hafta tell y'all about Bonnie and Clyde—"

"Captain Wiley! Not now!"

"All right, all right. Guess I better stick to business. Now honey, listen, just listen here a minute before you go off like a little tornado." He couldn't suppress a chuckle. "I want you to know the truth. I'd a told you earlier if I'd known you was in such a state about it. Jest odd for kids to be so worried about politics. 'Course, I was limited in what I could talk about before the trial. You sit back down here and let's palaver a minute."

He was finally going to say it. I grabbed Burt Charles' hand and crushed it to my breasts. I only glanced at him, but crimson traveled from his Adam's apple to his hairline. Sweat clung to the blond fuzz on his upper lip. I needed him too much to be concerned about his silly state of mind.

"Okay," I said. I filled my voice with as much dignity as I could muster.

"Your tío's a good man but he's had a, pardon my French, a helluva time with that brother of his. Oh, not that I didn't hate to see the man kill hisself—"

"*You* did not see him kill himself!" And then I was talking and I couldn't stop the words. "*I* was the one! I saw him kill himself."

Captain Wiley stared at me. "Good lord." That was all he said while he waited for me to finish.

The whole story gushed out. "What am I supposed to do if *he* goes off to jail? What about Mama and Aunt Hilda?" I whimpered. "Please don't get him in trouble. I just couldn't...." I blubbered and couldn't find a way to get control of myself. "It's my secret! Promise me you will never tell. Promise!"

"Now just hush a minute here. Listen to what I'm gonna tell you."

I let go of Burt Charles' hand and twisted my ring finger back and forth to stare at the kaleidoscope of colors radiating from the opal ring that Mama had repaired for me. Maybe the truth was like my birthstone—blue and green shot through with yellow, depending on the way you slanted the gem in the sunlight. And in the dark, there was no color at all, just a lump that promised nothing.

"Yes sir, Mr.....er...Captain Wiley." I glanced up for a second but I concentrated again on the ring. "I'm countin' on this being the truth. You know, sir, the real truth."

"Wouldn't steer ya otherwise, honey."

"Tell me."

"I reckon I know why there was such a ruckus between Atlee and George. From what I understand, your uncle just about lost the ranch trying to help his brother stay out of jail. Atlee was the youngest, you know. He loved his brother, right or wrong." Captain Wiley smiled like he knew how Tío felt. "You know what I mean?"

But I didn't really. Burt Charles was the closest I had to a brother. At that moment, I realized I loved him. How much I loved him. He was nothing like a brother at all.

"The real partin' of the ways came with all that Precinct 13 business. Some of the Feds questioned Atlee about his doin's with that election and he was pretty damn adamant about not knowing about it."

"Do you think he was telling the truth?" I wondered if Tío would lie to protect his brother. I might. I might lie to protect someone I loved. I knew I would.

"Now that's not for me to make a call on. I just know he wouldn't answer any questions about his brother though and since them boys down at the courthouse never could get an indictment against George, your uncle wasn't forced to testify. Embarrassed though, you could tell. When the ol' boys down at the Windmill Café took to expressing their opinions, he'd just get up and walk out."

"The reporters showed up here at the ranch!" Burt Charles intruded in the conversation. "We heard 'em didn't we, Izzie? They sounded like they knew exactly what was going on."

I nodded in agreement. "How come Tío would invite George to dinner if he knew he'd done all those bad things?"

Mr. Wiley clucked and shook his head. "Little girl, I know you don't have brothers or sisters so it's hard to understand, but I bet you will when you have kids."

"You got kids, sir?"

"Nope, brothers. Hard to separate yourself from your brother sometimes. Too much alike."

Burt Charles lost the ability to contain himself. "I heard Mr. García down at the store say the Parr brothers were cut from the same skin."

"See what I mean?" That had been my point all along. George and Tío were brothers and they were bound to be alike.

"Whoa. Hold on there, y'all. George and Atlee might be brothers, but they're as different as they can be. And finally, Atlee Parr had to take a stand…." Then with a laugh, he corrected himself. "Guess I should say he had to take *the* stand in this last income tax trial. I was there and I heard him."

Burt Charles jumped in. "You were there? Atlee testified against his brother?"

"Well, yes, he did, son. Yes, he did."

"Oh man!" said Burt Charles. "Was that where you were when we thought you were sick or somethin'?"

"That was the week."

I was silent, but I thought about the day Tío and Aunt Hilda drove behind the school bus and Tío really didn't make an effort to wave. They were driving home from the trial in San Antonio. I remembered how their door was closed that night and what a terrible day that was for them too.

Wiley went on. "Oh, not that I had anything to testify to in this ruckus, but I did want to clear my mind of some tangles, if you know what I mean. I usually stay out of the courtroom these days."

"What did Tío say? Did he testify against George?"

"I'm telling you right now, Miss Isabel Martin, your uncle went through the devil up there on that stand. He was about as upset as I've ever seen him."

"What did he do?"

"Oh, you know. Took a long time to answer questions. Like he just hated a doin' it."

"What did the judge ask him?" That long ago image of a God-like figure, only dressed in black, swept into my mind.

"Oh, it was the lawyer for the IRS that did the talkin'. You know, the Internal Revenue Service. The government office that makes sure you pay your income tax."

"Of course I know that!"

"And cheatin' the government gets you in bad trouble."

"I know that too." Did he think I was an idiot? "And George did?"

"Yessiree, George did. Tried to lay off some of his income onto Atlee. That was why Atlee had to testify. Turns out George leased some land from your uncle. Told him that instead of payin' the lease that he'd just pay your uncle's county taxes. Well, the county treasurer was in cahoots with George and issued a receipt for taxes that were never paid."

"George cheated Tío?"

"More than once, I'd say. After that, George irrigated that acreage with fancy equipment. Equipment he bought with county funds. Y'all have seen them things out there in the fields—them big rollin' wheels." Captain Wiley undid his thermos and took a swig, swirling water around in his mouth before he swallowed it. "He allowed as how all that machinery belonged to Atlee."

"The lawyer asked Tío about that?"

"Yep, he did. And your tío had to tell the truth. George defrauded the government and worse, he cheated and involved an innocent man. Not just any man. His brother."

Burt Charles sat with his mouth open, looking back and forth between Captain Wiley and me. "Man, George was worse than Daddy thought."

"Your daddy thought he was horrible?"

Burt Charles shrugged. "He sure didn't like the way Atlee had to bail him outta trouble all the time."

"So, little gal…." Captain Wiley stood with a grunt. "I guess that's about it. Just about saucered and blowed."

"Why didn't Tío just tell the truth from the beginning?"

"Why didn't you, Izzie?" asked Burt Charles.

And how would things have turned out if I'd confessed I'd seen the suicide? I twisted my hands in my lap.

"Well, now, see there? That's where people can go wrong. There's more than one kinda dishonesty in this world, ain't there?" Captain Wiley inhaled deeply and squinted up at the sky. "Not like you want to run out and spill your guts about every little opinion you've got, but you've got to learn to figure out when the truth is a good thing. Ain't an easy call."

I studied my fingernails.

Captain Wiley stood with one foot on the ladder and said, "No man in the wrong can stand up against a fellow that's in the right and keeps on a-comin'. That's the Rangers' Creed. But I guess I said that already. Anyhow, that means he defends his friends, and Atlee Parr is my friend. He's a good man. Now somebody better hand me my nails! I ain't never gonna get finished at this rate."

He stopped and gazed at the barn roof. "But I'm tellin' you one thing, honey. Trust ain't nuthin' someone can tell you. It's...it's a.... You ever heard of the word, insight?"

I said I thought I had.

"Well, it's something you got to dig out for yourself." Captain Wiley gave me a little half-hug. "Get diggin'."

Burt Charles obediently held the ladder with a grip on it that made his knuckles turn pale against his tan. The ladder wobbled. Burt Charles sucked in his breath.

Swiping my eyes with my forearm, I stood up and arranged the nails like a five-card poker hand and never took my eyes off them. And like in a poker game, I was glad I hadn't told Captain Wiley all that I knew. I'd left out the part about the package that passed between my uncle and his brother.

The Rustler

In truth, the dilemma of my uncle's involvement did not seem to hurt quite so much any more as the days went by. With the telling, a callus formed over my heart. Not like a pearl over a grain of ocean sand, but the rough scab on the inside of horses' knees. Chestnuts, we called them.

Burt Charles and I rode every chance we got on late afternoons. The rides were different now. I let him hold the bridle for me when I mounted up. I waited for him to come stand beside the stirrups when I slid down into his arms.

With the longer days, we wandered farther than we should. The adults still thought of us as mere companions—lookouts for each other who would report a horse gone berserk with snakebite or gored by a javelina. Never once did they imagine the horses pressed so close together they sometimes stumbled so that we could hold each other's hand. Never once did they imagine the fantasies that began to take hold of us.

It was late that afternoon when we rode out. The evenings were cooling off now and shadows fell long across the road. I watched our own shadows weaving in and out of the dust. Such an easy time.

We spent that afternoon with little talk, just the comfort of each other's company until a shot fired just south of us in the pasture beyond the mesquite break. It was the first and only time Canela ever spooked with me. Her haunches sank and for a moment I thought I couldn't stay with her, but she stopped as fast as she started. Burt Charles' horse bolted a few feet then quit.

"Oh, God, what was that?" It had the spiraling echo of rifle fire, but suddenly I was back behind the Chrysler on that early April morning.

Wide-eyed, hands clutching the saddle horn, Burt Charles said nothing.

We waited

Nothing.

The horses danced, anxious to get back to the barn. We turned back toward the sound but the horses spun to face the road home.

"We better go see," said Burt Charles.

"You can't mean that!"

"Somebody could be hurt."

"Somebody could have blown their brains out, too. I'm not going."

The horses turned again toward the barn.

"Look, it's not too far. We'll go up the back way where we won't be seen." He steered Jigsaw south. "I won't make you go in close. One of us may need to stay while the other goes for Atlee." Burt Charles nudged his horse into a trot. "I need you to help, Izzie. I promise I won't let you get hurt."

"Burt Charles." I let the words unwind in a long whine, but I followed him. Our roles reversed, he was the new instigator of our twosome. Canela argued but moved on at a very slow trot. Suited me. I wanted Burt Charles to get there first. And like he could keep me from getting hurt! *Oh, please.* We'd both be traumatized. One more disaster like I had already witnessed would probably ruin me for the rest of my life. I tried to make light of it, but despite myself, I dreaded what we might find.

We dismounted near the mesquites and tied the horses. There was nothing now but the cardinal's call and a soft intermittent scraping. In the field, a small, dark man stood over a calf. A cow pawed nearby and although she lowered her head and swung her horns, she did not charge the man. He took the calf by its back legs and pulled it toward the fence line where two children hung on to the windows of a pickup truck.

"A rustler. We gotta tell Atlee!" Burt Charles corrected his horse that spun again to make a run for the barn.

I took the cue. "I'll go."

But down the road to the north, the hum of an engine filled the silence.

The man jerked upright, listening. Motionless for a moment. Then frantic. He heaved the animal toward the truck. The calf's body caught on barbed wire and in a panic, the poacher took his knife and carved flesh off the bone in the attempt to get his prize through the fence.

Before the man could negotiate the wire, the Cadillac's noise filled the air and skidded to a stop, and Tío was out and at the fence line. The men faced each other. The children stared with great dark eyes wide with terror. The smaller one began to cry.

The man glanced at the children and back at Tío. "*Lo siento,*" he said. But the look on his face was defiant. He was anything but sorry. "*Para los niños, heh?*" He nodded at his children.

"*¿Sí, como no? Para los niños.*" Tío looked back over his shoulder at the mauled calf and saw us standing nearby. "Give me a hand with this heifer, son."

Burt Charles and I stepped out of the brush and walked toward them. I hung onto Burt Charles' arm all the way to the mutilated animal.

"Let's get this in his truck," said Tío.

"Sir?"

"In the truck." Then Tío added, "Izzie, hold the wire apart. See if we can't slide it through."

I did not understand the reason why we would help this man steal our calf, but I put one foot on the next to bottom wire and my hand on the line above it and pulled up with all my might. I whispered, "Tío, he's got a gun."

"I know he does, honey. It's all right."

The rustler must have understood. With a soft thud, he slid the rifle to the ground.

Tío and Burt Charles heaved the calf's body into the truck bed. Tío wiped the blood on his pants and stepped forward to offer his hand. The man jumped back against the truck door and reached for his rifle.

Tío held up both hands. "*Para la familia, hombre. No te preocupes.*"

The man dropped his rifle, his face full of disbelief.

"*¿Eres mojado?*"

"*No.*" The man stared at his children for a moment and then answered, "*Sí.*"

"*Vaya con Dios, amigo.*" Tío spoke so quietly that we hardly heard him.

The man backed into the car seat, never taking his eyes off Tío. Before slapping the truck into gear, he jerked his hat from his head and crushed it into his chest. His face crumpled and he spoke. "*Gracias, señor, gracias.*" His truck wobbled away over rows of coastal grass yet to be baled.

Burt Charles and I watched, our mouths open.

Tío was the first to speak. "Y'all ride with me. It's getting dark. We'll pony the horses back with the car."

Burt Charles and I sat in the back seat holding on to the horses with the reins out the window. The ride was silent and we all looked straight ahead.

Once again, I reviewed the history of my uncle's behavior and tried to make sense of it. Tío could be so wonderful to so many people, but more often than not, his kindness was against the law. He had not punished a trespasser, never mind rustler, never mind…. But then, a poacher might could vote if somebody paid his poll tax.

The Price of Beauty

Summer came again—its hot haze, its freedom. No more did I have to make an effort with my hair. Every morning I ran a brush through it and twisted it back into a ponytail. Out of my eyes and out of my way. More meticulous was my taste in attire. I rifled through Tío's closet and picked out a white dress shirt. He never said a word. Just shook his head with that wry smile of his. I doubted Estela was as amused. She would be the one over the ironing board early each morning before the day's heat made the task torture. I rolled my jeans up below my knees and donned bobby socks and loafers. It was hard to be any more sharply dressed.

Despite my confidence in my looks, Aunt Hilda swept her eyes over me as I skidded through the kitchen door and said, "The hair. Let me take a look at those split ends." Before I could snag a tortilla and head to the barn, she had my ponytail in a vice-like grip. "Call Dahlia's in Corpus. See if she can give you a trim. Oh, and wouldn't you love a permanent? It'll give you bounce and curls. I'll bet she has time to...."

"Do I really look like the Shirley Temple type, Aunt Hilda? Really?" I twisted my knuckle into my cheek, did a quick version of "The Good Ship Lollipop," and let the wrought iron door slam behind me.

"I'm making the appointment today!" she called after me. "Marisol can drive you. Maybe *she* would like a perm for when she goes off to school this fall. She could use a haircut at least. Her hair is past her fanny."

There was no stopping Aunt Hilda. I knew that, but maybe it would be fun to get to drive into Corpus Christi without an adult. I hoped Mari would turn the wheel over to me in that desolate stretch between Benavides and Kingsville. Most of all, I would get to witness her first professional cut. Probably her first haircut since she was born actually. I thought of all the years I have coveted that straight black mass she flaunted down her back. My own was dark, but it had a funky wave I finally learned was a cowlick. Hardly the dramatic locks of Jane Russell.

The drive took an hour and a half, but Tío recently had bought a new Cadillac with air-conditioning. We turned it and the radio up full blast. Marisol chose to follow instructions to the letter as far as who was in charge. She was. I was not going to get my fingers near the steering wheel.

Dahlia's was an exclusive shop that Aunt Hilda frequented for her perms. "Mrs. Parr called in our appointments. I'm her niece Isabel Martin and this is—"

Miss Dahlia's eyes widened. She started at Marisol's *huaraches* and worked her way up to the thin cotton skirt and finally to the long black hair. "Come here, darling," she said to me as she steered me by the elbow behind the reception desk. "Perhaps we misunderstood. When your aunt called and made an appointment for her 'little' niece, we set up a booster seat with our best stylist and well, we just *assumed* that the other appointment was for Mrs. Parr herself." Dahlia glanced up at Marisol and arched an eyebrow toward the stylist waiting with pursed lips and scissors poised. "And darling, ask your maid to wait in the car for you. I bet you just missed that sign by the entrance. It could happen to anyone." Her smile was beyond gratuitous. "Now if you'll just step this way."

"What sign? I didn't see any sign." I pushed my way past her and opened the entrance door. The heat from the South Texas noonday flashed against my face. *NO MEXICANS*, the sign read. How could we have missed it? Maybe Mari didn't miss it. Maybe she wanted to see what I would do. See me as the true gringa that I was. "Oh, but don't you see?" I turned toward Dahlia, her oh-so-red lips pinched, her eyes round as she nodded toward the sign. "We *both* have appointments," I said. "We came together."

"Oh now, sweetie, you just sit right down here and your maid can—"

"No, no she can't! C'mon Mari, let's get outta here." I headed out the front.

"Well, I hope you'll explain to your aunt that we...." Dahlia's voice trailed off to an embarrassed whisper.

"Don't look back," I said to Marisol. "Don't look back. We'll find someplace else to go. You know any good places?"

And she did—Pilar's. They spoke Spanish to me initially, but when I couldn't keep up, they smiled and just kept cutting. I left with a pixie cut. Somehow it seemed right. A new me stepped outside Pilar's that summer afternoon. Something inside me changed.

The Fourth of July

I was through talking about the *Camileño*. I had no intention of going over any of it again with anyone—except Canela, maybe or Boracho. They were my best bets. You could always count on them to keep their mouths shut. But one afternoon, in what I guess was an attempt to cement our fragile friendship, Marisol poked a stick in the anthill.

"I know you think I don't like you very much," she said. She stood behind me as I lay beside the pool. "I just thought I'd let you know, I've protected you every now and then."

I rolled over and shielded my eyes against the sunlight. "Whaaat?"

"Well, maybe not every now and then, but once anyway." Mari stalled as if she were waiting for an invitation to sit down.

I sat up and tried to pay attention.

She still stood with the sun behind her, blinding me if I looked up. I wondered if she did it for some halo effect or if she were even aware of it. I spun my forefinger for her to get to the point.

"You knew something all along, didn't you...the day George died?" Mari didn't whisper, but out in the hot, closeted air of July, her words shriveled in the heat.

"That was three months ago. I don't know what I knew, for goodness sake." I swiveled on my butt and stuck my feet in the water.

"You think I didn't see you, don't you?" she said. "You think you fooled everybody when you sneaked out of the house that morning, but I saw you heading out to the corral."

I began a slow kick in the pool water. My toenail polish swam like small red koi passing each other under the swirling water. I hummed.

"I *said* you were out there on your old horse and weren't supposed to be. Can't blame this one on me like you did when we took that little ride on Canela." She laughed as she bent and slipped her shoes off before sitting beside me and splashing her feet alongside mine.

I couldn't remember when I had heard her laugh. It surprised me. And there were our feet, nearly the same color now, together in the water.

"So why didn't you say something, tell on me? That's what you do best."

"It was the look on your face, chica. You shoulda seen that look." Mari glanced obliquely at me. "Ya wanna talk about it?"

"Can't."

"I get it. You never *will* talk about it, right?"

"Right."

"Then neither will I." She stood and shook the water off her feet.

Looking up at her again, the sun had moved. I could see her face clearly and saw in it what I most wanted to see—compassion. Just so long as it wasn't pity.

"Won't keep you from razzin' me, I guess." I worked at keeping my feet swishing back and forth.

"It's good for you, *Lizzie.*"

I laughed and shook my head. "Did you just call me...?"

She swatted my knee with her toes and walked away.

—⟋⟍⟍—

That night I spun around and around with my sparklers, one in each hand and called to Burt Charles. We ran laughing through the darkness, writing our names in the night with bright wands. I wondered if he would catch me at the edge of the orange tree orchard. I wondered if he would turn our chase into something more. Perhaps I would stumble and fall and he would fall with me and we would laugh and tumble on the lawn. I could make it happen—that accident of arms and lips and summer kisses. I could make it happen.

Hushed and expectant, we and the Villanuevas watched Tío light the fireworks. He fired off rockets that burst into fiery sprays against a moonless night, the sky deep in stars. The wisps of smoke and lights filled the air with the pungent odor of fireworks.

"I love that smell," I said. I expected Mari to say, in her best didactic tone, "Phosphorous and sulfur," but she didn't. She stood transfixed, her arms empty of her little sister now.

"*Luces de los angeles*" Mari's words were almost lost in the hiss of air flash. "*Sí, mijita,* angel lights. Just for you." I knew who she was speaking to—little Ana.

I slid one of the sparklers out of the thin cardboard and lit it with the punk. "More angel lights for you, Ana." I imagined handing Ana the spewing stick. She would giggle and wave it wildly in the air. I wished I had been kinder when I'd had the chance. I wished I'd done so many other things differently.

Mari observed me, but I could not quite read the look in her eyes. I wanted to believe it was the beginning of trust. "Here, Mari," I said, handing her some more sparklers, "Come go with us!"

She smiled, but stood there writing a word much too short for Marisol in the air. Ana. She wrote Ana. That moment broke my heart. I lit my sparkler from the tip of Mari's. The flash reflected in her eyes and I hoped she could see it in mine as well. Maybe it would kindle more than a sparkler. Stretching my arms far above my head and then dipping down to my feet, I wrote in the biggest letters I could make—*Ana.*

Estela

The next day I hung around the kitchen with Estela. Outside the air was still and hot. Cicadas reached a crescendo this time of day, their cacophony deafening. I wound the casement windows shut and strolled over to the icebox to open the door to peruse the contents. Milk was the only thing that looked good and when Estela wasn't watching, I took a long guzzle, and then rolled the bottle, chilled and damp across my forehead.

Estela flipped corn tortillas for tacos in the frying pan. I strolled up beside her.

"I can chop these onions if you want me to." I juggled two onions from hand to hand.

Estela cocked an eyebrow, but slid a knife my way. "*Ten cuidado, chica.* We both be in big trouble if you cut your finger off." She turned back to the tacos.

"You've lived here forever, haven't you, Estela?" I picked up a knife and peeled the onion.

"*Sí.*" She let the word trail out long and end with a lilt. "Joaquín, too. His family and my family, they come here when they were young. Long time working in this place." She lifted the crisp shell from the oil with tongs and held it in a curved shape till it cooled.

"Do you never get tired of staying out here all the time and doing all this work?" It dawned on me how much of her life she had spent taking care for others with so little to show for it.

"You work wherever you are. I don't mind. This is where my family is, my people. The Villanuevas, the Parrs." Estela's voice warbled like a mockingbird. "Sometimes you don't pick the place. Sometimes it pick you."

"But, it's hard here, you know?" I scooted a bar stool up to the kitchen island and sliced the onion. "It's not what I thought it would be. Not one bit."

"I know, *mijita.* But just the same, it pick you."

I stopped chopping and stared at Estela's back. It was too much to think about right now. I glared at the onions and chopped like a woodpecker knocking on a dead tree stump—like a conscience on a closed door.

"Listen to me, Isabel. I tell you something." Estela turned and reached out to still my hands. "I see you sitting there on your old Canela watching the sun go down. I do not know what you think, but you burrow like a baby armadillo. The hot ground, the cactus and mesquite? They will remember you and me and sing our story—to tell our children." Estela set down the last tortilla.

"How...?" I started to ask, but then gave in to her certainty.

She turned and took my face in her hands. "If you never know this, how can you find the truth? About *you*? And how do you ask forgiveness if you are always searching for a different place. Home is like your heart and it knows your name." And lifting her brows, she said, "It's a little bit hard to stay where everyone knows you, the good and the bad, but it is where you grow. ¿*Me entiendes?* You understand?"

I stared into her dark eyes for a moment. Maybe she knew me better than I knew myself. Maybe she knew I would thrive in this burnt land, throw down roots and grow little thorns. And it would be okay if I smelled a little like garlic and the sun basted my skin to the color of a wet pecan. Maybe I would speak the language like Tío did and then at last, some of whatever was missing in me would bloom.

Canela

On a hot night, I lay wide-awake long after the adults had retired. I left my bed and sneaked out to the pool. Sliding out of my bathing suit under the sun-warmed water, I swam slow breaststrokes under water. No waves. No sound, but for hushed bright rings when I rose to the surface. In the light of the moon, my skin polished bronze. I felt like a mammal, water-born, gliding through layers of light. I wondered what it would be like to have that boy I loved, blond and brown, here with me to practice underwater kisses.

The moon was full, its reflection shimmering across the dark wash and splintered only by ripples when I emerged to sit in the shadows. Wrapped in my towel I listened to the owl, the chattering cicadas.

I thought about the horses and how they looked last fall when we had found them at last. Keep the Change's stallion neck had still flexed, but his tail looked like it got in a tangle with coyotes and lost the battle. His mane was knotted, his hooves ragged. But now he was training to race again, his nobility regained.

Canela looked gaunt and exhausted when she had followed our truck back home. Now after ten months, her hips had rounded and filled out from the sharp angles that had been her haunches. She was plumper and shinier than I had ever seen her. I got to wondering if we should exercise her more or put her on less grain.

So Canela had an easy summer. We still kept her up near the barn. I could go check on her if I wanted and that night I did want to. Slipping into my boots and shorts, I tiptoed out into the night and called her name. Nickering she came to me, a slow moving form in the dark. A hard whistle of the Chuck-will's-widow and the stark white constellations punctuated the night. The mare's swollen center swayed as she approached, her coat a maternal glow, slick in the moonlight. Now I understood. I pressed my face into her neck and breathed deeply to take in that ancient earthy musk of horse. Unexpected tears stung my eyes. How long had I taken for granted the comfort she gave me? The long ambling walks, her ears twitching in recognition at my own long ramblings. Her patience with a child's too tightly gripped rein and flailing legs. She never left me even when gunshot stunned the silence of that April morning and despite her aversion to buttercups, she brought me back through them when we ran for home.

My uncle had never really given Canela to me. Maybe it was hers to choose when I became worthy. Of her and her baby to be foaled.

"I'm sorry, girl." I drew sugar cubes from my pocket. "I'll take care of you for a change." Like unraveling velvet, her muzzle quivered in my hand. Her flank trembled as I smoothed my palm over her belly. And across the two of us, swept a warm breeze full of longing and sweet promise that was almost too much to bear.

The Thumbprint of God

It would be August before the colt was foaled—a hot night.

"Mares have been known to take care of things all by themselves, you know." Tío reminded me. "And they usually drop their foals in the middle of night to keep prying eyes outta their business."

"No, Tío! You promised me I could be there. That this would be *my* colt to bring along."

"Oh yes. Now, I know. I know." He put his hand on my shoulder. "You'll be there to take care of the old mare no matter what crazy hour. Check her milk lately?"

"Yes, sir. It's kinda skim-milky." Tío had taught me how to gently milk Canela's udder just to be aware of the changes in her milk. It had gone from like yellowy floor wax to syrupy to skim. We had no idea exactly when she and Keep the Change, had mated, so we relied on the techniques of milk checking.

"Been feeding her the grain and alfalfa?"

"Yes, sir. And fresh water and I've got the towels and iodine solution." I nodded toward my foaling kit.

"Wash her udder? Wrap her tail?"

"Oh, jeez, no."

"I'll send Joaquín out to show you how to go about it. I'd say it was about time to get that done. When her milk goes opaque and white, and that's any day now, we'll have us a foal on the ground." He settled his Stetson on his head and started back to the car before turning with a grin. "Oh, I guess I'll give you a hand when the action gets going."

I tried to appear nonchalant about his being there. Even though he had given me advice on how to handle the situation, I was terrified I would do something wrong. Having taken prodigious notes, I studied them to the point of memorization.

By the time I mucked the stall again and fed Canela that evening, Joaquín was coming down the road toward the barn.

"*Hola, Joaquín. Bienvenidos.*"

Joaquín tried not to crack a smile, but I guess he'd heard my vow to learn to speak Spanish from Estela. I'm sure I sounded like a kindergarten Spanish lesson for gringas.

"*Un potro, eh?*" He cupped his arms as though around something small. I guessed a foal. He spent no more time trying to explain things to me, but took a small wet sponge and gently swabbed the crevices of Canela's swollen udder. Then he took out a tail wrap and went to work. I studied each revolution he made around Canela's tail and mimicked the turns of the cloth with my own hands.

----\m/----

Tío said the fewer the people at the foaling the better, but Burt Charles had to be there. Moral support. That's what I called his being a part of my life. I hated to admit how much I needed him sometimes. But there it was.

I picked up the phone. "Get out here this evenin', Burt Charles. Tío says it's any day now, and I'm gonna need a runner when her water breaks."

There was a long pause. "Okay, let me see. I am coming out to serve as your lackey. That right?"

"Do you want to see a foal being born or not?" But I sighed and let the truth out. "No, all right! No! I need you to...to help. I mean what if I do something wrong before Tío can get there?"

"Well, that's better. I guess I can talk Daddy into bringing me out after supper. Wait."

I thought I heard his fingers drumming on the receiver.

"What are y'all having?"

"I think it's enchilada night."

"Rice and refried beans, too?"

"Oh come on out for supper. Honestly, Burt Charles." But I relaxed more than a little. He would be there with me. What if tonight was the night? My colt. My very own colt. It had been my dream since my mother and I first came to South Texas. Maybe. Just maybe this time, my dream could come true.

An hour later we were just finishing up dinner. I rapped my fork on the table waiting for Burt Charles to finish his second bowl of Rocky Road ice cream. What was it with that boy and ice cream? I jumped up and headed for the door before he could put his spoon down.

Tío called after us. "Now, leave her alone a little. Just sit there and be real quiet. Some mares have their druthers about producing a baby with an audience watching."

Mama and Aunt Hilda mumbled something about not knowing why in the world we'd want to watch all that mucus and umbilical stuff.

Heavy with pride I turned to reassure them when I saw that funny twitch about Tío's mouth.

"Now don't you be like Prissy in *Gone with the Wind,*" he said. And in his best falsetto, "I don't know nuthin' about birthin' babies, Miss Scarlet." Then he was serious. "You hear that water break and you come runnin'. No sashaying down the walk clacking a stick on the fence rails like Prissy when she was supposed to be running for help for the birth of Miss Melanie's baby. I'll be there. We've got probably ten minutes till she goes down—Canela, not Miss Melanie."

I gave Tío a sidelong stare. "Funny. Very funny."

—⁓⁓—

Two nights had gone by and no breaking of the bag of amniotic fluid, but Canela was so restless that Burt Charles suggested I bring her out into the corral. "Let her wander around a little bit. She's making me nervous rocking back and forth in that stall."

I insisted on keeping a hand on her halter. "Well, what if she just drops down out here in the corral and we have to get her back to the stall?

"Has her water broke?" Burt Charles always managed to sound just a little superior.

"No, but...."

"Well then, I don't think we have to worry about her going down yet."

"What makes you the expert?"

"Just keep walking."

"I think I read somewhere that you should err on the side of caution."

"Walk!"

We paced past Keep the Change's stall and he gave the pregnant mare a little nudge. I was sure he meant to be friendly, but she squealed and delivered a hormonal kick at his stall door.

Back and forth, pausing for only moments at a time, she plodded until we brought her back to her stall. I had prepared a foaling area for her and mucked it twice a day. Joaquín shored up the walls. No cracks, no crevices for the foal to stick his hoof in. We packed a heavy bed of shavings. And waited.

"You hear that?" I jumped to my feet. Burt Charles and I peered through the slats of the stall.

"I'm pretty sure she just whizzed—you know, like a race horse."

Burt Charles' sense of humor failed to amuse me. "Well, how in the world are you supposed to tell the difference? Maybe you better go get Tío."

"Now just relax. I think that if the water breaks, it comes out in a big gush." Burt Charles pantomimed a dam breaking. "We're supposed to be quiet, remember? Sit down and hush up."

With as much drama as I could muster, I slid down against the stall door. I stared up at the night sky and thought of all the nights Burt Charles and I had sat on the roof of the hacienda and talked about God and life ever after. Now that we believed ourselves sophisticated near-adults, we stuck to lighter subjects and in some ways I missed those days when he was nothing but a friend. Stars were brighter out here over a hundred miles from any big city. Burt Charles reached out and covered my hand in his. Sweet. But it made me even more determined to say just one more thing.

"Remember when we used to sit on the roof?" I gestured toward the sky.

"Shhh," he said and kissed the palm of my hand.

—⁓⁓—

Six hours passed. We sat slumped against the stall. The crick in my neck woke me and I was just starting to unfold my cramped legs when it happened—a gush, like somebody dumped a five-gallon water bucket.

Burt Charles was on his feet and peering over the door. "That was it! I'll go get Tío!"

But I couldn't stand to wait alone. What if the foal came too fast? What if? "I'll go—I'll do it. You better take care of her!"

Burt Charles splayed his hands. "Well, what am *I* supposed to do? Go! Run!"

And I ran. I squeezed through the corral rails. The shirt caught and ripped down my back, but I was through and plunging over the hundred sandy yards between the barn and the house. Under my breath, "Tío, Tío." In seconds I was banging on his bedroom door.

"I'll be right along." How he could be wakened from a dead sleep and sound like he was halfway out the door amazed me.

"Okay, I'm going back!" In the light of the stars and no moon, I sprinted, my heart pounding. And with each exhale I begged, "Please, please, please." I dived back through the corral slats and stood gasping by Burt Charles.

"She's just standing there. She lay down once and got up again." He lit a lantern and held it up for me to see. "Whaddaya think?"

"Think?" My chest still heaved. "Think?"

"Your tío coming?"

"Yeah, he's on his way."

Canela pawed the ground and then on one knee and then the other, she eased down in her stall.

"Ah, jeez, now what?" I whipped the notes out of my back pocket. It says here we just wait. I scanned the paper and read aloud. "Through the sac we should see the front two hooves, one a little bit ahead of the other." I grabbed Burt Charles arm. "That's it! I see it."

And then Tío was there, the door of the Cadillac shutting with a quiet click. "How's it going?"

"Oh Tío! His feet! I can see his feet!"

"Quiet. Quiet. Now, let's just take a look here." He leaned over the stall door and smiled. "Looks like everything is going just like it should. Let's sit back down and be real supportive and not interfere. Canela's an old gal and she's workin' hard."

Difficult as it was, I did as I was told. Burt Charles tended to follow the rules, but it didn't come naturally to me. We waited.

The colt's hooves protruded even more and there in the sac wall poked the little muzzle of my colt or filly. The thrill…tonight.

"Uh oh." Tío squinted into the stall.

I gasped up at him. "What?"

Silence.

"What?" I grabbed my uncle's shirtsleeve.

"There's a tear in the sac. The foal's hooves must have punctured it prematurely."

I watched as between contractions, the colt's head sank out of sight.

"With the sac ruptured," Tío said, his voice low and measured, "it's gonna try to breathe, but there isn't enough room for its chest to expand.

Better give her a hand." Tío lifted the stall latch and we slid in next to
Canela. "Now listen to me carefully. This is your colt and I want you to
be able to do this."

Canela rolled her eyes around at us. And I spoke as kindly as I could.
"It's okay, girl. We'll help. We'll help." But my voice shook and without
taking my eyes off the mare, I appealed to my uncle. "What? What do I
do?"

"With the next contraction—I'll tell you when—you take both legs
and help the foal get far enough out of the birth canal so it can breathe.
We'll clear the sac away. Don't want the baby going back in the birth
canal if it's trying to breathe on its own."

The little hooves pointed toward me and I took hold. "Like this?"

"Like that. Just wait."

Tío studied the mare's flanks. "Now," he said. "Now. Pull!"

I caught my breath, leaned back and held on. The muzzle slipped
forward. I held.

"Just a little more. We need a little more before the contraction
ends." Tío reached around me and grasped the colt's forelegs. The scene
fell into slow motion for me. The blood—its rusty odor and the sweet
earthy smell of amniotic fluid. The ache and pull in my shoulders, the
heat, my uncle's arms around me.

"There! She can handle it on her own now. Tío put his arm around
me and pulled me away from the laboring mare.

Canela stretched her forelegs and released the foal into the world.
She rose to her feet and turned toward her baby. The umbilical cord
broke as she stood. I glanced in panic at Tío.

"It's good. It's good. Just like it's supposed to. We're just gonna be
invisible now."

My instructions came to mind. Free from emergency adrenaline, I
remembered the iodine solution. "Burt Charles, hand me the bottle." My
hand shook a little, but I disinfected the umbilical stump with a quick
dip.

We waited until the foal wobbled to a stand, staggered around a few
steps before falling and starting all over. At last, he found Canela's udder
and poked around at it till he was able to nurse just a little before losing
the technique and having to make adjustments to try again.

The next hour swam by in a haze. As Tío handled the afterbirth
delivery, I stroked the dark shining foal before me. He was a bay colt. All

white stockings except for one black one. "He's beautiful. Isn't he, Tío?" I ran my finger along his muzzle.

"Yes, yes, he is, Isabel." Tío studied the foal. Keep the Change throws some fine offspring." He gently lifted the foal's head and smiled. "And this…." He placed his fingers against a white smudge on the colt's forehead. "This is called the thumbprint of God."

—⋙—

The stars had faded and a fringe of pink lined the eastern sky before we walked back to the house. I thought I would be too excited to sleep, but I sank into the sheets and was gone within seconds.

Tomorrow, Tío had said last night. "Tomorrow, come out and just sit with Canela and…and what's-his-name. Establish yourself early as his partner."

I slept till noon. "Oh lord!" I tore away the sheets, threw on yesterday's jeans, which bore traces of blood, amniotic fluid and a little slime. Maybe baby would recognize that. I headed for the kitchen wondering if Burt Charles was awake. Last night, he'd staggered out to sleep in the guesthouse. And of course, there he was, sitting at the kitchen table, just having finished a four-course breakfast.

"My patience was runnin' thin." He wiped his mouth and stood. "But I figured I'd be in deep trash if I went out there without you."

I grabbed a Coke out of the fridge. "Let's go."

"Your tío said to tell you he'd be out later to give you a few pointers." Burt Charles huffed out the words on the jog to the barn. "I gotta be home by two. Mama's on the warpath 'cause I've been gone so much."

I really didn't mind. I wanted to sit alone with my colt. Time to think—to plan.

And there he was—like a kid in high-heeled shoes. He was steadier, but walking was still a balancing act. He nudged between the wall and his mama.

We watched him for a while before I got the nerve to ease into the stall. "It's okay. You can go on. I'm just supposed to sit here," I said to Burt Charles. "Oh, hey! Hey, wait a sec—bring me something to eat on your way home. Anything. Wait! See if Estela's got any leftover chicken."

"Yes, madam. Anything else I can tote for you?"

"You're my hero, Burt Charles."

"Uh huh. Right."

———ᘯ——

It was hours later when Tío drove up to the barn. I had fallen asleep and jumped when I heard the car door close. I tried to appear alert when Tío tapped on the stall door, but I expect I fooled no one.

"How's it going?" Tío nodded toward the foal who had folded up beside Canela and was now trying to unfold. "You want to let them out of the stall so they can have a little walk around?" He was already unlatching the hinge.

We watched as Canela and her colt headed for the open space of the corral. It was amazing how the foal gamboled about on those spindly legs.

"Got a name for him yet?"

"He's not like I thought he would be. I have to rethink some."

"Well, while you're thinking, I want you to understand what your responsibilities are."

"Oh, I know, I know. Muck the stall." I headed for the stall rake.

"That's the easy part. First off, just get him to where you can stroke him. Start while he's lying down and just ease over to him. Once he accepts your hands all over him—and that's gonna take a few days depending on his temperament—you'll get a soft rope and go over him with it. Soft like—easy. Pretty soon, he'll give to that pressure. That's what you want. And—"

Jeez. I was gonna have to get my notebook.

——ᘯ——

That night I went over my notes. Toys—I was to get him a ball, a hula-hoop and a tarp to blow in the wind so he'd get used to it. Then I'd be easing a halter on him and lifting his feet. And as he got a few weeks older there'd be trail rides—I was to take short walks on Canela and let him follow us through creeks and bushes, over dead trees. Let him get a good look at the cattle. Get him to follow his mama into a trailer. And help him get over a javelina busting out of the mesquite.

My Tío

The last full moon of the summer began to set outside my window. Its curved arc flattened out and sank, liquid-like into the horizon. I stood between the closed drapes and the window and wound myself up in a cranberry red comforter that I snitched from Aunt Hilda's dressing room chest. It was too warm, but the satin-wrapped down of it offered a sensual consolation that a plain blanket could not. I wrapped it around me tighter and promised myself that I would climb into bed the minute the moon dropped completely out of sight.

As I turned toward my bed, a scream rose and echoed against the stucco walls—*la llorona*! Or...or...Estela. Estela could be searching for her dead little Ana. It came again, a hard, agonizing scream in the night.

I whirled, twisting in the heavy fabric, and searched the room about me. I turned back toward the window and scanned the grounds for moving shadows. I could see nothing but the feathering limbs of the pecan trees and the fronds of the palms along the pool. No wind.

Out of long ago habit, I whispered his name—"Daddy." Despite his absence, he still had the power to protect me from nameless fears of the night. Even then, the irony was not lost on me.

I scooted across the room to the window, the comforter tangling at my feet. The silhouette of a man stood out against the night. The hat was familiar, a flick of a cigarette lighter flashed in the dark.

Again the scream. *La llorona?*

I shuffled flatfooted on bare feet to the door. Maybe Daddy had changed his mind after all and come to visit. I imagined him driving long dark roads to claim us at last. I imagined him trimmer, his rakish dark hair neatened with the fine-toothed comb of sobriety. The months of struggle with giving up the one thing that meant more to him than wife and daughter. He would have walked around the house with a prouder posture, sure in his gait. And he stood waiting for me to look out the window and see him there as though no time had passed.

"I knew you'd come!"

The heavy door grated against the floor and I pulled with a terrific wrench. The scream filled the night; its hysterical pitch, long and rasping, echoed from the *pasillo* walls.

"Daddy!" I cried out. The night fell quiet. So quiet.

Then so softly, "No, honey."

Arms reached around me, bundling up the comforter and me in one arm. "No, it's me, Tío. Just me."

How could I have imagined the handsome face of my father? Had I forgotten his dark hair that lost its precise part when a lock of it fell to his forehead? His Old Spice aftershave? Had I projected the image of my father onto the balding head of my uncle, his hawk-like nose and pale scars?

Stunned, I tried to reconcile my fantasy with fact. I could see now from the lamplight of my aunt and uncle's bedroom. To make light of my mistake, I attempted a chuckle. But it came out a sob.

"I...I...." My stammering was interrupted by another cry. "They say it's *la llorona*, you know." I tried for cool sophistication—a little bit of scorn to cover my fear, my mistake.

I could feel gentle laughter vibrate through his ribs, but with some effort he cleared his throat and hugged me tighter. "Nah! Now don't you worry about all that stuff. That's a cougar, honey, just an old cougar. The moon's gone down and the night's calm. That's when they'll get out to scare up dinner, but you know I'd never let anything get you."

Did I? Did I know for sure he could protect me from anything? It wasn't even humanly possible. But the thought—the thought was everything.

He pulled my cover a little tighter around me. "Where'd you find your aunt's goose down comforter? Aren't you a little hot in that thing?" Not waiting for an answer, he squeezed my shoulders and looked out to the ridge beyond our walls. "I'll have to admit, it's been a while since I've heard one up around these parts, but every few years, one or two will come up from Mexico. Big cats. You'll likely never lay eyes on one. They won't come anywhere close up to the house. It's a *llorona*, all right, honey. Just a big kitty *llorona*."

"So is there really a *llorona*, Tío? The Mexicans say there is."

He thought a long time before he answered. He was cautious and solemn and he said, "We all have our own truths, Isabel. Our own truths."

So here was my chance. The opportunity I had waited for. My heart punched my ribs like a fist. Just Tío and me. No one else would ever have to know. He would never speak a word of it. Neither would I. Between us—the bond of admission.

"I have a truth," I said. I took a breath like I was diving into cold water from the high board. And then in a hot rush of words—"I saw it all. The fight you and George had. I know I wasn't supposed to be there, but I was. I *was*. What you said when you handed him...handed him the...." I tried to read his pale eyes in the moonlight.

Taking me by the shoulders, he held me at arm's length. "That was something you shouldn't have seen. I could have gone to prison myself for that."

So. It was true. He *would* have gone to prison for handing George the gun. If I had told, the Rangers would have locked him up instead of just questioning him.

"It was found, of course, there on the car seat, but no one knew I was the one who bought it." He gazed into the night.

The owl called out—a brief monotone. Tío frowned at the silhouette of the old pecan. "Haven't heard her in a while," he said.

I searched the shadowed limbs. "George didn't have to kill himself, Tío. He could have gone to jail like he was supposed to."

"I think he finally just gave up when he couldn't have life the way he wanted it." Tío rubbed his temple, the skin sliding with his fingers. "His way or none, as usual. I loved my brother, but I never understood him. What I did was aiding and abetting. No way around it. That ticket to Mexico was the only thing left I could do for him."

"But I thought...I thought it was...." The image of George pressing that pistol to his head, his eyes daring me to watch had been the only truth I had known. And it was not the truth at all. "Ticket?" Like pieces of a jigsaw puzzle, the validity of the past months that had once fit together so convincingly, gave way to jumbled images. I blinked in confusion and stepped away.

Tío looked off. "The ticket and false passport in the package. And enough cash to get him started in Mexico. It would've gotten him across the border. I thought that surely he would jump at the chance and be gone before the Rangers found him. But then he could have never come back. Not ever. Either way...."

"He would be gone."

"Yes."

280   Mary Bryan Stafford

"It would have been a relief." I wrapped myself tighter even though sweat crawled from my armpits and sealed satin to my ribs.

"Yes." Tío waited a moment before he asked the question. "But you didn't see him pull the trigger. You didn't...?" A wish he made, not a question.

And here it was again in one night. A chance for the truth. Clear and shining. He had revealed his truth to me and now it was my turn. A gleaming confession to bind us. Honesty was all I had ever wanted.

And I answered.

"No," I said, my voice trembling. And then with conviction—"No."

He slumped. "Oh, thank God." Tío folded me in his arms. "I couldn't take it if I thought you had."

It was then I chose the definition of my uncle: his forgiveness when I rode outside the grounds, his handing out money to the poor, his patience with the wildcatters, a calf to the poacher, his arms around me when my colt was born. Most of all, I remembered that first summer long ago and his smile when he bent to welcome me to his world.

"Tío?" But I couldn't say another word. Captain Wiley had been right—insight. Box 13 no longer mattered. The package Tío gave to George did not matter. I had all the information I needed to know who my uncle was. I pressed my cheek against the fine weave of his gabardine shirt so I could feel his heartbeat.

The owl called once again.

—⚏—

Later, I lay in bed with the windows open and listened to the coyotes. I still loved the sound. Mama didn't. She said they were too desperate. She was probably right, but in my frame of mind, their urgency appealed to me. Even when their cries reached a frenzy, I knew they had found what they needed. This I understood.

I listened with fascination as the cougar gave one more scream into the night. Cats were different. Their screams were calls of anticipation. I recognized both the coyote and the cat. They reverberated in my chest and despite the dichotomy, the sound filled me up. Sliding from the sheets, I tiptoed to the open window. Beyond the shadows of the fig trees, the stars hung tremulous and brilliant.

I began to understand silences, the evasions. Protection from the truth. Not the best way, perhaps. Bandages instead. Sometimes that was all we could do for each other. Bandage.

About the author

Mary Bryan Stafford, seventh generation Texan and Daughter of the Republic of Texas, now makes her home in the Texas Hill Country outside Austin with her husband, three horses and two German shepherds.

CPSIA information can be obtained
at www.ICGtesting.com
Printed in the USA
FSOW02n0807060915
10541FS

9 780615 913636